# Mrs. Mike

The story of Katherine Mary Flannigan

## Benedict & [Nancy] Freedman

**Buccaneer Books**
**Cutchogue   New York**

A-1

International Standard Book Number:  0-89966-396-6

For ordering information, contact:

Buccaneer Books, Inc.
P.O. Box 168
Cutchogue, New York 11935

## CHAPTER ONE

The worst winter in fifty years, the old Scotsman had told me. I'd only been around for sixteen, but it was the worst I'd seen, and I was willing to take his word for the other thirty-four.

On the north side of the train the windows were plastered with snow, and on the south side great clouds of snow were whipped along by a sixty-mile gale. There was snow on top of the train and snow under the train, and all the snow there was left in the world in front of the train, which was why we were stopped.

"They're sending us snowplows from Regina, no doubt," the old Scotsman said.

I looked out the window, but it was no snowplow I could see, nor the road to Regina, nor even the coach in front of us, but only whirling, boiling, rushing gray-white snow.

"You'll be telling your children you were in the blizzard of 1907," the old man chuckled. "I was speaking to the conductor a while back. It's forty below and dropping. No, we'll not be in Regina *this* week." He opened his book and began to read.

We'd left Montreal March 5, eighteen days before, eighteen days spent mostly in pulling the engine out of drifts and scraping ice off the wheels.

It was because of my pleurisy I was being sent to Uncle John, who lived in Calgary, Alberta. Up till 1905 Alberta had been part of the Great Northwest Territory, and it gave me a real thrill to go to a place that had been officially civilized for only two years.

My mother had had her doubts about letting me go into such a wilderness. We looked it up on a map of North America, and Alberta seemed awfully empty. Our part of the country, which was Boston, was covered with winding black lines meaning roads, and barbed-wire lines meaning railroads, and circles of all sizes meaning cities and towns.

1

It was so crowded with these proofs of civilization that there was no room for the names, which were stuck out in the Atlantic Ocean. In Alberta there was none of this reassuring confusion. A couple of thin blue rivers, a couple of crooked lakes, and the map maker was through. My mother found the circle that was Calgary and carefully compared it with the circles of Massachusetts.

"A fine black dot it is, but not to be mentioned in the same breath with Boston," she said. Boston was a very distinctive city on our map, being a large dot with a ring around it. "And you'll bear in mind, Katherine Mary," she added, "that's as far north as I want you to go. Don't be letting your uncle take you up into this." She waved in the general direction of Mackenzie and the North Pole. "My own mother lived and died in the house where she was born, and all the traveling she did was to the oatfield and back."

We both sat and wondered at the size of the world until she folded it up and put it in the bureau drawer.

However, the doctors said the cold dry climate of Alberta would be good for my lungs, and Uncle John said it was a long, long time since he had seen one of his kin, and so at last my mother gave in and let me go.

She put me on the train in Boston, and for the twentieth time I promised I'd dress warm and keep dry and not go out into the night where there were bears.

"Now, there's a lot of snow up in those north places," Mother cautioned me, "and you'll always remember to wear your woolen socks. And when there's a cold wind blowing, on with your shawl and button up."

"Yes, Mother," I said. She kissed me, smiled and cried, and the train pulled out. Now here I was in one of those "north places" and the old Scotsman was calling to me from across the aisle.

One of the trainmen had wiped off the frost from his window. The Scotsman pointed, and there against the stock fence along the right of way were hundreds of cows and steers, blown across the prairies by that icy gale and packed densely along the fence, frozen and dead.

There was frost all over the window, except in the corner

2

where I'd scratched a clear space to look out, and except for KATHERINE MARY O'FALLON printed underneath, and except for where I'd drawn Juno's ears. Just then the train gave a jerk and started slowing down, making twice as much noise as when it went fast. They always do, and I can't figure out why.

I'd put Juno in the big lunch basket Mother'd given me. I had to keep him in there during the day because dogs were supposed to be kept in the baggage car and there was a mean porter on this train. Juno was the worry of my life. He had broken a strand of wicker, and I was always in terror that he'd stick that black nose of his out the hole.

The train was just about stopped now. I thought maybe it was another snowplow come to clear off the tracks, so I looked out. There wasn't much to see; snow on top of everything and not too many trees. There was a red silo and a house, and I was glad I didn't live there.

The basket with Juno in it started moving around in a very unbasketlike way. It finally fell off the seat and started rolling toward the aisle. I grabbed it back fast, opened the lid, and gave Juno a couple of slaps on the nose. This Juno wasn't like Mother's Juno; he was only a puppy and couldn't be expected to be as wise and smart yet. All our dogs were named Juno, and they were mostly cocker and black. The Irish Juno who had come to America with us had been red. I didn't remember that one because I was only two then. The first Juno I remember was the white and brown one, the one that howled when Uncle Martin played the violin. Uncle had his violin and his bagpipe (the Irish kind) from Denny Lannon, the great storyteller, whose great-grandniece I am. Mother used to say that Denny Lannon had a song and a story for every day in the week, and two for Sunday.

There I was thinking of Mother. And I mustn't. Otherwise how could I keep going through this white world of pale sky and frozen earth?

The wheels started again—the wheels that took me away from the three-story brick house and Uncle Martin's new sign saying in gold letters that we let rooms. But the room on the third floor Mother never let to anyone. It was the prettiest room in the house, always full of flowers. It was kept for someone down on his luck who would need a pretty room and flowers to cheer him up. Many a down-and-out actor had lived there, once a janitor out of work, and once a lady who took in sewing but couldn't do much any more because her eyes were bad.

I felt sorry for the lady whose eyes were bad, so sorry that I began to cry. I wasn't crying for her exactly, but for all the sadness in the world. And because right now, if I were home, I'd be feeding Pete, Mother's canary. But I wasn't home and someone else was feeding him, Mary Ellen or Anna Frances.

I blew my nose because I was determined to stop crying, but that didn't stop it. So I opened Mother's cookies. I'd been saving them for an emergency, and they were pretty stale. I ate them and cried some more because they were my favorite kind, small and brown and lumpy with bits of chocolate. *I* made that kind, too, only not so well. Mother said I didn't mix the dough thick enough. Anyway I sat there and ate cookies and cried. After a while the cookies were all gone, and there had been two dozen of them, so I knew I'd been crying for a long time.

"Regina! Regina!" Sure enough, we'd come to a town, a big one with yards and houses coming right down near the track, dogs and people and a little boy standing waving at the train. The little boy had so many clothes on and the top jacket was stretched so tight it looked as if it would split if he kept waving so hard. I wanted to cry about the little boy too, but I couldn't. He was too fat to be hungry and had on too many clothes to be poor.

We stopped, and I followed the people who were getting off to walk around and stretch their legs. It was awfully cold, and I'd forgotten to put my sweater on under my coat. Mother never let me go out in such cold weather for fear it would make my pleurisy worse. I hoped it wouldn't. I was afraid I'd be sick when I got to Uncle John's. I stared at the postcards on display, hoping that the scenes of sunsets and mountains and oceans would cheer me up. But I kept thinking of Mother and wondering if I'd ever be home again. The postcards blurred, and so did the station of Regina as I ran along it to the train, which was smoking and almost ready to

4

go. I climbed on the nearest coach and walked through to mine.

My berth had been made up, and I didn't see Juno's basket, I climbed in and searched frantically, looking into the most impossible places, under the pillows and behind the curtain. I ran down the car. I ran back and, throwing myself on my stomach, peered under the berth. There was the basket, tucked away next to my valise, but even as I pulled it out, I knew it was empty.

The wheels began to turn, and an awful feeling stabbed into me that maybe he was under them. I began a frantic search under seats, between bags, and around legs. A gray-haired man stopped me. "If you're looking for a black cocker spaniel, the porter has him. Carried him down that way." I started running. He was still talking, but I couldn't wait. Maybe they'd put him off. Maybe he was out there on the track, wandering lost around the station. The wheels chugged faster and faster.

I was at the end of the coach and pulling at the heavy door when I stopped. On the other side, the frightening covered part where the cars join, was Juno. He was sitting up on his hind legs because the mean porter was holding little bits of meat for him. I looked hard at the porter, and anyone could see that he wasn't mean, but only sad and thin.

I'd been sad and thin all day, too. But now I was only thin.


They called me early, but I was already awake. This was the day we'd be getting in, and I had a lot to do. First I got out the red plaid dress I'd been saving. I was sorry now I hadn't worn it because it was all in little lines that wouldn't fall out. It had been thirty days in that suitcase.

I combed Juno and then gathered up my clothes and took them into the ladies' room. I thought I looked very well in my new dress, even if it was wrinkled. People with red hair as a rule look awful in red, but my hair has enough brown in it to be called auburn. I tried to put it up in the figure eight my mother wore low on her neck. It was harder to do than I expected because my hair is curly and wouldn't co-operate.

5

But when I had it up I looked at least eighteen. Too bad I had to spoil it by putting a ribbon on. That was the way Uncle John was to recognize me, by the big blue ribbon in my hair.

When I got the bow tied there was still a couple of yards of ribbon left over. Back to my berth for my scissors, and then back to the ladies' room where they had the mirror. And all the time it was getting later. I tried the bow on one side and then on the other, on the front and on the back. Wherever I put it, it looked queer with my hair up. And it was so big.

People began coming in to dress. I was fascinated by a very fat woman dressing inside her nightgown. She had her hands underneath and pulled everything up from the bottom.

It was getting crowded near the looking glass, and the ladies began pushing. I had to decide where to put the ribbon. I fastened it on the right side and started back to my berth. The Scotsman shook my hands, both of them. "It's been a fine trip. I hope you meet your uncle all right. It's been a pleasure knowing you, Miss O'Fallon."

I said good-by to him and felt sad, the way you feel when you've shared something with someone whom you'll never see in this world again. When I got back to my seat, I tied a piece of the leftover ribbon on Juno. By now everyone on the train knew I had him, so there was no use keeping him in the basket. The train began to slow down. The windows were frosted over again so I couldn't see, but I knew it was Calgary.

Uncle John, Uncle John . . . I tried to fix the name with a body. Tall and dark, a lean face, Mother had said. What if he wasn't there? What would I do? What if he was there and didn't recognize me, and went away? What if he didn't really want me to come? What if he didn't like me?

The train was stopping. I grabbed Juno and put him in the basket. What would I say to him? What would we talk about? Should I call him Uncle John, or Uncle, or . . . ? Would he really be here? I couldn't believe it—John Kennedy, my mother's brother.

And just supposing he was here, would he know me? I put my hand up to the ribbon; it was still there. But he might not have received Mother's letter about the blue ribbon. Some people said I looked like my mother. I hoped he'd recognize me. I took a mirror out of my purse and changed the ribbon to the left side.

Ten minutes later I was standing on the platform, and a tall, dark, lean gentleman with eyes just like my mother's was smiling and saying, "Katherine Mary?"

Right then and there I put my arms around him and kissed him. Then I looked at him again. "I hope you're my Uncle John," I said.

"Yes, I'm your Uncle John." Then he looked at me hard. "Just like your mother." He kept looking at me. "Is it the custom," he asked slowly, "for young women in Boston, America, to wear two hair bows on their one head?"

"I added the second hair bow at the last minute because, Uncle, I didn't know which way you'd be coming from."

Uncle John had a big coon coat for me. I put it on right over my other coat, and it felt good. I climbed into the cutter, sat on a buffalo robe, and had another thrown over my knees. The buffalo robes excited Juno. He took a corner of one in his mouth and rocked back and forth, growling way down in his throat.

We started up. All Uncle did was pick up the reins, but those horses knew. It was like flying. We started up the snow on every side, and the wind blew a challenge. Juno was completely subdued and lay against me with his nose under my arm.

I snuggled into the furs and took a couple of quick looks at Uncle John. He was dressed in a coon coat too and fur mittens. And a fur cap pulled down over his ears.

"What kind of fur is that?" I pointed to the mittens.

"Beaver."

I could see Uncle John wasn't much of a one for talking. "And the cap too?" I asked.

"Yes."

Well, that subject seemed to be exhausted. I was about to settle back and look at things when Uncle surprised me. "How did you leave your mother, Kathy?"

"Mother's fine," I said. "She sends you her love."

Uncle John nodded his head and grunted. I tried to figure out what feeling that expressed, but I couldn't. So after a

7

while I gave up and just watched the town go by. Once I saw a street lighter reaching up with his long pole and making a light.

"And your sisters?"

The words startled me, coming out of the dusk and the silence with no other words behind them for two or three miles. Then I realized that two or three miles between words in this vast country was equivalent to a pause my mother would have filled with, "And who will have another biscuit?"

"And Frances and Mary Ellen are very well. Anna Frances poses for magazine covers. Mary Ellen is engaged. And I tap dance. . . ." I paused, but not for any two or three miles, just long enough to think if there were any more accomplishments we possessed as a family. There weren't. I glanced around for another subject. It was getting dark and pressing all around us were the silhouettes of buildings. "Calgary's a big city, isn't it?"

"Yes," Uncle said, "mighty big."

That was that. I tried another tack. "How far is it to your ranch?"

"Two days."

I nodded and leaned over the edge of the cutter to feel the wind in my face. We turned a corner and went down a hill, and Uncle finished his sentence, ". . . . but we aren't going there tonight."

"We aren't?"

"Well, no."

I waited patiently for him to go on. But I was about ready for another question when he spoke again. "We're stopping to see a woman."

This was interesting because Uncle John was a bachelor. "Who?" I asked.

"Name's Mrs. Neilson. Margaret Neilson."

The "Mrs." spoiled it. Except maybe she was a widow. I was still thinking about this possibility when we stopped. I shut Juno up in his basket and ran after Uncle John.

"Now remember, Katherine Mary, she just got out." Uncle John said this in a strange tone, as though he meant to say something else.

"Out of what?" I asked.

8

We walked up on the porch and Uncle rang the bell. "That's what we call it, Kathy. Coming out. It means out of the north country."

A middle-aged woman with a dirty dressing gown flapping around her opened the door. "Yes?"

"We'd like to see Mrs. Neilson."

I could see the woman's eyes light up with curiosity. "She's in her room. I'll show you."

"If it's the same one, end of the hall, I'll find it."

I followed Uncle John down the hall. The woman muttered something as we passed. Uncle stopped in front of a door. He turned and said, "Now remember, Katherine Mary."

What was I to remember? I didn't find out because the door opened, and a beautiful young woman stood looking at us.

"Mrs. Neilson . . ." my uncle began, and then stopped.

She was staring at me with large startled eyes.

"I'm Katherine Mary O'Fallon," I said.

"My niece," Uncle added.

Her eyes dropped to her hands. She wore a delicate little wedding ring. She turned it around and around. "Come in." And she smiled in a way that made my heart go out to her.

The room was dark and shabby, and I felt bad that she had to stay in it. But, as my mother would have said, she was a lady. She treated us as though we were in a palace.

When we were all seated, my uncle reached inside his coat, and then inside his jacket, and finally inside his shirt and took out an envelope. "It's your ticket."

She smiled.

"Your ticket," he repeated.

"You've been very good to me, Mr. Kennedy."

Uncle John didn't seem to know what to say to that. He took out his pipe and then put it away again. He cleared his throat. "Well, you'll be getting back, Mrs. Neilson. And that will be a good thing."

"Where are you going?" I asked.

"She's going to New York," my uncle said.

"I've been there. Mother took me."

"We were married there." She said it very softly.

"Is your husband there, or is he here, too?"

9

"He . . ."

I looked at Uncle John, and then I knew it was my fault no one was talking.

Margaret Neilson reached over and took my hand. Hers was like ice. "It's hard. It's a hard country. Men fight it. Men like to fight, but a woman . . ." Her voice got small and then stopped altogether.

Uncle stood up. "Mrs. Neilson, it's time we started. I'm taking Kathy up to the ranch."

She walked to him and took hold of his arm. "Don't go. Not yet." She looked at him in a pleading kind of way. "Have some tea first. I insist."

Uncle John sat down, a little limply I thought.

"Thank you, that will be real nice."

She smiled at that and hummed a little tune while she put the water to boil. Uncle took out his pipe, remembered, and put it back again. This time she saw him. "Mr. Kennedy, smoke your pipe. Please, I like a pipe."

She poured out the tea and served it to us in broken china cups. And then I saw it wasn't tea, just hot water. She must have forgotten to put the tea in.

"Sugar and cream?" she asked my uncle. "Or do you take lemon?"

"Lemon, please."

And there she was squeezing lemon into the hot water, and there he was stirring it around. Shouldn't someone mention that there was no tea in it, or was that impolite?

"And you, Katherine Mary, how do you like yours?"

With tea, I almost said. But I was glad I didn't, she enjoyed entertaining us so much.

"I'd like sugar," I said. And she gave it to me, two spoonfuls. I glanced over at Uncle John. He was drinking his. So I began to sip mine. And, holy St. Patrick, there's nothing worse tasting than hot water with two teaspoons of sugar in it.

Then she got her own cup and sat down. It's so silly, I thought. Now she'll find out, and wonder why nobody said anything. She'll think we're crazy, sitting here drinking hot water. I looked away just as the cup reached her lips because I didn't want her to see me staring. I waited for her to say something. She did. She said, "You must take Katherine

10

Mary to the hotel tonight. Then she'll be fresh for the trip up tomorrow." She took another sip, and this time I watched her. She didn't seem to notice anything.

We sat around drinking our hot water and not saying much until it was time to say good-by. She kissed me, and there were tears in her eyes when she did it. "I couldn't pull him out," she told me. "I couldn't."

We left early the next morning for Uncle John's ranch. Uncle tucked me into the cutter and started the horses on a fast, silent trot over the snow-packed road. For a long time I said nothing. I watched the clouds light up and the sun rise slowly and the snow gleam. I saw tracks of wolves and mountain lions crossing the road. I showed them to my uncle. He sucked at his pipe and said, "Rabbits."

I felt the inside of the buffalo robe that wrapped me and wondered how it felt on the buffalo. I breathed the sharp morning air and smelled the horses. But all the while in the back of my mind I was troubled. "Uncle John," I said, ". . . about last night . . ."

"Yes?"

"I felt strange in Mrs. Neilson's house. Didn't you?"

"No."

"Mrs. Neilson seemed so dreamy, and I always had the feeling she didn't hear a word we were saying."

"No great loss," said my Uncle John with a puff of smoke. This shut me up for a while, and I took to looking up at the clouds and figuring out animals and ships and islands there. The cutter skimmed along more like a sailboat than a sleigh, and the wind blew in our faces. I watched my uncle's pipe to see if he was angry, and finally I asked, "Have you known Mrs. Neilson long?"

"Eight months."

"Was she always like this?"

"No," Uncle John said. "People change." The road began to wind uphill. The horses slowed to a walk. "She was a bride when she came," my uncle said. "Neilson was a strong man, but stubborn. Did things his own way and never asked advice. Capable, though. Did everything himself. Wife adored him."

I nodded eagerly, but it was several minutes before my uncle went on. I tried to picture Mr. Neilson, the strong

11

man but stubborn. I could see his big shoulders and heavy hands, his square chin. Did he have light hair or dark? I never knew.

"Built his barn himself, no help. And a kind of shed, a milking stand on the west wall. People laughed at him for wanting the cow to get up on a stand to be milked, but Neilson was stubborn. He did things his own way. And after a while nobody gave him advice.

"Well, he went back East for a girl. You've seen her, Kathy. Pretty, but delicate, with scared eyes. Those women are not made for this country. Anyway, the house was all ready, and he brought her out to Lesser Slave Lake, and one night there was a blizzard. Snowed three days without a letup. When it snows like that, you can stick your head out of the window and all you see is the nearest snowflake. You can walk two steps out of your door and never find your way back to the house. But the stock in the barn have been three days without feed, so Neilson gets up and says he's going to the barn. His wife doesn't say anything, just looks at him scared. So he gets a little angry because he doesn't want to catch her fright, and he says in that stubborn way he has, 'There's two horses and a cow and a steer and two pigs—and I'll be damned if they'll starve!' Now she looks at him, pleading with her eyes. I suppose she wants to say, 'Forget the animals, I want you!' But you can't say that to a farmer. He'd die twenty times for those matched bays. He opens the door. Now, most of the fellows up here run a rope from the house door to the barn door during the blizzard season. When you have to tend to the stock, you don't need eyes; that rope is your compass, your chart, and your navigator. Neilson didn't rig a rope. I don't know, maybe he was too stubborn. Maybe he thought he was being kidded. A lot of the men around here were mad at his stubbornness, and they'd tell him things to do, like to plant wheat under the Northern Lights for a big crop, or to set out bowls of milk for the bears so they wouldn't pick up chickens, and a lot else, to see if he would bite. So when they told him about that rope, I guess he laughed and said he'd seen snow before."

My Uncle John looked down at me. "Comfortable?" he said.

"Go on," I said. "That's not the end. Go on."

He smiled. "All right. Neilson opens the door. He can't see the barn, but he knows exactly where it is. He's been to that barn ten thousand times. He pictures the barn. He pictures the door in the barn. He pictures the road to the door. And then he runs as fast as he can, so he won't swerve. . . . After two steps he disappears, and the snow is blowing in her face and she can't see or hear him, so she closes the door. She sits down, but her eyes never leave that door. She didn't even get a chance to kiss him or smile at him before he ran out.

"In her mind she follows him down the path to the barn, and she sees his hand reach out for the door, pull it open, pull himself in; she hears the horses whinny a welcome. 'Don't come back,' she prays, 'don't come back. Stay in the barn till it blows over. Stay where you're safe.' Two hours go by, and he doesn't come back. And suddenly she begins to tremble. She knows he isn't in the barn, he's lost, he's crying for help. She leaps up; she puts on her sweater, her coat, her boots, her gloves, her hat, she opens the door. . . . She stops. She almost laughs. He is there, he is surely there, safe in the barn. And here she was going to lose herself, wildly, uselessly. She can see him coming back slowly to the house in the final ebb of the storm to find her lying frozen in the drifts. Taking command of herself, she closes the door, sits down on a straight chair, and tries not to think. But after a while she knows he is dead, long dead, and she moans, and sobs, and screams. And there are still eight hours of night left.

"At seven in the morning the wind died. Half an hour later the snow stopped. Mrs. Neilson buckled on her snowshoes and went out. In a drift about four yards from the barn door she saw a boot. She pulled at the boot, but it wouldn't come. She went into the barn, harnessed a horse, and brought it out. She tied a rope to the horse and looped it around the boot. When we came by that afternoon, checking up, she was still trying to get him out."

It took us two days to get to Uncle's ranch. We were almost there when I noticed a difference in the air. It seemed warmer, and the sky flushed a deep rose. The glow spread

13

over everything. "Uncle John," I said, "my face feels warm."

Uncle smiled. When I say he smiled, I mean he smiled with his eyes. They twinkled and wrinkled, and that's about as much of a smile as he could manage. "It's going to chinook," he said.

"What's that?"

"You'll see soon enough, Kathy." After three days I knew my uncle well enough to know I'd hear no more about chinooks. I puzzled over the word a long time. It sounded Indian, I thought. Or maybe Eskimo.

"Well, we're here," Uncle said.

I looked around. We had turned off into an icy path, and I could see a fence. But that's all I could see.

"Up ahead." Uncle pointed.

Yes, there was smoke. Soon I was able to make out a large square house, log-built. A man waved and shouted and ran up to us. Juno began to bark excitedly.

"Hello, Jim," my uncle said. "Where's Johnny?"

Jim didn't answer. He was grinning at me. He even started to remove his beaver cap. Uncle looked at me with twinkling eyes. "I thought it better not to tell your mother that there's only one other white girl in these parts. This is Jim, one of the hands. Miss O'Fallon, my niece."

"Pleasure to meet you, I'm sure." Jim was still grinning.

We got out of the cutter, and it felt good to be standing on solid ground.

"Where's Johnny?" Uncle asked again.

Jim's smile broadened. "Out celebrating the Boer War."

Uncle grunted, and we went into the house. The contrast in temperature between indoors and outdoors was so great that I ripped my furs off before I said a word or looked around or did anything else.

Uncle showed me over the house. It had two bedrooms, a big kitchen, and a front room. It was very comfortable. Uncle had ten hands working the place, mostly looking after cattle. "They sleep in the bunkhouse," he said.

"Is one of them named Johnny?" I asked, because I was wondering about what Jim had said.

"No." Uncle took out his pipe and lighted up. "No, Johnny lives here with me. Does the cooking."

"Where is he?"

"You heard what Jim says, he's out celebrating."

"But Jim said he was celebrating the Boer War."

Uncle John puffed a while. "Yes," he said at last, "that's right. You see, we were in it together. That's where I knew Johnny."

I thought of all the snow outside, and the miles and miles of nothing. "But how does he celebrate?"

"Humph!" Uncle said. And that's all I could get out of him about Johnny.

I had gone to bed with Juno and a four-stripe Hudson's Bay blanket. Uncle had given me a white one because the Indians said the white were the warmest. But that night it chinooked, and I threw off all my blankets, for it blew hot and warm. The red glow deepened in the sky. In twenty-four hours the snow disappeared. I was glad to see the last of it, but that was because I didn't know.

"Uncle," I asked, "what's happened? Over night it's spring."

"Chinook," he said. "It's a current of air from the west, warmed by the Japanese current. It moves in over our mountains and down. It gets warmer and drier as it comes. And when it reaches the prairie, the thaw sets in."

At first I ran around and looked at everything. The earth was bare, with little grass blades pricking at it. What I had thought was field melted, and the Red Deer River ran its course. Juno and I took a long walk along its banks, looking into the swift, turbulent waters and listening for the different tones as it rushed at stones and boulders. We watched the ice break and disappear. The larger chunks were carried past like white rafts. It would have been a wild journey for anyone riding those ice cakes, for they whirled and stuck . . . and for a moment lay in the shelter of the shallows before another eddy spun them on again.

We left the river and wandered up near the cut banks. They were low beds that once had been mountain streams. Now they were dry, and cattle were grazing there, thousands of them. Juno barked and barked, but not one of the shaggy heads lifted to look at us. It is very fertile in these canyons, and the cattle graze all year around, even in the

15

winter, for the long thick bull-grass comes right up through three feet of snow.

But today the snow had gone. Everywhere, from all things, there fell a constant drip: from branches, from roots, from boulders, from eaves. I went to sleep my second night on the ranch to the uneven rhythm of that wet, pattering sound. In the morning the sun shone on the moisture-soaked earth, and a rainbow was made. The sound of wet air shaking itself into the Red Deer torrent made a subtle kind of counterpoint. This magic land . . . this was the North.

I walked again to the river. It was much higher than the day before. In some places water ran over the prairie, keeping pace with the strong current of the river. I saw men at a distance, driving cattle. They shouted and waved at me. But the wind carried their words away, and I couldn't hear. One of the figures separated itself from the group and came riding for me. It was Uncle John. "Back to the house," he yelled. "Get back to the house."

I wasn't used to being shouted at. Without answering, I turned and walked back.

No one was in the house. No one came for lunch either. I got awfully hungry, and when I couldn't hold out any longer, I looked around in the kitchen and ended by eating some dried fruit. It was four o'clock by then, and I was feeling very lonesome and neglected. Even Juno was no company. He kept whining, and every once in a while let out a sharp bark. That made me nervous.

At first I thought I imagined it, but then I sat very still and listened, minute after minute. I was not mistaken. A low mournful sound vibrated through the house.

It was after dark when the men came trooping back, tired and silent. I'd been mad at all of them, but when I saw them, the anger went out of me. I put some coffee on the stove. It was hot and black, and the men relaxed.

"How many you reckon we lost?"

"Hundred head, maybe."

"MacDonald's lost more," Uncle said.

"What happened?" I felt I could ask it now.

Uncle John gulped down more coffee. "Stock drowned."

"Drowned?"

16

"The men have been rounding them up for three, four days, since we first knew it was going to chinook. But there were a couple thousand head to get out."

I still couldn't understand. "But how'd they drown?"

"Ice jammed. Blocked the river. Flooded the prairie. We were working in three feet of water, and it was rising all the time."

I tried to shut out the picture of thousands of beasts helpless in the flood.

"Let's have more coffee, Katherine Mary."

I filled up the cups all around. They drank and warmed themselves for a few minutes. Then Uncle John went on, "You know how water seeks its level. Well, it did this time. Went rushing and foaming into the canyons where the herds were grazing. We rounded them out at fast as we could. Got most of them. Got more than some. MacDonald lost five hundred head."

I closed my eyes.

"Happens every year, Miss," one of the men said. "Most times we get 'em out. Sometimes we don't. It's the chinook does it."

I felt sick. Only that morning I'd seen them in the arroyos, red and white patches of them going on for miles.

I knew now what that strange monotonous vibration had been—the lowing of panic-stricken cows and steers struggling for a foothold, thrashing and churning till the water turned muddy. Men shouted at them, horses nudged them, water lashed over them, and their fear burst loose, stampeding them. The young fell and were trodden. The muddy waters turned red. They cried their soft low cry of terror, and the walls of the room had sounded with it. I looked at the eleven men sitting there in soggy boots. This, too, was the North.

## CHAPTER TWO

I was in the kitchen, making seven berry pies. They were currant—dried currants, at that. I'd never done this much baking before, and I was up to my elbows in flour. There

17

came an awful knock at the front door, as though someone were kicking instead of knocking at it. I walked into the living room and stood uncertainly looking at the door. The thumping continued.

"Who's there?" I asked. An extra kick was the only answer. I didn't know what to do. Uncle was out shooting, and I was alone in the house. "Who's there?" I asked again.

"Open the door—or I'll leave him on the porch!"

My first thought was that Uncle John had been hurt. I opened the door. A tall young man in a bright red jacket strode in. He carried a man on his back.

"Holy St. Patrick!" I cried. "Tell me quick, is he dead?"

The young man laughed and dumped his burden down on the couch. "Smell him," he said.

I did. The odor reminded me of John L. Sullivan, the fighter. He used to stay at our house. He had a watch with diamond shamrocks on the back, and every time he'd come in smelling like this, there'd be one less diamond shamrock on that watch.

"Who is it?" I asked.

"Johnny Flaherty."

So this was the missing Johnny. "Will you turn him over, please." I wanted a good look at him. He turned him, and I saw a little man with a big, shaggy mustache and a pale face with a yellow tinge to it.

"He needs some black coffee. You'd better be putting it on."

I whirled around. I was five feet, four and one-half inches, but I had to look up, way up. "I thank you kindly for bringing him back, and I'll thank you to be on your way again, for I'm taking no orders from an English soldier."

"An English soldier, am I? And what gave you that idea?" He frowned down at me, and he was very good-looking.

"With that red coat, you're either off to a fox hunt or you're a British peeler, or maybe you're both."

"You little chit—look at the size of you and you insulting the uniform!"

That made me mad. He could have noticed my naturally curly hair or my eyes, instead of my size.

"Well, if you're not an Englishman, who are you?"

"I'm Sergeant Mike Flannigan, of the Northwest Mounted."

I never could really have thought he was an Englishman, not with the lilt he had to his speech.

Johnny Flaherty moaned from the couch. I had almost forgotten him.

"Miss O'Fallon," the sergeant said patiently, "will you get the poor man some coffee?"

I decided to let this Irish cop know whom he was dealing with. Without a word I walked off into the kitchen. I heard Mike Flannigan singing in a good, and certainly big, baritone, something that went, "Heave ho, heave ho!" at the end of every line. I paid no attention but started the coffee. In a moment he came in with Johnny Flaherty on his back again.

"Whatever are you doing?"

Mike backed up to the pump and slid Johnny off his back, then whirled to catch him as he sagged limply on the floor. Mike Flannigan braced him with a knee and a hand against the wall. With the other hand he pumped. "Got to sober him up before your uncle gets back."

The water came in a sudden stream. He pushed Johnny's head under it and continued pumping. For a moment there was no reaction except a feeble sputtering. Then suddenly Johnny let out a whoop and began thrashing wildly in all directions and using the same words John L. Sullivan used.

Flaherty's arms and legs flayed out at every angle. The only stationary part of him was his head, which Mike held relentlessly under the pump. Profanity and water ran down the dripping mustache into the drain. And all the time Mike soothed him in a low soft brogue.

"Shut your mouth, Johnny Flaherty, there's a lady present."

"To hell with her!" bubbled out from the pump.

Mike gave him a good ducking for that. But his words came all the more gently. "I'd be ashamed, Johnny Flaherty. Just as John was counting on you to help him welcome his only niece."

"To hell with him!" yelled Johnny, getting his head free of the pump for a second and glaring savagely around with water-clogged bloodshot eyes.

19

Under he went again. It was funny and sort of pathetic to see the little man squirming while the one big hand of Mike Flannigan held him under. Mike went on in a mild, reproachful voice, "So you've let him down, and now look at the sorry impression you're making on the young lady."

"To hell with you, you son of—" He didn't get to say it. A full minute passed. He began yelling something that sounded like, "I'm drowning!" But if he was, it didn't seem to disturb Mike. He went right on pumping and lecturing. "What have you to say for yourself, Johnny Flaherty? I suppose you'll be telling me next you were out celebrating?"

Johnny sputtered something that Mike took to be an answer.

"Don't tell me you were celebrating an honorable historical event like the Boer War by getting completely and disgustingly drunk?"

"That's what I was doing," said Johnny. "I was celebrating the war." His speech was no longer thick, and he didn't slur his syllables so much.

"Yes?" asked Mike, who still held him firmly by the collar. "And what's it an anniversary of, this time?"

"Mafeking," Johnny said. "The Battle of Mafeking."

"Uh-uh," Mike said. "You celebrated that last time, only six weeks ago. How many times a year does a date come around?" And he began pumping again.

Johnny watched him. "Kimberley," he said desperately. "It was the glorious Battle of Kimberley."

Mike laughed. "I sometimes wonder if you were really there at all. Kimberley was fought in February. What month is this?" His pump hand started working, "What month is this?" he repeated evenly.

"Isn't it February?" Johnny asked. "That's right," he screamed, with his head halfway to the pump. "It's April! Must've got mixed up for a moment."

"You must have," Mike said, and then, in his most beguiling tone, "What did you say you were celebrating, Johnny?"

"The victory of Ladysmith," Johnny said, and they both started laughing. I remembered vaguely from history class that Ladysmith had been a Dutch victory. Johnny grabbed

20

a towel and started rubbing his head and face, and then wound the towel around his neck.

He turned to me and gave me a sheepish grin. "I feel rotten, Miss Katherine. Besides which, your uncle's going to be like the black Satan for the next few days. I hope you can bring yourself to overlook the disgusting spectacle I've made of myself, and not be too hard on me."

"She shouldn't forgive you, you old toper, and that's a fact."

"Keep out of this, Sergeant," snapped Johnny, without taking his worried, red-veined eyes off me.

"Mr. Flaherty," I said, "I'm sorry to learn you're a drinking man. My mother always said it was the curse of the Irish, but if you like your coffee as strong as your drink, it's ready for you."

He seized the cup avidly in his hands. "And God bless you for this and for your forgivin' ways. It's an angel, in truth, has come to live with us." He drank the coffee down without taking breath. "I'll have a second cup, Miss, and then I'll go to bed."

/ Johnny drank down his second cup, as he had his first. The front door slammed. "It's your uncle!" Johnny was terrified. "I'm in bed! Tell him I came home peaceful and went straight to bed." And Johnny was out the one door before Uncle John was in the other.

Uncle walked right up to Mike Flanagan and shook him by the hand. "It's good to see you, Mike. What brings you into our part of the country?"

"Well, John, rumor has it that a young lady has been seen in these parts, and I thought I'd better check on it." He laughed and flashed his eyes at me to see how I was taking that.

"He came to bring Johnny home," I said.

Uncle stopped laughing and his mouth clamped into a line. "Johnny home?" he asked.

"Yeah," Mike said, but he didn't seem to want to say anything more than that.

"Come home walking?"

"Sure," Mike said.

"Sergeant Flannigan," I began, "you know very well—"

"I'm not saying he didn't need a little assistance," Mike put in, and looked at me in a way that made me know I'd better shut up. I did.

But Uncle John was mad. Plenty mad. He didn't say anything. Just walked into the room he shared with Johnny. We could hear them in there going at it. Uncle John would start quiet and end shouting, and then Johnny would shout too, so that neither one could hear what the other was saying. And that was probably just as well.

I was embarrassed that Sergeant Mike had to be here to hear it. But he seemed to be enjoying it. Every time there was an extra loud "God damn" or "bastard," he'd throw back his head and laugh.

I went on preparing the dinner and setting the table and pretending I didn't know what those words meant, although I did from John L. Sullivan. I was getting madder and madder at Mike Flannigan, so mad that I put two sets of spoons on the table and no forks. He noticed when I took off the extra spoons and laughed harder.

I stopped squarely in front of him. "What do you find so amusing, Sergeant?"

"A young lady like yourself in Alberta Territory."

I didn't know what he meant by that, so I looked at him sharply as though I did know. "Will you please tell my uncle that dinner is ready?"

"What about the hands?"

"They've eaten, all ten of them." I must have sounded tired, for he went for Uncle right away.

They came back, Uncle John not saying much. I didn't say much either because I was mad, and Mike didn't say much, because he was eating. After a while, when I'd stood it as long as I could, I asked my uncle, in a very polite voice, if he'd care for more potatoes. He put down his fork. "Katherine Mary," he said, "I think you're not too favorably impressed with my friend Johnny Flaherty?"

"I'm not," I said.

"Well," my uncle said, "he takes a lot of putting up with, but it's worth it to have the best cook in the Northwest."

I remembered the mud on Johnny's clothes and hands, and his face going from green to purple under the pump.

"He can cook," I said, "but it's a question in my mind if I'd care to eat it."

The men smiled. "You're a very fine cook, yourself," said Sergeant Mike, though I noticed he hadn't touched the currant pie. "But all the women in the world and their grandmothers couldn't cook the way Johnny Flaherty does. Why, he learned the trade from the fiends themselves, the way they cook the sinners in the volcanoes."

They both laughed, but I turned to my Uncle John and said, "It's funny now, but a few moments ago you weren't laughing, Uncle John. You were telling Johnny Flaherty to go to—to where he learned to cook." I wound up, blushing, because Mike's eyes were on me.

"True," my uncle nodded.

"And how often does Mr. Flaherty celebrate?" I continued.

My uncle sighed. "Ah, there never was a war like the Boer War. A battle nearly every day, and all critical."

"And you get mad every time they bring him home?"

My uncle nodded soberly, but Mike was roaring at some joke I didn't see. His laughing made me angry, so I said, "Then why do you put up with it at all?"

My uncle took a bite of currant pie. A strange look came into his eyes, and he laid the fork down.

"Hmmm," he said. What he meant by that I don't know, only he ate no more pie.

"If it was me," I muttered to myself, "I wouldn't let him come back."

"Kathy," said my uncle, "do you know what a flapjack is?"

"It's a pancake," I answered with some contempt, "made with eggs and flour, nothing very special."

"Tell her about Johnny's flapjacks," Uncle John said to Mike.

"My mouth waters and tears come into my eyes to think of it," said Mike solemnly, while my uncle listened with a very pleased expression on his face. "It is a pancake to make the deaf and dumb speak and the Irish women, God bless them, to eat and be silent. Johnny's cakes are as rich and fine as the food of the saints, and so light that when you throw 'em in the air they stay there. I wish I had a dozen now."

"You may think he's exaggerating about Johnny's cooking," my uncle said, "but I'll tell you a story to prove it. Johnny and I were buddies in the Boer War. He's a little man now, and he was a little man then, and not a hair on his face but that mustache like a kind of cord to hang him up by.

"We were out on patrol, and a Dutch column, horses and wagons, came down the road and cut us off. So we lay down behind a boulder in the field and put mud on our backs and lay still as stones, which in truth is what we seemed to be at fifty yards. Our heads and arms were up close to the boulder and pretty well hidden from the road, so after a while Johnny says, 'Are you hungry?' I snorted. 'And so what?' I asked. Johnny pointed to a flat stone at the edge of the boulder. The sun had been beating down on this stone all morning, and it was hot. 'We'll make it hotter,' says Johnny, taking out the captain's field glasses, which we had, being on patrol.

" 'What are you thinking of, Johnny?' I asked.

" 'Flapjacks,' says Johnny.

" 'You are mad with the heat, Flaherty,' I say. 'Let's eat our condensed rations.'

" 'Condensed rations!' " says Johnny, and spits.

"He was right, so I spat too, being careful not to move the mud on my back and legs. On the road they were pulling field pieces past, and Johnny and I kept count.

" 'Of course,' says Johnny, 'this is not the five-burner stove me mother had in Ireland, and it will not accommodate large pancakes. But I will roll them thin.' So he reaches into his knapsack.

"You understand, Katherine Mary, it was the patient work of a half hour to move his hand to his knapsack. But out come dried eggs and pancake flour and condensed milk. Well, he mixed the batter in the palm of his hand, which added to the flavor, I'm thinking, and he rolled it out thin with his forefinger, and cooked it on the hot stone with the captain's lens. And they came out flapjacks no bigger than a shilling, but tasting like manna from heaven. And all

24

this time we moved nothing but our hands and our mouths. Our hands very slowly and our mouths very fast.

"It got dark and we started to make our way back, but there was a sniper waiting for us in a tree. The first we knew of him, there was a shot, and we both rolled into the ditch. It was not exactly a ditch, but a damp stream bed, wet and dirty.

" 'Did you see where it came from?' says Johnny.

" 'No.' I had not. Neither had he.

" 'Then we stay here to eternity,' says Johnny, 'because he knows where *we* are.'

"I looked at Johnny and said, 'It is not the fate of a Kennedy to spend the rest of his life with his face in the mud. I'll stand up and draw his fire, and you kill him.'

" 'A very good plan,' says Johnny approvingly, 'but it is I who will stand up. I am a smaller man, and there are not so many places to kill me.'

" 'That may well be,' I replied, 'but as it was my idea, it is my right to try it.'

" 'Like a Kennedy to hog all the glory,' Johnny snickers. 'You invented the plan, I will carry it out.'

"I began to be worried. I saw the prospect of a long, lonely hike back to camp, with nothing to eat but condensed rations. 'Johnny,' I said, 'if he kills you, there will be no one left to make the pancakes. And your pancakes are my only satisfaction in this hot and dirty land ten thousand miles from Ireland.'

" 'And much good it will do me to make pancakes,' says Johnny bitterly, 'if you are too dead to eat them.'

"So the argument continued, and finally we threw dice to decide it. But they were Johnny's dice, and he could make them come out thirteen if the mood was in him, so it was no surprise to see that he won and stood up and was shot in the shoulder before I brought the Dutchman down.

" 'Are you all right, Johnny?' I yelled.

" 'My left arm,' he says holding it.

" 'Praise be to the Mother of God,' I said, 'it's not your flapjack arm,' and we got up out of the ditch."

My uncle pushed back his chair, and so did Mike. "Wait till you eat them," he said. The men stood up.

I was getting used to my uncle's stories. I soon learned

that when it came to spinning a yarn or telling a tale, he had a touch of the genius of Denny Lannon the storyteller, whose grandnephew he is. And I suppose the reason he was so sparing with words in between times is that he was saving them up for his next story.

"Well," said Mike, "when are you going to teach Kathy to shoot?"

"You mean go hunting?" I couldn't believe it.

"Johnny bought her a twenty-two in town," Uncle said.

"You won't be needing any ammunition," Mike said, and grinned at me.

"Why not?" I asked.

"Well, you can use the currants in those seven currant pies you baked."

Was there really something wrong with the pies? I'd been saving mine for later because I was full. But I walked to the table and took a big bite of it to show him. It was as if I had pebbles in my mouth. I wondered what was wrong. But I wasn't going to ask them because they were laughing at me and because my mouth was too full of that currant rock pile to talk. To spit them out would be defeat, so I made a fake gulp and tried to hold my mouth naturally as if I had swallowed them.

Mike said good-by. I didn't answer because I couldn't. He took my hand and leaned toward me till my hair brushed his cheek.

"Spit 'em out," he said softly, "and next time, cook 'em."

I did no more cooking for a while. Johnny was back on the job, and he would only let me in the kitchen to sniff. But I made him promise to let me get the dinner if ever Sergeant Mike Flannigan returned.

Oh, it was a fine revenge I was preparing for him! I would make currant pies with currants so soft and juicy they would melt in the mouths of the men, but his I would fill with buckshot. And while the others ate and enjoyed, he would break his jaws. Then I would say, not to him but to the walls, "It is weak teeth these redcoats have."

Or maybe he'd come knocking at the door in the middle of a storm, with mud all over that fine uniform, and a slow step, and weariness in his eyes (for he had ridden night and day without rest), and bleeding from a wound in the shoulder, where a crazy 'breed had shot him. I'd help him in and take off his boots, and give him hot tea and whisky, and get him into his bunk. He'd say, "Thank you." I'd say, "Oh, I'm just a litle chit." And I'd laugh carelessly to show it didn't make a penny's difference to me, one way or another.

Sometimes I brought him home with a bullet in his shoulder and sometimes limping from frostbitten feet. But today his leg was broken where a horse fell on him. He was leaning on me and I was helping him to the couch, when a girl rode up on a pony and banged on the door.

I opened it, and she strode in, tall and blonde and swift-moving. She was the first white girl I'd seen since Calgary.

"I'm Mildred MacDonald," she said. "And you're Katherine Mary. You're very pretty. You don't resemble your Uncle John at all. I would have come over earlier, but I was in Calgary. Do you like it here? Have you seen Johnny Flaherty? Can you ride?"

I said, "Yes," meaning I could ride. As for the other questions, I'd lost track.

I guess she'd lost track too, for she snapped back, "Then let's go. That's my pony outside, Name's Squaw."

"I'll go get Rosie," I said. "It'll just take a minute."

Mildred went into the kitchen to talk to Johnny, and I went to the stable to saddle Rosie.

Rosie was a red-and-white Indian cayuse, and Uncle John had told me Rosie was mine for as long as I stayed with him. But he hadn't told Rosie. She was more trouble than a bag of wildcats. Some days she acted as if she had swallowed a pint of pepper. She dashed here and there, trotted and galloped and jumped ditches, whether I wanted to or not. The next day she would mope. A slow walk was her fancy now, a slow walk that grew tireder and tireder and at last stopped altogether. If I kicked her, she'd go into a bumpy jog, two steps walking and two steps trot, and the moment my attention wandered, Rosie stopped.

Hard as it was to ride Rosie, it was harder to saddle her. I threw a blanket and saddle on her back. That was easy. But the moment I threaded the end of the cinch strap through the rings, Rosie's eyes met mine, her nostrils twitched, she sucked in an enormous breath, and her stomach swelled up like a sausage balloon. Pull as I would, I could barely fasten the strap. I mounted her, out came her breath, the saddle slithered around, and the blanket worked loose. I'll be lucky, I thought, if a stirrup doesn't come off.

It was this, I think, that lost me the race. It's a hard thing to race a horse when you're running a private race yourself to stay on her back. Rosie was faster than Mildred's Squaw, but more independent. And when Rosie zigzagged, it was all I could do to make me and the saddle zig and zag with her.

If only Rosie had let me saddle her right, and had run fairly straight, and not stopped once to take a quick bite out of a shrub, I could have won the race long before my pleurisy got me. As it was, Mildred was sailing ahead on Squaw when my pleurisy stabbed my side and chest with long twisting pains.

Mildred caught Squaw up short and wheeled her around. They came galloping back. She reined the pony in. "What's the matter, Katherine Mary, don't you feel good?"

"I'm all right," I said. "I'm just not used to riding. I bounce all over." I slid off Rosie's back. I felt shaky, and the pains were still in my chest.

"Put the reins forward over her nose." Mildred got off Squaw. "They think they're tied then and won't bolt for it."

"Will they just graze here?"

Mildred nodded. She was still breathless from the chase. I sat down with a rock to lean against. The meadow and the sky were fuzzy, as if they were made out of cloth, and they leaned at a queer angle. I closed my eyes, and when I looked again, the meadow was level and the sky was where it ought to be.

Mildred flopped down beside me. "That was fun. I love to ride. So does Dick." She stopped, looked at me, and laughed.

"Who's Dick?" I asked, because I saw I was supposed to.

"Dick is Richard Carlton. He's a lawyer with brown eyes that I'm going to marry."

"Are you really going to get married?" She seemed more wonderful to me now than ever.

"He lives in Calgary, and we've been engaged for three weeks."

"How do you have to feel about someone, to marry him? I mean, do you think about him all the time and try to remember how he looks and what he's said . . . ?" I stopped. Mildred was looking at me in a strange way.

"Are *you* in love?" she asked.

I felt my cheeks getting hot. "Of course I'm not in love. Why, I don't even know what it feels like. That's why I asked you."

"Well, you gave a pretty good description of it."

"I just thought you'd have to feel something like that if you were going to marry someone." I felt I was stumbling around so I quit talking and watched Rosie and Squaw munch grass, then amble slowly, still chewing, to a more tempting spot, pull up and digest the most tender of the young blades.

"Dick has his practice in Calgary," Mildred went on. "I was in last week with Mother, and he took us to lunch. Dick knows your Uncle John."

"Does he know a lot of people?"

"Oh, Dick knows everybody."

"Well," I hesitated, "does he know Sergeant Michael Flannigan?" There, it was out and said. Mildred didn't seem surprised. It was just conversation.

"Of course he knows Mike. So do I, so does everybody in Alberta, I guess. In fact, Mike and I had a long talk about you in Calgary."

"Oh!" I tried to seem casual. "What does he do in Calgary?"

"He's on some sort of detail work. Anyway, he said I was going to have a girl friend, a very pretty one, at that."

"Oh, he didn't! He thinks I'm skinny."

"I'm just telling you what he said, Katherine Mary."

"Well, he thinks I'm skinny too, because he called me a little chit. As a matter of fact . . ." I pulled two wide grass blades, placed them together and tried to whistle through them, but it didn't work.

"As a matter of fact, what?" Mildred asked.

"Oh, nothing. I was just going to say I don't think much of Mike Flannigan."

"Why not?"

I considered. "Well, for one thing, he's too cocky."

29

"And he's a big brute of a man too."

"Oh, I like a man to be big." Then I saw she was teasing me. "Mildred," I said, "don't you ever tell him I said that."

She smiled. "I won't, Kathy. Why, I'd bite my tongue off before I'd repeat a thing like that to Mike Flannigan or any other man. They're conceited enough as it is." She squeezed my hand. "But you do like him a little, don't you?"

I thought about that for a while. "Well, I like some things about him."

"What things?"

"His eyes."

"They are nice," she agreed.

"Mildred, they're so blue you could swim in them."

## CHAPTER THREE

We were in the kitchen. Johnny had shot a deer and was skinning it. It was bloody and messy, and I tried not to look. Johnny tossed a piece of fur at Juno, who dragged it into a corner and worried and fought it.

The other men would go off on long hunts, be gone all day. But not Johnny. He'd go out to the ravine about a mile behind the house and just sit there until a deer came by, and then shoot it. He was telling me that moose meat was better, that it tasted like beef, and that next time he'd bring down a moose.

"Especially the nose; great delicacy, the nose."

"I don't think I'd like to eat anything's nose," I said.

"Yes, you would. You'd like moose nose. An Indian dish, great delicacy. Another favorite with the Indians is bear paw. They bring in beautiful bear skins to the Hudson's Bay Company, but all the paws are cut off. Could get a lot more for their skins if they wouldn't mutilate them— but they'd rather take less and eat bear paws." He took the carcass outdoors. Juno and I followed him and watched with great interest as he tied it in a tree.

"Keep the flies from it."

"Don't they fly as high as that tree?" I asked.

But Johnny was more interested in food than in flies. "Tell you something else that's a great delicacy, that's beaver tail. Yes, sir, that tail is real sweet. On the other hand, a porcupine tastes terrible."

I followed Johnny back into the kitchen.

"Ever make a mulligan stew?" he asked.

I had to admit I hadn't. "What do you put in them?"

"Everything. You can watch me." He took pride in his cooking, just as any artist would, and it was a treat to watch him. He let me collect the vegetables for him while he cut up the meat. Everything in one pot. That was the principle, Johnny explained. I watched enthralled as caribou, grouse, pork, rice, potatoes, dehydrated corn, canned tomatoes, macaroni, and celery followed each other into the pot. Johnny laughed.

"The more the better. Everything flavors everything else in a real mulligan." Johnny stopped talking to stir. Soon the smell of it was in the air, and the look on Johnny's face was one of reverence.

"What about the deer in the tree? Is it going to be a mulligan too?"

"No, it's going to be pemmican."

"What's that?"

"Just dried moose or deer meat."

"I haven't seen Mildred for ten days." I said "Mildred" but I was thinking "Mike" and there must have been something in my voice because he stopped stirring and looked at me.

"Is a moose like a deer, only bigger," I asked quickly, "with bigger antlers?" That wouldn't have fooled a woman, but it fooled Johnny. He was right back on moose.

"They're not the same thing at all, different animals. Take a moose, now. It will never gallop like a deer. Just swings along at a sort of pacing trot. But it can outdistance the fastest horse going."

Had Mike gone back to the country he'd come from without stopping to see my Uncle John? Or was he still on duty in Calgary? Would he be coming by the ranch again? I suddenly realized that Johnny had stopped talking. The last word I'd heard had been "moose," so with a great deal of interest in my voice, and none at all in me, I asked, "Is a moose a clever animal?" It sounded like a stupid thing to

31

say, even to me, but it was enough for Johnny to be off again.

"Well, now, clever—it's hard to say. It's got poor sight. But it's clever enough when it comes to smelling or hearing." He interrupted himself long enough to put a spoonful of mulligan in his mouth. With his cooking and eating and eating and cooking, it's a wonder to me so much ever came to the table.

I began to think of the time that I had cooked and Mike had eaten. But it was hard to think around Johnny when he was telling stories, and he was telling one now.

"It was a blizzard storm I was out in. Mighty trees such as fir and spruce crashing down and branches breaking off and flung by the wind great distances. It was in such weather and on such a day that I was stalking a giant moose with an antler spread of fifty to sixty inches. Now, mind, he was over a hundred yards from me at the time, and all around were the trees and the branches crashing to the earth. And here I was sneaking up on him, trying to get my sights on him. But there was too much brush between us, and he was taking cover in it, not because he suspected I was around, but because that's their instinct. Well, I was moving gently as I could through that gale—but didn't my foot step on a twig and snap it! Well, it was a little twig, and mighty trees were splitting and falling, but the big fellow heard that twig and he let out a 'bell' and was out of sight before I could get my gun to my shoulder. That's a true example of their powers of hearing."

I guess it was true, all right, and a little more than true. But that's the way Johnny tells things.

"Help me dish out the mulligan." And Johnny reached down three bowls.

"There's only two of us." I started to put back the third bowl, but he stopped me.

"Mildred's here," he said.

"*What!*" I ran to the window. She was tying Squaw to the porch. I turned and looked at Johnny. He was grinning.

"Heard the pony," he said. "Our men would've come in all together."

"Johnny, you've got hearing like a moose."

Mildred came in and ate mulligan stew with us. It was

32

wonderful because, as I said before, Johnny was an artist. He would no more let anyone drop a vegetable in his stew than Michelangelo would have let a student sculp the finger of one of his statues. No, you could not help Johnny cook. About dishwashing he wasn't so much of an artist. He let Mildred and me help him. And then pretty soon he was off altogether.

We were glad to have the kitchen to ourselves. Up to then we'd just been skirting around things and giggling when we got too close to the important ones, as when Mildred said, "Done any more swimming, Katherine?"

Johnny said, "What do you mean—any more? There ain't no place to swim around here."

We both laughed, and Johnny looked kind of disgusted, and that's when he said he had chores.

Mildred was just waiting for me to ask her something, and I wouldn't. Finally she had to say it herself. "I was in Calgary again to see Dick."

"How is he?"

"Who? Dick?"

I thought that was mean of her. "Of course, Dick. Isn't that who you were talking about?"

Mildred smiled. "Oh; he's fine; in fact, he's wonderful. Mother and I shopped in town all day for my trousseau. And then in the evening Dick took me dancing. Oh, it was fun!"

It sounded like fun. I imagined myself shopping with Mother and picking out beautiful filmy white gowns because Mike and I were going to be married. And then in the evening Mike took me dancing.

"You're so quiet," Mildred said. "What are you thinking about?"

I realized I'd been drying that bowl for an awfully long time. "Nothing. Just about what a good time you must have had."

"Oh, and guess who we saw?"

My lips formed the word "who," but I don't think I ever got it out.

"Ted Russell. Oh, that's right, you don't know Ted, do you? Mike Flannigan was there too."

"Where?"

"At the dance."

Words, just plain words, strung together in a sentence can slash to pieces the make-believe and the dreams. They cut into mine. The black wavy hair and the tall red coat were the same. But those eyes, those blue eyes that had been smiling at me, smiled now at someone else.

"What was she like?" I must have asked out loud because Mildred answered, "What was who like?"

But now I didn't want to know. What did it matter whether she was tall or short, thin or fat? I wasn't she, and never would be. It would be this girl I didn't know, but who was much prettier than I, who would bandage Mike when he came in wounded. It was she, this girl who maybe had wavy black hair and blue eyes too, who would cook surprises for him, who—

"Katherine Mary, who were you talking about?"

"Nobody," I said and threw a shower of knives and forks into the drawer. "Let's go out on the porch." I thought this would change the subject, but I was wrong.

We were out there and sitting on the swing when she asked it again. "I know you were talking about somebody. Now who was it?"

"I was just wondering about the dance, and what you wore and what Mike's girl wore."

"Mike's girl?" She gave me a blank look.

"Well, you said he was there, didn't you?"

"But he didn't bring anybody. He just called the dances. Why, he didn't dance once."

Words, it was just words again. Or maybe it was all in myself. I had made the unhappiness, and now I made the glad feeling that was all through me. I thought about it for a while. Words that I could spell, and a few that I couldn't, were back of all feelings that anyone in the world had ever felt.

"Mike asked about you." These words were so wonderful that they bounced me right up in the sky.

"He did?"

"Yes, he thinks you're awfully pretty."

"He does? Did he say so?"

"Well, he didn't say it exactly like that. He said he'd never seen such a head of hair on any female."

34

I was a little disappointed.

"But, Mildred, that doesn't mean he thinks I'm pretty. That just means—well, that I've got a lot of hair. And anyway 'female' isn't a very nice word."

"What's wrong with it?"

"I guess there's nothing wrong with it. It just sounds like animals, that's all."

Mildred laughed. "You should be glad 'cause that shows he doesn't go around saying nice things about all the girls. 'Cause if he did, he'd know how better." I thought that was a very fine bit of reasoning and my affection for Mildred increased considerably.

"He said something else, too."

"What?"

"He said your eyes were as gray as the breast of a dove."

That was poetry, and it thrilled me. "Did he really, Mildred?"

Mildred hesitated. "Well, he said gray as a whisky-jack."

"A what?"

She looked at me helplessly. "A whisky-jack; it's a bird too."

"But not a dove?"

She admitted that it wasn't a dove, but a thief and a scavenger.

"Wherever did it get such a name as whisky-jack?" I asked.

"It's the kind of call they have. It sounds like they're asking for whisky."

Well, I didn't know whether I liked Mike's compliments or not. Of course, you had to take into consideration that he was a woodsman, and it would be natural for him to compare a girl with things he knew. He'd probably never seen a dove, and a whisky-jack he saw every day. Even so, working hard at it, I couldn't make myself like it. Then, suddenly a terrifying thought struck me, and I looked at Mildred. Why had he mentioned my eyes, the color of my eyes, unless . . .

"Mildred, you didn't tell him?"

"Tell him what?" She asked it right out, as if she had nothing to hide. But now the suspicion had entered me, I

35

could not be sure. "You know, what I said about his eyes being so blue you could swim in them."

Mildred looked hurt. "Why, Katherine Mary, you know I'd never breathe a word. Why, I'd bite my tongue off first."

The way she said it made me feel very ashamed and unworthy of her friendship. But still I couldn't help thinking it was funny he'd said anything about my eyes.

Mildred stayed all night. I was supposed to ride her back in the morning, but we slept pretty late. And then Johnny took his gun and went toward the ravine. It was a perfect chance. We decided to make apple pies. I knew how to do that. Mother had taught me. I intended to make twelve of them all at once. I figured I'd have to, with that many men eating them.

"We've got a case of apples, Mildred. How many do you think are in a case?"

"About thirty pounds," Mildred said.

I looked inside and held up a very wrinkled-looking object.

"Is this an apple?" I asked Mildred.

"Of course. It's a dried apple."

I'd never used dried apples before, but I proceeded as if they had been regular apples like the ones Mother bought in Boston. I put the thirty pounds of apples into the washtub in relays and soaked them. Then I put them on to boil.

"Haven't you got an awful lot of apples there?" Mildred asked as she watched me fill container after container with apples and set them on the stove.

"Don't forget I'm feeding twelve men," I said, and that shut her up.

I was sorry I had snapped at her, and I said, "I suppose you're a good cook yourself, Mildred."

"I've cooked for Dick lots of times when he was up at our ranch. I think that's one of the reasons he proposed to me." She laughed, and then stopped all at once. There were tears in her eyes. "Oh, Kathy, I don't know when we'll be married."

"Why?" I asked, slipping my arm around her. "What's the matter?"

"Oh, nothing. It's just that—well, it's harder to marry a lawyer than a Mounty."

36

"What's so hard about it?"

"A Mounty can't marry till he's been in the service five years. And a lawyer can't marry till he can feed a wife. At least that's what Dick says. And it's so hard to get started."

"It's always hard when you're young," I said, and I said other things that we had both heard people say. They seemed to comfort her. Not the words, but that she knew I was sorry about her and Dick, and that I wished they could get married right away.

Mildred snatched off her apron. "Come on," she said. "That's enough. You can ride me home now."

We raced each other over the low meadowland, and that seemed to restore her spirits. But I kept thinking about something she had said—that a Mounty had to be on the force five years before he could marry. I wondered how long Mike had served.

I didn't stay at the MacDonald ranch because of the boiling apples. On the ride back I just let Rosie lope along. I only pulled at the reins when she stopped to eat grass, which she did as often as she thought she could get away with it. Suddenly I jerked her up so hard and short she rolled her eyes and flicked her ears at me. I hadn't meant to, but coming over the hill to the north of me was another rider.

In such wild and open country you rarely meet anyone, but it wasn't that that made me pull at Rosie. It was that even at that distance I could see that the rider was tall, and that he was dressed in red. I told Rosie that there were other Mounties in the world, and it probably wasn't Mike at all. But I didn't believe myself, and my heart pounded fast and made more noise than Rosie's hoofs.

He was close enough now for me to see it was a uniform—red jacket, dark blue riding breeches with a yellow stripe, long brown boots, spurs, holster, beaver cap on top of black waving hair, and blue eyes, the bluest I had ever seen.

I looked up into them and kept on looking. No words came to my head. The way I'd planned it, I was going to bandage him or feed him, but here in the hills, I couldn't do either. So I smiled the smile I'd practiced in the mirror.

"How do you do, Sergeant Flannigan?"

"Get off your horse," he said. That was certainly not the

37

way to greet a young woman you hadn't seen in three weeks. I gave him what I hoped was an icy look and dug my heels into Rosie, who shot off.

Mike wheeled his horse and took after me. It was a short race because he rode that big black horse of his right in front of Rosie. She stopped short; I went pitching forward and, would have fallen if Mike hadn't reached out and grabbed me and set me back in the saddle again.

He dismounted. "Get down," he said.

I sat there with my lips pressed hard together, thinking things I could only have said if I'd been Johnny or John L. Sullivan.

Sergeant Mike reached up, put his two hands around my waist, and lifted me down. For just a minute I was standing awfully close to him, and for that minute I couldn't do anything.

But I pulled away. "Mike Flannigan," I said, "you're not to push me around and pull me off horses. I'll tell my uncle, and he and Johnny and the ten hands will ride you down and even if you are a Mounty, they'll hog-tie you and—" I had started out in a low, frigid voice, but by now I was yelling, and he stood there and watched me, slightly amused, as if I was putting on a show for him.

"Katherine Mary, you're the hardest girl in the world to do anything for."

I looked at him a little uncertainly. "What did you want to do for me?"

"I want to teach you to manage a horse."

There he was telling me again.

"I know how to manage my horse."

Mike laughed. "If you could have seen yourself bouncing all over, like a jack-in-the-box, you wouldn't think so."

"Mildred says I ride very well."

"You would if you'd tighten your cinch."

"But Rosie—" I changed my mind. I wasn't going to give him the satisfaction of showing me or telling me anything more.

"But Rosie blows out her stomach when you go to pull it tight. Is that it?"

"How'd you . . .?" Then I saw the grin on his face. "Yes, that's it."

38

"Well, look. Here's what you've got to do." He undid Rosie's cinch and held it ready to tighten. Rosie took her usual big breath, blowing out her belly till it looked like a barrel. When she had it completely extended, Mike cracked her across the back with the flat of his hand. Rosie was so surprised she gave a sort of gasp, and all the breath went out of her. Her sides deflated like a punctured balloon, and in that moment the cinch was pulled in and tightened.

"There," said Mike. "Now you do it."

I tried to, but the first time I didn't hit hard enough, and the second time I forgot to pull the cinch, but finally I got it.

"Did I do it right?" I asked, knowing very well I had but wanting a little praise out of him.

"Now, another thing," said Mike. "You're riding English on a western saddle. You've got to let out those stirrups." He fiddled around with them and slipped them in a lower notch. "Try that," and he handed me up.

"How it is? Comfortable?"

I had decided to say it was all wrong, but he asked me so eagerly that I had to let him be right. "Yes, it's much better."

He looked at me and smiled, not that teasing grin, but a sweet, gentle, kind smile.

We looked at each other for a few minutes. Then I began to realize neither one of us was talking. And that he was looking at me in a queer way. Of course, the sun was in his eyes, and it might have been that.

"It's a lovely day," I said, "but warm." And before he could answer, I let out a cry that startled all of us, including Rosie, who started off like a mad thing. I kept her going, too, urging her ahead.

Mike never did catch up to me. He had to catch his horse first; it had bolted when I shrieked. He kept shouting questions, but at the speed Rosie was going there wasn't enough breath in my body to answer him. Besides, how could a man understand what it is when you've left your apples boiling too long!

I pulled up in front of the house and jumped down. The dried apples met me at the door. They had boiled up and over. The floor was covered with the messy things. I stood aghast, looking and not knowing where to begin.

Mike came up behind me and looked too. He didn't say anything, just took off his coat, rolled up his sleeves, and went to work. We filled a washtub and a bucket with puffed dried apples. I was embarrassed that a thing like this had to happen when Mike was here. But it was funny, and I couldn't help laughing. Mike laughed too when he saw me laughing. I guess he didn't dare laugh before, for fear of hurting my feelings.

He reached for the last apple, but it slipped out of his hand almost at my feet. I stopped to get it just as he did, and we bumped heads with an impact that sent us both sprawling. We really laughed then. We laughed so hard we couldn't get up. Uncle John and Juno must have heard us because they came in to see what was going on. There we were, Mike and I, lying on the floor and roaring. Uncle looked down at us, and we looked up at Uncle. It was a long way up Uncle John's six-foot-three of height, and by the time you reached his face you were at a psychological disadvantage. I suppose Mike thought so too, because he got to his feet.

"Hello, John." He said it a little breathlessly, but with one of his most ingratiating grins, which Uncle John did not return.

"Katherine Mary," my uncle said, "you will please get up from the floor?"

Mike came forward to give me a hand, but Uncle stepped in front of him and helped me up himself.

Mike looked upset. "We were just—er—picking apples." He .waved toward the linoleum and repeated the word "apples." Uncle John looked at the linoleum too. But all the apples were picked up, all but the one we had fallen down over, and Juno must have eaten that because there wasn't an apple in sight. Uncle, Mike, and I stared at the blue and gray linoleum.

"We were picking apples," Mike repeated stubbornly.

"Hmmm," Uncle said.

And that was all he said until dinner, when he told Johnny that in *his* day they picked apples from trees.

Mike was back in a few days. He stood in the doorway smiling and holding out a present.

40

"You didn't need to bring me anything," I said, but was very excited that he had, so excited that I couldn't get the string untied.

"Here——" he took it out of my hands—"I'll do it." He snapped the cord and handed the package back to me. I opened it, looked at Mike, looked at it, and looked at Mike again.

"Well, put them on," he said.

I lifted out a pair of heavy mackinaw pants. "But they're men's," I protested.

"Put them on. I'm not taking you hiking in *that*." And he pointed scornfully at my blue polka-dot dress.

"Are you taking me hiking?"

"Yes. Hurry up and change." I grabbed up the trousers and started for the bedroom. Then I remembered. After all, they were a present.

"Thank you very much," I said. "They're lovely."

Mike grinned. "Put 'em on."

We tramped along a stream, past the foothills and up into the mountainous country. I liked the way Mike walked. I liked the freedom in his body. I kept up with him too because he had just said that he hated to walk with women who minced along. Mike led the way up the path. For a while I watched the tops of the tall silver trees, but I stumbled, and then I watched the ground. It was dappled with moving dark shadows of leaves and with bright sunny patches. It was a strange day. The air would be very quiet, and then up ahead you would see a fluttering of the leaves. A moment later the little gust of air would pass you, and it would be still again.

We entered the gorge of a mountain stream. The sides loomed steeper and steeper. Rock ledges shot up to meet perpendicular cliffs. A sharp black shadow shrouded our path. The sun and sky disappeared and leaning out over us at a crazy angle was a giant gray bluff.

Mike looked back over his shoulder. "Notice the sheer rock faces. See how one juts out above the other. I think the Indians must get their patterns for blankets and baskets from the design in these rocks."

I was glad, though, when the cliff didn't hang over us, but

41

slanted back the way it was supposed to and let us have the sun again.

"Thirsty?" Mike asked.

"Yes."

He flopped down on his stomach on a low flat rock and, reaching into the stream, he cupped water up into his hand and drank. I lay down on my stomach too and cupped my hands and filled them with water, but the water dripped through my fingers, and by the time I got my hand to my mouth all I could do was to lick a slightly wet palm.

Mike laughed. "I guess you'll have to get your face down in it. Inch forward a little so you can reach it."

I looked at the frothy swirling water. "I'll fall in."

"No, you won't."

"My hair will get wet."

"I'll hold it." He caught back my hair, and I got a very good drink. I stood up laughing and blinking water out of my eyes. Mike opened his hands slowly, and my hair fell back around my shoulders.

"Is your hair red?"

"It's auburn," I said and tossed my head a little so he could see the lights that auburn hair has.

He turned away. "Come on."

I followed him back to the trail. He'd thought my hair was pretty; I knew he had. Why wouldn't he tell me?

We passed a tiny tree growing out of a solid mass of rock. "Look, Mike."

Mike slowed down and looked. "It's got guts," he said. "In another twenty years it will be a spruce."

We walked on again, and I swung my arms like Mike. Up ahead he stopped and held a brier that would have snapped back and struck me in the face. He watched me as I came up to him and ducked under the branch.

"You walk like a boy," he said. I knew that was meant as a compliment, the first compliment that Mike had ever paid me. I was glad now that I had strained every muscle to keep up with those long legs of his. But after a moment I had to lean against a rock to catch my breath.

"I wonder what makes a mountain?"

"Upheavals in the earth, but it's the water that cuts the

42

levels and ravines and determines the character of the mountain."

I loved to hear Mike talk. He put himself in the place of whatever he told about. When he told about mountains, he was the mountain talking. I glanced up at him. He was shading his eyes and looking upstream. There'd been something on my mind, and for days I'd been thinking of ways to ask it. Finally I decided the best way was to ask it straight out. Then it would seem to be a question like any other, or at most a desire to make conversation. So I said it.

"Mike!" He turned and looked at me, but I asked it anyway: "How long have you been a Mounty?"

"Since I was a kid. Let's see, it's been about seven years." He looked at me with a question in his eyes.

"I was just thinking," I said hastily, "that that's why you know about mountains and what makes them, and things like that."

"Well, when you live in 'em, you get to know 'em. As a person knows his house because he lives in it."

I nodded, but I was thinking . . . seven years. And Mildred said all a Mounty needed was five years on the Force. I stopped myself right there. My heart pounded the blood into my face.

"Let's go on, Mike," I said, but he caught my hand and pulled me back.

"We've got to go quietly from here on. Follow me and don't make a sound. I've got something to show you where the stream bends up there."

"What?" I asked, but he motioned me into silence and, leaving the trail which branched away from the river at this point, made his way silently and nimbly over the stream bed. Those wet rocks were slippery, and slimy moss grew on them, so I followed much more slowly, and he waited twice for me to come up to him. The second time he nodded toward the forest of silver trees scattered among the rocks and thickening into a dark tangle of woods.

I looked and at first could see nothing. Then I noticed one or two and finally a dozen trees that had been felled in the oddest manner. The stumps were not sliced straight across as a saw would leave them, but were whittled into a conical shape, the tip ending in a sharp point.

"Beavers," Mike whispered.

"Is that what you were going to show me?" I whispered back.

"That's the way they cut trees. One working at each side. They slice the wood through with their teeth. Their dam's just ahead."

We crept forward a few feet more. Mike pulled me down beside him on a rock ledge, and I stared at the blockade of wood, stones, twigs, and mud that dammed the stream and turned it into a large pool.

We were silent a long time, waiting and watching. My foot began to cramp under me, but I didn't dare move it. And then, up to the surface of the pool bobbed a beaver. He swam across, using his tail as a rudder. He scampered upon shore, and we lost him among the rocks. He was about three feet long, and one-third of him was tail. His hair started silky gray and became a coarse, thick, reddish brown. When he jumped to the rock, I saw that his hind feet were webbed.

"We were lucky to see him," Mike's voice was very low. "In the spring they are usually off roving the forest, but there is a break in the dam. See, where that little trickle of water is coming through." Mike stopped talking suddenly and jerked his head toward where the beaver had disappeared. Here he was, back again. He came walking on his hind legs, carrying stones and pebbles in his paws.

"He looks like a little man," I whispered.

"That's what the Indians call them, 'the little people.' "

The beaver walked out on top of the dam and, reaching over, stuffed his stones into the opening and patted mud carefully around. Mike reached impulsively for my hand. I followed his eyes, and there at the foot of a large elm was another beaver. She was chewing busily at a branch and didn't seem to be helping in the construction work at all.

"They eat the pulp of branches, and water-lily roots, leaves, things like that, and berries too." Mike's hand was still over mine, and I wondered if he knew it.

"How many beavers do you think there are?" I whispered.

"Usually there are about four adults and eight young."

"How old does a beaver get?"

44

"Oh, they live to be twenty or thirty years old."

The beaver that had been eating dropped her branch and came down to the edge of the pool to watch her mate. You could see that she carried young. The little fellow working on the dam had dived in the water. He was submerged for several minutes.

"They have a lodge down there with dozens of rooms that are connected by water. They're very busy, these little people. They fell trees in the summer when they're building a new dam, and when the tree's ready to fall, they whack the ground, with their tails. It's their warning, like a lumberman yelling, 'Timber!' Then in the fall they build their lodges. Sometimes there's as many as a hundred of them working, laying in supplies of wood for food and building material." Mike smiled at me. "In fact, they are the only creatures, besides man, that do so much building and engineering. They like to change the looks of the world, and so do we." He stared into the water. "They are very human. I have heard stories of Indian women losing their babies, who have suckled young beavers to bring them comfort."

I saw the dark head of the beaver as it broke the surface. He swam the pool and climbed up on the bank beside his wife. And what a performance he went through after his bath! He squeezed the water out of his coat with his hands, much as we would wring out laundry. It was very funny to watch him, and I almost laughed out loud. Then the two of them began to tussle. They wrapped their arms around each other and rocked back and forth, then round and round, but never sideways. They looked like fat little furry men wrestling. I looked at Mike to see if he was laughing, but he wasn't. He was looking upstream, and his face was angry. He jumped up. The beavers stopped romping, stared at him, and scampered off.

"Mike!" I got up too. I was mad at him for frightening them away.

"Stay here, Kathy." He spoke so emphatically that I did what he told me. I stood watching as he made his way along the rocks by the beaver pool.

But I was curious to see what he was after, and anyway why should I stay here just because Mike Flannigan told me to? So I followed him over the rocks and sand, past the

45

pool, and then I saw what I couldn't see before because it hung gray against gray slate rock. A pole like fishing pole had been set low over the water. It had a clamp on the end of it. A mother beaver had swum into it. The trap had sprung, swinging the pole high into the air. And there the beaver hung by her forepaws, whimpering. A large hawk swooped low, and I cried out. Mike wheeled around.

"Get back!" I saw then what he did not want me to see. The eyes of the beaver had been torn out of their sockets. Mike broke the pole and laid the animal on the ground. Then he carried me into the edge of the wood. There he sat me down with my back against a tree. He had faced me in the other direction, so I heard him go but did not see him.

That note of distress was in my ears. I sat there seeing the empty sockets ooze blood. Then I heard the shot, and my hands unclenched themselves. I heard Mike coming back, but I couldn't stop crying. I could see the toes of his boots standing beside me. He bent over and touched my hair, very lightly.

"The hawk did it, and the beaver was still alive!" I sobbed through the woods.

"Kathy, don't think about it. I never thought—" He stopped, and when he went on his voice was calm again. "No real hunter would trap, this time of year. An Indian wouldn't. Most others wouldn't either."

I shook my head because I couldn't talk.

"They wait till June anyway, when the young are born." I knew he wanted me to answer him, but I couldn't. I just couldn't.

"And it isn't like this, as a rule. Almost all the fellows set traps under water, that either drown the beaver or let it get away without mangling it. These spring poles are nasty contrivances, and not many use them. Really, Kathy."

"How—how long had it hung there?" I choked over the words.

"Not long." But I knew he was lying because the blood had clotted.

"What did you do with it? Just leave it there?"

Mike looked embarrassed. "That paw that it was caught by was almost pulled out anyway, so I put it in the beaver pool."

46

I looked at him in horror. "You mean you cut off its foot and put it in the pool?"

Mike avoided my eyes.

"It's one of those crazy Indian customs that white men that live among Indians fall into. You feel sorry for the beaver you've had to trap, so you leave part of him, any part you can spare, in the place where he has lived, so the spirit coming back will find it and understand that the hunter made what reparation he could." Mike spoke as though he believed this. What a strange man he was!

"I've known trappers who have worked hours boring a hole through the ice of a beaver pool to give back to the spirit a portion of what he had taken."

A furry body hanging by a mangled forepaw, a hawk biting and tearing away the helpless thing's eyes . . . His words had fallen gently, like a curtain shutting those pictures from my mind. He took both my hands in his. He felt badly. I knew he did. And we had been having such a nice day. I forced a smile and then looked up to show it to him, I hadn't known he was so close. My face was streaked with tears, but he reached down and kissed it. I let him kiss me. It was something I had not known, this melting away into feeling.

## CHAPTER FOUR

For a week I had been after Uncle John to get his permission to go to the O'Malley's dance with Mike. And all I could get out of him was, "I'm thinking it over."

I made a face to myself, but he caught me.

"And what's the matter, Kathy?" he said. "Don't you believe I'm thinking it over?"

I fired up. "You've been thinking it over night and day for a week," I said. "It's a wonder you've had time to attend to the cattle and the house and the accounts."

"Well," he said, "when's the dance?"

"Tonight."

"Your mother might not be wanting you to run off to dances at your age, even if it is with a Mounty, so I'll have to continue to think it over." He turned toward the door. "But get your clothes ready, just in case . . ."

When Mike came to pick me up, Uncle John was still thinking it over. He said he'd let me know his decision when we came back.

We laughed together as we saddled our horses.

"Your Uncle John," said Mike, "never says anything straight on. Always hits it sideways."

We rode off over the muddy road. A light irritating rain was falling, and I kept reaching down to make sure none of it was trickling off Rosie's back into the saddlebag. In that saddlebag was my dance dress, very carefully folded, with round twists of newspaper in the folds to prevent creases. In my mackinaw pants and beaver coat I looked like Mike's kid brother, but bouncing on Rosie's side I had a dress that would remind him that I was a girl. Blue and shining it was, with heavy ruffles and a slender waist; and my blue shoes that matched were at the very bottom so as not to crush anything.

The O'Malley barn could be heard long before it could be seen. As we rode up the hill we heard the shrill notes of a fiddle start up, and the laughing and talk die down. Two Indians galloped by us in a wild silent race. The rain stopped for a while, and there was a pale gleam in the west where the moon was trying to break through. Mike stopped at the barn and told me to go up to the house to change. But I wanted to look in at the dance first.

Four or five Indians were standing around the door. They were dressed in dark blue suits; and, although the suits were all the same size, the Indians weren't. Mike opened the door, and I peered into the huge dimly lit room. A few smoky oil lamps hung from the rafters, throwing long, flickering shadows on the floor. They were dancing a fast and furious square dance, but as far as I could make out there were ten men to every woman on the floor, and a few hundred more men lined up along the walls. Three fiddlers played wildly in the back, and near them a tall ferocious 'breed with a dirty handkerchief around his neck plucked at a guitar. I heard the caller yelling above the racket, "Join hands round for a Birdie in the Cage! Get your partner and swing her off the floor! Join hands round—Birdie fly out and Hawkie fly in! Hawkie fly out, give Birdie a swing! Everybody join hands and swing her all around!"

48

A space cleared in the center of the floor, and I watched a heavy-shouldered giant of a man swing his partner around and around with everybody clapping and stamping. Her beaded moccasins barely touched the floor, her skirts billowed out, and her head was thrown back, eyes closed. I was frightened and excited and anxious to join the dance myself.

"I'll run up to the house and change," I told Mike. I walked out, and the four Indians in their blue suits looked at me and grinned. Mike appeared, glaring.

"I'll take you," he said.

When we came back to the dance, it was even more crowded. White trappers, 'breeds, and Indians fought over the few Indian girls. I felt eyes staring at me from every corner. Before I threaded my way through the first square dance, I had received twenty proposals, including marriage. I was the only white girl there.

I never had time to sit down and catch my breath. Sometimes in the patterns of a dance I would be swept away from Mike. Arms would tighten around me, and faces would flash by—dark Indian faces, gleaming with sweat and grease; red Scottish faces shining with heat; small French faces secretly smiling. The music flew by in wild, erratic rhythm, the laughter was loud and excited, and the floor of the barn shook under the heavy steps of the men.

Unexpectedly I heard Mike's voice in my ear. "Come over to the side," he said taking my hand. "There's going to be trouble." I followed Mike's eyes and saw a pale man standing uncertainly by the door, scrutinizing the dancers. Some of them stopped and watched him curiously. He had a vague abstracted look that made you think of a sleepwalker or someone who had been lost for a long time. And yet he was young, and his hair was black and thick, and his face would have been handsome had he smiled.

"George Bailey," Mike said. "And Bull MacGregor is here with the girl."

"What girl? Who's Bull MacGregor? Where?"

But my questions were answered quickly. Nearly everyone had stopped dancing, and a path opened. At one end of it I could see the giant who had whirled his partner in the air during "Birdie in a Cage." A six-foot-four Scotsman he

49

was, with dirty red hair and an uneven beard. At the other end of the hushed dancers stood George Bailey. He didn't look at Bull MacGregor or the slender Indian girl, half his size, who stood next to him, staring at the floor. Instead, he looked over at Mike, and you could see he was annoyed by the attention he was drawing. There was whispering and talking from the crowd. Someone snickered, and the musicians went at their fiddles in an effort to start the dance again.

Mike and I watched Bull MacGregor swagger insolently past George Bailey on his way to the door. His girl half-ran, half-walked along with him, Bailey did not move; his hollow face showed no expression. MacGregor opened the door, and the wet air blew in. But the girl had turned around and stood staring at George Bailey. Her face also was expressionless, but her whole body was tense and expectant. MacGregor tapped her on the shoulder, but she did not feel it. He said something in a low voice. The girl didn't move. He flushed from his forehead into the neck of his open shirt, and he hit the girl in the face, a hard short blow.

We all watched George Bailey. He was crossing the floor, slowly, steadily. His mouth was slightly open and his hand trembled, but he didn't quicken his pace.

"No knives, George," said Mike.

Bull MacGregor waited, leaning forward, swinging his huge fists, heavy as sledges. The girl scrambled to her feet and seized his arm. MacGregor flung her off, and she fell toward me and Mike. Her lip was bleeding, and there was a long purple welt on her cheek.

"Do something, Mike!" I pushed him. "Put him in jail."

"Yes, yes, in jail," the girl sobbed, clinging to me. "He kill him, he kill him!"

George Bailey was about ten feet away. He stopped uncertainly, hesitated, but MacGregor rushed him with a bellow that made me understand why they called him "Bull." There was a flurry of punches. Mike and two other men stepped into the struggle, and it was all over in a second. Bull's right arm was slashed and bleeding, and Bailey lay on the floor, shaking his head queerly. The two men helped him to his feet and pulled him away, while Mike stood in front of MacGregor talking in a low voice.

"I'll forget the scratch," Bull said, "but if I see him around again, I'm going to let the dirty 'breed have it."

He turned toward the girl. "And now *you,* come on!" He put his hand on her shoulder and sprayed blood all over us both.

She held my hand and repeated hysterically, "No go! No go! He kill me!"

"Let her alone," I said. "Let her alone, you big coward. It's easy enough for a man the size of a buffalo to beat a little mite like this." And I put my arm around her, though she was a bit taller than I.

"Sergeant Mike, put him in jail," the girl pleaded. "He beat me, he choke me, he try kill me! Look . . ." and she started to undo the collar of her dress.

"Let her alone for tonight, Bull," Mike said, "and go home."

MacGregor growled something and turned toward the door. The blood was still trickling down his arm, but he ignored it.

"How's the cut?" Mike said.

MacGregor pushed his way out without answering.

"Don't let him go!" the girl screamed.

"Shhh," I said. "What's your name?"

"Mart'."

"It's all right now, Mart', " I said.

"Please, Sergeant Mike, put him in jail."

Mike had an annoyed look on his face.

"Mike," I said angrily, "do something for her. That big bully! I'd just like to have seen him lay a hand on me."

Mike grinned. "All right," he said to the girl, "he beats you?"

"He try kill me all the time."

"And you're through with him for good?"

"Yes, yes, through, finished."

"All right. Come in in the morning and sign a complaint, and we'll arrest him."

"Yes! Yes!"

"And you can stay here tonight. I'll speak to the O'Malleys. They'll put you up."

51

Mike signed to an older woman, who came over and took Mart' away. Her fingers clung to me, and she repeated, "Yes—in jail, in jail!"

I watched till the door shut behind her. The fiddles started up again with renewed vigor, trying to erase the impression she had made. But I wasn't interested in music or dancing any more.

"Mike," I whispered, "you *will* put that man in jail?"

He smiled. "She won't come in to sign a complaint. She won't even stay here tonight. In an hour she'll go home to Bull."

"No!" I cried, horrified.

"It's happened before," Mike said calmly. "They always go back."

"Well," I said turning a little red, "if any man ever struck me, if he just laid his littlest finger on me, I'd get the biggest sharpest knife in the kitchen, and I'd whet it all day on the grindstone; and it's my belief, Sergeant Flannigan, that man wouldn't sleep long in my house."

Mike burst out laughing and swung me onto the dance floor.

It rankled in me. I mean, I didn't like Mike's callous attitude, and I didn't like that bully's roughness, and I didn't like her weakness if she went back to him, and I was just irritated all around. So I guess I acted a little cool to Mike, and soon he seemed to draw into himself and become dignified, and then we were riding home in silence.

Finally I said, "It was a very nice dance, and I thank you."

And he said, "Yes."

I said, "I certainly enjoyed all the people, and the Indians, and the music."

And he said, "Yes."

I kicked Rosie, hard. We began to trot.

"You're not much for talking this night?"

"No."

"And what is on your mind, Sergeant Flannigan?" I said.

He turned his head and looked at me, and began to talk, fast and earnestly. "You think I'm hard and cynical, that I'd stand by and let a man strike a woman and do nothing about it, but you don't know the story behind it, so I'll tell it to you, and you're not to interrupt until I'm done." He reined in, and the horses settled down to a walk.

"The girl's name is Marthe Germaine. Her mother was pure Indian, her father some kind of mixed 'breed, a man no one liked—neglected his wife, neglected his kids, ran off and disappeared one day. You remember that man who knifed Bull MacGregor? George Bailey, he's called. Part Indian. Used to be a very nice fellow, but he's changed a lot. Anyway, then he was young, good-looking, a hard worker, made a lot of friends. He fell in love with this girl, Marthe, took her up north to his trap line, made her his girl. They didn't get married, there's not many marriages like that. I mean it's rare for a man to marry an Indian girl with the priest and everything. But George loved her and was good to her, and she adored him, and worried over him, and mothered him, the way women do. George had a partner, this Bull MacGregor you saw, and as long as George was there, he kept away from the girl. MacGregor had nothing but contempt for George; he could crumble him with his bare hands. But the man was his partner, and MacGregor had his own peculiar code.

"Well, one day George had to go down for supplies. Supposed to back in a month. Didn't return for six months. Ran into all kinds of bad luck and trouble. Bull waited two months, then he took the girl. I guess he figured George was never coming back, so she was his by inheritance. Of course, he never asked *her* how she felt about it, and if she made any objection, I suppose he smashed her in the face. After all to him she was just an Indian *klooch*. But Marthe was pretty, and capable, and MacGregor grew fond of her; so when George Bailey came back, Bull wouldn't give the girl up.

"Now, here's where the story gets peculiar. Marthe hated MacGregor, hated him as close to murder as an Indian woman can think, and she loved George. But she was afraid, if it came to a fight, that George would get killed. So she told him she didn't love him any more, that she'd always loved Bull, and she sent him away. That was that, for five years.

"Then Bull brought her down here. She was miserable.

53

He knocked her around the way you saw tonight. Well, one day Bull beat her up worse than usual, left her unconscious, and a neighbor sent for Constable Vincent. He locked Bull up for the night, and I told the girl that if she wanted to, she could sign a complaint, and I'd hold Bull there for a month, and she could clear out. I tried to convince her that in a month she and George could lose themselves, and that Bull would never follow, it didn't mean that much to him.

"She thought it over, and then said she was going back to Bull, he was her man, he brought her food, he built her house, she was his woman. And then she said something very funny. She said she hated George because he hadn't the courage to fight Bull like a man. Now, that I haven't figured out to this day. After all, *she* was the one who stopped George. And yet, tonight, remember the way she looked at him, as if daring him to come on? Well, I don't know how it's going to end, but someone's going to get hurt."

"Well, all women aren't like that," I said.

"No." he smiled, "but they're unpredictable creatures, all of them. For instance, right now you're sulky, and in a minute you're going to laugh." And he leaned over and squeezed my hand. I laughed. I couldn't help it.

But then that was all. He didn't say another word. He didn't squeeze my hand again or try to kiss me. We just rode ahead under the dark clouds. And what *I* say is, men are unpredictable creatures, all of them.

Flashes of lightning ripped the heavens, and a torrent of rain blinded our horses. I turned my face to the sky and laughed because the things you enjoy can't hurt you. That's what Mike always said. In spite of that my boots felt soggy, and the wet penetrated my heavy mackinaws.

I thought about the Indian girl and wished George Bailey would fight for her and get killed. I thought about Mike too. He kept looking at me in a worried way. I know he didn't like my being out in this downpour. Oh, yes, he was fond of me. There was no doubt about that, but he was fond of his horse too.

Once we had passed the broken-down fence that marked Uncle's property, the horses took heart and began to gallop.

"Ride right up on the porch," Mike shouted. "I want to

54

get you out of the rain." So I rode Rosie under the shelter of the eaves and got off.

"I'll take them around to the barn," Mike said. "You go to bed."

"I've had a very nice evening," I said.

"Katherine Mary, get in the house and get out of those wet clothes." I went into the house, but I gave the door a good slam so he'd know I was mad. And there was Uncle John sitting up.

"It's a quarter to one," said my uncle.

"It's a wonder we ever got here in this rain. The horses almost got mired."

"Where's Mike? Didn't he come in with you?"

"He's seeing to the horses."

"We can't let him go on a night like this. He'll sleep in the bunkhouse."

There was a long pause. I waited there, miserable and shivering, because I wanted Mike to come in and see that I hadn't done what he told me.

At last my uncle said, "Did you have a good time, Kathy?" I went over and kissed the top of his head.

The door opened and slammed, and Mike strode across the room, leaving puddles of water behind him. He nodded to Uncle. "I told Kathy to get into some dry clothes."

I faced him. "I was just saying good night to my uncle. Any objections?"

Mike was looking grim, and Uncle interrupted. "He's right, Kathy. You're wet to the skin."

What were the two of them—a couple of grandmas? I flounced out of the room.

"You can say good night in the morning," Mike called after me. I didn't even turn around.

I dried all over with a rough towel. It felt good. Then I got into my nightgown. I was still chilly, so I put on my robe too. Then I got into bed and pulled up the covers. I didn't feel sleepy, and my behavior troubled me. After all, Mike had taken me out, and I'd had a wonderful time. And poor Uncle John waiting up till all hours. Then I'd acted like that.

I got out of bed and opened the door to the living room. Uncle was still there by the fire, and I could see a section of

Mike, a section of kitchen, and about an inch of stove. I came out and walked to the fireplace. Mike stuck his head around the corner of the kitchen door.

"I'm cold," I said, and held out my hands to the fire. I wanted to say, "I'm sorry," too, but Mike started yelling because I didn't have any slippers on, and when he got through I didn't feel like saying it any more.

"What are you doing in there anyway?" I asked him. "I thought you were supposed to be in the bunkhouse."

"Well," said Mike, "I was warming up some water for a hot bath. But as long as you're still up, you're the one who's going to get it." I simply laughed.

Mike said nothing more, but poured the heated water from the kettle into a large washtub. Uncle John watched with interest. I pretended to be staring dreamily into the fire.

Mike came to the door. "It's all ready," he said.

"Uncle John, can you make out any salamanders in the flames?" I punctuated that sentence, with a shriek, for Mike lifted me off my feet, carried me to the chair, set me down in it, rolled back nightgown and robe till they reached my knees, then stuck my feet into that tub of water.

"It's too hot!" I screamed.

"It's good for you."

"Uncle, Uncle!"

Uncle was shocked into movement, not much, but a little. He stood up. "Mike, I think this has gone too far." I think he meant Mike pulling my clothes around my knees.

"It has, John," Mike agreed, "and I want to talk to you about it right now." He looked down at me. "You stay where you are." He walked out of the kitchen and shut the door behind him.

I stepped quietly out of the tub, dried my feet with a dish towel, walked without one creak of the floor to the door, and stood listening, hoping to hear Uncle John bawl Mike out. But it was Mike who was doing the talking. I listened to one sentence, then another, and then I realized what he was leading up to, and then I heard him say it. At least I think I did because Mike pushed the door open.

"I thought I told you to stay in that tub." He scooped me

up and set me down again with my feet in the hot water. I had my arms around his neck, and I didn't let go.

"Mike, do you?—do you?—"

"Yes," he said, and put my hands back in my lap. He walked over to Uncle John, who was shaking his head and talking to himself. Mike stopped in front of him. "Well, John?"

"I can't give my consent, Mike. The girl's too young, only sixteen. And she's not well. She was sent here because of her pleurisy, and her lungs aren't too strong."

"I'll look after her, John." And we both knew he would.

"You'll be going back to your wild North, and you can't take a delicate girl like Katherine Mary into a country like that. You know you can't."

Mike looked from me to my uncle. "There's two ways of thinking, when it comes to that. To my mind, the country would harden her, make a strong woman of her."

There was silence between the men.

Finally Uncle said, "There's no man I'd rather give her to than you, Mike Flannigan, and you know it well. But she was put in my charge by her mother. And her mother would not approve. She's too young yet, and she has no strength. I'm thinking she could go back to Boston."

I stamped my foot, forgetting it was in the tub, and the water splashed all over. "Have I nothing to say about this?" I asked the two of them.

Mike looked at me reproachfully. "Your uncle's too good a friend for me to be talking a matter like this behind his back."

"And what am I? I hope at least you think as much of me as of my uncle."

"Kathy, of course I do."

"Well, then, you just say it. If you love me, you tell me right here and now. And if you want me to marry you, you ask me, and then maybe I will and maybe I won't."

Mike came over to me and crouched down by my chair so he could see my face. He spoke low so my uncle couldn't hear. "I love you, Kathy. I always have, and I think you've always known it."

I couldn't stand the look in his eyes, the earnest almost

57

pleading look. I turned away from it. I, a sixteen-year-old, had demanded that this sergeant of the Northwest Mounted humble himself, and he had.

"I'll make you happy, girl. I'll give my life to it. I want you for my wife." He didn't touch me. Didn't even take my hand. But I felt and knew only Mike.

"I'm going to marry you. I'm going to marry him," I said to my uncle. But my uncle was no longer there. Mike stood up, drawing me with him. We held to each other, and I had never had him so close.

I shut myself in my room. All night long I had gone over it and over it with Mother, and sometimes she cried and sometimes she laughed and sometimes she didn't do anything at all. And that's what I was most afraid of. I could see her opening my letter. She would read it twice, because the first time she wouldn't believe it. Then she'd know I wasn't coming home, that I was going to marry someone named Sergeant Michael Flannigan and go up to those "wild north places" with him. I had to stop her worry and her fear by telling about Mike. "He's a man," I wrote, "twenty-seven years old, responsible, who'll look after me." To know he was kind and good and capable—that would help her. And she would hear the same thing from Uncle John, who had promised to write also. Maybe I could make her know about Mike; but about the country he was taking me to—never.

And when would I see her? I knew mother hadn't the money to come on for the wedding—and Mike already had his orders; we would leave immediately for Hudson's Hope. The pain of a separation that would be for years, and maybe forever, must run between us the length of the Saskatchewan.

Things would be different between my mother and me. I would be Katherine Mary Flannigan, a woman, and my mother would be Margaret O'Fallon, another woman. The mother and the child were somehow gone. But these things couldn't go in a letter. We must tell each other the good things and the things we hoped would be good. I looked down at the words I had just written . . . "We will be married here at the ranch on October 20, that's next Sunday.

58

Uncle will give me away, and Johnny will be best man. I have a beautiful dress, all white with lace at the throat and on the sleeves."

I couldn't put it off any more. I began a new paragraph, writing the words that had to be written. "Then we are going to Hudson's Hope, where Mike is stationed. We'll take the train from here to Edmonton. From Edmonton we must travel seven hundred miles by dog sled. Mike says the trip will take two or three months."

I looked over what I had written and crossed out the part about seven hundred miles and the words "two or three months." Then I crossed the whole thing out and started over.

"Hudson's Hope is quite a way from the nearest city, Edmonton, but we will make the trip in easy stages."

Then I told her that my pleurisy didn't bother me any more, and that I was much stronger. I thought writing it down like this would help make it true. Because I really was a little worried that I would fold up on Mike somewhere along those seven hundred miles to Hudson's Hope.

I put that thought away, along with worries about what to take with me, what kind of punch to serve at the wedding, and what if Johnny didn't stay sober long enough to stand up with us when the time came.

I returned to my letter. It was slow work, choosing the words to hurt my mother. If only I could have written about Mike's hair, and eyes—and his straight nose, and how tall he was. Well, I had, a little, but I knew she was interested in other things about him. So I told her how the Canadian Government supported us, gave us house, clothes, horses, food, and a little money. I thought it better not to tell her what Mike said about money not being much good up there.

"Everything is trading," he had said. "Food you can eat, horses you can ride, skins you can keep warm with. But what can you do with a paper dollar?" Yes, I knew my mother better than to speak disrespectfully of money.

"I want for you to be here so much," I told her, "but I know you can't leave the house, and that anyway the trip would be too expensive. And we have to leave right afterward because those are Mike's orders."

I felt important, writing about orders. It was all new and

59

strange. "But you'll come and see me when we're up there,"
I continued. "And then we'll come to Boston to see you."

While I was writing it, I thought it was true. But then I
looked at it and knew it wasn't. It was far, across a conti-
nent. I felt afraid. No one would know that, not Mother and
not Mike. I'd keep the fear pushed down inside of me, and
no one would know it was there.

"I'm awfully happy," I wrote.

I was. Awfully happy and awfully in love, and tomorrow
I was marrying Mike.

## CHAPTER FIVE

We had to leave Juno. He was too civilized to live on the
trail. The sled dogs would tear him to pieces. Mike warned
me. "I'll get you another Juno when we get to Hudson's
Hope," he said, and I left Juno with Mildred. He was the
last tie with Boston and home. From now on the Northwest
was home.

We took the train from Calgary to Edmonton and set out
for Lesser Slave Lake as part of a dog-sled caravan. There
were thirty-six sleds of traders, trappers, and Hudson's Bay
Company men.

Two nuns were riding on the sled of a trapper named
Baldy Red. They were bound for the Mission at Peace
River Crossing and had no visible money or supplies. The
older one had come to the camp where the caravan was
assembling and asked if there was room for herself and the
other sister. The men talked it over for a while, but no one
semed able to spare the space. Each sled was heavily laden
with equipment and goods.

At this point Baldy Red walked into the meeting. He
was a short, stocky man with a fringe of bright red hair
circling his bald spot. His neck was red, his face was red,
and his nose was bright red. He wore his shirt open at the
throat, and no cap was on his head or mittens on his hands.
He pushed his way through the group of men and walked,
or rather lurched, over to the nun. Mike said he was drunk,
but he didn't speak like a drunk, and I thought what he said
was nice, and nicely put.

"Sister," Baldy Red addressed the nun, "my friends here say there's no room. That's a true word. But I will *make* room. It's women like yourself this country needs. To bring the word of God to the heathen, and the hand of mercy to the sick. And God bless you for the good work you're doing, and, God damn me—I mean God help me—I'll make a place for you and the other holy sister on my sled."

And the Sister said, "Thank you." She looked him over carefully and then asked, "Are you Catholic?"

"Sister," Baldy said, "I don't know. My parents never told me. I've never gone to a Catholic church. But," he added appeasingly, "neither have I gone to any *other* church."

The nun smiled a little. "My friend and myself will be glad to ride with you. God reward you for your courtesy."

Baldy Red with a very gallant air led the nun to his cutter, and they drove in for Sister Magdalena.

"Well, I'm glad of that," I told Mike. "I was getting ready to ask you if we could take them."

"We're loaded to the brim," Mike laughed. "If we had another passenger, I'd have to harness you with the team."

"He's a very nice man," I said. Mike said nothing, but he smiled, I thought, queerly.

The next day we started. Baldy Red made a seat out of two packing cases and up-ended three more to make a back rest. He covered the cases with buffalo robes and seated Sisters Margaret and Magdalena on their improvised throne.

The day was cold, fifty below zero, and no amount of of covers could keep me warm sitting on the sled. So I'd get off and run until I was warm and tired, and then get on and ride until I was rested and cold.

Baldy watched over the nuns as if they had been truly his sisters. He found them extra robes and made ear muffs for them out of a pair of old mittens.

"Something's up," Mike told me. "That old rascal never spoke to a nun in his life."

"You don't like him," I said.

"Sure I like him," Mike said, "but I don't trust him. That old Baldy has never made a straight move in his life. Even if he blows his nose, there's something crooked about it."

"I don't believe it." I said.

"There was the time he sold a Dutch farmer his horse." Mike said thoughtfully. "The farmer, Humbert his name was, paid Baldy eighty dollars for the horse; for, while it didn't look any too handsome, being sort of mottled brown with white spots, it was sound in wind, fast, and well trained. Humbert bought the horse, and he says for a day or so he watched that horse with fear in his heart, waiting for its teeth to fall out, or for it to go lame, or get vicious or come down with the glanders—because, you see, he knew Baldy.

"The third day he went in to brush the horse, and the horse was gone. He rode to town, and Baldy was gone. Humbert didn't waste any time, but came to the barracks and swore out a complaint, charging Baldy Red with the theft of one six-year-old horse, brown with white spots.

"A week later we caught up with Baldy. He had two horses. We brought them both back. One was a ten-year-old gray mare. One was a six- or seven-year-old brown horse, brown but with no spots. Farmer Humbert stood a long time looking at his horse, and then he started to swear. Claimed Baldy Red had stolen the horse and covered up the white spots somehow. Baldy just laughed and said the old guy was crazy, this was a different horse. Humbert opened the horse's mouth and said he recognized the teeth. Baldy sneered and asked him did he see any spots before his eyes. Well, we were stuck. Humbert had identified the horse as brown and white, and this horse was just brown all over. We washed and scrubbed him with soap and turpentine and naphtha, but brown he was and brown he stayed. Humbert nearly went crazy. He said he recognized the teeth, the ankles, the eyes, and the gait of that animal. But, as Baldy pointed out, that's not much good as evidence from a guy that can't tell the difference between brown and white. So we had to let Baldy go."

"Well, then Baldy *was* innocent, and you were just picking on him," I said. Mike looked at me, and at the glee in his eyes a doubt grew in my mind. "Where *did* the other horse go, the brown and white one?" I asked.

"There was only one. The brown part went with Baldy," Mike said, "and the white part went with a little paint remover."

62

The first village we came to was Athabaska. The weather was changing; there was a tension in the air, and heavy clouds piled in the east. The sun was already low when a circle of pale, silvery light sprang up around it. A little later, within this giant loop, four smaller shining circles appeared. In each circle a small unreal but gleaming image of the sun shone. Looking up at the five tangent suns gave me a weird and alien feeling. I seemed to be on the plains of a distant planet, gazing into a dream landscape. The silver circles became hazy, the mock suns flashed evilly, the daylight seemed to flicker, and then the vision vanished, and the true sun sank into a mountain of dark clouds. Even the dogs seemed upset, and we rushed on at a furious pace until we whirled into Athabaska, and I tumbled off the sled, my face stiff and my eyes dull with staring.

"Sun dogs, they're called," Mike told me. "I've seen as many as sixteen surrounding the sun, like puppies around a bitch, and shining every bit as bright as the big one. Sun dogs. The Indians are scared of them. They think they are evil stars trying to kill the sun, and they beat pans and raise an awful racket to scare the sun dogs away. It generally works. The whole illusion is in the atmosphere, and I guess the noise shakes it. Anyway, when you see those things, ten to one there's a blizzard by the morning."

There was. We were stuck in Athabaska two days. In that time I saw a lot of Baldy Red.

The cabin we occupied was long and rambling, with two stoves and twelve beds. The one assigned to Mike and myself was at one end, and Mike hung a blanket as a sort of curtain because, he explained to me gravely, we were newlyweds. The nuns slept next to us. As a mark of respect. Baldy Red had dragged in three of his heavy chests and improvised a table where the nuns took their meals, away from the men. When I saw Baldy, face purple and sweating in the sub-zero cold, lug those six-foot packing cases into the cabin, half break his back propping them up so that the three cases would make a level surface, and then cover it all with a gaudy cloth he'd dug up somewhere, my heart went out to him, and I turned to Mike and said:

"There's a man with a kind heart. I think it's sweet and pathetic the way he built that table for the nuns. He even

63

thinks that horrible rag is a pretty tablecloth. And look at the way he worked, dragging those heavy cases in."

"They *were* pretty heavy," Mike said, and winked at me; why, I didn't know.

I set about making friends with Baldy Red. First I spoke to the nuns. They were just about overcome by his attentions.

"And yet they say he has a bad reputation," said Sister Margaret.

"Evil tongues!" said Sister Magdalena.

While the blizzard roared outside, and I chatted with the nuns, Mike and the men were grouped around the big stove discussing the weather, though, as far as I could see, that didn't change it any.

Baldy Red came over to ask the sisters if there was anything they wanted, and I took the opportunity to talk to him.

I guess the story Mike had told me was on my mind, because right in the middle of a perfectly innocent conversation I asked him if he'd sold any horses lately.

"I sell horses right along, Mrs. Flannigan," said Baldy without hesitating in the least.

"I'm not the best judge of horseflesh in these parts," he went on grinning, "but I'm the best judge of who's the worst judge . . . and that's the way I keep body and soul together."

Throwing a pious look at the nuns, he made his way back to the stove. He smiled at us all the way, with his cheery, innocent red face, but I was beginning to doubt him too.

I went back and threw myself on my bed. I could hear the wind beating against the walls. I pulled back the curtain over the one tiny window in the north end of the cabin and looked out into flying snow. It reminded me of that terrible night when the train had been stalled before Regina, a long time ago. I couldn't make myself believe that it had been less than a year. It seemed as if I had lived the longer half of my life since that day. I was suddenly overcome by the same loneliness and hatred of the cold and snow as on that night, and to comfort myself I began to draw a dog's ears, Juno's ears, in the frost of the windowpane.

Well, another Juno was behind me. The train Juno would

be scrambling over Mildred's ranch. The Boston Juno would be curled up in my mother's bedroom, where her grandmother, the Irish Juno, had had her first pups. And I was going to make Mike give me a Northwest Juno as soon as one of our sled dogs had a litter. For a second I was worried because it seemed to me that only male dogs could do that hard-sled-pulling. But then the only dogs I'd seen in the North were sled dogs, and if they were all males.. . . so I reassured myself and went on drawing Juno.

It had taken a long time to get used to these northern dogs. Not dogs, but half-tamed wolves they seemed. Pat one on the head, and you'd lose a finger. I've seen Black-Tip take a bite out of the one in front of him while pulling the sled on the dead run. The greatest and most unbelievable confusion in the world is when dog teams go at each other, and snarl the traces like a wet fishline, and pile the goods in the snow, and mill around in growling fury.

About the only one with a gentle disposition was Black-Mittens. The half-breeds and the Crees seemed to think highly of the black parts of a dog, and so they were named Black-Ear, Black-Foot, Black-Socks, Black-Mittens, Black-and-White, Black-Patch, and so on, up to the magnificent leader of the team, Black-All-Over.

In the morning we were on our way to Jussard. Baldy Red was snowshoeing beside our sled and joking with Mike. "And what are they sending Sergeant Flannigan into our territory for?" he said. "Is it to give him a rest?"

"Why, to put down crime," I said, a little proudly.

"Crime!" Baldy laughed. "There's no crime to speak of in the Northwest. Oh, a few shootings, and once or twice a week a throat cut over a woman . . . or maybe Scotch Bobby taking a pint too much and burning down a house. But as for thieves and pickpockets, and such bothersome rascals, we've none of them." He grinned at me. "Why, Lady, you could take a sack of gold from here to Fort St. John, and not a man would stop you. You're as safe as in the Lord's pocket."

"A place *you'll* never go, Baldy," Mike said.

"Now, there's a houseful of redcoats at Jussard," Baldy Red continued, "but what use in the world are they but to smoke the government's tobacco and eat the government's food, and interfere with the movements of the government's best citizens?" This meant himself, for he shook his head in a self-righteous way.

"Redcoat is a name I don't like," Mike said stiffly.

"You'll not deny if you fell on your knees you'd look like the sun setting over the hills," said Baldy with a wink at me.

"Some day you're going to get your whiskers singed, Baldy, my boy," Mike said. "And it's a pity I'm not on duty this trip, or I'd do it for you."

"Would you now?"

"Yes," said Mike. "And the first thing I'd do would be to have a look in those wooden chests of yours, if it wouldn't be disturbing the comfort of the holy sisters."

"Oh, but it *would* be disturbing their comfort," Baldy said, with what I thought was a kind of weak smile. "And the Lord knows that's the least we can do for women that bring such a blessing on this God-forsaken country. Have you ever heard of the Mission at Grouard?" He turned to me.

"No," I said.

"A wonderful place," said Baldy, and launched into a description of the Mission, the nuns, the school, and the gardens.

Mike waited till he had finished. Then he grinned and said, "Baldy, you're so fond of the nuns, why don't you give them something? One of those chests of yours would make a beautiful seat for the schoolroom. Yes," Mike said, warming up, "five or six kids, maybe seven if they were small enough could sit on them, and if they didn't kick their feet too hard, they couldn't be breaking the glass."

"What glass?" Baldy Red shouted, and it was comical how pale his face could become and yet leave his nose shining red above.

"Why, I have a picture in my mind of your chests being filled with rows and rows of bottles."

"The only bottles I ever carry north are empty bottles," said Baldy solemnly, "for castoreum." He turned to me and explained that this was a panacea made by the Indians from two small glands under the beaver's tail.

"In that case, everything is okay," Mike said. "There's no law against bringing in empty bottles."

66

"The bottles are empty," Baldy said stubbornly and returned to his nuns on their chests, where he sat down and eyed Mike and me suspiciously.

"What's wrong with bringing in full bottles?" I asked immediately.

"To Baldy Red, the only full bottle there is, is a bottle full of whisky. And the law says—no whisky north of the fiftieth parallel."

"Are you going to arrest him?" I demanded, thrilled because I had yet to see Mike make an arrest, and yet a little sorry for Baldy, who seemed so nice and friendly and had taken all the trouble to explain to me about the Mission and the beaver-tail medicine.

"No," Mike said. "I'm just guessing. Besides, I'm not on duty. We'll see what the boys at Jussard will do."

But the Mounted Police at Jussard couldn't cope with Baldy and the nuns. They searched the sleds of the caravans thoroughly for liquor, firearms, and other contraband, but they gallantly refused to disturb the two nuns on their cases of whisky. And so the five packing cases that made up the sisters' throne were untouched, and we pushed on to Peace River Crossing. There we left Baldy. We were starting our three-hundred-mile trek upriver to Hudson's Hope in the morning. Mike said good-by to Baldy Red, and the crimson old man winked back slyly. "Like I said, Sergeant, empty bottles—just empty bottles."

That night, our last at Peace River Crossing, Mike whispered to me, "It's a shame to let all that rotgut liquor poison the Indians, and it would be a worse shame if that noble Baldy Red were a liar." So Mike sneaked out of our cabin, and what he did I don't know, but after we came to Hudson's Hope, word reached us that Baldy Red had spoken the truth after all. When he came to open his five cases of bottles, they were, in truth, all empty.

## CHAPTER SIX

Mike said the air was so cold he was afraid it would freeze the lungs of the horses. Maybe that's why every breath hurt me. I was tired. The going had been slow all day, and Mike was up ahead with the runner. Another mile, and he dropped back to my sled.

"How goes it, Minx?" he asked, and squeezed my hand. I laughed and said, "Fine."

He gave me a sharp look and then began telling me what a good rest we'd have tonight. "This isn't a trapper's cabin. The Howards have a big home with an organ. They had it freighted in."

"Have you stayed with them before?"

"Sure, they've put me up whenever I've been in the territory. Everybody's glad of company up in these parts; they try to get you to stay on and on."

"Who are the Howards?" What I really wanted to know was: was there a *Mrs*. Howard? I thought how nice it would be to talk to a woman. Mike jogged along by my side, and his forced breathing punctuated his speech. "Howard's a lumberman. Got a mill up there at Taylor Flats."

"Is he married?" I asked.

Mike laughed. "Well, all I know is they've got four sons."

I smiled to myself. I was a married woman, and Mike said things like that to me sometimes. But the smile went out of me, for the cold was cutting at my insides with every breath. Pain was white, white and cold, and it was around me like a winding sheet. Something beat at my ears and dripped into my mind. At first I thought it was snow, but after a while it made sense and I knew it was Mike talking.

"We'll be there soon . . . soon, darling."

By breathing very regularly, I was able to push away the white and see the troubled blue eyes of Mike Flannigan. "Did Mildred tell you what I said about them?"

"What, Kathy? What, girl?" He bent very close to me because my words hadn't come out as loud as I thought them.

"I told Mildred. I said, 'His eyes are so blue you could swim in them.'" The words poured out on a swell of pain, but it was suddenly important. I had to find out. "Did she, Mike? Did she ever tell you that?"

"Yes, darling. She told me. Now don't talk. Rest. We'll be there soon."

"But what did you think of me?"

"I loved you, Kathy."

68

I sighed and turned my face in against his furs. I tried to remember when he had gotten into the cariole with me—but after a while I forgot to wonder, and then I think I slept.

The motion stopped. I sat up and looked around. We were in a clearing. Ahead of us was a house, and a charred barn stood a little to one side. All over the clearing were neat stacks of firewood. Mike picked me up. His steps shook me and hurt.

He set me down inside, and the sudden heat almost choked me. There were a lot of people, all talking in whispers. A woman helped Mike undo my furs. "The poor child," she said.

I remember being put in an iron bedstead, and Mike feeding me soup and then lying down beside me. I thought it funny he had on all his clothes and wondered why he didn't come under the covers.

When I opened my eyes it was daylight, and Mike wasn't there. I sat up carefully to see how I felt, and I knew I was much better. My clothes were folded over a chair, and I began to put them on. I saw the door handle turn very softly, and the door open very slowly. Mike looked in. "Kathy," and he was over by me in a step. He was so close that his worry and his fear and his love were mine too, and in me.

"I'm all right, Mike," I told him before he could ask me. "Shhh," I said, "It's all over. I'm well now."

Mike laughed shakily. "You'd think I was the one who had been sick."

I laughed too. We sat on the bed and laughed with relief that things were better, and not worse.

Then Mike went into the other room and came back with something that looked like a dog harness.

"What's that?"

"It's for you," Mike said. He looked at the leather straps in his hand and then at me. "A Mounty's got to be a bit of everything, Kathy. Up in this country, where there's no judge, no policeman, no forest ranger, I have to be those things. I have to be a doctor too." He looked at me and smiled to reassure me. Then he said, "You've not been well, Kathy. And I think it's a collapse of the right lung you've got. Now, don't look scared, darling—because I've got the

69

thing here that's going to help you." And he waved the dog harness.

"That?" I asked.

"It's a brace that will keep your shoulders back. Haven't you noticed how you're leaning forward all the time? Why, the air your lungs are meant to be filled with never gets where it should, on account of your hunching your shoulders forward." I must have looked unconvinced because he added, "A good posture will keep you from getting so tired, Katherine."

"But, Mike, I don't want to wear a brace."

"You'll give it a chance, won't you?"

"Well, if I can wear it under my clothes."

"Sure and you can. I've made it that soft it won't chafe."

I took off my shirt and undid the top buttons of my underwear. "You'll have to put it on me, Mike. I'll never figure out how it works."

"Lift up your arms, then, and I'll slip it on." I did. But instead of slipping it over my arms, it was himself he slipped between them. He kissed me in the hollow of my throat, and it was a long time before we got those braces on.

I rested in my room all day, and that evening I met the Howard family. Mike had spoken of the Howard "boys," but the youngest was five years older than I.

I went into the kitchen to ask Mrs. Howard if there was anything I could do. She was shocked at my wanting to help. "Eyes and hair," she said, "that's all you are; eyes and a mop of hair. The only thing you can do that will be of any use is to wash up for dinner." So I pumped water over my hands and then looked around for a towel.

"Up there on the wall." Mrs. Howard pointed. "We got one of those roller towels. Henry brought it back when he was out about a year ago."

I could see that the towel had not been changed in that length of time. It was black and grimy, and as it hadn't occurred to Mrs. Howard to change it, I could hardly suggest it. I took hold of the towel with as small a grip as it was possible to get and still spin it around. As it whirled I looked for a clean spot, or at least a light gray one. There didn't seem to be any. I turned it again, very slowly, to make sure. By that time, my hands were dry.

"Ma," one of the boys called in, "where's dinner?"

Mrs. Howard looked harassed. She was stirring four or five pots and keeping a weather eye on twenty pairs of socks that hung over the stove. The line was strung too low, and every time she reached for a dish, the socks flapped in her face. The main course was beans, and she let me put them on the table. They had a very long table, and the Howard men and Mike were seated at it. Everything in the room was homemade—except a gilt organ. It was highly polished, and a candle gleamed at either end, giving it the appearance of a shrine, which is what it was to this family.

Beside each man was a brass spittoon. The six of them lolled back on hind chair legs, chewing tobacco and spitting. The idea seemed to be not to spit in your own spittoon, but in your neighbor's. There must have been some skill to the game because the floor was spotless. Mike looked up and gave me a sly wink. "What are we eating?" he asked.

"Beans."

A chorus of groans went up. "Ma," Mr. Howard called to the kitchen, "is it beans again?"

"Never you mind, Henry Howard." She came in with meat in one hand and a pot of prunes in the other. "We got dessert tonight." She set the prunes on the table. "These here are known as lumberman's strawberries."

"You see, they're dried," Mike explained. "Easy to keep up here."

"Aw, heck," one of the boys said. "I thought when you said dessert, you maybe meant candy."

"Now where would I be getting candy?" his mother asked as she set some dried eggs beside the dried prunes. "It's all gone three months ago." She turned to me. "Last time Henry went out, he was supposed to bring me some cups. My china ones I started housekeeping with all got broke. And all we got left is that tin one you see."

I looked where she pointed and was horrified to see a tin mug of water making its way toward me. Each man gulped thirstily, wiped his greasy lips with his hand, and passed the cup on. It was refilled at frequent intervals. It came to me; a bean was floating in it. I tried not to think how it had gotten there, but passed the cup quickly to Mrs. Howard. "Aren't you thirsty?" she asked.

71

"No," I said.

"Well, anyway, I was telling you about how we haven't got no decent china. Know what this Henry done? He bought candy. Now, some men can't be trusted. They'll go on a drunk as soon as they hit town. Well, Henry'll go on a spree, too, only with him it's candy. What does he do but eat it and stock up on it until all the money is gone, including the money set aside for my cups."

"I hated to touch that cup money," Mr. Howard interrupted, "but it's a terrible craving, Mrs. Flannigan, just terrible."

He had called me Mrs. Flannigan, and I glanced significantly at Mike. He still wasn't used to my having the same name as his mother.

I was startled by a low wailing cry that rose to a shriek. No one seemed to notice it or even look up. But it started Mr. Howard on a new train of thought. "Hear about our fire, Mike?"

"Noticed your barn was charred. Lose anything?"

The wail had been taken up and answered again and again in a maniacal crescendo of sound. I shuddered with it long after I stopped hearing it. Then I was hearing it again, a low minor wail that built and built until the final shriek tore through you.

"What is it!" I knew from the way the heads swung toward me that my voice was out of control.

"It's nothing," Mrs. Howard said. "A wolf pack's out there crying to get at the bodies of the horses. They smell the cooked flesh, and it's driving them crazy not being able to get at it."

"Yes," one of the boys said, "we lost five horses. Barn was ablaze before we knew it. Couldn't none of us get near it. The horses just roasted, that's all."

"It was terrible," Mrs. Howard said. "You could hear the poor things screaming."

The screaming of the dead horses and the screaming of the wolf pack blended, swelled, receded. I followed the curve of the rising inflection, and when it reached its shrill wailing peak, I screamed too. I jumped up and screamed on the same note as the wolves and the horses.

72

The men looked at me. I screamed and screamed.

There was a frantic rush for the door. Chairs overturned as the men fought to get out. Away they went, every male Howard, into the night. Mike was on his feet too. He took me by the shoulder.

"Katherine Mary, stop it!" He spoke with a sternness I'd never heard before, and I did stop it. But the wolves didn't. They kept it up. The shrill note of their cry hung in the air, faded and came again. At the window I saw the frightened faces of the Howard men. I began to laugh, it was so funny. They could listen to tortured horses and wolf pack in full cry, and it didn't bother them. But a girl's screams had chased them from their home in stumbling panic.

"Katherine Mary, stop it!"

I tried to say, "It's all right—I'm just laughing," but I was laughing too hard to say it, and Mike didn't like my laughing any more than he had my screams. Tears were running through my fingers. I guess I was crying too.

Mrs. Howard went to the door, "Freddy!" she called. "Come on in here and play something on the organ. It will calm her." There was no answer from the outside.

"Freddy?" she said again. And Freddy slunk in. He gave me a quick furtive look and sat down at the organ. The tones came low and mellow, but the howling pack held their pitch—making weird dissonant chords. The boy began another song, "I Wandered Today Through the Hills, Maggie." It was my mother's song, one she sang as she fixed flowers for the best room and hummed when she hung the clothes to dry. Maggie was the girl's name in the song, and Maggie was my mother's name, too, Margaret Kennedy O'Fallon, but everybody called her "Maggie."

And then I knew what it was all about. It hadn't been the wolves. Their cry had the loneliness in it, and that was why I had to scream and cry with them. I was lonely too because I didn't have any mother. The two-storied house and Uncle Martin and my sisters and Mother's canary—and even Uncle John and Johnny and the little Juno I'd left—were in my thoughts, but under my feet these two months had been only the trackless white of this dead and frozen land, empty with loneliness.

Mike could see that the music wasn't cheering me up any. He leaned over me and very gently lifted me to my feet. "We'll get you to bed, Kathy," he said.

Upstairs I tried to tell him that it was just that I hadn't felt well, that it really didn't mean anything. Mike's face was full of misery, and I knew an unhappy determination was in him. But he held it in and would say nothing. I put my arms around his neck. "I'm happy, Mike. I love you and I'm happy."

He pushed my head against his shoulder and stroked it.

"Really, Mike," I whispered into his jacket, "I am happy. I don't know why I act like this. I guess I'm crazy."

Mike still stroked my hair. "I'm taking you back in the morning, Kathy."

Mike and I lay awake with our own thoughts. And in the morning he took me on, not back. It was that night that I really became his wife, for I knew that this white land and its loneliness were a part of Mike. It was a part I feared, that I didn't know or understand. But I knew that I had to know it and understand it, and even love it as Mike did. Because I wanted to be like Mike and then, after our lives had been lived, maybe I'd be Mike.

When he held me, we were crushed into one, one body with one heart beating through us. And that's the way it had to be with our minds and our feelings. It was much harder because they get tangled in thoughts and caught in emotions. But in the end that's the way it had to be.

So I lay there, my second night in Taylor's Flat, and told myself, "If you love Mike, you'll love the things that go with him. And if you can't love them, you'll understand them—and until you do you'll keep the fight to understand them in yourself, and not be carrying on and worrying him like you did tonight." I was cold and trembling under my covers for fear I'd talked to myself too late, that Mike would really send me back.

But Mike must have been talking to himself as hard as I was to myself, and he must have decided that I was still worth the trouble I caused, because in the morning he said nothing about sending me home.

One night cannot dispose of a feeling or settle an attitude.

74

and many a night on the way up to Hudson's Hope I had to fight back the thoughts of my home and my mother and the tears that came with them. . . . Yet it was a happy time and an exciting one, full of love and adventure and a new life opening up. The fears grew smaller, and all they could do was peck at my happiness.

The country, as we approached Hudson's Hope, became more beautiful. We traveled up the frozen river bed, and hills large and small rolled away from us on either side.

Mike told me I was stronger. I knew I was.

"The brace helped me."

"And you've adjusted quickly in a country that is usually too hard for women." He was proud of me, and he acted proud in front of the men because where were *their* wives?

On the north side of the river there were few trees, but on the south side there were forests of poplar and jack pine, large sections of which had been lumbered over. The river bed sank deeper and deeper and finally became a gorge with cliffs of white rising up as walls. We left the ravine and traveled on higher ground over a trail Mike said he knew well. Our dogs were climbing.

"When we reach the top you'll see the flag. Then we're there, Kathy."

There was a flag in front of every Hudson's Bay Company in the Northwest. It meant hot food, rest, fresh supplies, conversation, people, a little oasis of humanity and comfort before going on through the white void. Only this time it would mean more; it would mean our home. After almost three months of travel, we'd have a home. We hadn't reached it any too soon, either. For it was February, and the thaw set in during March. There was no traveling in this country in spring and summer, except by canoe. But we had made it in time. There was the flag coming into view, showing that the log house behind it was a branch store of the Hudson's Bay Company, not one of the half-dozen trappers' cabins that hid themselves among the drooping, snow-laden trees.

I took Mike's hand without saying anything. It was beautiful. The few cabins were grouped on a plateau, and below them hills rolled away, carrying white armies of poplar and pines on their backs. To the north and facing the village was a fifty-foot drop where in spring and summer the Peace River ran the gauntlet of dark bluffs.

We pulled up in front of the store, and Mike pushed against the door just as it was thrown open by a big brawny giant from the inside. The two men collided, laughed, and gave each other a couple of pokes, the way men do. He was as tall as Mike, only thicker and bulkier. He was half in and half out of his furs.

"Son of a gun, son of a gun," he kept saying, and all the time hitting and poking at Mike with his big beaver mitts. Then suddenly he caught sight of me. "I'll be . . ." he said and stood there staring. I got out of the sled and came over to them. Mike took my hand. "Kathy, meet Joe Henderson." I smiled at him and said, "Hello," but the big man was without words.

Mike laughed. "How long are you going to keep us standing out in fifty below, Joe?"

Joe mumbled something in his beard and kicked the door open. No sooner were we in the house than Henderson found his voice.

"Uaawa!" he bellowed. "Uaawa!" A dark Indian woman appeared from the back room and stood poised like a wild thing.

"Where the hell did you go running off to?" And then, as she continued to stand there with frightened eyes, "We'll want some tea, so get busy with it!" His voice lowered from a bellow to almost a whisper. "You see," he said to me, but without looking at me, "you've got to think out every step for them. We'll want food too, and she could be getting that while the water's boiling. Only you can't never explain that to them."

He sighed and sat down on a packing case, leaving the two chairs to Mike and me. I looked around curiously. The woman worked in the center of the room over the stove. I looked away at once, for she seemed to wince under my glance. I concentrated instead on the room. There was the usual counter with shelves mounting to the ceiling behind it, and a tangle of goods piled and stuffed and jammed into the shelves. Wild masses of cascading flowered cottons tumbled over jelly glasses. Knives speared spools of wire, and a rusty alarm clock sat on top of twelve cans of beans. On the floor were piles of soft, gleaming pelts, and on one of these a naked baby slept, its tawny body blending with the skins.

"What a beautiful baby! Is it yours?" I asked the woman at the stove. She lifted her head to be sure I meant it, to be sure the white woman spoke to her. When she saw that both these things were true, she smiled, a half-smile that came into her eyes.

Henderson reached for an empty bottle. He had thrown it at her, and she was picking up the shattered pieces before I realized what had happened. A cut over her eye bled onto her hands as she worked. Henderson had not watched to see whether his bottle had landed a blow or not but had turned back to us.

I stood up. "Mike," I said, "I want to see our house."

Mike stood up too.

"But wait." Joe Henderson was upset. "You must eat. You've come a long way today."

I walked toward the door and began putting on my furs. Mike stood uncertainly. No one said anything. The woman looked across at me and then back to the water which had begun to boil. It was to the water she spoke.

"It bring much honor to house if Sergeant Mike and Mrs. Mike eat."

I unbuttoned my jacket and sat down. Preparations for the meal went on. But the woman did not speak again.

After a while the child on the pelts stirred. I took him on my lap, but he wriggled off and walked on fat, unsteady legs to Joe Henderson. I caught my breath as I saw him grab hold with a small brown fist to the giant's pants leg. The child said something, whether in Indian or gibberish I wasn't sure.

"Does he talk?" I asked.

Joe Henderson gave me a strange look.

"Yes; in the language of the Beaver Indian, he calls me 'Father.'" There was a mocking note in the man's voice, but it was very gently that he stroked the dark head of his son.

"Tell the lady your name."

The child turned in his father's hands and regarded me a moment with serious eyes. "Siwah," he said.

Henderson scowled, then turned to the woman, speaking unpleasant sounds in her tongue. She gave no answer, and

77

the motions of her work were not interrupted. He turned to his child. His voice was no longer harsh, perhaps it was the change back into English. Again he said, "Tell the lady your name."

The reply came promptly. "Tommy Henderson."

"He's a fine little fellow," Mike said.

I was surprised. I didn't know Mike liked children. There were so many things about Mike I didn't know. But about this I was glad.

The Indian woman served us silently, but did not eat herself, and Henderson did not ask her. I was glad when it was over and we were out of the hot room with its smell of food.

Mike grinned down at me. "Which way do you think our house is, right or left?" I looked in both directions. Coming in from the top of the hill I'd seen some cabins, but now a forest of pine hid them.

"Right," I guessed.

Mike laughed. "Right it is. Come on." But I still stood there.

He looked back, trying to understand. "Excited?"

"Yes," I said. "But that Joe Henderson, he mistreats her. Why, you could kill a person with a bottle like that, couldn't you?"

"Well," Mike said, "maybe."

I could see he was disappointed because he thought I wasn't excited about seeing our house. So I put Joe Henderson and Tommy Henderson and the Indian woman into the back of my mind. And I put my fur mittens into Mike's fur mitten.

"Mike, are you really taking me to our home?" He looked at me with blue eyes shading into all the blues there are.

"And does a little chit like you have a house and a husband? And do you think you're going to set up housekeeping with us?"

I laughed. Then I stopped because he had.

"Kathy—I hope it will be all right, the changes I have made in your life!"

"Mike, I love you." It wasn't an answer to his words, but it was the one he wanted.

"It's been all right so far, hasn't it?"

78

"All right?" I threw my arms around him. "It's been wonderful."

"Come on then, I'll race you to the house."

He's shy, I thought. Yes, he really is, that big hulk of a man. But I said, "How can I race you, when I don't know where it is?"

"Follow me," and he was off on long legs.

"This isn't any kind of race," I said, running after him.

Mike turned into the pines. Ahead of us in a clearing stood a cabin. I stopped running. I approached it, trying to know it all at once, the trees and the rocks, the ground rolling under my feet. This was home. Mike put his arm around my shoulder.

"Don't look so awed, darling, it's just my office."

"Office?" I repeated the word blankly.

"Well, sure. I've got to have some place to lock up the criminals. Unless you want to keep them in the spare room."

He pushed the door open, and there was a large shabby desk and two chairs, one comfortable and one uncomfortable. There was a cupboard too, all padlocked. It didn't look anything like a jail, and I couldn't see why the prisoners couldn't get out of the windows.

"Do you really keep prisoners here?"

Mike laughed. "Never have. In the first place, there's very little crime. The Indians never give trouble unless there's been liquor smuggled in. The 'breeds are a little wilder. Every once in a while there's woman trouble, squaw stealing. Then I bring 'em in and put them to work."

"What kind of work?"

"Oh, usually cutting me a winter's supply of wood."

"Well, if nobody's locked up in it, what do you need an office for?"

Mike made a serious face. "Katherine, you don't realize I'm a big man up here. That's why I stay here. Sit down, girl, and I'll tell you all about it." He pushed me into the comfortable chair.

"This office is the Hudson's Hope court and hospital." He unlocked the cupboard at the back. It was filled with rows of neatly labeled bottles.

"Medicines?"

"Not much. Quinine, disinfectants."

"You mean people really come to you when they're sick?"

Mike said slowly, "We're seven hundred miles from civilization or a doctor."

"But do you know anything about it?"

"Not much. I bought some books in Calgary."

I looked at this man that I had married. There was more here than a red coat.

"Where's the house? I want to see that."

"It's behind the office." He caught my hands as I started for the door.

"Kathy, I hope you won't be disappointed in it. It's just a house, you know; Government-built."

"I'll love it, Mike." And I did. It was set cozily among the trees, and through a side window I could see Mike's office. There was a large front room and two bedrooms. There was a combination stove and heater, the kind they all had in this country. Logs to keep the room warm were shoved in the back, and the front was a wood stove for cooking meals on. The chinks in the wall were stuffed with moss. Over the bed was a buffalo skin.

"They still have them in these parts."

"Buffalo?" I asked.

"A few herds. Wood bison, we call them, but they're dying out."

I forgot to answer. I ran around and looked at things and planned the cleaning I would give everything, and how I would have more room by moving the table against the wall, and that I'd make new curtains. I whisked by Mike with a head full of ideas, but they were spilled out, for he reached out a sudden hand and caught me to him.

"Like it?" he asked. But how could I answer, with him kissing me so hard?

The rest of the day was spent in cleaning, scrubbing, and scouring. Top and bottom we went over that house, and we went to bed very tired and happy. We were excited, too excited to sleep. We lay there whispering to each other how it would be.

"You'll make me a book case."

"Yes," he said. "In the summer there is the river, and in

80

winter we walk on snowshoes over the white world." I was feeling very drowsy and contented. I closed my eyes and snuggled under Mike's arm. But a face came before my eyes, the dark sullen face of the Henderson woman. I closed my eyes tighter to send it away. I was happy and sleepy, and I didn't want any ugliness from the world to get into our cabin. I couldn't keep it out. I saw again the flash of the bottle as it left Joe Henderson's hand—saw the blood falling in a thin stream to the floor.

"Mike . . ."

"Hmmm?" said Mike in a very sleepy, faraway voice.

"Is that Indian woman Joe Henderson's wife?"

"You might call her that."

"But he acts as if he hates her."

There was a long silence. I thought Mike had fallen asleep.

"Yes, I think he does," Mike said slowly, into the pillow.

"Hates her?" I asked.

"Yes."

"But why?"

"Because of the boy. Everything is because of the boy."

"Tommy?" I asked.

"Yes," said Mike, and then he added, "There were two Tommys." I lay still in the dark, waiting for his voice to continue.

"You see, there are many reasons why a man comes to live in a wild land like this. We come, you and I, Katherine Mary, because here we can live the real life, the life men were meant to live. But there are men who are used to the cities, who would never leave them except that they are driven. Joe Henderson was driven when Tommy died.

"He had only the one child, and he idolized him. But the boy was not strong, and Joe quarreled constantly with his wife—I think her name was Isabel—because he thought she ran around too much to parties and lunches—and didn't give Tommy proper care. Well, maybe she was a bit flighty, but it certainly wasn't her fault that Tommy caught diphtheria. The child came down with it, that's all. Well, I guess the little fellow didn't have much resistance. He was really just a baby, about two or three years old, the size of this Tommy. Anyway, he was dead in four days. And Joe Henderson never spoke a word to his wife. He looked at her when she cried and sobbed and held the little body—just looked at her.

"From that day on he was driven. He drifted through cities and towns, working only to eat and never long at one thing.

"It was only when he struck into the Northwest that any peace came to him. He seemed to take a sort of satisfaction in the rigor and the hardships. At least he had something tangible to fight—the cold. He prospered for a while, and he did pretty well. He came to be known as a steady man, one that left the Indian women strictly alone. Every three or four months, of course, he'd go on a binge. Then he'd talk about Tommy to anyone who would listen.

"Well, the Hudson's Bay Company needed a man here, and Henderson got the job. He's been here four years now. The first year he lived alone. He hated women — you couldn't trust them. Hadn't his own wife killed Tommy? But you've seen him, a big fiery man with red blood in him.

"I was glad when I came in from a couple of months on the trail to find Uaawa with him. I thought it might soften him a little to have a woman around again. And it did, for a while. But as soon as the baby was born, he changed. Of course, he shouldn't have called him Tommy, but he did. And I think it hurt him every time he looked at the child, to see the dark Indian face of him. The other Tommy had been fair.

"He blamed Uaawa for a lot of things—for the boy's black hair and brown face. Then she is a woman, and he didn't trust her. He questioned how she dressed him, what she fed him, where he played. The woman is Indian, and maybe that saved her from going out of her mind. She didn't fight back, not when he beat her and kicked her around, and she didn't go back to her people. That wasn't her way. She was too Indian. And she chose a typical Indian revenge, or maybe it wasn't revenge at all. That's the trouble with the Indian mind, you can't understand it.

"She began by giving this child, this Tommy Henderson, an Indian name. Of course Joe was furious. But in spite of the beatings he gave her, she continued to call little Tommy by his Indian name. When Joe isn't around, she speaks to the child in the Beaver language, and the boy has come to understand that language. He knows the myths and legends of his mother's tribe. There's no doubt the woman is making an Indian of Tommy Henderson.

"It's probably very simple. She sings the songs that were sung to her by her mother, and tells her son the only stories that she knows. Or it may be a pride in her own people. Perhaps she doesn't want the boy to be ashamed before white men. Yes, perhaps it is only that she wishes him to understand her people, to have pride in them. Or perhaps it is as Joe Henderson says—the woman is jealous and spiteful. The child has all his love, she none of it. For the child, Joe will do anything. He's Tommy, and he loves him. Being Indian and being a woman, Uaawa knows this giant of a man who kicks and curses her can be made to suffer through his son."

I thought it all over, a long time.

"I think he's made a mistake. I don't think he's fair to the Indian woman. You're right, though. It's all because of the first Tommy, and you can't help but be sorry for Mr. Henderson."

Mike didn't say anything. The complicated, tangled pattern of lives, where they touch and intertwine—it's impossible to unravel it. I was sorry I had tried. Who can know anything about anything? Especially when they're sleepy.

## CHAPTER SEVEN

Mike left early for his office. I promised to be over as soon as I'd done the dishes and help him straighten up out there. Well, with only two of us it didn't take long to get the dishes out of the way. Then I had a good idea. I thought I'd put up a lunch, and we could eat in the office. It would be fun, a sort of indoor picnic.

I began slicing bread for sandwiches. Suddenly I whirled and faced the room. There was nothing there, of course, but I felt that there was, and I worked uneasily. The feeling of being watched became stronger. Again I turned, this time toward the window, and I laughed with relief; for there,

83

staring in, was a round-faced girl about six years old. I opened the door gently and smiled, so she wouldn't be afraid. But she bounded off like a deer, stopping a safe distance from the cabin to turn and stare.

"Wouldn't you like to come in?" I called.

She just stood there regarding me silently with enormous black eyes.

"Come on," I coaxed. But as she didn't move and it was cold with the door open, I shut it and went back to making lunch.

She came silently, so silently that I hadn't really heard her, but I knew she was out there. I went to the door again, this time with a sandwich in my hand. I opened it and held out the sandwich. She looked at it and held out her hand. I gave it to her, and she fingered it carefully all over, then stuffed the whole thing in her mouth. I had decided that she knew no English, so I motioned to her to come inside. She watched my gesture with intent, curious eyes. But the only response was the continued chewing of that sandwich. Again the cold drove me in.

I counted over the sandwiches and tried to guess how many Mike could eat. I felt a cold gust on my back. The door was open. I continued working and waited for the slight click the door gave when it was closed. The click came. I smiled to myself.

I didn't hear her move, but pretty soon the dark head was at my elbow and the dark eyes on the food. Excitement throbbed in them at the sight of the thick, buttered bread and the slices of meat. I reached down another sandwich to her. Again it was fingered all over with wonder and awe before it was popped whole into her mouth. Two other sandwiches followed. But the last one was not eaten. She carried it off. Stealthily, quietly, she was gone from my elbow, and when I turned to look, gone from my house. My stock of sandwiches being pretty well depleted, I started to work on some new ones. I had finished and was wrapping them when my door opened again.

A brave in full Indian dress with much beadwork nodded solemnly at me, stalked to the best chair in the house, and sat down. Behind him followed aunts, sisters, uncles, and cousins. Each gave me a nod or a grunt and then sat in

84

my chairs. The last chair was finally occupied, and still they came, seating themselves ceremoniously on the floor.

When they were all in, you couldn't have stepped for Indians. They sat there regarding me steadily and silently. I didn't know what they wanted or why they were here, or what I was expected to do about it. Some fifteen children were gathered in the doorway, chattering excitedly, and in the middle of the group was my little friend, waving her sandwich triumphantly, and at the same time protecting it from the sudden onslaughts of the other children.

"Holy St. Patrick!" I said aloud and stared hopelessly at the thirty expectant faces and the sixty hungry eyes that stared back at me. Could it be that they expected me to feed them?

I couldn't just stand there with my mouth open, I had to do something. I was Sergeant Flannigan's wife. I had a position to keep up in the community. I thought of a speech, saying I was not settled yet but that we'd all have a nice party soon. But, looking into the rows of swarthy, stolid faces, I was convinced that they wouldn't understand my speech, that the only thing they'd understand was food. It was plainly my move, and thirty people were waiting for me to make it. I did. I put on a gracious smile.

"What a lovely surprise! I am very glad to see all of you here."

While I was saying this in a loud voice, I was rapidly counting noses. Twenty-eight grownups and twelve children. I had seven sandwiches. By cutting each sandwich into four parts, I would have twenty-eight pieces, each an inch long. Well, Mother had served *hors d'oeuvres* that weren't any larger than that. And there was still a little meat left. The children could have that. I would put on tea. That, at least, there'd be enough of, except, of course, they'd have to drink in relays because there were only ten glasses.

Well, it was the strangest and silentest tea party ever given. I cut up the seven sandwiches and passed the pieces around. They were accepted gravely and gravely swallowed.

But the ice wasn't really broken until tea was served. Then the noise of much sucking and gusty sipping was punctuated by a few belches. This was evidently their idea of a good time. So I smiled and beamed and asked who would have some more tea. This was the only thing I said which they seemed to understand.

When they had had all the tea they could drink, the gentleman who had led the procession rose, grunted at me three times, and left. This was the signal for general departure. The women smiled shyly, and when the last one had pushed the last child out before her, I had to keep looking at the ten glasses, the crumbs, and the spot in the corner where one old crone had kept spitting to assure myself that I had just given a tea party.

In March the thaw set in. The snow had become pockmarked. Millions of tiny, shallow holes appeared in it as it sweated. The winter was almost over. We had missed the last mail delivery. There were only two during the winter, and when Mike told me there were none at all during the summer I cried.

But whenever I got awfully homesick and lonesome for Mother, something happened. And something happened now to take my mind from thoughts of home. I stooped down in the snow and examined the prints carefully. By putting my fingers close together and jabbing them into the snow, I tried to imitate the impression there. It wasn't a dog track because it came in from the woods and circled the house again and again, each time drawing in closer. I remembered how the dogs had whined last night. I was excited now, and I ran back to the house.

"Mike! Mike!" He came to the door. "Look at the tracks! What is it?"

He bent down as I had, to study them. But to him they meant something.

"Wolf," he said, straightening up. "You wouldn't think he'd come so close to the house. But you never know what a wolf's going to do. I saw one once that seemed to be dying. He just staggered along, and overhead a raven watched him. Finally the wolf sank down in the snow and lay still. The raven swooped down, settled on him, and prepared to eat—only it was the wolf that ate the raven."

86

"You mean a wolf is smart enough to pull a trick like that?"

"Yes, and I wonder what deviltry brought this one so close to the house."

Mike looked up. Overhead the trees had lost their silvery-white finery, and their bark was black and wet where it had melted.

"How'd you like that hike I've been promising you, up to the Bull? The snow's gone now except for these few inches."

I had been wanting to go to the Bull. I'd heard about it from the Indians who dropped in regularly once a week for their treasured tea parties. It was a gigantic rock shaped exactly like an enormous buffalo head. It guarded the entrance to the Ne Parle Pas Rapids a few miles up. Whenever I teased to go, Mike had put me off, saying the snow was too soft and treacherous for our snowshoes this time of year.

"What do you think about that wolf coming so close?" I asked as I swung off with Mike.

"It's an interesting thing." And it was interesting to me that he could talk and walk at such a pace. "But it's really the prairie chickens that are making them so bold."

"Prairie chickens?"

He grinned. "Rabbits to you."

It made me mad, his making such a mystery of it. "Go on," I said.

But he didn't go on. We had struck the high ground above Hudson's Hope. And from there the eastern Rockies could be seen, Backbone-of-the-World, the Indians called them. There they were, range after range of them, shading from purple to the faintest blue. The mist rose about their base, making them look like sky islands. Mike held my hand very tight. It was wonderful to share things like this, especially as I always got kissed.

We walked on. The spruce rose in dark towers above us, and everywhere and from everything the snow was going. After a while I remembered about prairie chickens.

"Well, every seven years or so there's a disease that breaks out among them. It seems to be some sort of head and throat infection. Anyway, they die off like flies. And of

87

course both the timber and the black wolf feed mostly off them. So when the prairie chicken gets scarce, the wolf goes hungry."

"But can't a wolf eat other things besides rabbits?" I asked.

"Oh, yes, they hunt caribou herds, picking off the young, the sick, the crippled. And if they're ravenous, sometimes they will attack a full-grown animal. They go after mountain sheep and goats and even moose. But those herds are always on the move, and if they don't happen to be in the same vicinity, old wolf gets vicious. He has to be either ravenous or mad to come into the post."

"Do you think ours is mad?"

"I hope not," Mike said. "I don't want our dogs coming down with hydrophobia."

I must have looked pretty sick when he said that because he reassured me at once. "Don't worry, Kathy, I'll put out meat with a little strychnine rubbed through it. That ought to get him."

But I didn't like that either. Now I was sorry for the wolf.

"Maybe he'll go away," I said, "or die naturally."

"Wolves don't die except three ways—mange, distemper, or poison."

"Can't they be shot or trapped?"

"Not as a rule. They're too clever. They're so trap-shy that hunters can keep them away from a carcass of a deer by laying a piece of metal on the ground."

"I still don't like it. I hate to poison him."

"If we don't," Mike said, "he'll start ripping our dogs to pieces."

I sighed. Things weren't like this in Boston.

"But, Mike—" My hand was gripped so hard the bones ached. I looked at Mike. He relaxed his grip and pointed. I followed the direction of his arm. I saw nothing. Just a snow bank. But I kept staring at it very hard. I knew there was something there, and I wanted to find it. I wanted to be a woodsman like Mike. Then I *did* notice something, a thin stream of vapor rising from the drift. Mike led me away. When he considered we were far enough from the drift, he stopped.

"You saw it, didn't you, Kathy?"

"I think so. That little bit of moisture rising up?"

"That's it!" Mike was jubilant. "And can you guess what it is?"

Well, I couldn't, so he told me. "It's a bear hibernating. The thin little trickle of steam is his breath. He'll be waking up any time now, though."

I marveled at Mike. He had the sharp sight and the cunning of an Indian.

He pointed out the Bull to me, and, sure enough, the great rock was a perfect buffalo head, even to the shaggy neck which we began to climb. It was fascinating, this world of Mike's. But I was too much of a stranger in it yet.

A crunching like glass splintering filled the air. What now, I thought, and looked at Mike. He gave a triumphant shout into the face of the Bull. And the Bull threw the cry back to us. Again and again we heard it sounding in the crevices.

"Now you're going to see something." And Mike pulled me up to the top.

Below us a long strip of white earth heaved like a huge writhing snake. White sandstone cliffs looked down as it pushed up on itself, splitting cakes of ice loose. In the open space water moved. It was the Peace River crunching and gnawing at the ice layer that covered it. Blocks of ice and frozen snow were beginning to pile up on themselves, and a chunk as big as my head was struck from both sides and sent catapulting thirty feet into the air. Then larger pieces went flying and popping—one ice block the size of our double bed jumped past us into space and then fell back, cutting a jagged hole through which water foamed and spurted. Tormented, the river strove to free itself. Faster and faster now the cakes were being shot into the air. All around they leaped and fell. The noise was deafening. For miles up and down, the Peace spat out gleaming ice that flashed a moment in the sun, then crashed heavily back.

"The river's angry," I whispered, but even through the din Mike heard me.

"Not angry. It shakes winter off as we rub sleep from our eyes."

"How did you know, Mike?"

"About the breaking up? It comes about this time every

year. And when you've been in the country as long as I have, you can usually hit the day."

"But how? I don't see how."

"Well, the snow starts to melt, and when there's just a bit left and it's just so soft, well, then you figure it's time for the breakup."

I had to laugh. He sounded just like Mother, a perfect cook who could never tell anybody how she made things.

The barrage of ice blocks continued as more and more river broke loose. In half an hour it flowed freely, carrying the melting blocks along. The ice cakes still jostled and whirled against each other, but only occasionally now did a piece get lifted into the air.

This experience made things different for me. Things I had thought of as static, lived, had a violent insurgent life of their own. The river was like the bear; it hibernated for the winter.

I tried to tell Mike a little of what I felt about it.

Mike was a woodsman. He understood. "All of it, the forests and the mountains and the rivers, they've got their moods and their feelings, just like a person. The Indians recognize this—just as they know some places are good and some are evil. Why, there are places in the forest you couldn't pay an Indian to go into."

"Because they're evil?" I asked.

"Yes, or cruel, like the rapids *qui ne parle pas*. That means the rapids that don't talk. That's why they're so treacherous. Usually you hear the murmuring of rough water well in advance and are able to do something about it. But here there is no sound, no warning. The first thing you know you're in them. The water drops two hundred and forty-three feet in a couple of minutes, and no one has gone through it alive. Once they put an empty boat in the rapids and waited down below to see what happened. Not even a board or a splinter of that boat came through. It must have been pounded to pulp."

I looked down into the freed water. It was swift-moving, even here. I drew back from the edge.

We walked over the rock to the side we had climbed. Climbing down is always harder than climbing up, and

90

Mike gave me a hand to hold to. But I won't climb down unless I see where I'm going. So I faced out and waved my foot back and forth in hope of finding some place to set it. Mike was watching me and laughing very hard, which was one of the reasons he didn't see them first. The other reason was he was climbing down with his face against the side of the Bull the way you're supposed to. Anyway, men, dogs, and sleds suddenly appeared over the hill.

"Mike, Mike, look!"

We climbed back up and watched the men and teams surging over the plains below us. More and more sleds spread out over the valley until there must have been fifty men racing each other over the waste.

"Those are our neighbors, Kathy. Hudson's Hope men, all of them."

I stared down curiously at them. They were coming home after a winter's trapping. That would bring the population of Hudson's Hope up to about one hundred thirty-five people, including the Indians on the reserve.

The sleds were piled with dark furs.

"How much do they make from a winter's trapping, Mike?"

"I'd say six hundred dollars is a pretty fair season. But most of them owe a good part of that to Joe Henderson. He outfits the men up to a hundred and twenty dollars . . . on credit."

"That's very nice of him."

"It's business," Mike explained. "He won't trade with them until he gets paid."

'Breeds, whites, and Indians ran forward beside their sleds, waving their arms and yelling. I turned to see what they were yelling at, and from the other direction came the women, running all together.

As the two groups neared each other, I began making out the faces of the women. There was old Ookoominou, who had spat in the corner at my first tea party. There was Ninalakus, running on light feet ahead of the others. I tried to guess to which man each was calling. A tingling thrill of anticipation was in me. These women had not seen their men for seven months.

The tension grew. The men and women were close enough now to recognize each other, and eyes passed quickly from face to face.

A few caps went sailing into the air, and a few hurrahs were heard from the men. The women stopped running; one or two walked forward slowly, and the rest stood still.

The men were among them now, circling in and out and through them. Here and there a man ran forward and caught a woman to him. But when that happened, the man was always white, and the woman always young.

For the most part a woman would walk to the man's side and he, many times without a word to her, would throw heavy pelts from the sled into her arms. She, bracing herself, received skin after skin until her body bent under the weight of them. Then the man would raise his whip and the dogs would start, the woman keeping pace.

Bit by bit the women fell behind. Once again, men and women were in separate groups.

I couldn't understand, and I couldn't keep it in me any longer. "Mike, why do they do that?"

Mike didn't look at me. "Their dogs are tired from the long trek. They wanted to lighten the sleds for them."

"But the women!"

Mike said nothing. I followed his eyes and couldn't believe what I saw happening. An Indian had unhitched one of his dogs and was harnessing his wife to the team.

"Mike!"

"His dog's gone lame," Mike said.

I couldn't answer him. I watched, horrified, as the woman strained with the beasts, and the sled moved slowly after the others.

"Indian women are toughened to it, Kathy. That's all they've known for a thousand years. Why, it's only recently the braves have even turned professional trappers. Used to be the men only hunted to eat. There was no such thing as profit. And the occasional hunting they did was their only contribution. The women have always done the work, the lifting, the hauling, the skinning, the cooking and home building."

"But it's terrible. What kind of a life is that?"

"It's changing," Mike said. "Very slowly, of course, but

92

it *is* changing. When the Hudson's Bay Company first came into this territory, it was the squaws they had to hire to bring the furs those seven hundred miles into Edmonton. They often carried a hundred and fifty pounds of goods on their backs, over fourteen-mile portages without a rest. Now, of course, the men have taken over, and there's come to be plenty of 'breeds and whites too. But at least it shows there is hope, that things are gradually changing for the women."

They'd have to change a lot more, I decided, and I was busy with plans and revolutions all the way home. I didn't do any talking because I was thinking hard. Uncle Martin was always discussing the exploitation of labor, and he said organization was the only way to fight to it. To Uncle Martin organization meant strikes. I considered the idea of getting the Indian women to go on strike against the men. But I decided they weren't advanced enough. They were savages, and they wouldn't understand.

I would have to devise something else. If I was going to live among these women, I was going to do something for them. I didn't know what yet, but . . .

Mike broke in on my thoughts. "Did you have a nice walk, Kathy?"

I looked at him surprised. Is that what we had done today, taken a walk? A walk here didn't mean around the block on a cement sidewalk, as it did in Boston. It meant wolf tracks, bear breathings, rivers throwing ice at you, and Indians, and . . .

"Yes," I said. "It was a very nice walk."

### CHAPTER EIGHT

Mike had said of the mosquitoes, "They are the first to come and the last to go." But I hadn't realized what mosquitoes could be. I hadn't realized that every act of ours would be governed by them. When winter ended, I looked forward to getting out of my heavy mackinaw pants and into skirts once more. But I was never to wear skirts in this country; for spring and summer, and all during the mosquito months, I wore overalls as protection against those vicious swarms of insects. Mike tacked a fine cheese-cloth over every window. The mesh of ordinary screening was not small enough for those tiny, whining pests. The dogs were made miserable. We had to keep smudge pots going, and all day long they huddled about them. Even wild animals were sometimes driven mad by the swarming, biting hordes. The nights were cold, and it was then we had our only relief from mosquitoes.

Mike had given me gloves to wear when I worked in the garden. I decided privately not to be bothered with them, but ten minutes out of doors, and my hands were red and swollen twice their size. So now I never went out without them. Another necessary piece of mosquito-fighting equipment was my hat, a big hat with a wide brim from which hung a cheesecloth veil that was carefully tucked into the neck of my waist.

As I bent over my field peas I was conscious of the thin whine of a thousand small wings. The sound was so constant and so monotonous that usually I didn't hear it, but now for some reason I did. The mosquitoes lay in dark shifting clouds over everything, and I was proud of having outwitted them with so many clothes.

There was something in my red clover patch I decided not to pull up because there was just a chance it might be red clover. I'd have to ask Mike when he came. He should be here pretty soon because he was taking me to the Indian Reserve. I straightened up. This gardening was hard on the back.

"Kathy!"

I ran around to the other side of the house and watched Mike come to me over the tall grass.

"Are you ready, Kathy?" he called. I was, and fell into stride beside him.

"I know it's longer by the river," I said, "but it's prettier."

Mike smiled, and we turned toward the river.

"How long do you think it will take me to speak their language well, Mike?"

"Not long. You're picking it up fast."

"The grunting I can do already," I said, "and the solemn looks."

94

Mike laughed. "Let's hear the grunting."

But instead I showed him a wild canary. It was pale yellow with black on its wings, not at all like Mother's canary. Mike had pointed one out to me a few days ago, and I wanted to show him I remembered.

Mike stopped me suddenly with his hand.

"What is it?"

"Nothing. You look pretty against a Manitoba maple. It sort of goes with that red hair of yours."

"Auburn," I corrected.

I was very happy, and I was doing good too—doing the kind of work missionaries and people like that did.

"That cheesecloth is going to make a big difference in the lives of those Beaver Indians, isn't it?"

"It should," Mike said.

It struck me this wasn't a very enthusiastic reply. But I forgave him because last week he had spent two hours talking to the Indians in their own language, telling them that the mosquitoes could not get through the cheesecloth I had brought them. He had explained patiently that it would be sanitary and comfortable, and they would have less sickness if they fastened this thin stuff over their windows and across the entrance of their tepees.

"What messages of civilization are you going to bring them today?"

Mike was teasing me, but I answered very seriously, "I'm going to teach them to wash."

"Wash what?"

"Everything. Themselves, their children, and their houses."

Mike laughed from there all the way to their river, when he got interested in telling me how we could make a million dollars. He pointed to the low island formed of sand, gravel, and silt that collected behind log jams and in other sheltered places. He stooped and picked up a handful of the sand.

"There's gold here," he said, waving it at me.

I poked at it with interest and turned over a few bright-flecked pieces that might have been gold. "Why don't we mine it?"

Mike threw the handful away.

"Too fine, no profit for hand panners. Some day, though, somebody will invent a machine for mining this stuff and make himself a million dollars."

We walked on silently, thinking about gold. After a while Mike said, "It would ruin the country, though. All those prospectors coming in." And then, without change of inflection, "Watch that elk, Kathy."

I looked out across the river. It was narrow at this point, not a quarter of a mile across. In the middle, heading for the shore, was a giant elk breasting the water majestically. His antler stalk rose from his head like a young forest.

"Look, he's treading water. Something must have frightened him."

"Maybe he saw us or smelled us."

"No," Mike said, "the wind's the wrong way, and elk can't see at this distance. But he's scented something he doesn't like. He's turning back."

And sure enough, the animal turned and headed back for the opposite shore.

"There's the fellow that scared him. Look, Kathy, over there on the other side of the shoal."

I shaded my eyes and peered across. A large brown bear was making hooking motions with his paws in the water.

"Is he fishing?"

"Sure. See him? He's throwing the fish up on the bank."

Mike was right. Every few seconds the bear would scoop up a squirming fish and toss it on the shore.

"That's what the elk scented, all right."

"But Mike—" I watched as the beautiful creature swam toward the bear.

"They'll do that," Mike said, "every time. I've seen it happen with deer and with wolf too. When they're startled midstream, they'll swim back to the side they started from, no matter how close they are to the other bank. Even if the danger comes from that original side, back they go."

The elk veered again and swam on a slant. He landed well upstream of the bear and plunged off into the woods. The bear never looked up; he was busy devouring his catch. We watched as he poured the wriggling, flipping things down his throat.

"They're whitefish," Mike said.

I gave him a quick glance. He couldn't possibly see what kind they were, clear across the water.

"You see," Mike explained, "they were coming in the shoal water to spawn. That's the only reason the bear was able to catch one after another like that. And it's the season for whitefish."

I reached up and kissed him through the cheesecloth. "You're wonderful!"

"It's my business," Mike said seriously.

"To be wonderful?"

"To know these things. It's a business just as banking or farming is a business."

"But you know it well," I said.

"Sure I know it well," he agreed.

While we had been kissing, the bear had gone away. We walked on beside the river. We were close to the Indian village when Mike pointed. "Another fisherman."

There was an Indian boy in the bottom of a canoe. He leaned over, his head close to the water, and peered down intently. In his hand was a dart, poised and ready.

"They spear the fish," Mike said. "Look, Kathy, he's got a partner." Up above circled an osprey. Suddenly his wings folded back, and he dived, or rather dropped, into the water. He came up gulping and swallowing the last of a still-thrashing tail. Mike called something to the boy, who grinned and held up a fish in either hand.

"What's he fishing for?"

"Anything he can get—pickerel, trout, giant pike. We'll go fishing with the Indians some night. They burn torches at the end of the boat to lure the fish."

The boy in the canoe shouted a shrill word to us. It sounded like "Muskinongi." Mike jumped to the edge of the water and stared down. I ran over too, just in time to see a dark sleek head dive beneath the surface.

Mike laughed. "Muskrat." Although we stared for several seconds, it did not reappear.

We left the river. Some Indian children were racing each other in the woods. They played silently like animals. Heads looked out curiously from houses and tepees. The women and the children stopped work to watch us. Inside, the braves reached for their eagle headdresses and then stalked out to greet us. As we walked toward the house of Mustagan, the chief, the group around us swelled. Boys left their arrow-making, young men put down the paddles they were fashioning, girls left their spinning and their beadwork. Mustagan came forward from his door to greet us. He was a tall, strong-looking man. And behind him moved Oo-me-me, his wife. She was soft and pretty, and her name meant "Little Pigeon." Mustagan spoke words to Mike and raised his hand in ceremonial greeting. He led the way to his house, a cabin very much like ours.

Oo-me-me spread two bright blankets on the ground outside. Mike and Mustagan sat upon them, and the other men squatted in a circle around them. Oo-me-me brought the pipe to her husband. It must be passed around and smoked. It was beautifully carved, with a long eagle-plumed stem and a smooth bowl. But I didn't like the strong, acrid stink of it. I tried not to think of the mouths it had entered and the teeth it had lain between. Mike got second puff at it, and as there were thirty or forty men, I was glad he was accorded this privilege.

Still, there was dignity in these men, hunters of the tribe, warriors. The circle was impressive, dark bodies rising naked out of velveteen cut from Joe Henderson's bolts. But over the store-bought goods were laid trappings of beadwork; images and colors flared against copper flanks.

On the nearest copper flank a mosquito settled, gorged its fill, and flew away. Mike said the Indians and the mosquitoes had lived here so long that they were used to each other. The 'breeds suffered like the whites, but the full bloods seemed more or less immune. But they weren't immune to the diseases that go with the fly and the mosquito, and I looked at the windows of Mustagan's house. No cheesecloth of mine was hanging there, and the only curtain was made of the beating wings of insects.

"Oo-me-me," I said sternly.

She looked at me with smiling eyes. I beckoned her away from the council of men and into the house. I pointed at the bare windows. "The netting, the cheesecloth Sergeant Mike put up, where is it?"

She smiled again and spoke her Mission School English slowly. "Him much fine, much pretty."

98

"Yes," I said, "but where is it?"

She looked at me a moment as though trying to understand what it was I wanted. "Me bring, yes?"

"Yes." I was glad that at least she still had it. Mike would have to hang it again, and I would have to explain again. "These things take time," I said to myself—"and patience," I said to myself, only harder.

A whimpering sound came from the room Oo-me-me had entered. I walked to the doorway and looked in. A baby lay in a nest of rags and clothes that had been heaped on the floor for it. It waved its chubby legs, driving a flock of mosquitoes and flies into the air. On one leg was an open cut, angry and red. When the leg stopped twitching, the insects settled down on it again, biting into the raw flesh.

Oo-me-me had found what she was looking for. She returned to me with an armful of what the French call *parflêche*. It's a kind of dried hide, and half a dozen skirts, mostly velvet and velveteen, were wrapped in it. She undid the package with care, and I saw that each dress was edged with a thin strip of cheesecloth.

She was so pleased and proud of her dresses that I didn't say anything. Then I looked at her baby, turning and twisting under its covering of biting bull flies and mosquitoes.

"Oo-me-me," I said, "you have done wrong."

She understood that word. She must have known it at the Mission, for a hurt, puzzled look came into her eyes.

"It is not yours, that netting. It belonged to the windows."

She looked sullenly, almost defiantly, at the windows. "For what they want pretty dresses?"

At that point Mike came in. I showed him the dresses and started telling him the whole thing very fast, so that Oo-me-me wouldn't follow it. I don't think Mike could have followed it either if the dresses trimmed in cheesecloth hadn't been there as evidence. I could see from Mike's expression that the whole thing struck him funny, and I think he would have laughed if my voice hadn't gotten a little shaky at the end. Instead, he called in Mustagan and told us about Father Lacombe and the garbage can.

"You see," Mike lit his pipe, and began in Beaver, slowly, so I could follow. Mustagan's eyes never left his face. An Indian is the most patient listener in the world. "Years ago, when the first Mounty rode into Calgary, there was nothing there but a tent. The tent belonged to Father Lacombe, the first white man to come into the Territory. That little tent was the first Mission in the Northwest. Well, the Indians there were Blackfeet, and Father Lacombe taught them and lived among them and became a brother to them, and spoke to them much of their elder brother who was God's son, whose name was Jesus. Also he spoke to them of other things. There was one habit in particular that he spoke against, and it was this: when food and filth filled a tepee so that a bad smell came, and there was no place to step, the Blackfeet would leave that house and build for themselves a new one that was clean and fresh—for a while.

"Now, in the nation from which the good Father came, it was the custom to collect waste foods and bones into a neat pile, to hunt out the dirt from all corners of the lodge, gather it together, and burn it. He spoke to the Blackfeet of this white man's custom, telling them it was good medicine. But to the women this custom brought more work, and as it was the day was not long enough for their labors. So, though they listened with pleasure to the voice of Father Lacombe and watched his gestures with admiration, still did the waste matter and the filth lie on the floors of their tepees.

"But the Father did not despair of teaching them, for he knew the ways of women, and that their hearts followed after beauty. So he wrote on a piece of paper. And this paper was carried by dog sled and runner into the city that is called Regina. And back into the wilderness came a large thing of *cylindrical* shape." Mike's hands molded a cylinder in the air, and Mustagan nodded. "It was wrapped in many layers of heavy paper and guarded always by ten braves, for it was known to be the good medicine of Father Lacombe. And after many months it arrived in the camp of the Blackfeet. The drums beat, and the people of the tribe gathered around. Father Lacombe stripped the wrappings from it, and a great cry went up, for the thing flashed silver in the sun and was beautiful to behold.

"The Father then showed them how the top came off,
100

easily as the scalp from an enemy's head. And the tribe filed by and looked within. When he saw that the eyes of the women glowed to behold this thing of beauty, Father Lacombe spoke and named the thing of shiny silver, *'garbage can.'* He explained that within its mouth would lie all the decaying food and gnawed bones in the camp.

"The Blackfeet were well pleased with this silver gift and wished to make gifts in return. But the Father would not take their skins, their bows, or their weapons; he said only that they must put his gift to good use.

"Now there was sickness in another tribe, and Father Lacombe journeyed ten sleeps away to bring them comfort and medicine. When he returned he went, before taking rest or sleep, to look at the floors of the lodges. Great was his disappointment, and bitter were the eyes he turned upon the Blackfeet; for still did the filth lie ankle-deep in the tepees, and nowhere did he see the garbage can.

"He went then to the chief and asked that the council fires be kindled. And when the blankets were laid and the people assembled, great was his surprise to see two braves enter the circle with the garbage can in their arms. It was placed in the center of the council, and the chief took his seat upon it.

"For a moment the Father knew not what words to call upon. But finally he asked why they had not filled his gift with trash, as he had asked them. And the chief made answer for the people, saying they would not fill so beautiful a gift with such dishonorable objects.

"We would no more throw bones at the present of Father Lacombe than we would throw them at the Father himself."

Mustagan nodded in silent approval.

"And so," Mike concluded, "the chief ceremonial seat in a Blackfoot council is known still as *gabajcan.*"

Oo-me-me looked with awe and wonder at Mike. And Mustagan said, "A storyteller, him bring gladness to all hearts."

I was feeling better too about the cheesecloth. Greater and wiser people than I had not succeeded any better. How clever Mike was! He would not offend Mustagan and his wife by mentioning the cheesecloth directly, but had hinted at their error with the involved circumlocution an Indian loves. I wondered if Oo-me-me had understood the parallel.

I said, "Next week when I come I will bring you more cheesecloth."

Oo-me-me looked puzzled. "But no more have I dresses to put it on."

A brave entered the house. An Indian never knocks on the door, not even on the door of his chief. Though he held his voice low, the words that he spoke to Mustagan came from him in a sort of pant. The man's excitement spread to the others. Oo-me-me stared with wild eyes at his face. Even I, who could not hear him, felt trouble.

"How long ago?" The words burst from Mike in English. He changed them quickly into Beaver. The Indian answered, and Mike stood up. Mustagan also rose, and the Indian, taking it as a sign of dismissal, darted off.

Mike turned to me. "Chief Mustagan will send someone back with you, Kathy."

"What's happened?" I couldn't keep the fear out of my voice.

Mike hesitated. "A white woman lost on the trail."

"A white woman around here?"

"Maybe not. We don't know where she is. She and her husband started by boat from Peace River Crossing. I know him slightly, a Frenchman, Jacques Jellet. He's a trapper."

"How did she get lost?"

"They'd been traveling four or five weeks, camping at night. They didn't want to overload the boat with provisions, so he shot their meat on the way. Well, three days ago he went off a ways hunting, and when he came back she was gone. He saw the fire was low, nothing but a few embers. So he figured she'd gone after wood. He waited a half hour or so, then he began calling her.

"Two days later he stumbled into a Cree camp, still calling her. At first the Crees ran from him. They thought he was some kind of spirit. His clothes were half torn off him, his body was cut and bleeding, his eyes were wild, and over his head he waved a burning torch."

"Was he mad?" I asked.

"No, mosquitoes."

102

The Indian who had brought the news was back at the door with a horse. Mike took the reins from him.

"How did our Beaver Indians hear what had happened in the land of the Crees?" I asked.

"Haven't you heard of the moccasin telegraph?"

"Yes," I said, "I've heard of it, but I don't know what it means."

"It means," said Mike, "that the print of the moccasin is on every trail, and by the moccasin comes the news." He swung into the saddle.

"Mike, dear, be careful."

"She couldn't have gotten far," Mike said. "There's really no chance she could have wandered as far as my territory, so this is just routine. They'll find her body a hundred miles east of here."

I caught his leg and looked at him. "Her body? But, Mike, she couldn't be dead! She's only been lost three days. You can't starve to death in three days."

Mike looked grim. "She's dead, all right."

"But how?"

He paused, then said the word again, "Mosquitoes."

## CHAPTER NINE

They had taken the Union Jack from in front of the Hudson's Bay Company and were flying it down by the pier. It waved good-by and so did we to the men in the boats. There were three large canoes piled with the winter's catch of furs. The men would take the pelts three hundred miles by water to Peace River Crossing, from where they would go by overland trail another four hundred miles to Edmonton. That trip had taken us three months in winter. In summer, traveling by water, it would be longer. I felt sorry for the wives of the men who were leaving. They did not talk or wave as much as the others.

The trappers crowded the pier, pointing with pride to the canoes, identifying their own furs, laughing and telling stories of how that beaver and that mink tangled with their lines. "Look how low is *bateau* in the water, eh! Heavy with the winter's work. *C'est bon.*" And they waved their sweaty, bright-colored handkerchiefs at the Indians in the canoes, and yelled messages at them: "Tell that little *klooch* at Grouard that I'm still thinking of her!" Or, "You get to Peace River Crossing, you tell one Baldy Red I cut his heart out he no pay me that five bucks!" I laughed out loud when I heard that. I'd almost forgotten Baldy.

Mike undid the ropes that shoved off the first canoe. A great shout went up. It shook the air, from every throat it burst—that is, from every throat but one. Atenou sat glumly, his face in his hands. I watched him as Mike shoved off the second and third boats. His expression of woe did not change. His eyes stared mournfully as the canoes flashed past him, but he did not move his head to follow their passage.

Something was wrong. This was not like Atenou. He was one of Mustagan's best hunters, a man whom the Indian women watched with their slow eyes, for he had not yet taken a wife.

I walked over to him. "Atenou, is something wrong?"

He lifted his eyes to me, then they closed from the exertion.

Maybe he's sick, I thought, but I didn't want to ask that because Indians are very susceptible to suggestion. Instead I said, "What is it?"

A low moan, that was all. It frightened me, and I called Mike.

"What's the matter with you, Atenou? You look like the last rose of summer."

Atenou answered Mike as he had me, with a wavering moan. Mike tried again, this time in Beaver. Atenou took his hands away from his face, and one cheek was swelled out like a balloon.

"Toothache." Mike pronounced the word first in English and then in Beaver. Atenou held onto his jaw again. Mike forced his hands away and his mouth open. He asked questions which the Indian answered with grunts and groans. Mike's hand was in Atenou's mouth by now, and he did something inside it that brought a bellow. A pretty half-breed girl going by asked, "Atenou is singing with the tooth ache?"

Mike turned to me. "An abscess. The one in the back.

104

All I did was press on it." He hauled Atenou to his feet. "Come on!" He marched off, piloting the brave toward the office.

I ran after them. "What are you going to do?"

"It's got to come out," Mike said.

"But . . ." Mike's look warned me into silence.

Atenou was completely docile. I guess he thought nothing worse could happen to him than what he was feeling now. But he was wrong.

Mike sat him in the big chair. "It's your wisdom tooth," he said. "It's got to come out."

Atenou gazed dully at him and made no answer. Mike went to the back of the room and unlocked one of the cupboards.

I followed him. "Mike," I whispered, "you don't know how to pull teeth!"

"Shh!" Mike whispered back. "Do you want him to lose confidence in me?"

"Oh, Mike, I don't think you should try it."

Mike got out a bottle of liquor and rummaged around until he found a whisky glass. "Here, pour some out for him. Give him as much as he'll hold."

I took the bottle from Mike, and maybe my hand shook or maybe I looked a little white around the mouth, because Mike grinned at me and said, "Pour yourself a glass too." I ignored the suggestion.

Atenou looked very surprised when I handed him the forbidden firewater. But he drank it down and asked no questions. Every time I asked if he would have some more, he grunted acceptance. I don't know how many glasses of whisky I poured him. Finally I got tired and left him the bottle.

I walked back to see what Mike was doing. He was very busy. In front of him was spread a case of vicious-looking instruments supplied by the Canadian Government. Also supplied by the Government was the thin paper book of instructions which Mike was reading.

"What are you doing?" I asked with disapproval.

"Trying to find out if it's a bicuspid."

I recognized that dogged note in his voice, and I knew that Atenou's tooth was as good as out.

"All right," I said. "How do you go about it—just pull?"

Mike consulted the book. "Pull with a twisting motion, it says here."

"Twisting?" I asked dubiously.

"Certainly. You know what twisting is—a, a twist."

Poor Mike, I could see he was scared. Well, he's got a right to be, was my first thought. My second was more wifely: "What can I do to help?"

"You can help me tie him if he's drunk enough."

He was drunk enough. He lolled back in the chair, humming a war chant and hiccoughing. We passed the rope back and forth over and under Atenou's body until, as Mike said, we had him hog-tied.

Then Mike told me to bring him the case of instruments. The sight of those dozen sharp hooked implements seemed to bring Atenou out of his drunk. Mike nodded toward the whisky, and I poured another two glasses down his throat. On the third glass his head fell back, his eyes clouded over, and the stuff dribbled down his chin.

Mike took off his jacket and rolled up his sleeves. We walked silently to the pump out back and washed our hands.

"Open a fresh roll of cotton," Mike said. I nodded and followed him into the office. It took an awfully long time to find the cotton, and almost as long to open it. When I brought it to Mike, he was rereading the directions in that thin paper book. There was sweat on his forehead. He fingered through the instruments and picked out a pliers.

"Open your mouth," he said to Atenou. But Atenou was too drunk to understand him even when he spoke in Beaver.

Mike turned to me. "Hold his nose, Kathy."

"What?"

"Hold his nose. He'll have to open his mouth then to breathe."

I could see Mike's point, but I didn't relish holding the nose of that drooling, drunken Indian, even if he was tied.

"Hurry up!" Mike said.

I moved close and bent over Atenou. The smell of him was indescribable, part whisky and part—I don't know what. I took a deep breath, which I intended to hold until that tooth was out, and pressed the end of his nose between my thumb and forefinger. Nothing happened. I pressed harder, and the mouth fell open. In went the silver pliers and Mike's hand up to the wrist. In a moment they were both out, but there was no tooth between the pliers.

"Holy St. Patrick, did he swallow it?"

"No," said Mike. "I haven't pulled it." He looked away from me. "I was thinking—" He stopped.

"Yes?" I said.

"I was thinking that maybe I could do with a small gulp of that whisky myself."

It somehow pleased me, seeing Mike Flannigan in need of a drink like any other Irishman. Well, he had one. And it was no small gulp that he had, either.

"Now it's your turn, Kathy."

I looked at him, then I looked at the dark shining nose I had to hold again. I took it straight from the bottle like a man. I coughed and choked and made a face, but a warm comfort spread inside me. I grabbed Atenou's nostrils and squeezed. Again the mouth dropped open, again the pliers and Mike's hand entered. I saw it give the twisting motion and the pull. I saw it give the twisting motion and the pull again. Mike braced his foot against the chair—twist, pull, a jerk, a yell from Atenou—and the tooth came out in the pliers. Mike waved triumphantly in the air. I guess maybe he was a little drunk. I guess maybe I was too, but whether from whisky or relief I don't know.

But Atenou was sober and feeling gingerly around in his mouth with his tongue. When he came to the hole, he let out a cry that could be heard in the Red River Valley.

Mike and I rushed to him, untied him, bathed his face, gave him whisky, and plugged the vacant spot with cotton. All this time he never stopped yelling. Suddenly I realized the impossibility of yelling with your mouth filled with cotton and whisky. I looked at Atenou. His mouth was closed. The screams were coming from somewhere else. Mike must have reached that conclusion too. He ran to the door and started yelling, "Drop it, you damn fool! Drop it!"

I ran to the door too, but Mike pushed me back. I ducked under his arm and looked. The horse I saw seemed to be one of the four escaped from the Apocalypse. Its coat shone with sweat, its eyes rolled in terror, its lips were flecked with foam, its ears were flattened and twitching, its nostrils flaring. The screams of the man were mixed with those of the animal. For there *was* a man on its back, a man clutching something wildly, desperately, in his arms. I strained to see. Even Atenou watched with interest from the window. What the man seemed to hold was a ball of fur. It couldn't be that. I craned forward and before Mike pulled me back I had seen it. A bald-faced grizzly was running almost at the horse's flank. She was the same coloring as the fur ball the man held—her cub, of course. Now I understood Mike's hoarse cries of "Drop it! Drop it!"

The man turned toward us a ghastly face. Mike cupped his hand. "You idiot, drop that cub!"

For a moment it seemed that the man had not understood, for horse, rider, and grizzly streaked by us. I caught my breath, for the grizzly was gaining on them. Its bared teeth were even with the mare's thin, white-stockinged shanks. But the man *had* understood, for his arm went out from his body in a queer jerking motion. At the end of them the cub dangled and was dropped. It rolled over and over. The mother grizzly turned to it, nuzzled it with an inquiring nose. Then, picking it up in her mouth, she set off at a dignified trot for the woods.

The horse stopped and whinnied uncertainly. The man went limp in the saddle. He seemed to have caved in from the stomach up. His shoulders dropped, and his head sank between them. Mike ran for him. "Katherine Mary, get out that whisky."

There was no need to get it out. It was still sitting on the table. I filled the glass full. When Atenou saw me at the whisky, he clapped his hand to his cheek and groaned pitifully. I poured him a glass too.

Mike returned with a pale-faced young man leaning on his arm. The stranger crossed the room unsteadily, smiled wanly when Mike introduced me, and fell into a chair. Mike handed him the whisky. He drank it down obediently in one gulp, as though it were medicine. He coughed a little, but already the color was coming back to his face.

Mike sat on the edge of the table and lit his pipe. He blew a few thoughtful puffs into the air. "Now let's have it."

"Have it?" The young man looked startled. "Oh, you mean about the bear?"

"No," said Mike. "I mean about you. We'll get to the bear in good time."

"Oh, me?" The young man smiled a rather ingratiating smile. "Peters, Ralph Peters."

"All right, Mr. Peters. What are you doing in this part of the country?"

Mr. Peters sat up straighter in his chair. "Just passing through, Sergeant. I'm a prospector."

I followed Mike's glance. He was looking at the young man's hands. They were well kept. The nails were cleaner than mine and had been buffed until they shone.

"How much prospecting have you done?" Mike asked in a slow drawl.

Mr. Peters seemed embarrassed. He shifted slightly in his chair. "I guess I exaggerated a bit when I called myself a prospector. I haven't done any mining as yet, I'm on my way north. Yukon, matter of fact, to try my luck."

"You must have got in this afternoon. That's the only way I figure I could have missed you—in all that confusion when the fur brigade left."

"A good guess, Sergeant. I came in just afterwards. Met the canoes about a quarter-mile before sighting the dock."

"You're American, aren't you?" Mike asked.

"Why, yes, Detroit."

"And what did you do in Detroit?" Mike was still looking at Ralph Peters's hands. They seemed to fascinate him.

"I sold shoes. Thomas & Bailey's main branch, Tenth and Church streets."

Mike grinned. "Well, I guess you can tell us about the bear now, Mr. Peters."

At the mention of the word "bear" the color drained from Mr. Peter's face, and he reached for the whisky glass. I filled it for him, he took a sip, coughed, and set it down.

"It was a terrible trip, by canoe, you know. I thought I'd stay here a week or so and get the cramps out of my legs. Well, first thing I did was borrow that horse and ride around a bit. Wanted to see the country."

"It's a beautiful country, isn't it?" I asked.

109

He looked at me a little blankly. "Oh, yes. But full of bears."

Mike laughed. "It's the season for them. Summer and spring."

"Yes," the young man said slowly, as though marking those seasons definitely in his mind. "Well, I was just walking the horse, so as to see everything better, and as you say, ma'am, it *is* pretty country; rolling and mountainous, and the leaves new and fresh. I was remarking to myself that things are a lighter green when they first come out, sort of a lime or yellow-green, I guess you'd call it."

"Where'd you find the cub?" Mike asked impatiently.

Mr. Peters looked at him reproachfully. "In a yellow-green thicket. You see, the horse had stopped to browse when suddenly its ears went back, and it stiffened up. At the same time I saw a movement in the thicket. Well, I was curious. I pushed back the bushes with my gun. If it was anything dangerous, I figured I could shoot it. But all it was was a little bear cub crouching there. When he saw me he made a noise in his throat that was supposed to be growling. He was awfully cute, you know, round and chubby like a chow puppy. I got off to have a better look at him. He whimpered a little when I picked him up, but he didn't put up much of a fight. Had the thickest fur I ever felt in my life. I thought it would be fun to take him back to camp.

"My horse smelled bear and didn't want to let us up, but I finally got me and the cub on her back. I'd just turned her and headed her for home when a whirlwind of fury crashed through the thicket at us. The horse lunged forward like a crazy thing, but it couldn't pull away from that she-demon of a bear.

"Do you know, we must have galloped five miles with the creature at our heels. I could hear it panting. Once I looked back at the blur of mottled fur, at the open mouth drooling saliva, at the bared teeth. The lips were rolled back and the teeth snapped, closing on air, but always snapping closer. I thought I would fall from the horse. Only the thought of falling under that creature kept me on its back."

"Why didn't you drop the cub?" This from Mike.

"Drop him?" said Mr. Peters. "I didn't know I had him. I didn't know anything but those blazing red holes of eyes.

110

My head was filled with a terrible screaming. I guess it came from me."

"It did," Mike said. And then he made a practical suggestion. "Finish your drink, Mr. Peters."

Mr. Peters raised his well-cared-for hand to his mouth. It was white, and the blue veins stood out in a strongly marked pattern. He thought it held a drink. It didn't. There was no doubt of it. Mr. Peters was badly shaken.

To take his mind off bears, I began to talk about Atenou's tooth. Atenou listened appreciatively as I told about his pain and his courage. He was beaming by the time I got to the extraction.

"Where is that tooth, anyway?" Mike asked.

I looked at the table. The pliers were still there but the tooth was gone. I turned to Atenou. He grinned and pointed to his chest; there, on the end of a buckskin thong, swung a small pouch.

"It's in there?" I asked him.

He dumped the contents of the pouch into his hand. First came a silver button, then a packet of herbs tied together, and finally the tooth. The blood was now dry on it. Atenou lifted the tooth carefully in two fingers and extended it toward Mr. Peters.

"The tooth of wisdom," he said slowly.

"Wisdom tooth," Mike corrected.

"Same thing. Yes?" Atenou asked.

"Well—"

"Yes." Atenou decided for himself.

Mr. Peters drew back slightly from the tooth. "What do you want to carry it around with you for?"

"It good medicine—powerful."

Mr. Peters laughed. "Indian superstition."

Atenou, who did not understand such a long word, was nevertheless pleased by it. "Yes," he said. "Much strong. It make cure of pain between bone."

"Rheumatism," Mike explained.

"Oh, really?" Mr. Peters winked broadly at us. He was beginning to enjoy himself. "And what else does this tooth do?"

"It make love in heart of loved woman," Atenou declared gravely.

111

Mr. Peters thought this especially funny.

"Him also great protection against bears."

Mr. Peters stopped laughing. "Really?"

"Strong medicine against grizzly."

Mr. Peters turned to us. "You know, I sometimes think these native superstitions are worth looking into. After all, they live in these places and have survived."

"Bear no come where is this tooth. No like, strong medicine."

I was proud of Atenou, the chief hunter of Mustagan. He drove a shrewd bargain with the shoe salesman from Detroit.

### CHAPTER TEN

"Up here," Mike said, "there are no signposts or traffic cops. During the day you've got the sun, and at night the stars. From them you'll learn to tell time, direction, and to some extent, the weather."

It was my first astronomy lesson in the clear black night of Hudson's Hope, and the stars crowded in on us, a million times brighter, closer, and more real than the stars of Boston. The Big Dipper I knew, and that was all. Somewhere, I was sure, there was a Little Dipper, but it was hiding. "About the only other thing I recognize is the moon," I admitted.

Our necks were stiff from craning, so Mike laid out a blanket and we lay on our backs, gazing up. I remembered the verse from my mother's Bible, "And God made the firmament. . . ." This was the first time it had really looked like a firmament.

"The two end stars in the bowl of the Dipper, they're called the Pointers because they point to the Pole Star." Mike's hand traced out the line. "Roll your head closer to mine so we'll be looking the same way," he said.

I smiled. "Are you flirting with me, Sergeant Flannigan?"

"Not at all, Mrs. Flannigan," he said, putting his arm under my head. "This is an astronomy lesson, and you'll kindly point out the Pole Star for me."

Well, that wasn't so easy because, to tell the truth, for all

112

it has such an important name, and is (Mike says) the basis of navigation and direction-finding, the Pole Star is a pretty mediocre-looking star and hard to find.

"There's the Big Dipper," I said, "and there's the Pointers, and there's the Pole Star." And, glory be to the saints, just as I pointed, out jumped the Little Dipper, hanging from the Pole Star like a pot on a hook. "And there's the Little Dipper!" I cried out, much to Mike's amazement.

"So you're learning by yourself, redhead," he said, and hugged me.

Then he showed me the Dragon that curls around between the Dippers, and Cassiopaeia's Chair, and the Hair of Berenice, which the Indians call Owl's Eye, but which I would call Dinner Plate, because that's its shape.

"You're to remember," Mike said, "that the Pole Star is the North Star. It's in its place every night, all night. The North Star never moves from there, but all the rest of the stars turn around it.

"Why is that?"

"Shall I give you the scientific explanation or the story the Beavers tell?"

"It's too lovely a night for the scientific explanation," I whispered. Mike sighed and smiled, but he knew I was right. This cold, clear, enchanted night was no place for mathematics and physics. Right ascension and declination and the ecliptic would have to wait for an evening with an indoor star chart. On this black, bright-jeweled chart that was flung over our heads, only magic and mystery could move.

Mike said, "The story was told to me by an old chief of the Beavers, on my long patrol three years ago. I heard it twice after that, once among the Blackfeet, once in a different version among the Crees. But it always began:

"It was in the days of before-the-before. Before the day of the first chief of the tribe, before the builder of the first tepee, before the father of the first Beaver. Yet even in those days there were men on the earth, and they hunted. And when they died, they went to the plains-above and hunted there forever.

"Now, then there was no sky, and the sun lighted up the plains-below and the plains-above equally. On the plains-below men hunted buffalo and moose, and on the plains-above the spirits hunted smoke-deer and bison of fire. It happened that the men on the flat of the earth became discontented, as all men do, and took to watching the hunts of the spirits and envying them. And it's not hard, my darling, to see how that was. For what is buffalo meat and moose meat and the skin of the beaver compared to the magic meat of the fire-bison and the flashing skin of the sky-eagle! One day Onowate, a man with the strength of three bears, threw his hatchet into the air and killed a sky-eagle. The spirits were angry and complained to the Great Spirit. And he hid the plains-above from the eyes of men with a blue curtain.

"During the day the sun shone on the plains-below, and during the night it shone on the plains-above. And men continued to hunt deer; and the spirits, deer of smoke.

"At that time there also lived Ayoo, a woman with the cunning of three mountain lions. And she was curious. She wished to see the hunt of the spirits in the plains-above. So she urged the men of the tribe to climb the trees and cut holes in the blue sky-curtain. Now, beloved, the trees then were not like the trees now. They were as large as a mountain, and tall. A hundred men holding hands could not circle the base of such a tree or see the top. The upper branches of these trees rested against the sky-curtain. And the men persuaded by Ayoo's cunning, the cunning of three lions, these men cut holes in the sky. And when night came and the sun shone on the plains-above, the light leaked out and twinkled.

"The men spent their evenings peering through the holes and spying on the hunts of the spirits, and Ayoo sat on the highest branch feeding her curiosity. One night, Onowate, the man with the strength of three bears, reached through his opening and caught a fire-bison by the leg and pulled it through. Onowate's arm was seared to the shoulder and two of his fingers turned to ashes, but that night he feasted on the dinner of the spirits.

"Once again the spirits complained to the Great Spirit, but the Great Spirit refused to repair the curtain. It seemed that he was angry with the men and yet pleased by their audacity. But at last he yielded to the pleas of the spirits,

114

and with a twist of his hand set the sky-curtain spinning.

"No longer could the men look through the holes they had made. No sooner would one put his eye to the opening than it would begin to move, and he either stopped looking or fell off the tree. Of course, the spinning has slowed down by now, but keep your eye on the stars, and in half an hour you will notice that they have shifted.

"So the men on the plains-below gave up their gazing and returned to hunt buffalo and moose and the skin of the beaver. And Ayoo was unhappy because her curiosity was not full.

"Now, Ayoo was a woman with the cunning of three mountain lions, and she had a plan. She went to Onowate, the man with the strength of three bears, and whispered her plan. And one night he went to where a tree grew that was the greatest tree on the flat of the earth, and its name was Gorikan, which means 'unbendable.' This tree Onowate climbed. And when he came to the top he took the highest branch of the tree Gorikan and thrust it into the nearest hole in the sky. And it stuck there.

"Round and round that branch the sky-curtain whirled, but that point never moved. For it was held there by the tree that was unbendable.

"Then the spirits that hunt in the plains-above became angry. They complained once more to the Great Spirit. But this time He laughed at them. And so they sent fire.

"The fire burned the man's skin, and it burned the woman's hair, and it burned the bark of the tree. But Onowate beat out the fire, and Ayoo put grease on his wounds, and Gorikan stood straight.

"So they sent water. The water loosened the man's grip, and it filled the woman's mouth, and it rotted the trunk of the great tree. But they held firm.

"So they sent stones, and thunder, and iron, and lightning. Nothing worked. The tree stood, and still the sky went whirling around that one point, and Ayoo fed her curiosity.

"In the end, the spirits aroused the terrible Snow Spirit that lives in the below-the-below. And he came with his winds and his rains and beat upon the three. Ice formed on the arms of Onowate, and even with the strength of three bears, he could no longer lift them. Hail beat against the head of Ayoo, and even with the cunning of three lions, she could not think. And snow and more snow piled on the branches of Gorikan, until with a great crash the unbendable tree broke, and fell, and all were buried beneath the snow.

"Yet to this day the sky-curtain turns around that one point in the north. And sometimes at night Ayoo stirs under her blanket of snow and whispers cunning into the ears of Onowate, and with his great strength he starts to lift the tree once more so that she may look in on the hunt in the plains-above. And then the spirits unchain the terrible Snow Spirit and rout him out from his cave in the below-the-below, and we have such storms as make men tremble."

I lay very close to Mike, and we looked up into the sparkling holes in the sky-curtain and dreamed of the man and woman buried beneath the snow since the days of the before-the-before.

"You are very strong, Mike," I said as he tightened his arm around me. "You have the strength of three bears," and I hugged him back.

"And you, little one, have the strength of one bear, or maybe half a bear," he laughed.

"I am much better now," I said. "I'd forgotten." And I suddenly realized that I was healthy and strong, so healthy and strong that for weeks I had forgotten all about my chest and my cough and my pleurisy. I had even forgotten to put my brace on.

And so I thought this would be a wonderful time to tell him, now that I was well, and the sky was full of stars, and his ear was close against my lips.

"Mike," I said, "we're going to have a baby."

He jumped a little. "Is it true?"

"I've known for some time," I said.

"Well, you certainly kept it hidden from me," he said. I laughed. "That wasn't hard."

"You imp," Mike said joyfully, "you have the cunning of three lions."

And we looked up and watched the sky turn.

## CHAPTER ELEVEN

A wind had sprung up—Meyoonootin, "fair wind," the Indians called it. I'd been working in the garden all morning. I was a little tired and didn't want to overdo because of the baby. I leaned the hoe against the house and sat on the steps. I shaded my eyes and looked out across the hills. Meyoonootin bent and lift the grass in rhythmic waves like the waves of an ocean, a green sea breaking around the roots of a forest.

A little gray mole ran out from the grass at my feet and scurried blindly up on the porch. He ran first one way and then the other. I didn't want the dogs to get him, so I cornered him and set him free again. The grass shook and trembled as he made his way through it, then fell again into its easy indolent motion.

The air was heavy and full of haze. The sun seemed half obscured, but it shone with more color. It was a strange, flaming orange. I took in a deep breath. Smoke, that's what it was. Not haze. There was a fire somewhere. It had been such a dry spring. Things were brittle. A fire now would be bad. I felt uneasy. I wished Mike was around. I decided to get him.

As I ran toward the office, I heard one of the dogs behind me. I turned to call it, but it wasn't a dog. It was a cat, a giant cat with a tawny coat, and only a few feet behind me. I braced myself to meet it, my arm lifted to protect my throat and face. The animal's tongue lolled out over its teeth, the eyes were glazed. As it came abreast of me, it veered slightly and raced on. I fell against a tree, bewildered. A small striped badger scurried after the lynx. I began to laugh. There was something wrong with the laugh. But there is something wrong with everything when a wildcat is chased by a badger.

I caught my breath, for I realized now what it was that forced the wild things of the forest to take suddenly to the paths of men. Only one thing could make the badger run with the lynx, and that one thing was fire.

I ran on toward the office, and three gray rabbits ran with

117

me. The smoke was thicker now, and hot ash and cinders sifted down on the path. But the animals were running *with* me. That meant the fire was behind us. I wondered if it would reach the house. Why hadn't I brought the dogs with me? But they were smart. They'd run the right way.

I saw the red of Mike's jacket as he ran toward me. He didn't say a word, just grabbed me tight against him.

"Thank God!" he said, over the top of my head. Then he pushed me arm's length from him.

"Get to the river, Kathy. Its widest point is just opposite the store. Wade out to the middle and stay there." His hands tightened on my arms. "Stay there till I come for you. Promise me you'll do that."

"Yes," I said." "I will. Oh, Mike, is it going to be bad?"

"There's a wind," Mike said, "and a forest fire's never any joke."

"What about you? Mike—I'm so frightened you won't be careful!"

Mike pulled me to him; his hands were in my hair a moment. "I'm fine. You know that. You do just what I tell you, Kathy. Don't be frightened, don't get panicky, and don't leave the river. No matter how bad it looks, don't leave the river. It's safer there than anywhere else, and the minute it isn't I'll be there to take you out."

He gave me a push. "Hurry, Kathy!"

I ran so that Mike would see that I would do everything as he told me. The brush broke behind me, and in a moment Mike was running at my side.

"I'm going with you, girl—as far as Henderson's. He's going to be worth ten men to me now."

I stopped running. "But, Mike, he's not there. He's hunting."

"Damn! That's right, went south, didn't he? That means he's cut off. All right, darling, I'll leave you here then."

"Be careful and—a blessing, Mike." But already he was gone. He had left the path and struck out in the direction of the reserve. I stood and watched the red of his jacket as it moved through the filigree of laced branches and brush that already separated us. I turned away.

"Dear God, don't let anything happen to Mike! Please, God. Please, please, please!" And by God, I meant God and the woods and the mountains and the unknown old gods that the Indians knew. I walked in that prayer all the way. The air was a blue blur, and the rest a dark blur full of many colors, all blending—and I was alone, knowing for the first time in my life, knowing through anguish how I loved Mike Flannigan.

I saw the flag in front of the Hudson's Bay Company. I saw it clearly and distinctly, and everything else came into focus for me. Women, dragging children, pulling children, holding children, were crowding the river banks. Some had waded into the river and were standing waist-deep. The children cried and whimpered and stared with frightened eyes past the store, where clouds of smoke circled up and bright flashes leaped among the pines. Two little boys were not crying. They thought it was fun to be in the river. They made faces at the dark column of smoke and then dived under so the smoke couldn't get them. I went down to the bank and walked into the river. The water was cold, and I waded up and down the edge until my ankles were used to it. The hottest day cannot warm water the ice has imprisoned all winter. It felt strange, sloshing into my shoes. I thought of taking them off, but the bottom was too rocky.

It was terribly hot. The wind was no longer Meyoonootin, fair wind, but Sou-way-nas, the fierce south wind. It blew hotly over us, bringing us gray ash that was our homes and our forests.

There were more people crowding down to the river. Oo-me-me waded out in water past her waist. In her arms was the child. I went over to her. "Oo-me-me," I called.

There was no response. Her eyes were on me and were very quiet. She had resigned herself. She was waiting for the known or the great unknown.

"Oo-me-me," I said again, "did Sergeant Mike tell you to come here?" There was no answer.

I had to know where he was. "Oo-me-me, please! Was it Sergeant Mike who sent you and the others down here?"

Her eyes were past me now. As I looked into them I saw reflected the smoke and the darting flame. Nothing more.

Of course it was, I said to myself; it's Mike directing things. He's sending everyone where he told me to go, the widest part of the river. But maybe he hadn't reached them.

119

Maybe something had happened to him. The Indians would probably come here anyway.

The wind whipped the smoke wall. It beat the flames and made them dance. They reached out golden arms and leaped into new places. I strained my eyes. Little black figures darted among the smoke, but whether one of them wore a red coat I could not tell. I remembered my prayer and began saying it again.

Someone was calling my name. It was Lola, the 'breed wife of one of the men who had left with the fur brigade. She held a baby in either arm, and a third at her skirts, crying.

"Mrs. Mike!"

"Yes," I said. "I'll take him."

I lifted up the baby that sat crying in the water. I rocked him in my arms and talked to him. After a while he forgot to cry, and then he fell asleep. It was good to hold a baby in your arms and to have quieted him.

It was terribly hot. I waded deeper into the river. Lola followed me.

"Why did everyone come here? Did Sergeant Mike tell you to?" I asked.

She shifted one of the babies onto her shoulder. "No, him send three fellers to tell everybody come and be safe in river. One, she go reserve; me, I live by there, so I hear, too. Other two, they warn cabins. One go east, one west, tell all women, children, come."

It was good to hear this news of Mike, to be able to follow his movements, to know that then, at least, he had been all right.

"You think we die in damn river?" Lola asked.

"No, Lola, we won't die. Sergeant Mike has all the men together by now. It looks to me like they're going to try to stop the fire at the lumbered-over spot behind the Company store. See, you can see them over there, a little to the left of the big smoke." It helped me to hear these words even if I had to say them myself.

"Look!" said Lola. A red fox dived into the water from the cliff above. The wind brought to us the smell of his scorched coat. He swam until he was just within his depth, and there he stayed completely submerged, with only the

120

top of his nose showing. There were twenty or thirty dogs around, but they paid no attention to him. I looked for our own dogs and saw Black-Tip, the team leader. I called to him but couldn't coax him past where he felt bottom.

The fire had entered the back door of the Hudson's Bay Company. The building broke into flames; fire poured from every chink and opening. The roof fell in. They had not checked it at the clearing. The river was the next natural barrier.

The wild things, hesitating at the brink of the river, hesitated no longer. Moose, deer, otters, mink, bears, wolves, lynx crowded into the river with the humans. The smoke had thickened. The only sky to be seen was a dense, thick, curling, shifting gray. The baby woke gasping. I waded farther into the river. The current was swift there, and I had to brace myself against it. I bathed the child's face and wet his hair, but still he cried.

"I do not see Ookoominou, my mother," Lola whimpered. The smoke stung my eyes and obscured the faces around me. I could no longer see who was here and who was not. But there were not as many as there should have been. This threw me into a panic. If they were not all here, Mike would try to get them through, and it was no longer possible.

The flames shot up along the river like a ragged fringe. Everything was bright, terribly bright, but because of the smoke I could no longer see. I closed my eyes, but I couldn't shut away that brightness.

The child screamed terribly. I lowered him until the water was at his chin. Hot ashes were falling and burning me. The air blistered my face. My eyebrows and lashes were singed. My face and throat burned; my body was numb with cold.

The fire danced on the edges of the river; the water was gold. Ripples mirrored the flames, glittering red and orange. Everything was intensified. Color! There had never been such color. The world writhed in searing, burning color!

Sound was the only thing that could travel through that color and live. Animals and humans cried with the forest, with the trees as they strained, as they broke, with the trapped creatures.

121

I tried to guess how long it had been, how long I had been in the river. Was it day or was it night? I could not see the sky. I did not know. I only knew the torturing heat and the smoke. I tried to figure it out by deciding whether I was hungry. But the skin of my face seemed to throb and swell, and food was a word I remembered from a long time ago.

I saw the fire leap the river. It burned, a bridge of flame, from shore to shore. That was farther up, where it was narrow, but it was blowing down on us. The heat cracked my skin open. I couldn't stand it. Mike! I thought: Don't let this happen to Mike. I covered the baby's nose and mouth and ducked both of us under the water. It felt wonderful, cold and wonderful on my blistered face, and if I was dying I didn't care. The child struggled, but I kept my hold until there was no breath in either of us. Then we came up, gulping for air, but the air hurt us. I clapped my hand over the baby's face before he could breathe out. Once again we were under. I lost count of the times we came to the surface. I'd wait until my lungs were bursting, then up, to let the burning air rush in through nose and mouth. The child still struggled, so I knew it lived.

I don't know when I realized the air no longer hurt to swallow. The smoke and fire were still there. But hadn't they always been? Wouldn't they always be? I was too tired to think about it. I only knew that for some time I hadn't cooled our faces in the water. The river went past, went past, went past—it was time moving by. It flowed without stopping, it was silvery now with no brightness in it.

Mike picked me up. I don't know where he came from. He picked me and the baby up. He was taking the wet clothes off me. When he came to the shirt, I tried to help him by holding my arms up, but I couldn't. I was too tired. With his hunting knife he cut the clothes from me. The next thing I remembered was feeling warm, under blankets and drinking hot soup. I was dressed again, this time in skirts, Indian skirts and a man's shirt. It was day, a different day, the next day, Mike said. I looked at everything; there was a sky over my head, not a roof. My blankets lay on the ground. A smudge was burning at my head.

"Am I all right?"

Mike grinned. I don't know how I knew it was Mike. His

face was black with streaks of skin showing where the sweat had run down. The red coat had gone and the shirt under it. He laid a hot compress over my face and throat.

"It hurts," I said. "What is it?"

"Tea, strong tea. Best thing in the world for burns. The Indians use it."

"Mike, Mike!" I sat up and threw my arms around him. "Mike, Mike, Mike!" I wanted to say, "Are you all right? I love you. Were you careful?" I wanted to tell him, to ask him about the baby, the fire, what had happened; but the only thing that came out was "Mike."

Mike held me. He whispered little words to me, pet words. He told me I was fine and that the baby was fine. "You were just tired, Kathy. Chilled and tired, and you got second degree burns on that pretty face of yours."

"Yesterday," I said, "you just went to the office. We might never have seen each other again. . . . Oh, Mike, it can happen like that!"

Mike's blue eyes looked hard. "It has happened like that for some of them."

I had forgotten there were others. For a moment there had been only Mike and me, but now suddenly there were those others, almost a hundred and fifty of them.

"Mike, were many—" I stopped. The drawn look on his face told me.

"It's not your fault, Mike."

He looked at me for a long while. "I don't know," he said slowly. "I haven't been able to think that out yet. I don't know yet if it was my fault, but it was my duty to protect the people against this country."

He had told me once he was a policeman, not against man, but against Nature.

"Tell me about it, Mike." I knew it would be better if I could get him to talk.

"We got the fire under control in fifteen hours. It's still not out." He was reciting facts, making a report. He was judging now, and his voice was impersonal.

"I needed every man if I was to stop the fire at the river. I wasn't able to do that. At one place the fire jumped. But where the Peace is wide, there at the bend where you were, Kathy, we stopped it. I had forty-seven men. I needed a

123

hundred of them. I sent three, took them from their stations. Young Eagle I sent to the reserve with orders to evacuate all women and children to the river. Pierre and Scotty I sent to cover all the outlying cabins. Pierre went east of the store, Scotty west. Scotty got through."

"Pierre?" I asked.

Mike shook his head. "He never came back."

"Mike, you can't blame yourself."

"I should have sent two men," he said. "One would have gotten through."

"But you couldn't spare them."

"No."

I put my hand over his big one.

Atenou walked toward us over burned ground. Mike rose to meet him. One question was asked and answered. Mike turned to me.

"Will you be all right, Kathy?"

"Yes," I said, and tried to get up to prove it.

Mike pushed me back. "Rest, Kathy. You've got to be careful. It's been a shock and a strain on you."

"Where are you going?" I asked him.

He hesitated. "I'm going to the cabins east of here to see what can be done."

He kissed me swiftly.

"Be good, Minx."

I rose up on my elbow and watched him stride off. I'd forgotten to ask him about our own home, if it was standing.

"Atenou."

He looked down at me.

"Our home, Sergeant Mike's home, is it burnt?"

"Burnt," he said.

"Completely? I mean, there's nothing left?"

"Him burnt."

Somehow I couldn't picture it. I saw it as I'd seen it last. My wedding dress from Calgary hanging in the closet, Mike's map of Canada tacked to the bedroom wall. That big iron stove, *it* couldn't be gone, I thought. And my garden. The field peas were just coming up.

"What about the reserve?" I asked Atenou.

124

"Some place fire eat up. Some place strong medicine, fire him no go."

That was good. At least the village hadn't been completely demolished. It could probably be rebuilt.

I came to the question I feared. "And the outlying cabins?"

"Many gone, some not."

"And the people who weren't in the river?"

"On gray wings went they."

"How many?"

Atenou told off the names. He held the endings, drawing out the sound of it. The effect was a chant, a death chant. I shuddered. Most of the names meant faces to me, sometimes words, sometimes laughter. Children and women, all of them, and all from cabins east of the shore. Atenou stood like the angel of death, slowly intoning. He must have counted off forty names, a third of the people. The last named were men who had died fighting the fire. There were only three of them, and the last was Pierre, the man Mike had sent to the east.

"They found him?"

"Found," replied Atenou. "Him under tree on way to cabins, him back crack like kindling."

"But didn't the people try to do anything when they saw the fire coming?"

"Ground show some get through to river. Fire she come between—those who were afraid to go; now they cannot, they take children, go hide down wells, in root cellars."

"Did—did that save any of them?"

"Sergeant Mike him take bodies from there now."

I turned my face against the blanket. It was rough. It hurt my skin, it made me cry.

My arm was seized in a powerful grip. I was half shaken to my feet. The face I looked into was mad.

Joe Henderson twisted my arm under me. He glared at me from green glittering eyes over which were neither lashes nor brows. Both had been singed from his face. His lips were cracked and swollen, they were caked with blood. They twisted and grimaced before the word came out of them. The word was "Tommy!"

Still I could only stare. The clothes had been torn from

125

him. His body was a network of gashes. He must have crawled miles on his hands and knees; they were pulp. And his side, his entire right chest was burned and blistered.

His mouth twisted itself for another effort. "Where's Tommy?"

"There were so many people, such confusion . . ."

"He was in the river. He must have been. You saw him." He commanded me to have seen him, but I hadn't.

"There was so much smoke I couldn't be sure." A film spread over Henderson's eyes.

I tried to reassure him. "But he must have been there. That's where we were right in front of your place—" I stopped suddenly and remembered something from a long time ago. No, from yesterday morning. Uaawa taking an east trail with little Tommy.

Joe Henderson's burnt mouth got ready to say "Tommy" again. I couldn't have stood it, so I told him, "Yesterday morning you went hunting, Joe. I know, because Uaawa came past my house with Tommy. I called to her, and she said you'd left and she was going to visit her sister."

"Her sister—the Bonnard cabin. East—she took him east into the fire. Tommy . . ." His voice broke over the name and he started running. He staggered like a drunken man, he almost fell from the cliff into the river.

"Mr. Henderson!" I called. "Joe!" He didn't hear me. I got up. I felt pretty good, just dizzy, and he couldn't go alone. He was in no condition to. It wasn't hard to catch up with him because he wasn't walking straight. I took him by the arm, and I think several times I kept him from falling.

It was witches' country, black, burnt over. Trees stood hollowed, empty of their life, with only stark charcoal wrappers left. It was hot underfoot; the fine ash burned through our shoes.

Along the dead shore and over the smoldering ground a woman walked, looking into the Peace River and calling. We came closer. The woman was Lola, and it was my own name she called, "Mary!"

"What's the matter, Lola? What are you doing here?"

She did not take her eyes from the water. "Did you come by river, Mrs. Mike?"

126

"Yes," I said.

"Did you see my baby, my Mary, Mrs. Mike?"

"Oh, Lola!"

"The river took her, damn river. I held them both. I slip on bottom, on damn rocky bottom, and river take her from my arms. You no see her, no?"

"No," I said, and turned to Joe Henderson, but he was not there. I plunged into the forest of black stumps.

"Mary!" called the woman on the shore. "Mary, Mary!" I ran from the sound. I ran to Mike.

I came to the clearing. There should have been a cabin there. There wasn't. I ran on. I almost fell into the foundation of a house. The root cellar was half-filled with smoking ash. I heard voices now, somewhere a man crying. Two Indians passed me carrying something charred and black in a blanket. I didn't know what it was when I looked at it . . . but when I thought about it, I knew. I saw Joe Henderson standing in a knot of Indians and 'breeds. I walked to them. I had run all the way but now somehow it took me a long time to reach them.

They were gathered about a well whose stone sides were blackened like an outdoor oven. From down inside the well came Mike's voice, hollow and full of echoes. "Give me a hand there!"

Mustagan bent over the edge and stretched out his hands. A brave reached to steady him as he received the burden. With a grunt he lifted the body over the side and laid it on the ground. There was a general movement forward. Only Henderson stood rocklike, his eyes rested a moment on the figure. It was a woman's. There was no face. Joe Henderson looked back toward the well. One of the men called down to Mike, "Anyone else?"

It was a moment before Mike answered. "Yes, two, I think. I'm sending up the child."

Again Mustagan reached into the well. This body was very small. He laid it at Henderson's feet. This time no one moved forward. They were like a well-trained chorus, their eyes fixed on Henderson, waiting for him to cry or sob or scream. But he didn't do anything. Just stared.

Mike handed up the third body, again a woman's. Joe

didn't look at it, not once. He didn't lift his eyes from the body of the child.

Mike climbed up from that death hole. I was almost surprised. The rule, I thought, was that Mustagan had to lift you over the edge and that you had to be dead with your face burnt off.

Mike looked angry when he saw me, but he just said, "Sit down, Kathy."

There was no place to sit. The ground was too hot. There was only the wall of the well, and I wasn't going to sit on that. I shook my head, and Mike turned a little wearily to Joe Henderson.

"I'm sorry, Joe," he said.

The words seemed to rouse Henderson. For the first time he looked away from the boy, looked straight at Mike. He spoke very quietly. "It's not Tommy."

Mike didn't say anything.

I looked down again at the boy. Of course it was Tommy. The face was there, all but— Anyway, there was enough to see. There could be no doubt that it was Tommy Henderson.

"It's not Tommy," Joe Henderson said again. Then all at once he fell beside Tommy and grabbed him in his arms. The small blackened shoulder turned flaky and crumbled under his touch. He didn't seem to notice.

"Don't be scared, Tommy. Don't be scared. I won't let anything happen to you, not this time, not again! I saw the smoke, Tommy, I came up by canoe as far as I could. But it crossed the river, Tommy, cut me off. But I went by land, Tommy, right through it. So don't be afraid, Tommy. Tommy?" He let the body fall from his hands. "No, that's not Tommy. I won't let it be Tommy!" And he turned up an agonized face. He saw me. He began explaining very fast.

"You see, my store is right by the river, the widest part of the river. Uaawa would bring him to the river." He repeated the name Uaawa to himself. Dark shadows swam in his eyes. Then they became still with uncertainty.

"Uaawa," he said again, as though that explained everything to him. He looked over at the body of the second woman, his hands clenched at his sides.

"So she sneaks out as soon as my back is turned—takes

128

Tommy to her sister. They talk to him in Beaver, sing to him in Beaver. They feed him Indian food, tell him Indian stories. She tried to make an Indian out of my son, out of Tommy Henderson."

He stopped and laughed, or maybe cried. It was a strangled sound in his throat that he choked back.

"She hated me, all right. She knew I had no use for her, and she hated me. The damn *klooch!* She knew she could get at me through Tommy. I was a fool. I should have known she'd do this. But he was hers too, and I didn't think she could."

Mike took him by the shoulder. "What are you saying, man?"

"That she murdered my son."

"You mustn't be thinking things like that."

Joe Henderson spoke again.

"The many times I told the woman what to do in case I wasn't here, and Tommy was bit by a snake! What to do if he cut himself, what to do if he got sick on those tins they send us, and what to do if there was a fire. 'Put him in the river,' I told her, 'right in front of the cabin it's deepest and widest.'"

Mike spoke soothingly to him. "She didn't know there would be a fire, Joe, when she started off to her sister's."

"It was hate that made her take Tommy to that Indian cabin. Hate that made her put him down the well."

"Joe! Joe, it was too late by the time she saw the fire. It was between them and the river. She did what she could for Tommy. He was her child too."

"Hate was her child. Mine is dead."

The graves were dug all day. I worked with the women. Thirty-seven wooden crosses we made and whitewashed. We cooked mush in the cabins and tepees that were left. The fire had skipped around like a child playing hopscotch. Without reason it had taken and it had spared. Mike fell asleep while he was eating the mush. I shook him and he finished. Mustagan had asked us into his cabin. He shook hands with Mike after the custom of white men. "The Sergeant, him save the people of Mustagan."

That was all, but it was enough.

## CHAPTER TWELVE

I trailed my hand in the water. It looked like the hand of a sea nymph who had somehow drifted into the Peace River. The current was carrying our canoe along swiftly, and the Indian in the bow held his paddle upraised, watching for snags. I let the water run through my fingers and kept my eyes on the woods, hoping I'd see a bear. I loved to watch bears—from a distance. The day before, I had nearly sat down on one. The men had pulled the canoe on the bank for some minor repairs. I walked over to a flat rock, curled up on it, and there was a black bear eating red willow berries. He backed away, but stopped to turn up a rock and lick off the insects and bugs clinging to the bottom. That's when I jumped up and ran. A bear that will eat grubs off the bottom of a stone will eat anything, I reasoned, and that anything might be me.

Mike wasn't impressed. He said black bears were friendly, lumbering old cusses, and that the only ones I need worry about were grizzlies. Just the same, it was a shock seeing it, and from then on I was doubly careful. I didn't want my baby born with a face like black bear's.

Mike thought I was becoming unusually scary and fanciful. "It'll be a good thing when you have the baby and get over all this," he'd say.

But I continued to give way to my moods, and right now it was my mood to take my hand out of the water and flick drops in Mike's face. He grinned down at me and splashed me with his paddle.

"How's my cabbage?"

That was his new name for me. He said that's what I looked like, a little round cabbage. I dipped down for more water to splash back. He laughed, caught a crab, and almost lost his paddle.

I lay back among the cushions and half-closed my eyes against the sun. It was lazy and peaceful after the excitement of leaving. Ours was the last boat of the season, and already Hudson's Hope was weeks away.

We had been rebuilding our house on a new site. The

other was too charred; it would be years before anything grew back. Mike had dug the foundation when the letter with Government seals came through to us.

"We're transferred to Grouard," Mike had said. "Well, at least we don't have to worry about packing."

And that was a true word. We had the clothes on our backs, and that was all. The fire had cleaned us out.

One by one, 'breed and Indian, they came, and at our door each left a gift of food. The canoe was given us, and enough provisions for the six weeks it would take us to reach Grouard; and these people faced a long, hungry winter.

Everyone came down to the river to see us off. The flag was flown at the pier just as it was the day the fur brigade left. At the last, Mustagan stepped forward and presented me with a suit of white caracul. To Mike he gave an ornately beaded quiver full of flint-tipped arrows. We shoved off, and I looked back at the waving hands, at the waving flag.

Tonight, as I laid our blankets on somebody else's bed and hung that somebody else's blanket up as a partition, I wondered about all these cabins we'd been sleeping in for the last few weeks. The owners of them we rarely saw. But on the wall or over the stove was usually a crudely painted sign. The one here said, "Make yourself to home, stranger, and shut the door when you leave." In the North no one ever locked his door, not even when leaving for the winter.

Every night we stopped in a cabin where wood had been stacked, matches left, and canned goods laid out for the chance traveler. All the unknown host received in return was a scribbled note giving our thanks, any news we could think of, and our names. This whole system of northern hospitality was a gigantic chain, for while we were eating this man's beans, he was undoubtedly farther up the trail, eating somebody else's.

I lay awake listening to the snores of the Indians who were rolled in their blankets on the other side of our partition. The baby was moving in me. It moved a lot now. It was strange to think I had a person in me, a person who some day . . . I snuggled in against Mike. It was then I felt my first pain. The cramp grabbed hold, turned and twisted in me like a live thing. I clutched Mike.

He was awake instantly, bending over me. "Kathy!"

131

"It's the baby!" I tensed myself against the pain, but it had stopped. I began to cry.

"Kathy, darling; girl, what is it? What's wrong?"

Nothing was wrong now, but I was scared. So was Mike.

"Kathy, are you—? It is bad?"

I cried harder, but against his arm, so the Indians couldn't hear.

"I don't want to have my baby here! You promised me we could get to Grouard, you promised me."

"Darling, I thought we could."

He began stroking me. I jumped away from him and said very viciously but very quietly. "You keep away from me!"

"Kathy." Mike said it in a stunned sort of way.

"You lied to me," I said into the pillow, "and now you can just leave me alone."

I knew I was unreasonable, that Mike had done his best. But I couldn't help it. I wanted a woman to help me. I would be ashamed in front of men. Oh, Mike was all right—but not those two Indians.

"Kathy," Mike said soothingly. "Kathy, girl."

"You've got to send those Indians away. I'm not going to have it if they're here. I won't, that's all. I just won't!"

Mike took my hand. "I'll send them away. I'll take care of you myself. It won't be anything, kitten. All women have babies. Haven't I always looked after you, darling? And I will now. Don't be afraid, girl, trust me."

"I don't trust you," I said, and pulled my hand away. "You said we'd get to Grouard, you said I didn't have to have it on the trail. You promised.

"Kathy." There was decision in Mike's voice. "Tell me exactly how you feel. Do you have any pains now?"

"No."

"And how many did you have before?"

"Well, one."

"You'd be having them fast and close if you were near birth. I can get you to Peace River Crossing by morning. There's a Scottish woman there, Mrs. Mathers, who used to be a trained nurse. Do you want to chance it?"

I threw my arms about his neck. "Mike, you're so good to me!"

In less than ten minutes we and the two bewildered sleepy

132

Indians were in the canoe. Sometimes I slept and sometimes I looked into the dark water. It was a silent, unreal trip. The paddles dipped together. An owl hooted through the forest. I would rather have my baby beside the river, with the wind blowing clear and sharp, than have it in that close and musty cabin. But there were no more pains. I dreamed that all the Junos we'd ever had were leading a beautiful little girl toward my mother and saying, "This is Katherine Mary's child." And I kept saying, "No, no, she hasn't been a baby yet, she hasn't been a baby."

When I opened my eyes the stars had faded out and the sky looked soft and pink. I reached up and kissed Mike's hair.

"Where's that baby?" he said and laughed.

We were no longer running in a gorge, but beside a grassy bank rising in terraces from the river bed. It was sunny meadowland, and there were wild flowers, blue and red, and after a while a yellow kind. It was four hours before we came to Peace River Crossing. The Indians call it Eteomami, which means "Water Flowing Three Ways," because here the Hart, the Smoky, and the Peace come together.

"It's civilization," Mike said. "They've even got a telegraph."

He helped me out of the canoe. The ground felt unsteady under my feet. I held onto Mike and thought of one thing: getting to Mrs. Mathers's house. Twice Mike's name was called, and both times he answered without stopping.

"Here we are," he said, and we walked onto a porch that squeaked and moaned with every step. Mike knocked, and we stood there waiting. He knocked again, and the door opened a grudging crack.

"What do you want?" The voice was high-pitched and querulous.

"It's Sergeant Flannigan, Mrs. Mathers. I've brought my wife to you."

The door opened farther, and at first sight I didn't like her. She was a woman of fifty, with a lot of flesh, loose and gray. I tried to do away with my impression. Mike says it's a bad habit of mine, judging people right off by the way they look. But is wasn't the way she looked, exactly, it was her voice too.

"You poor dear," she said. "Come in."

The house looked like her—big, rambling, and untidy. It smelled of food, and not only of today's food, but as though every meal had left its grease and its smell behind. She was telling me to take off my things. I did, but I felt uncomfortable the way she was looking at me. "This is silly," I told myself. "The woman's a trained nurse, she's got to look at me if she's going to help me." So I smiled and told her how we'd traveled all night to get to her.

"My dear," she said, "I don't know how you stood the trip. I know of many a miscarriage brought on by less than you've been through."

Mike frowned, but she didn't seem to notice.

"Bed's the place for her, Sergeant. I'll let you know when she's all tucked in and comfy."

Mike gave me a reassuring grin as Mrs. Mathers led me off.

She turned back the bedding and smoothed the rumpled covers. I stood and looked at the room. A cracked slop jar and basin, a dark dresser, and a straight-backed chair were the only furnishings.

"Do you want me to help you out of your things, dearie?" The plump fingers reached toward me.

"No," I said, drawing back a little. "I can manage fine, thank you." But I didn't, not with her watching me. I fumbled at every button. I'd taken off my boots and my mackinaws when she came toward me with a string in her hand. At the end of it was tied a button.

"Now," she said, "stand still, Mrs. Flannigan, and we'll see something."

"What?" I asked.

"Well now, we'll just see," and she hung the string in front of my stomach and stilled it with her hand.

"If it's a boy, the string will move forward and backward. If it's a girl, it will swing right and left."

"Oh, please, I'm so tired. I want to get into bed."

She was indignant at that. "Well, if you're not even curious!" She handed me a flannel nightgown which from the size of it was hers and watched me as I slipped it on.

"You're not built right," she said.

"What do you mean?" I felt frightened.

134

"You're just not. Too small all over."

I got into bed and pulled the covers up high.

"Some women aren't made for child-bearing, and you're one of them."

"My grandmother had fourteen children," I said, "and my mother had three."

"What did I tell you? See how they're dwindling off?" She brought her face against mine. "It's a bad month too. August is the eighth month of the year."

I made an effort to overcome the repulsion I felt. "Augustus must have thought it was lucky when he called it after himself."

"Too many eights," she said. "Eighth month of 1908 . . . and today, do you know what today is? The twenty-*eighth!* It's bad luck, terrible. I doubt if we'll take that baby out of you alive."

I shrank back against the sheets. "You mean I'll have a dead baby, a stillborn baby?" Just then it moved in me, and that tiny precious movement gave me the strength to lash out at her. "Don't you say things like that! Don't you dare! My baby's all right. My baby's alive!"

"Of course your baby's all right. What are you talking about, Kathy?" Mike stood in the doorway. "Kathy, what's wrong?"

I tried not to cry, but I did through every word. "She said I can't have a baby. She said—"

"What?" The word dropped from him like a bomb.

Mrs. Mathers began talking very fast. She scuttled over the words like a fat prairie chicken. "I said it would be a hard confinement, Sergeant. There's no use fooling ourselves, it will. And I was telling your wife that we always try to save the mother. If needs be, let the child go and save the mother. So you see, there's nothing for her to worry about, nothing at all, if the worst comes to the worst—"

"Get out!" Mike said, and his lips barely moved.

Mrs. Mathers stood and looked at him as though she hadn't heard right. Mike didn't say anything more. He didn't have to. Just looking at him made me want to hide under the covers.

Mrs. Mathers must have felt that way too, because she said, "Humph!" and started for the door. It wasn't until she

135

was safely out of the room that she muttered something about "my own house!"

Mike closed the door and came back to the bed. He spoke in a stern voice. "Forget that nonsense."

"Mike," I said, "she's the one you're mad at, not me." But even this wouldn't make him smile.

"Of all the fool, ridiculous things to tell a girl!"

"But maybe she knows. Maybe she's right. After all, she's a trained nurse, Mike."

"You see, she's got you half-believing those bogey stories. You'd think a nurse would know better. But I guess being a nurse can't change a person's character. She's a gray woman with gray sayings."

"A crape-hanger."

"Yes," Mike said.

But I couldn't keep it up, not even for Mike. My baby was going to die—and I wanted it so much. I turned away from Mike and cried for the little Mike, the woman's words repeating themselves in my mind.

Mike took my hands away from my face and kissed them. "Listen, Kathy. This idea of bringing you down here wasn't so good. But it was because I didn't know anything about the woman—just that she was a trained nurse. That impressed me. I wanted you to have a trained nurse. I want you to have the best. And, by Heaven, you're going to get it."

I tried not to smile. "Another idea, Mike?"

"And this time it's good, kitten. I'm going to telegraph Mrs. Carpentier to come up from Grouard and look after you."

"Mrs. Carpentier, who's she?"

Mike smiled. "Mrs. Carpentier is a good witch, a fairy godmother. You'll love her, Kathy."

"But who *is* she?"

"Well, she's Cree, full blood, married to Louis Carpentier, a 'breed trapper. Wonderful person. Been midwife to every woman within a hundred-mile radius."

Anything was better than Mrs. Mathers. I coudn't have stood her handling me. "Could she be here in time?" I asked.

136

"She'll have to be."

Two nights later my pains began in earnest. Mrs. Carpentier was somewhere on the trail. Mrs. Mathers sulked in the next room, and it was Mike who sat with me. The pain ripped and tore me. I'd hold onto his hands and scream. He tied a sheet to the bedpost. I'd pull on it and pull until it stopped. Then I'd lie panting, gathering my strength to meet it again. Mike would wipe the sweat from my face. Sometimes I remember a cool cloth on me.

It was one of these times when I lay exhausted, gasping for breath, that she came. I didn't notice that the door had opened. She was just standing there, looking down at me. Sarah, I thought, it's Sarah, from the Bible. I sighed and closed my eyes. I felt peace. The fear had gone.

It began again, seizing, grabbing, tearing. Then she spoke to me. "Sarah . . ." I tried to say, but only wild screams came.

Her voice went on, like an undertone of river water, slow, strong, and clear. I clung to the sound. I held to it. The pain swept me into a black gulf that was wet, that was sticky, that was blood, that was sweat. But I knew that in the voice and behind it was the world. If I held on, I could get back to it, into it, through to it.

The pain let go of me then, suddenly and completely. I didn't open my eyes. When you're tired as this, you've got to be dead. And a weak tear rolled out because I didn't want to be dead.

Something fragrant, slightly pungent, was in front of my nose. It smelled of the woods. I opened my eyes to see. Sarah was holding a glass for me. I drank. It was bitter and yet sweet.

The pause had been shorter this time. It grabbed me faster. The words stayed with me again, they were telling me, "Grow in the moist soil . . . running streams." Swirling pain, rising pain, but it could not pull me down into the darkness.

"Yellow flowers," she said, "small, bloom in June." I was being broken, split into two pieces.

"Mike, stop them!"

137

"From root come medicine. Make nice baby come fast. Make mother strong. Grind the root, crush . . ." Crush! That's what they were doing to me, crushing.

"Mix with water. Name is squaw root. Squaw root for help squaw with baby." That was all. I lost the words, everything. Then Mike was kissing me, stroking me, putting the wet cloth on my face again.

"Darling, it's all over. We have a girl."

I smiled at him. I could hear Sarah moving. After a long time I was able to turn my head and watch her. She was rubbing oil on a tiny mite of a baby. They put her beside me, tucked her in my arms.

"A lovely girl baby," Sarah said.

I looked at Sarah. She was big, big as a man. Six feet tall and strong. There was a grace and dignity in her, and a kindness and a knowing that sixty years had brought. I thought of what Mike had called her, the good witch.

The little thing in my arms stirred. The movement gave me a happiness and a joy I had never known. I smiled at Mike, I smiled at Sarah.

"Tell me about squaw root," I said.

"It have seed like big pea, can make much good drink . . . like coffee."

The little mouth opened against my breast.

"What else can it do?" I asked.

"Squaw root beside make well the squaw, make well the hands-swell-dropping sickness, the shaking sickness, the laugh-and-cry-without-reason sickness, and the pain-in-joints sickness that is called rheumatism."

I touched the baby and touched Mike. My family, I thought. I was so happy. I didn't want to spoil the enchantment this good witch had brought, so I asked her, "Tell me more about squaw root."

But instead she told me about my baby. Moss, she said, was softer than cloth. And she diapered it in moss, held in place with little pants. Talcum powder you couldn't get up here, but she knew something better, pounded tea leaves.

"You must have had a lot of children," I said.

"Seventeen of my own. Many others, maybe hundreds, I brought into the world."

"So many?" I asked her.

138

She nodded. "I brought my sister into the world when I was ten years old. And always after that, more children, and more. I never lose mother, and I never lose child, except once . . . in this house."

"In this house?" I held my own baby tighter.

"Yes," she said. "He was dead baby I take from Mrs. Mathers."

Mike's hand tightened over mine.

## CHAPTER THIRTEEN

We called the baby Mary Aroon, after my grandmother, Bridget Aroon. Mary is the sweetest, most beautiful name there is, and I was always grateful to my own mother for squeezing it into my name.

Sarah left for Grouard two days after Mary Aroon was born. It was the day she went that I showed her the name Sarah in my Bible. I told her how Sarah had been the mother of a race. I told her that in my delirium, when I saw her standing in front of me, I had felt she *was* Sarah. Her hands had been strong, her voice gentle, and for me she had been that ancient mother of Israel.

"Mrs. Carpentier," I said, "I want to call you Sarah. May I?"

She ran her finger over the name in the book.

"It is the name between us," she said.

In a week I was strong enough to make the trip. Mike bought a cart and padded it with blankets. I lay in it and bounced the long way to Grouard. Many times I told Mike I'd rather be riding the horse, but he would smile and tell me I had a fine view of the sky.

I had never before looked forward with such eagerness to a place as I did to my new home, Grouard. When I had come in to Peace River Crossing, my only desire had been to lie down and hide. Now all my fears were turned inside out, a new life opened before me, and I knew that when I came to Grouard I'd start living it.

Sarah had told me how I would come to the village: "First up over Black Bear Hill, and down below, way on

139

the ground, is piece of shining rock like stone for arrow-head, only rough around the edges. It is far, far away, and when the wind blows you see it is not a rock, but Lesser Slave Lake. The Crees, they call it Slave Lake because the Blackfeet, that once lived here, made slaves of captured people. And tears of slaves make this great lake. When you see it, you will soon be in Grouard, and your friends will be there, Mrs. Mike."

And so it was. The hill, the lake, and new friends to welcome us. Two men came riding up the trail to meet us. Constable Cameron had seen the smoke of our last campfire. The Indians, as usual, had known all about it even before he did. They told him it was Sergeant Mike, Mrs. Mike, and Mike's girl-child. So as we came over the top of Black Bear Hill, Ned Cameron came galloping up the other side, pulled in his horse, and saluted.

"Constable Cameron, sir. And this"—pointing to the slim youngster who rode behind him—"is Timmy Beauclaire, and I think, Mrs. Flannigan, he has a present for you."

"A puppy," the boy said. He pulled it out of his jacket. "Like it?"

"Very much," I said, and before I knew what I was doing, I showed him the baby, bundled in her fur bag. "Like it?"

He nodded, and we both laughed.

Mike and Ned Cameron walked their horses and exchanged news. Timmy leaned from the saddle and handed me the puppy.

Timmy Beauclaire was about thirteen then, very thin and eager, with curly brown hair and sharp eyes of the color people call hazel, but really twinkling blue, brown, and green. I was his friend from the first minute and mothered him in a way that was laughable when I remembered I was only a few years older. Truly I felt that I had lived a hundred years and could give advice to my own mother now.

Timmy asked me what I would call the pup.

"Juno," I said.

"That's a funny name."

"It's Irish. All my dogs were called Juno, and it's brought
140

me pretty good luck, and so this one is going to be Juno too."

"Don't you want to see whether it's a him or her first?"

Well, I did, but not with him around, so I said, "Makes no difference. He's still Juno."

"You mean *she's* still Juno," Timmy grinned, and Mike came up and we drove off for Grouard.

The part of Grouard I saw first was the little white cemetery on the hill, and it was so bright and sparkling it hardly dampened my spirits. The crosses were whitewashed and salted against the rains; this I knew from Sarah. The tall gray stone cross was Black Eagle's, the first important chief converted to Christianity; this Timmy told me. I thought the cemetery quaint and pretty, and only for a moment did a shadow of the future fall over me. There was the tiny distant figure of a woman walking through the graveyard gate, and for a second I thought it was me. Then we turned a corner, and the cemetery was gone. Cabins began to appear, and Ned Cameron shouted to me, "Grouard!"

We passed the boat landing in the cove, the Hudson's Bay Company store, and the trail turned into a hard-packed dirt road.

"There's a friend of yours, Mike," Cameron laughed as we came upon a most curious building. It was a gigantic cage made of saplings stuck in a circle in the ground and bent in on themselves. In one corner was a little shed or lean-to, and next to it a heavy gate. A man stood in front of the shed, grinning and waving at us. It was Baldy Red.

"Our jail, Mrs. Flannigan," Cameron said.

"What's he done now?" I asked.

"Baldy? Oh, he's back to his old trick of letting cows follow him. Other people's cows."

Baldy had come to the edge of his cage. "Welcome to Grouard, Mrs. Mike; and you, Sergeant, I'm counting on you to get me out of this thing."

"See you in the morning," Mike shouted back. We were past the jail, past the barracks, and driving up to a little cabin in a hollow. There were half a dozen people standing in front, waiting for us. There were tall trees bending over the house. And there was a garden of the strangest, most beautiful flowers I had ever seen. This was home.

141

Sarah was the first to greet me and help me out of the cart. She took the baby from my arms and led me into the house.

"You sit down, rest first," she said. "I have soup ready and tea. Plenty of time meet everybody. Madeleine take care of baby." Sarah handed Mary Aroon to a dark plain girl of fourteen or fifteen.

I sank back into a chair, but I wasn't tired, just taking everything in—my new home, my new friends . . . and the flowers. I could see them through the window, row upon row of colors, soft and bright. And not one of them could I recognize. Who, I thought, had been caring for my garden? Who had planted and cultivated these lovely flowers months before I came? I wanted to ask Sarah, but she was too busy feeding me and introducing my guests.

"This is Timmy's mother, Mrs. Beauclaire. Mrs. Constance Beauclaire and Mr. Georges Beauclaire, her husband, and Madeleine and Barbette are her daughters, and the baby—of course the baby is yours," Sarah concluded gravely.

Georges Beauclaire twitched his mustache, grunted something, shook my hand and left, clearly relieved at the chance to join the men outside. He was a heavy, broad-shouldered man, rough and awkward in his movements, yet with a certain good-natured big-bear grumpiness about him that almost made me laugh. Beside him Constance Beauclaire seemed delicate, shadowlike, and almost as young as their daughters. There was a foreign grace about the way she stood and walked, and her soft eyes had a veiled, preoccupied air that you find in people who live in the past. When her husband left, she drew up a chair and silently took my hand. The light fell more fully on her face, and I saw the strength and character I had missed. I saw a small, proud mouth, a slender straight nose, as rare in the north as a princess's coronet, and deep, brooding eyes of an unearthly blue. It was the lavender-blue that lights a lake for a moment after the sun has set. This was no trapper's wife.

"Katherine Mary," she repeated my name softly, and it sounded unusual and elegant in her liquid French speech. "I would have wished to know you ten, twenty years ago.

142

You will never understand, I hope, what it is to be one white woman, *the* one white woman." Constance smiled. It was more the remembrance of a smile than a smile itself. "You must tell me about Winnipeg and Montreal and Boston. Not much, what you can remember. They are not the cities I remember, but they will do."

"My mother lives in Boston," I said. "You are very much like her."

Sarah was bending over me, another bowl of soup in her lean hands. "Nice party?" she asked me.

"Yes," I said. "The best there ever was."

The sun was low, and its rays spread across the room, twinkling in the dust of many feet. Almost in a dream I spoke to Constance, and Sarah, and Sarah's husband, shy silent Louis Carpentier, and the McTavish brothers, and Old Irish Bill, with his long hair and elfin eyes ("the finest mathematician in Canada," Constance said), and Madeleine cradling my baby and scolding Barbette, who wanted to play with her too, and Mike standing behind my chair, smiling at them all. When they had gone I went to the window and looked at my enchanted garden with its rows of flowers that never grew in a garden before.

"It's been lovely," I whispered to Mike. "They were all so sweet, even poor Baldy in his cage. And I'll never finish thanking the one who planted this garden. Mike, who was it?"

Mike seemed uncomfortable. "They say it was Mrs. Marlin. She wasn't here tonight. She's not very—she's not very well." Then abruptly he said, "Look, Kathy, don't get upset about those flowers," and he started to explain something. I never heard it. I'd fallen asleep in his arms.

It had been an evening of magic, but the morning was quite down to earth. The baby woke me, squalling; the puppy, Juno, got into a sack of flour; and a bear walked off with a bucket of milk I'd hung outside the window. I walked out into my garden—and they were all dead, every single flower, lying dead and withered on the ground. The enchantment was gone, the fairy wand broken. I ran into the house and shook Mike awake.

"Mike," I sobbed, "my flowers!"

"I know, Kathy." He dressed quickly and drew me out to

143

the garden. "Look." He pulled up one of the poor faded things. It came right up out of the ground. No roots, no stalk, no leaves. It was just a blossom, cut and stuck in the earth.

"She's not right in the head, this Mrs. Marlin," Mike said unhappily. "She thought it would be a pretty welcome, Kathy," he said. "They're mostly wild flowers. They grow in the woods, in swamps, in very difficult places. She must have spent all day finding them, and then she put them in the ground to make you a garden."

I pressed his hand tightly. Suddenly I knew the enchantment hadn't gone. I thought of these people. None of them knew me. Yet Timmy brought me a puppy, and Sarah saved my life, and Old Irish Bill sang old Irish songs for me, and crazy Mrs. Marlin spent a day in the swamps so that I might have a pretty garden for an hour. I kissed Mike hard and walked back into the house. I picked up the baby, and she stopped crying. I dusted the puppy off and gave it a piece of dried fish. And as for the bear, if he liked my bucket of milk, he could have it!

## CHAPTER FOURTEEN

Constance Beauclaire had come to borrow liniment for her husband's sprained foot. The baby woke up and began to cry. Constance bent over the crib and lifted her into the air. Mary Aroon laughed, and Constance laughed back. I had never seen her laugh freely before. Constance lowered the baby to her shoulder and patted her. Her hands were beautiful, so slender and fragile. It seemed strange to me that such a creature should live in this wild country.

She smiled across the room at me, and again her smile made me sad. "She is very like my Suzanne."

"Suzanne?" I said. I knew she had another son besides Timmy, and then of course the two girls, Madeleine and Barbette, but I hadn't heard of Suzanne.

"Another daughter?" I asked.

"A baby like this. It was a long time ago." She laid little Mary gently in the crib. "My first family."

I didn't understand. "Your first family?"

144

She looked at me with those great lavender eyes. "Katherine Mary, you are so young."

That was no kind of an answer. "I'm almost eighteen," I said.

"Almost eighteen," she repeated, and she smiled that smile full of pain and tenderness. "I was almost eighteen when I came from my country, from France."

France, yes—that's where she belonged, rare perfumes, and full swishing skirts, a box at the opera, a carriage with plumed horses.

"We came over on a small boat, my father and mother and five sisters and brothers. It was strange how it happened. The sailors blamed the captain, and the captain blamed my father, and he—well, he was dead by then, and so were the others."

"They died on the boat, your family?"

"Yes."

"All of them, the five sisters and brothers?"

"All of them. You see, my family had been well-to-do. We lived in Paris. I went to convent school on the Riviera. Later I had a governess, English."

This woman of faded beauty sitting before me in heavy mackinaws and a man's shirt, worn and mended, had known things of another world, another life. I hadn't dreamed them up, the opera and the horses with plumes; they had existed.

"My father speculated and lost everything. Of course, I didn't know that then, I just knew we were going to America. I thought of it as a holiday, and so did the others. I didn't even look back at the house because, you see, I was almost eighteen, and looking forward. When we came to the ship—it was a large sailing vessel—the captain was pacing the deck, and when he saw my father he began cursing. My father was very angry and ordered us below so we should not hear the captain's words. Later, when my father came down, he said the captain was an unreasonable ruffian. And that was all we could get out of him. But my brother, Renè, who wished to become a sailor, and who was always bothering the crew, said the captain's temper was due to my father's arriving three hours late. To my father time was of no concern, he was master of it as he was of everything

145

else. But the crew was surly. The maledictions called down on my father's head would bring bad luck.

"We were two days out when Florence, my youngest sister, sickened. My father insisted it was the food, but it was smallpox. When she died, the captain slipped the body overboard quietly at night so the crew wouldn't know. We were forced to keep in our quarters. Food was left at the door for us. The hands were told we were quarantined for measles.

"Then we began dying inside our cabins. I shared a room with my two remaining sisters. The morning of the fifth day, I found they'd locked us in. From then on we did not know if our parents and our brothers were alive or dead. When my sister Viola died, I pounded on the door and screamed for my mother. No one came, no one answered me, no one brought food. The whole ship is dead, I thought. And I held onto Jeannette, who tossed and moaned; and begged her to stay with me. But she died too. I covered her with one sheet, and Viola with the other. But I was frightened of the still bodies, and I began throwing myself at the door. I dug my nails into the wood and screamed."

She turned her eyes on me, soft, wounded eyes. "I hadn't eaten in two days. It was hot in that little cabin, and the smell of death was there. I closed my eyes and prayed to die fast. When I opened them I was lying on the berth, and there was a tray of food in front of me. My sisters were not there. I got up and tried the door. It was open. Suddenly I knew it wasn't real, that I had dreamed it, that I alone had been sick and dreamed these things. I ran to my mother's cabin, holding to the wall of the passageway. I tried the door, and it opened. There was no one there; even the trunks were gone. I ran on to my brothers' cabin. The berths were made up. It was neat and tidy, no clothes around, nothing." She stopped talking and looked at me.

"That's the way it was. It had struck the men too. They had fallen from the ropes and the rigging. A third of them died. The whole crew had been demoralized. They had forgotten our food, they had forgotten everything, had prayed and sung and wept. The boat somehow looked after itself.

"It took two months to reach America. And, as I said,

the crew blamed the captain for the curses he had called down, the captain blamed my father, and he was dead."

Constance smiled at me. "Don't look like that, Katherine Mary. It happened such a long time ago, twenty-five years. I can talk about it now, tell it as if it were a story, because so many years of living have passed between me and that little French girl. She was called Constance too, but the language she spoke is not my language. The things she learned on the Riviera I do not remember."

"What did you do, all alone?" I asked her.

"I got a position as a maid. A housemaid. I was very fortunate. Did I tell you even the trunks had been thrown overboard, for fear of contagion? But I was fed and clothed and given a day off once a week. I would go to church, and then walk. I walked and walked all over the city because there was only a small empty room to go home to. One day, on my day off, while I was walking, I heard my name called. I recognized him at once, Georges Beauclaire. He had been our groom. A great man with a horse, my father said. I was so glad to see him I almost kissed him. It was as though a part of my family had been restored to me. He knew my name, he knew theirs. When he asked me about myself, I cried. I had not been able to cry all that time.

"I married him that afternoon. He told me he had nothing. Well, that nothing of his was enough to get us into Canada. Georges dreaming of this immense wild country where a man worked for himself and had no master. And because I had no dreams of my own, I shared his. At Edmonton we bought a horse and loaded him with our supplies. He went lame in two days and had to be shot. We spread out our goods there on the trail. Georges took a gun and cartridges, a knife, matches, and a fifty-pound sack of flour. I took a fifty-pound sack of sugar on my back, and we walked. We walked till our shoes fell apart, and then we walked barefoot. We ate the berries along the way, and at night I cooked the flour with sugar and water. It kept up our strength.

"We'd been on the trail six weeks when the first snow fell. We had no other clothes. We had nothing. We thought we would have to die. But we didn't say that to each other,

147

we didn't say anything, we saved our breath for walking. And came to a trapper's cabin. He was a Russian. Gorgin his name was. He was leaving for his winter's trapping, and he took Georges along as partner. I stayed seven months in the cabin alone. My first baby was born there. It didn't live."

"Oh," I said, "was that Suzanne?"

She shook her head. "No, the first was a boy. I never named him. What was the use?"

She got up and walked to the window. A dying sun lit her features. My mother told me there were people in this world born to sorrow. Constance was one of them.

"You asked me about my families. Women up here speak of their first family, their second family, their third family. Counting the baby boy I lost that first winter, I've had four families. Nine children. "They're out there." I knew what she meant, the little graveyard we'd passed on the way in.

"When Georges came back that winter, we had money for clothes, a team, and provisions. We came here to Grouard. We built our house. The Indians helped us. And I had my second family, three children. It was the little girl, Suzanne, that reminds me of your Mary. I raised one of the boys, Paul."

"What happened?" I asked, glancing nervously at Mary Aroon, who was asleep in her crib.

"Measles, that time. Whole tribes were wiped out with it."

"But the other times? You said you had nine children."

"Once it was scarlet fever, and once it was typhoid. The winters are hard up here. There is no doctor, but I raised four. You saw my girls. Paul is married; he lives in Edmonton. And Timmy you know."

She turned from the window. "A nice family. It's enough for any woman. But sometimes I think of the others."

I didn't know what to say. I closed the window and fastened it, to give me something to do. She watched me, and when I had finished she said:

"Katherine Mary, we're going to know each other very well, for many years, I hope. You'll see, you'll come to

148

understand. These big things, these terrible things, are not the important ones. If they were, how could one go on living? No, it is the small, little things that make up a day, that bring fullness and happiness to a life. Your Sergeant coming home, a good dinner, your little Mary laughing, the smell of the woods—oh, so many things, you know them yourself." She took my hand.

"You know I didn't come to talk about myself—but you are the only woman to come in in all these years; the others, the 'breeds, the Indians, even my own daughters, have never been out. It makes a difference, so you'll forgive me."

"Oh, no, it's been . . . I mean, you've been—" I stopped. I wanted to say, "How wonderful you are, how beautiful . . ." But I didn't know how. She picked up the bottle of liniment.

"Thank you, Katherine." She walked toward the door and then paused.

"You haven't seen the Mission. Perhaps you and the Sergeant would enjoy the midnight mass. I usually walk. The woods are very peaceful at night."

Before I had time to answer, Mike kicked the door open. He and Constable Cameron were half-supporting, half-dragging Timmy between them. Constance rushed past me. The boy was sobbing. She lifted his head and looked into his face.

"Is he all right?" she asked Mike. Mike nodded. They brought Timmy into the house, and Mike pushed him into a chair. None of us looked at him. He was trying to control his crying, and long rasping breaths shook him again and again.

"You went to my house first?" Constance asked Mike, and I was amazed how calmly she spoke.

"Yes," Mike said. "Georges was there, soaking his foot. He's got a pretty bad sprain. Anyway, he said you were with Kathy."

Constance turned to Timmy. His dark, tousled head was in his hands, but he seemed quieter.

"What happened, Tim?" she asked.

"Mish-e-muk-wa . . ." the word was muffled by his hand.

149

Mish-e-muk-wa was the Cree name for bear. The Indian word startled me. I thought of what Constance had said—none of her children had ever been out.

"As near as I can figure it," Mike said, "Tim was out hunting with Jerry West. They were on their way back with a few rabbits when they bumped into Doug and Ray Lamont and Dennis Crane. They'd been fishing, hadn't they, Tim?"

"Yes." Tim choked out the word without looking up.

"So they all walked back together," Mike went on, "and the men were kidding Tim and Jerry about their hunting, asking them why didn't they really bring down something, like an elk or a mountain lion, when all at once Doug lets out a whoop and grabs Tim's rifle, for there's a grizzly. You see, they were coming back along the lake, and this grizzly's on the other side of Miller's Cove. So Douglas says this is his kind of game, and he lets the grizzly have it. It's at long range, clear across the water, but he hits the bear."

"But he didn't kill it." Timmy looked up at us, his face streaked with tears. "It went into the water and swam toward us, right across the cove. And Doug kept pulling the trigger and it just clicked because it was empty, but he kept pulling it anyway."

"Didn't the others have guns?" his mother asked him.

"Fishing poles." Timmy's lips twitched, and for a moment I was afraid he was going to laugh.

"It kept coming, and Doug kept clicking that empty gun at it. And Jerry, he dropped his rabbits and started running. The bear wasn't swimming any longer; he was touching bottom. His neck and shoulders were out of the water." The terror in Timmy's eyes grew.

"Don't tell it, Tim," Constance said. But he had to tell it.

"We ran, all of us. There was a shack, no one lives there now, they used to make liquor in it. You know, Mother."

Constance nodded.

"We ran for that and—Jerry fell—" Timmy looked at his mother, faced her as though he were facing God. "I didn't stop. I could have picked him up, but I didn't." The anguish that darkened his eyes darkened hers. She didn't say anything.

Mike spoke up then. "The others didn't stop, Mrs. Beauclaire. Grown men, and none of them stopped. There wasn't time."

"Yes," said Timmy, "there was. We ran into the house, and Dennis slammed the door. Then Jerry got up and ran to it. The grizzly was behind him, its mouth open. Jerry grabbed the door and tried to pull it open. But they held it. I tried to open it; they pushed me away. Jerry was pounding at it and calling to me—to me! And I couldn't make them open it. I begged them, I begged them . . . and then Jerry began to scream."

Constance put her hand on his shoulder. "Timmy," she said. But Timmy didn't hear her, he heard Jerry screaming.

"He's dead?" Constance asked Mike.

"Yes," Mike said.

"God, you should have seen him," Constable Cameron said. "His face was torn apart."

"Ned!" Mike said. And Constable Cameron stopped talking, but bears were on his mind, and I was sorry when he said he would go to the Mission with us for midnight mass.

It was, as Constance had said, very peaceful walking in the crisp cool air. Timmy walked silently, his eyes on the ground. Mike was talking to Constance, but talking so Timmy could hear.

"When you're overwrought like that, things go on happening, and it seems that they're taking a long time about it. But really everything took place in a matter of seconds."

Timmy's hands clenched. "Mike," he said, "cut it out."

"All right, Tim. I just want you to know that after talking with the others, I'm convinced that it had to be done like that." Timmy didn't say anything, and we walked on. It had been a long evening. Mike had visited the shack, and he and the Constable had made out a report. Supper had been silent. I looked up. Black trees against a midnight sky.

"Sure," said Ned Cameron, "it was just a case of one or all." No one said anything. The leaves stiff with frost crackled under our feet. It was again Cameron who spoke.

"Yeah, a wounded grizzly's a mean animal. Ordinarily they're pretty easygoing and shy. But they're desperate fighters when they're wounded or when you get them cornered. How big was this one, Tim?"

151

Tim didn't answer.

"Remember the one McTavish got last summer? Weighed over a thousand pounds. I never was lucky enough to get one of them big fellows. Mine have always been right around four hundred pounds. But this fellow the Mc-Tavishes got, front claws were six inches long. They trapped him, you know. It's pretty easy, once you find a bear trail, because a bear will always step squarely in the print of his own tracks, so there are well-worn footsteps, almost like stairs in the hills. But the ground between isn't broken down at all because it's never walked on. So what you do is set the trap right in the middle of a print, and you got your bear."

I glanced at Timmy. Shadows crossed his face and lay in his eyes; from the trees, I thought.

"Another thing about real bears. That's what the Indians call 'em, real bears . . ."

"Ned," Mike said.

"I was just going to say, it's too bad it isn't six weeks later. The whole thing could never have happened then because they hole up about the time the first heavy snows hit us, and that's usually November. Have you noticed there's frost on the ground already?"

We came into a clearing, and the moon struck Timmy's face. Constance was watching him anxiously. I slowed my steps and smiled at Constable Cameron.

"Mike showed me once where a bear was hibernating in a drift."

"They'll do that, north side of a snowbank. But usually they den up in a watee about five feet high, six feet wide, and say ten feet deep."

I had stopped to pin my scarf tighter. We were far enough behind now so Timmy couldn't hear.

"You notice the grizzly didn't eat the kid, just mauled him up. As a rule, you know, they'll eat anything. But about a month before they den up, they quit eating. They go into hibernation with a clean belly and intestines. Their stomachs are drawn up in a solid lump like a chicken's gizzard." I gulped and nodded.

"That grizzly may be wounded worse than they think.

I'm going to have a look around tomorrow. If the fur's in good condition, they fetch quite a price."

I was glad when we reached the Mission. It was the largest building I had seen; in fact, it looked a little like a fort. It had a stockade surrounding it, and inside were the gardens.

"They raise their own food," Mike said. "They took the prize last year in hard wheat. Bishop Grouard is a fine man, Kathy. I'm anxious for you to know him. Grouard's named for him, of course. This Mission was the first building on Lesser Slave."

"It took God to beat the Hudson's Bay Company," said Cameron, and laughed.

"There are eighty children living here now, and they keep the place up. Each one has his job, gardening or sewing or whatever it is, and they take a pride in it, as you can see by the look of things."

The service had started, and we slipped in quietly. The pews were logs split in two. They rested at right angles to one another, forming seat and back. Candles made little pools of light, and shadows wavered on the rough-hewn walls. They were strange shadows, pointed and long—an eagle headdress . . . rounded shadows like a turkey's back, made by the women as they pulled their blankets around them. But the dark faces were lifted, their bodies yearned forward, and the words reached quietly into the corners of the chapel. The softness of the Cree language, with its deep musical notes, was very restful. I felt peace steal over me. I looked at Tim. There were tears again on his face. But the words drew me, and I turned toward the altar.

The bishop was a white-haired, vigorous-looking man. Thick hunter's boots showed beneath his black cassock. He stood straight, like a sturdy old oak, and when he prayed it was a gentle conversation. Closing my eyes, I felt the answering response. In the hush and the quiet I felt I couldn't pray. I could only feel a happiness and a contentment. I opened my eyes and looked into the face of the Mother of Sorrows. She was carved in wood. The work was crude. It looked as though it had been done with a hunting knife. But the face was not cold, like expensive marble faces. A great

153

beauty was there, a great love and sincerity that made you forget its awkwardness and the strangeness of its proportions. The purity of the expression haunted me, the sorrow of the eyes, the sweetness of the mouth. I knew it. I had seen it before . . . I turned away, but the face was still in front of me. No, it was Constance Beauclaire, and her eyes rested on Timmy. Mother of Sorrows, I thought; and now my prayer came.

## CHAPTER FIFTEEN

Mike wanted me to take a girl from the Mission to help with the house and the baby. I had completely forgotten my pleurisy, but every now and then I would catch Mike watching me with a worried eye. I still didn't stand straight enough or breathe deep enough to suit him.

"You don't have to take too much on you, Kathy," he said. "You can have one of the young girls at the Mission give you a hand with the housework."

"How young?" I said.

Mike laughed. "Fourteen, fifteen, sixteen," he said. "At what age do you get jealous?"

I gave him a push. "Who's jealous of you? You think you're such a dashing figure of a man in your red coat and all!" I looked him over and I had to admit, "Well, you are."

"Now look, Kathy," Mike said seriously, "you think I don't know about your sneaking down to the cage, taking Baldy Red things to eat, and squeezing in through those saplings to fix up his shed. If you want to do it, that's okay. But pampering Baldy Red with hot meals and clean sheets adds to your work."

I was mad that he had found out about it. I lashed out. "It's disgraceful! That filthy place, and the horrible things he cooks for himself!"

Mike didn't answer me, so I gave in a little. "If I have a girl to help me, can I go on fixing up Baldy's cell?"

"As long as I don't know about it officially," Mike said.

So we decided to get a girl, but somehow I didn't get around to it, and then Baldy was released, and it wasn't until he had been clapped back into the coop right after Hallowe'en that I finally went to the Mission.

I knocked at the door. It was opened by a cheerful-looking, red-faced Sister.

"I'm Mrs. Flannigan," I said.

"Don't stand there in this chill weather, child. Come inside."

She wouldn't let me talk in the hall, either, but took me to an inside room. Tea was served by an Indian girl of twelve or thirteen, primly dressed in long black stockings and a gingham pinafore. It was not until Sister Teresa had poured me a second cup that she felt she could ask my errand.

"I want to bring a girl home with me. I have a baby, and my husband says I should have a girl to help me in the house. I'll take good care of her, and we have an extra bedroom."

"I see," the Sister said. "Would you want her to do the cooking?"

"Well, I don't really care. It would be nice if she could do a little of everything, cook and keep house and look after babies. And then we could trade off doing things, take turns at it."

The Sister nodded. "You'd want one of our older girls, then. Well, the best thing to do is to let you meet them." She rose, and I followed her into the hall. "We've eighty children here at the present time. All ages. We've classes every morning. They're taught reading and writing. And Old Bill gives them a lesson in music or mathematics whenever he can spare the time. A good man is Irish Bill."

We entered the kitchen. Four girls were at work there. They smiled shyly at me. But when the Sister told them why I was here, they stole little glances at each other. And I was afraid that as soon as I left the room, they would laugh. When we were in the hall again, I asked the Sister to what age they kept the children.

"Until they're eighteen," she said.

I was glad of that, because I was eighteen already, and it was with more assurance that I walked into the next room. Here there were thirty or forty children, all sizes, all ages, and all busy. There was cleaning and scrubbing going on.

There was a lesson on the blackboard, there were looms, there were girls knitting, sewing, crocheting. There were children with books, and children with games. There were big girls looking after babies. The Sister explained that this was the recreation room. All those who had no classes or special chores at this hour played here.

"It's supervised play, of course. They are taught useful and instructive things." She stopped by one of the older girls.

"Amy here is an expert needlewoman." She held up a patchwork quilt. The stitches were tiny and regular.

"It's beautiful work," and I smiled at the girl.

She looked at me appraisingly with black shoe-button eyes and did not smile back.

We walked to another group. The eyes of the children followed. Some of the little ones laughed and pointed. The bigger ones looked down at their work as we came up to them, but their heads lifted as we passed, and I felt them staring after me.

"Louise is very good with children," the Sister said. "Quite dependable." She spoke of them as if they weren't there. Louise looked away, then back shyly, uncertainly. More girls, trustworthy, good housekeepers. I was getting them mixed up. Smooth braided hair, dark eyes, black stockings.

The Sister opened a door at the back of the room. Wails and sobs came from the dark interior, and I drew back nervously.

"It's punishment row," she explained.

The room was a linen closet with only one window very high up. A bench was placed in the center. On it sat three small children crying their eyes out, and a big girl looking pensively at the floor. At that moment Sister Teresa was called back. As soon as the door closed behind her, the children stopped bawling, and began pulling at the big girl. "Go on, go on, Mamanowatum!"

The girl looked at me and smiled.

"What did Fleet Foot do then?" one of the little boys asked her.

"He went then alone into the forest. At his side ran the black wolf—" The door opened, the cries went up from

156

the three simultaneously, and Mamanowatum's eyes rested modestly on the floor.

The Sister went right on about punishment row. It seemed Gerald had stolen from the apple bin, and Luke and Veronica had kicked each other and called names. The Sister hesitated when she came to Mamanowatum. "And Anne," she said, "has acted in a very foolish way."

I realized then that their Indian names weren't used. If I had named the girl, I wouldn't have called her Anne, but something light and wild and full of laughter.

"We rarely find it necessary to punish the older children." She looked reproachfully at Mamanowatum, and turned toward the door.

I said suddenly, "I'd like to take Anne home with me."

We were all surprised, the nun, Mamanowatum, and I. But the Sister recovered first. "She has a lovable disposition. But I feel I must warn you, Mrs. Flannigan, she's wayward, and her needlework isn't what it should be. Still, she's very good with children." I pretended not to see the twinkling glance Mamanowatum shot at me.

"How old is she?" I asked.

"Fifteen," the Sister said and, clearing her throat, she added, "I think it would be best if you discussed your choice with our Mother Superior."

"Of course," I said. "But I want to ask Anne—Would you like to live with me? You could have your own bedroom, and there won't be too much to do."

The girl looked at me earnestly. "Yes," she said, "please."

I sat alone in the room where the Sister and I had had tea. It was important to me now. I wanted Mamanowatum. I was afraid they wouldn't let her come because she was being punished. Then I wondered why she was being punished. I didn't think she would steal or kick people on the shins, but of course I didn't know.

The Sister came back, accompanied by the Mother Superior, a tall austere woman. "Mrs. Flannigan?" she said and nodded courteously. She sat and motioned me to be seated.

"I'm glad that you have come to see us. I'm sure you will give one of our girls a fine home."

"Yes," I said. "Anne."

"I have already been informed of your choice." The voice was cool and level, the eyes were cool and level.

"I'm curious, Mrs. Flannigan; what made you pick Anne? In so short a time I would think it impossible to judge if she possessed more virtues than the others, or more talent."

"I don't know," I said, and I didn't. I mean I wasn't clear in my own mind why I wanted her, but I did . . . enough to fight for her. "I like her," I said.

The Mother Superior seemed puzzled. "My dear," she said, "I think perhaps you were sorry for her."

"Oh, no!" I had interrupted her. That immediately made me young and impulsive-sounding. The Mother Superior appeared not to notice. I admired her for that.

"Mrs. Flannigan, I think you are a very generous person. I think you felt pity—" I started to deny it, but she stilled me with a glance. "Pity is one of the greatest qualities with which the human soul is endowed. Do not be ashamed of it.

"As I say, you felt sorry, seeing Anne sitting in punishment row along with the four- and five-year-olds. Having aroused such an emotion in you, naturally she stood out in your mind."

The shrewd gray eyes fascinated me. Was she right? Was that the way I felt? Then into my mind popped the merry face of Mamanowatum and the story she was telling about Fleet Foot.

"Well, my dear?"

I looked at the Mother Superior. "Can't I have her?" I asked.

She smiled at me; even the gray eyes smiled. "Mrs. Flannigan, I'm determined this conversation shall proceed in a logical way. If you don't intend to ask why Anne is being punished, I shall have to tell you."

I must have looked surprised, for she said, "My dear young lady, perhaps this girl is an incorrigible liar or a thief. In that case it would be as well to know it before taking her into your home."

"Of course, you're right." I was angry with myself. I'd been acting like a child.

"Well, to put your mind at rest, she is none of those

158

things. She is intelligent, charming, and completely capable. In fact, she is admirably suited for your purposes."

The woman was twisting me in her words.

She went on, "Anne has a fault, however, a serious fault —that of being too young."

"It's a fault she'll outgrow."

The Mother Superior didn't notice my joke. "Anne is young enough to imagine herself in love."

"She's in love?" I asked. And then, "Is that why she's being punished?"

"We have no reason to believe Anne has been immoral. Otherwise we couldn't keep her here among the other girls. I believe that she is merely headstrong."

"Is she too young to marry?" I asked.

"She's only fifteen."

"Yes," I said, remembering that I had been only a year older.

"Of course, Indian girls mature early and marry young. If it were anyone else, well, maybe. But as it is, it's quite impossible."

"You know the boy?" I asked.

"He's Jonathan Forquet," she said, as though that explained. "'Son of Raoul Forquet.'" And then, a trifle impatiently, "My dear, you've heard of the Riel Rebellion?"

"Yes."

"Then you know it was an uprising of the half-breeds against the Canadian Government, an attempt to set up a government of their own in the Northwest. Riel himself was apparently a mild-mannered man. In fact, he was a schoolteacher. Nevertheless, he was the brains behind the revolt. But in the massacre that followed he lost the reins, was merely swept on in something he lacked the power to stop. He became the figurehead in whose name blood flowed and crimes of all descriptions were perpetrated." The Mother Superior looked at me from beneath severe brows. "Forquet, Raoul Forquet, the father of Jonathan, was one of the brigands who seized command. He was relentless, unfeeling. Completely so. He murdered, destroyed—and called himself a revolutionist. Of course, the whole thing was impossible without the Indians, and the Indians refused to join the 'breeds. So it ended as those things usually end, with the

159

hanging of the leaders. Then men soon lost heart and disbanded. However, in this particular section they did *not* disband, for Raoul Forquet had not been caught, and he was still carrying on a war with Canada and Great Britain. A handful of lawless, ragged men followed him in his private war. But some were caught and some ran off because Raoul Forquet, to do him justice, refused to allow them to pillage and steal." There was a pause.

"That's all," the Mother Superior said. "When he was caught, there were three followers and an Indian girl with him. The men were hanged. I tell you this so that you may understand Jonathan's character. And why it is not possible for Anne to marry him."

I thought about Raoul Forquet. "He was a very stubborn man."

"Exactly, and Jonathan is like him, very like him. I don't know when he saw Anne first, but he began waylaying her. I understand he has even met her inside the Mission walls. Perhaps," the Mother Superior said, "all this strikes you as romantic. Perhaps your pity is again aroused for the two lovers. But I wish to tell you that I have talked to Jonathan Forquet here, where I am talking to you now. I made every allowance for him. I granted the fact that he is three-quarters Indian, that he was raised in squalor by an Indian mother, that this same mother undoubtedly fed him on tales of his father's greatness. But nothing could excuse his arrogance, his defiance. He laughed and refused to answer my questions. Only when I asked him to leave Anne alone did he answer, 'She be my *klooch*.' That's what he said, and that was the word he used to me, '*klooch*.' Mrs. Flannigan, I can't tell you what I felt. It was as though his father were standing before me. The same relentless determination." The Mother Superior unfolded her hands and then folded them again.

"I wonder if you realize what the word *klooch,* as Jonathan used it, implies? Tragedy for our Mission-trained girls. The tragedy of filth, dirt, ignorance, and superstition. Our girls read and write. Can you turn them into pack animals, to live in tepees, to haul and lift all day for a man who kicks and beats them? You see the impossibility of it. You see the tragedy of it. You see why Anne cannot marry Jonathan."

160

"Yes," I said, "I see."

"Now that I have explained the situation, Mrs. Flannigan, the decision rests with you. And the responsibility, of course, if you decide to take her."

I knew I was getting into trouble. When you see trouble as plainly as I saw it, there's no excuse to go walking out to meet it. But I remembered Mamanowatum, and how grave her pretty, happy face had gotten when she looked up at me and said, "Please."

The gray eyes of the Mother Superior made me hesitate, but I knew I was going to do it.

"My husband, Sergeant Mike, can take care of that Jonathan. And I'll look after Anne."

The Mother Superior rose. "Very well, Mrs. Flannigan. I hope both you and Anne will find happiness in the arrangement."

Before I could thank her, she was gone. The plump Sister, after telling me she would get Anne packed and ready and send her down to me, trailed after her. I was alone now with nothing to do but think about what I'd done.

## CHAPTER SIXTEEN

I was congratulating myself on how well everything had turned out, when it happened. In the first place, everyone had taken to Mamanowatum. Mary Aroon cried to be picked up by her, and Juno followed her around the house. Mike was pleased with himself for having thought up the idea—and she was a great deal of help, but mostly she was a great deal of fun. Mamanowatum, her Indian name, means "Oh-Be-Joyful," and that is what we called her.

When I told Mike what the Mother Superior had said about Jonathan, he just laughed and said, "I don't think we'll have any trouble in that direction."

But he was wrong.

It was about an hour after he'd left the house that I went out to shake the rugs. And there on our front doorstep was a pile of the most beautiful skins I'd ever seen. Beaver, mink, otter, and lynx were stacked in a neat, gleaming pile. I couldn't believe my eyes. There must have been two hundred dollars' worth of pelts there. While I was standing, staring, Oh-Be-Joyful came out too. She gave a little cry and gathered the skins in her arms, burying her head in the soft pelts. She whispered into the warm fur in her Cree language.

"Oh-Be-Joyful, do you know whose furs these are?"

She lifted shining eyes to me. "Yes, Mrs. Mike, they are mine."

"Yours?" She hugged them to her some more before she would answer me. "Are they not beautiful?" she asked. "Are they not the best of furs?"

"Yes," I said. "They are. They're expensive. Too expensive to be lying around on the porch."

Oh-Be-Joyful examined each pelt, stroking it and exclaiming over it.

"So young is the season for so pretty furs. He is clever, no?"

He? So that was it. "Oh-Be-Joyful," I said sternly, "where did these furs come from?"

She looked at me with such happiness that I was troubled.

"From Jonathan," she said, and when she said it the name was beautiful, the most beautiful I'd ever heard.

"Who's Jonathan?" I asked, to gain time.

"He called Jonathan Forquet. He is maker of canoes. From the land of the Blackfeet and the land of the Beaver come men to buy from Jonathan the canoes."

"Really," I said in my coolest tones.

"The *bateau* sings the song of the currents, and the waters race to catch it. For Jonathan, he know the time to cut the birch bark. In the almost summer does he make the cut beneath the lowest branch, and another above the roots. With his knife he makes the line between, and with the flat side of his knife lifts the birch bark and takes it away in one piece, without breaking. This I have seen him do."

I didn't want to take her pride and her happiness from her, but the word *klooch* made me do it.

"When did you see him making canoes?"

"In the almost summer." Her hands were still in the furs.

"When you were at the Mission?" I asked.

162

Now she understood. We looked at each other a long time.

"Why did they call me 'Anne' at the Mission?" she asked slowly.

"I don't know. Why?"

"Because they did not wish me to be joyful."

"No," I said, "that's not the reason. They name all the children with the names of saints, so they will try to be good also."

She shook her head. "They did not wish me to be joyful," she said again.

"They did not wish you to be bad or wicked; they did not wish you to be a *klooch.*"

Her black eyes studied me. "Mrs. Mike, I *am klooch,* The word, she mean woman, Indian woman."

"Oh-Be-Joyful," I said almost angrily, "you're neither a *klooch* nor a woman; you're a fifteen-year-old girl."

Her full lips went stubbornly together, but she made no answer.

"And while the good Sisters at the Mission took care of you and taught you, it was wrong to sneak away and be with Jonathan."

Her eyes were round with wonder at such a thought. "When I first look on him I know my home is where he is. He tell me of the four winds, he tell me of the forest spirits, on the hill he dance for me the dance of good harvest."

This Jonathan that told such stories, that danced on hill-tops, was not the cold, relentless young man I had pictured. I could only think that Oh-Be-Joyful was a child yet and no judge of character.

"Are you happy here, Oh-Be-Joyful?"

"I love you," she said.

It wasn't easy to harden my heart against that, but I wasn't going to let this pretty, bright-faced child become the squaw of Jonathan Forquet.

"Then you must promise me that while you stay here with us you won't see Jonathan." She bowed her head and did not answer.

"Promise me, Oh-Be-Joyful, and I'll never mention it to you again. We'll forget the whole thing."

She raised sad eyes to mine. "Can I forget him who

163

brings me the joy my mother, who is dead, want me to feel?"

I was angry, but I made myself remember that she had never defied me before. I said as quietly as I could, "If you don't promise, I can't keep you."

"I love him," she said.

I went right on, "I'll have to send you back to the Mission. They will keep you for three years yet; they'll watch you."

She smiled at that. "Jonathan, he go where he want."

"I want you to stay with me, Oh-Be-Joyful. And all I ask is that you promise me."

"No," she said.

I was afraid I was going to cry in front of her. I turned away and walked to the end of the porch.

"I'll help you pack. There are some things of mine I'd like you to have." Saying that made me realize I was sending her away. I felt awful.

"If you change your mind," I said and stopped, because I was choking over the words. Oh-Be-Joyful began to sob. I ran back and put my arms around her.

"Oh-Be-Joyful, don't cry!" But she cried harder.

"Do you really love him so much?" I asked.

"Yes."

"Oh, dear," I said, "I wish Mike was here."

It occurred to me that we would look pretty silly to anybody walking by, holding onto each other like that and crying. It was up to me to pull myself together. I did, and decided that as I couldn't do anything with Oh-Be-Joyful, Mike would have to handle Jonathan, scare him away from the place or something.

When I thought about it a while I was sure that Mike could manage it, and that Oh-Be-Joyful wouldn't have to go back after all. But of course I couldn't tell her that I intended to get rid of Jonathan. So after I had jumped up, feeling everything was solved, she continued to sit there staring down into the pile of furs.

I wanted to get her busy at something. "Help me tie up these pelts. We'll take them over to the Company store, and they'll give them to Jonathan next time he's in."

164

She gathered the furs in her arms. "They are mine," she said.

"Oh-Be-Joyful, the furs are Jonathan's. You can't accept a present worth several hundred dollars from him."

"When brave lay gift before door and woman take it in, it mean she have him as husband."

"Then you most certainly will not take it in."

"I take," she said.

"Oh-Be-Joyful, you give me those furs!"

Her grip tightened on them.

"You're a mean, ungrateful girl, and it will serve you right if you marry Jonathan Forquet. You'll have no one to thank but yourself."

There were tears in her eyes, but she said nothing.

I walked back into the house. I felt confused. I wasn't so sure that the Mother Superior had been right. And I wasn't at all sure that Oh-Be-Joyful was wrong. I'd once heard an Indian refer to me as the Sergeant's *klooch*. If having a baby and a little home made you a *klooch,* it wasn't such a bad thing to be. It seemed to me that it all came to this: what was that relentless, stubborn, determined boy, that maker of canoes, that storyteller and dancer on hilltops, really like?

I walked back out on the porch. Oh-Be-Joyful still sat there, her eyes big with misery. I put my hand on her head and stroked the thick black hair.

"What's he like?" I asked her.

She caught my hand and pressed it. "He tall and straight as young fir tree. He walk in the ways of our people. He hunt alone, no brother sit at his campfire. He is silent like the woods, and when he speaks it is with knowing. With much care he take bark from tree, that tree is not hurt. Yet great fierceness is in his soul, and around his neck hangs the teeth of Mish-e-muk-wa. I want much, but never him speak love to me. Now today he lay the furs before the door as my father lay furs before the tepee of my mother. Should I send them back to the lonely campfire?"

"Oh, dear," I said again. "I wish Mike was here."

But when I thought about it, I was glad he wasn't. What I needed was a chance to talk about it with him alone. So I packed up a lunch and took it to his office. There was a great deal of loud talk coming from the office, and as I passed the window I glanced in. A swarthy 'breed with a dirty yellow handkerchief knotted around his head was saying, "He try kill me every night."

"Now wait a minute," Mike said. "Let's get this straight."

I decided I'd better not interrupt them, so I sat on the step and waited for yellow handkerchief to go. But he was a long time about it, so I took out a sandwich and began to eat. Also I wondered who was trying to kill yellow handkerchief, and why, and if they would succeed. They must have moved nearer the window because their voices became suddenly audible.

Mike said, "Then you don't know why Jonathan wants to kill you?"

At the name Jonathan, I choked on my sandwich.

Yellow handkerchief's voice was surly. "I tell you, no. Him hate me very much. Him make up this lie."

"About you stealing from his trap lines?" Mike asked.

I was so excited and upset that I opened another sandwich.

"Yes," yellow handkerchief's voice came again, "him tell that damn lie to my face."

"You're sure it's a lie?" Mike asked.

"You think I steal from trap line?" yellow handkerchief roared. "You think I thief? Then good-by!"

I drew myself to one side so as not to be crushed as he stamped out. But he didn't stamp out, for Mike said quickly. "Now look here, Cardinal, let's not be so touchy. If your life's been threatened, I'm on your side; but I've got to know how matters stand before I can take any steps."

"How they stand?" Yellow handkerchief was beside himself. "I told you how they stand. That snake Jonathan Forquet come every night to my house and shoot at me with bow and arrows."

"How many nights has he done this?"

"Three."

"And how close does he come?"

"Damn close. He pin my sleeve to table, him let fly arrow one-half inch from my head. Last night arrow she hitting between my fingers."

166

"It sounds like he might just be trying to scare you," Mike said.

"He try kill me," yellow handkerchief said with conviction.

"Well, whether he is or not, he can't go around shooting at people."

"I tell you, him try kill me. Him come and say to me, 'I kill you, Cardinal, you dirty dog, you steal from my traps.' And it is a lie and he knows it, but he shoot anyway. Every night he try kill me."

"All right," Mike said. "I'll bring him in."

"What that mean, you bring him in?" yellow handkerchief asked suspiciously.

"It means, Cardinal, that I'll handle it my own way."

"You put him in jail, yes?"

"Now look, Cardinal. I want you to keep out of this. I'll talk to Jonathan and see what I can get out of him. But if he sees us together, he'll shut up like a clam."

"Okay, okay, so long you put him in jail."

"I'm not promising that."

The door opened so suddenly that it almost knocked me off the step. Yellow handkerchief's boots left gray prints on the thin layer of November snow.

Mike looked at me sternly. "Kathy, what's the idea, sitting out here in this rotten weather?"

"I had to talk to you about Jonathan."

Mike walked back in and sat down with a sigh. "Then you might as well have joined the party. That's all I've been doing, talking about Jonathan."

"Is he really a killer?" I asked.

Mike grinned.

"Well," I said, "I couldn't help but hear some of it, with yellow handkerchief yelling like that."

"Yellow handkerchief?" Mike laughed. "Oh, Cardinal."

"Listen, it's no laughing matter, because Oh-Be-Joyful loves Jonathan."

"Yes," Mike said, "you told me about it."

"But now it's worse. Today he dumped a whole bunch of skins on our porch."

At last Mike looked concerned. "He wants to take her off, huh?"

167

"Yes," I said. "That's what it means. And I couldn't get her to promise me not to. You've simply got to do something about it, Mike. You've got to talk to him, tell him to keep away, and put the fear of God into him so he'll do it."

"Jonathan doesn't scare easy," Mike said.

"That's too bad for him. Then you'll have to put him in jail as Mr. Cardinal suggested."

"Good God, Kathy, I can't put a man in jail because he's in love!"

"But he's dangerous. Suppose he kills Mr. Cardinal, how would you feel? And how would I feel? Because by that time he would have run off with Oh-Be-Joyful too. Mike, it makes me just sick to think of it, a potential killer."

"Kathy, you're working yourself up over nothing. In the first place, I don't believe Jonathan is a potential killer. I think that Cardinal *did* rob his traps. And Jonathan took this way of scaring him off. Trap-stealing is the most serious crime in the Northwest. You can see why. It's a man's livelihood."

"Then why didn't he come to you?"

"He's Indian, that's why."

It seemed to me Mike was being unfair. "You're taking Jonathan's side against Mr. Cardinal's," I said.

Mike said very evenly, "I'm trying not to take any side until I know more about things."

"You don't like Mr. Cardinal."

"Of course I don't like him. He's got a reputation that smells like dead fish, a whole stinking trail of it, from here to Calgary."

"What's he done?"

"Laudanum," Mike said.

"What's that?"

"It's a drug. They use it for anaesthetics; it puts you out. Cardinal served a year in Calgary for peddling it. I've just checked with the Calgary authorities because someone's been bringing laudanum into my territory."

"Oh, Mike, how do you know?"

"You remember the day Jerry West was killed by the grizzly outside that old shack?"

"Yes."

"You remember I went down there to investigate? Well,

168

on the way I met Cardinal. He was carrying a box of fishing tackle, but no pole and no fish." Mike's voice had sunk lower. He was talking to himself by now.

"I'd give anything if I had opened that box of tackle. But I didn't suspect then. It was only as I walked toward the shack that I noticed it was where Cardinal's footprints had come from.

"Now, the way I figured it, Cardinal must have heard what had happened with the bear, and while I was taken up with Tim he went to the cabin and probably took something away in that box of tackle. So I had a look around, and I noticed a peculiar thing. The window by the door was knocked out, and there were pieces of glass lying on the ground. It made me wonder why Jerry West pounded at the door until the grizzly got him. Why didn't he jump through the open window? The only reason I could think of is that the windowpane wasn't knocked out then. I began to suspect it was Cardinal who had knocked it out. But why?

"Then I noticed an interesting thing: a few pieces of the window had shattered and fallen inside the room. I bent down to examine them and found that they were not window glass at all. They were tinted a light green. I became conscious then of a sweet sickish smell. I felt around, and the floor beside the green glass was damp.

"Then of course the whole thing came to me. I was sure the smell was laudanum.

"What I think happened was this: Cardinal had hidden his supply in the shack. The shack was used as a distillery in the old days, but since that was broken up, no one's been near it. A perfect place to hide the stuff. Of course, when he heard about the grizzly killing, he knew I'd be down to investigate, so he had to beat me to it. He did. He packed up the vials of laudanum in his tin box, and in his hurry one of the bottles broke. He kicked the glass into the corner where no one would be apt to notice it. And if they did, so what? The place used to be a distillery. But the smell was noticeable in the shack, so Cardinal knocked out the window, and it was dissipated in the fresh air." Mike looked at me and grinned.

"Why don't you arrest him?" I asked.

"It's all supposition," he said. "I haven't got a fact in the world to back it up with. But it makes a nice story."

"And you make a nice detective." But after I'd thought about it a while, there was one thing I didn't understand. "What do people in this country want with laudanum?"

"On first thought you can't see it. Mountaineers and trappers don't seem the type to take to narcotics. But there are plenty of snowbirds up here, and plenty who aren't, who like to have a supply of the stuff on hand. The reason for it is a pretty grim one."

"What is the reason?" I asked.

"Well," said Mike, "a lot of miners pass through here on the way to the Yukon, and miners travel alone and work alone. Anyone who thinks he's onto a rich vein doesn't want a partner around to cut his throat. Then there are plenty of trappers who work alone, too.

"Now, there are many things can happen to a man alone on the trail. And the man who falls and breaks his neck is a lucky man. But suppose you don't break your neck, suppose you just break your leg? The vulture starts circling above, and the wolves stand in a circle, and every time you look they're closer. You can keep them off for a while until your ammunition's gone or until you fall asleep. Well, that's when the little three-ounce phial you wear around your neck's going to stand you in good stead. Because it's going to put you to sleep, painlessly and soundly asleep. You won't feel it when the hungry circle closes in. You won't feel the first crunching bite. You won't feel the others rending and tearing and fighting each other for your still-living flesh."

"Oh, Mike, it's horrible!"

"Not with laudanum," he said.

We sat in silence for a moment, then Mike reached for the lunch basket.

"How can you eat?" I asked him. "I feel absolutely sick."

Mike opened the basket and looked in. "Sure you do," he said. "You've eaten all the sandwiches."

I couldn't believe it. Not even when I saw the empty lunch basket. "It's a nervous habit," I said with dignity. "I always eat when I'm upset."

Mike set out the next morning to find Jonathan and bring

170

him in. I don't know how Oh-Be-Joyful knew it, but she did. We were silent and avoided looking at each other. When I fed the baby, there was no calling back and forth about the new tooth, or any laughing over the way she talked to herself. Oh-Be-Joyful used to pretend Mary Aroon was speaking Cree, and she would answer everything the baby said. It was very funny, but there was no fun in anything today, and no happiness. While I was peeling the potatoes for dinner, I came across one that looked just like a little fat man with big ears. I held it up.

"Look, Oh-Be-Joyful, at my little man."

I thought that would make her laugh, but she burst into tears and ran from the room.

It had been such a long day, and now it was past suppertime and no Mike. So many things can happen to a man on the trail. Especially if he's out to bring someone in who, maybe, doesn't want to be brought in.

Pictures crowded into my mind. Mr. Neilson, a strong man but stubborn, his boot sticking up out of the snow and the girl with the delicate wedding ring pulling at it. Burnt bodies lying by a well. A beaver with its eyes gone, swinging from a pole. Timmy sitting in the little church, his face wet with tears. I lighted a candle and set it in the window. It would be a welcome to Mike. It would make things more cheerful.

Oh-Be-Joyful came silently into the room and sat in the corner most filled with shadows.

"I wonder what's keeping Sergeant Mike," I said. And just then I heard him clumping with his snowshoes on the porch. I opened the door, and a gust of snow swirled in my face.

"Mike," I called. He grabbed me to him in a rough snowy kiss. Not until he bent to unstrap his snowshoes did I realize there was someone with him, standing silent in the dark.

"Come in," I said. The Indian boy followed closely behind Mike. I slammed the door shut against the wind and turned to them.

"Kathy," said Mike, "this is Jonathan Forquet."

Jonathan nodded courteously, but there was no smile on his lips. I noticed this because I noticed his mouth in par-

171

ticular. It was full, with a clean sweeping outline. He held himself well, proudly or perhaps defiantly. His long dark eyes swept over the room. They came to rest on Oh-Be-Joyful who stood in the farthest corner, hardly breathing. Jonathan's face did not soften. He gave her no sign, but he looked for a long minute.

It was Mike who roused him by demanding dinner in a loud voice. I was angry with Mike, terribly angry, for having brought Jonathan to the house. I wanted a chance to tell him so, so I said, "You have to help me carve the meat," and I led the way to the kitchen. As soon as the door swung to behind us I turned on him, blazing mad.

"Mike Flannigan, what on earth are you thinking of, bringing that boy here? Didn't you see the way he looked at Oh-Be-Joyful? Oh, you're crazy, just crazy!" The tears that had been close to the surface all day spilled over, and I wiped them away furiously with my apron.

"Kathy, I brought him here because I didn't know what else to do with him. And I think," he added slowly, "that that's what you would have wanted me to do."

"Oh, Mike, if they hear about this at the Mission, they'll take Oh-Be-Joyful back. They'll think you're deliberately encouraging it. And you are."

He took me by the arm, but I shook him off. Then he grabbed me tight by each shoulder, so tight I couldn't have shaken his hands off or pried them off either. He swung me around to him.

"You're going to listen to me, you little minx. I brought Jonathan here so you could put a meal into him. The boy is starving. He fainted on the trail coming in."

"Is he really starving, Mike?"

"When I found him, he was peeling the bark from a jack pine and sucking at the sap. You've got to be pretty hungry to do that."

I couldn't believe it. "But if he could shoot at Mr. Cardinal, why didn't he shoot food for himself?"

"He's sick," Mike said. "That's why it took me so long to bring him in. He's too weak to travel, really. But he's a plucky kid. Jumped away from that jack pine like a shot when he heard me coming. Afraid I'd guess what he was doing. And on the trail, not a word out of him. I didn't realize there was much wrong, he walked along with me quietly enough, and then all at once just crumpled up on the snow. He lay there as if he were dead. I built a fire and erected a kind of lean-to to shelter him from the wind, and all that time he didn't move. I started chafing him then and loosening his clothing. I noticed that his skin was discolored around his waist. I opened his shirt and found that his whole body was terribly bruised. For a while I thought that one of the ribs was broken. He must have been kicked fifty times in the side. That's the only thing that could account for it. I began to see why he was shooting at Cardinal."

"But if he was so weak, how could he?"

"I had a look around Cardinal's cabin on my way to pick up Jonathan. The cabin's on the hill, and I noticed a wide strip of underbrush had been crushed and tufts of weed and bush pulled up by the roots. At the time I couldn't understand what could make a track like that, but after I saw Jonathan, I knew. He's crawled up that hill every night for three nights. Where the vegetation's pulled up by the roots, that's where he rested or maybe fainted. How he could hold on like that I don't know, but he must have."

I thought of Raoul Forquet and his war with Canada and Great Britain, and I understood how Jonathan held on. "You think that Cardinal beat him up?" I asked.

"Yes," Mike said, "that's what I think. I visited Jonathan's trap lines, and there were signs of a scuffle. There have been heavy snows since then, but once a man sets foot, or in this case, snowshoes, on a snow-covered rock or a fallen tree, he leaves an impression no snowfall will obliterate. And that's what happened. There were the close-footed prints of the Indian Jonathan. And the impression of white or 'breed steps, wide apart, straddling on the web of the shoe."

"But Jonathan's a 'breed. That is, his father was a 'breed."

"He's Indian for all that," Mike said. "More Indian than many a full-blood. When he found his traps had been meddled with, he lay in wait. Cardinal came by to take a look at the traps, and Jonathan caught him at it, confronted him, and probably demanded the stolen skins. Cardinal must have knocked him down. I think one blow did it. Jonathan

173

must have struck his head on something, or maybe the blow knocked him out. But if there'd been any real tussle, his face would look like his body. It's a pretty ugly picture, Cardinal standing over an unconscious boy and kicking him. If Jonathan had been white, he would have died in the forest. But, being Indian, he ate the sap of the jack pine and lived. Not only lived, but crawled to the house of his enemy every night to shoot at him."

"He just meant to scare Cardinal, didn't he?"

Mike shook his head. "He meant to scare him, all right. But a cat scares a mouse, worries it, before she pounces. Jonathan may be intending to pounce."

"Well, that brute deserves to die, and I wouldn't blame Jonathan a bit for killing him."

Mike looked at me with that teasing smile of his, and then his face grew grave. "If I could prove Cardinal was a trap-robber, the whole Northwest wouldn't be big enough to hold him."

"But it's proved," I said excitedly. "Jonathan's your witness. He actually saw him."

"That's what I *think*," Mike said. "But that's not what Jonathan says."

"What does Jonathan say?"

"Nothing."

"You mean when he came to, he wouldn't tell you how he'd gotten hurt?"

"He wouldn't," Mike said.

"But why?"

"Because of that devilish pride of his. He got the worst of things, didn't he? First Cardinal robs him, and then he beats him up. Jonathan wants revenge, and he doesn't want me spoiling it by sending Cardinal to jail. My job is plainly to keep the boy from becoming a killer."

"And mine," I said, "is to feed him before he faints in my living room."

I carried the dishes to the table. Jonathan stood leaning against the door. He spoke a low word to Oh-Be-Joyful and she jumped up to help me. In the kitchen, Oh-Be-Joyful caught my hand in hers. "Jonathan, he is sick, yes?"

"He'll be all right," I said, "once he gets a good dinner in him."

174

"You are sure, Mrs. Mike? You are sure?"

"Of course I'm sure." But I wasn't. I didn't like to see Jonathan leaning against the door that way. He wasn't the kind to lean if he could stand. I set down the platter of meat.

"Well," I said, "I guess we eat."

Mike turned to Jonathan. "Pull up a chair."

Jonathan smiled slightly and shook his head.

"Come on," I said. "Things will be getting cold."

Jonathan did not move. He said, "Already I eat much today."

"Of course you have," I said, "but you've been out on the trail with Mike for hours. I know Mike's always starving when he's been out all day like this." I cursed the evil little luck that made me use the word "starving," for Jonathan said, with that half-smile on his face, "Me, I do not starve."

Oh-Be-Joyful spoke softly to him in Cree, but he would not look at her.

"I'll feel very sorry if you do not accept my hospitality, Jonathan," Mike said.

"And my cooking," I put in. "A cook likes a little appreciation, and the best appreciation is eating."

Jonathan held that little mocking smile on his face and said nothing.

I sat down abruptly with my back to him. It was a terrible meal. Who could eat anything with that hungry boy watching us silently? Oh-Be-Joyful didn't touch a thing. Mike ate steadily without once looking up from his plate. I stood it until the meal was nearly through, but when Oh-Be-Joyful pushed away the stewed plums which were her favorite dessert, I pushed back my chair and said, "Jonathan Forquet, you've spoiled everybody else's dinner by your stubbornness, and I hope you're satisfied!"

His eyes met mine. They were young and troubled. "I—I did not know," he said.

"Well, you know now. Next time I cook a meal, and you're around, you're going to eat it whether you like it or not."

"Kathy," Mike said.

"I don't care, it's perfectly ridiculous. Jonathan is pretending he isn't sick or hungry, and we're pretending with him." Somewhere in the middle of this I heard Mike groan, but I went right on, "I'm going to feed you, Jonathan, and then I'm going to put you to bed. And in the morning when you wake up, I'll ask you if it was all right that I did it."

Jonathan moved from the door and stood straight and tall in front of me.

"I don't care," I said again. "It's your own fault. It's the only way you let a person treat you."

He smiled at me, and his eyes were friendly. "Mrs. Mike, I ask you, please you give me to eat, yes?"

"Nothing's hot now," I said, "but the meat's just as good cold."

He sat at the table and ate my dinner. He ate with his left hand. It was stiff, and he had difficulty raising it, but the other hand hung at his side, unusable. He ate slowly and very little. When he had finished he looked to Mike and me and said gravely, "I have eaten in the house of my friends."

"Yes," Mike said, "you have."

Oh-Be-Joyful was filled with delight by what had happened. She smiled secret smiles to herself and moved busily around the room. Jonathan watched her with pleasure.

"She is too young," I whispered. "You will let her stay a while with me." I waited.

The words came so low from him I scarcely heard them. "It is well."

There came a rapping at the door that somehow shattered the peace and the friendliness. Mike opened it, and Cardinal stepped inside. He wore the same dirty yellow handkerchief, this time under his cap. He looked quickly around, and when he saw Jonathan he grinned in a very unpleasant way and clapped Mike on the shoulder.

"Ha!" he said. "You got him. Good!"

Jonathan jumped to his feet. He looked from Cardinal to Mike. There was a curious expression in his eyes.

Cardinal crossed the room and planted himself before Jonathan. He stuck his neck out, bringing his face very close to Jonathan's. The boy did not move.

"So!" Cardinal said. "Sergeant Mike, we did good to arrest this fellow, no?"

"Arrest!" Jonathan looked at Mike.

"Jonathan is not under arrest," Mike said.

"Him murderer!" Cardinal cried. "Him try kill me all the time."

Jonathan watched, apparently indifferent, but Mike was mad.

"I thought I told you to stay away, Cardinal. You're not doing any good here."

"I know what you want, Sergeant. You want by nice talk get out of him how he try kill me. I know better way." Again he brought his face close to Jonathan's. "You tell Sergeant Mike you shoot arrows at me."

Jonathan looked past Cardinal at Mike. He spoke slowly for the thoughts forming in him were painful. "Sergeant Mike light fire on trail to warm me. In his house him give me food. Is it that he want I speak of shooting arrows so he arrest me? Tell me now, this thing is true?"

Mike returned Jonathan's steady gaze. "The thing is not true. If I had wanted to know about the arrows, I would have asked you. There was no need to ask. I knew you had shot at Cardinal. But I had a different reason for bringing you here, Jonathan. I wanted your side of what happened between you and Cardinal. Of course, I must also warn you: there must be no more shooting."

"No!" bellowed Cardinal. "This is all wrong. Him try kill me. How I know tomorrow night he won't shoot straighter? Do I got to be dead before you put him in jail?"

Mike spoke to Jonathan. "There's to be no more shooting. I want your word on that."

"His word! What you think he is? Some damn good school-boy? Him murderer, murderer!"

It was difficult to ignore Cardinal, who was practically frothing at the mouth, but Mike did ignore him.

"Well?" he asked Jonathan.

Jonathan looked fiercely ahead of him at nothing.

"I can't let you go around shooting at people," Mike said.

Jonathan stood there without answering.

"Jonathan," Mike said, "if you shoot at Cardinal again, I'll be forced to arrest you."

Jonathan's gaze rested almost gently on Cardinal. "Then my next shot, she be my last."

Cardinal turned pale. "It's a lie about the trap lines! It's a lie!"

Jonathan did not answer him. Instead, he said, "One moon ago, I follow Mother May-Heegar, gray wolf, to den. She lie down and die of wounds. From inside come little May-Heegar. Them cry like puppies. I take skin from Mother May-Heegar and eat her. I give pieces little May-Heegar. They eat her too. When skin of Mother dry, I put in den. Little May-Heegar like sleep there. Then I tie my shirt over opening. They scared of shirt, no go out while it still there. Next day I come, feed little May-Heegar. Them so little, I must chew food for them. After we eat, I paint little May-Heegar faces with bright paint, like I paint canoe. That show they mine. Every day now I go play with them. But one day I take rag from opening, they no run out. They dead. They mostly eaten. I feel bad. I look around, see mark of Pee-Shoo. Follow track into forest, see Pee-Shoo spring into tree." Jonathan touched the chain of bear talons that hung around his neck. "Mish-e-muk-wa die with one arrow through heart. But Pee-Shoo, big cat, killer of cubs, did not die, but went with beating heart through forest. My arrows, they follow him, they let him not to rest. In terror must he live now until the day my pity, she guide arrow into the wicked, frightened heart of Pee-Shoo."

Jonathan looked at us. He did not look longer at Cardinal than at the rest of us, but when he had gone, Cardinal fell heavily into a chair.

The next morning we heard that Cardinal had left Lesser Slave Lake. He had gone in the night to do his winter's trapping farther north.


### CHAPTER SEVENTEEN

Winter was long and quiet. The men were away from the village, trapping. The women stayed in their houses. In my own I had made a new friend—my daughter, Mary Aroon.

Now that she was over five months old, Mary Aroon had decided to take charge of the household. She had an uncanny eye for spotting things I needed, and yelling till I gave them to her. That was the end of my red pot-holder, and my green taffeta ribbon, and my spool of coarse thread, and nearly the end of Mike's shaving brush. Mike himself had to interfere to save this and argue it out with Mary Aroon.

This love of bright colors she got from me, along with her red hair. But her appetite came from Mike. Better than a clock, she was. Did I wait two minutes past her feeding time, she'd bang on the walls of the crib; that was warning. Next minute the house would be filled with screeches that should have come from a mountain lion. There was no answer to that. Mary Aroon was fed.

I expected another baby sometime in July. I was determined that this one would be just as strong and healthy as Mary Aroon. The bitter pessimism the women of Grouard had adopted didn't touch me. I wasn't resigned to losing six children to raise three. Every one of mine was going to grow up!

This was good country, I felt. I had come here weak and pale, coughing, hunched over, with shooting pains in my chest. Now I was well, I ran my own house, I had a child and would have more. Surely in this cold clean air of the North my children would thrive. I tucked the blanket up over the back of my baby's neck, kissed the top of her head, and gave her a nice bright green piece of cloth to play with.

Sarah had given me a small bottle full of brown powder. I secretly gave Mary Aroon a pinch in a little water, once a week. I was afraid Mike would disapprove. After all, I didn't know what the brown powder was. Probably a doctor from the outside or a pharmacist would have laughed and said it wasn't anything, meaning anything in their books.

But Sarah told me, and I believed: "Better, Mrs. Mike, to give medicine for sickness before than after. This way, when sickness come into baby, medicine is already there waiting."

So I took the scratched little bottle, which from its shape was probably once an iodine bottle in a prospector's first-aid kit, and I put it on the back of the shelf behind the salt and pepper and sugar.

179

"Sarah," I had asked her, "how do you know all these things?"

"Mrs. Mike, I know from my mother and from many old men and women who knew from before; I know from trying and mixing, myself; I know from the look of the plants; I know from things I am told when I sleep. You give your baby this now, she will have good stomach, good liver, she will never be sick. And you come yourself," looking at me critically, "come in January, and I start giving you squaw root. By the time your new baby comes, it will be quick and easy, like that!" And she brushed one hand swiftly against the other.

Therefore in January I dutifully walked down to the Carpentier's cabin on the lake and called for Sarah. She appeared at the entrance of a shed which ran along the south side of the cabin. She looked very tall and commanding. "Come up here," she said.

I had been down to her cabin only three or four times, and I had never been in the shed. I had never wanted to go into the shed.

Things grew and hung in that damp musty place that belonged at the bottom of swamps, under rocks, or in nightmares. From the door I could see thick, fleshy stems, slightly hairy, spread over a rack to dry. On the ground in front of me was a long-dead stump with strange warts on its dried-up roots and unhealthy-colored toadstools like shelves on the sides. One of the toadstools, thin and crumbling in its rottenness, was carefully supported by a network of string. Along the side of the shed was a long table, completely bare except for a dead muskrat pinned to the wood. The air was full of the smell of decay. Even the sunlight was transformed into a weird silvery light by the curtain of cobwebs which hung over the lattice. I shivered a little as I stepped into Sarah's workroom.

"Sit down, Mrs. Mike." She pulled a chair out of the shadow for me. I sat down, looking around me nervously. I wondered if I was imagining things moving in the dark corners.

"My plants," Sarah said. "Beaver oil for put beaver smell on trap, I sell to trappers. Rub on trap, lay trail on ground, fool wolf. Wolf not get man smell, get beaver smell, come

180

fall in trap. White trapper use musk, fish oil, other things, but beaver oil best."

I turned my head, and something curved and sharp swung against my cheek. It was a clawing foot with nails protruding. It hung from a buckskin thong.

"Nothing," Sarah said. "A lion's claw. When bad things grow in the body and swell it, it is good to hang this claw by the bed and pray to the maker-of-claws to tear out the evil."

She reached under the table and picked up a large tin can. She tilted it to show me the pale brown chunks it held.

"Touch it," she said. I touched. It was rubbery, yet soft. "I take plant, squeeze out milk, dry in sun, becomes like this—good for heart, good for liver, makes to cough." She pinched off a piece, swallowed it, and coughed, a dry sharp cough. She smiled broadly and offered the can to me. I shook my head.

"No, I don't feel like coughing," I said, trying to laugh. The next moment I jumped. Something had moved in the gray corner across from me. I couldn't see well. It was in the shadows, but it seemed about the size of a puppy, it hopped like a toad, and a hoarse cry came from it. Sarah picked up a large cardboard packing case and put it over the thing.

"Nothing, an animal," she smiled.

"Yes," I said.

"Mrs. Mike," she said, taking my hand, "never be frightened of things because of their looks. Ugly mud flower"—she tilted the can again—"make well the heart. Pretty root"—and this time she picked up a long curling tuber—"kill a man.

"You don't like this room," Sarah continued, "because she smell a lot, because she is dark, because these things in it not your friends. But I like smell, I like dark, and all things here my friends—even him." She reached out her heavy foot and gently touched the box. There was an answering thump from within, and again that cry. The animal under the box began moving around restlessly. Was it a beaver being prepared for an operation to remove the precious castoreum? Was it a monstrous toad whose withered skin was a prime ingredient in magic? I was afraid to think about it. I forced myself to look away.

"You told me to come, Sarah," I began.

"Yes, you think of your next baby. I have ready for you." She reached over the table and fumbled in an open cupboard. "Many hundred babies I am the first to see. And only one die. Every one I save with squaw root." She chuckled. "You take every day, and I tell you, when baby come you not even know it, no! Once I play good joke on Louis, my husband, I am near my time, big like vinegar barrel. I am cooking dinner. I say, 'Louis, we need wood!' He say, 'We have plenty.' I say, 'Louis, chop wood!' He look at me and shrug his shoulders. I turn my back, take big chew of squaw root. He pick up ax, walk out. Let me tell you, when he come back with split wood, there is twins in the bed, and I am back cooking dinner. But he is a man, he is blind, he sit down and eat. 'Coffee strong enough?' I say. He say, 'Yes.' Then both babies cry. He look around! *Sacre bleu!* he say French. He run to bed. Where they come from? He hit his head with both hands. It was good joke, Mrs. Mike, best joke I ever make."

Sarah handed me a little box made of bark. "You laugh now, Mrs. Mike?"

I smiled. The atmosphere of the place had changed. It was still a witch's den, but a den of white magic, sorcery that ended in a joke. I followed Sarah down the shed while she exhibited her treasures to me: bearberry leaves drying on a plank, starweed soaking in a bucket of water, peels of slippery elm bark stacked in a corner, stalks of trumpet weed crushed in a stone bowl. Here were remedies for sore throat, for rheumatism, for snake bite, for unreturned love, for headache, for a broken leg, for a balky horse, for bad hunting, for all the ills and addictions of man. Sarah's catalogue fascinated me so much that I forgot all about the wet cobwebs, the toadstool, and the animal under the box. Curiously I asked her if she had any deadly poisons.

"Much easier to kill than make well," she said. "Anyone can pick up rock, crush in head of a man. Take wise man to fix. I could go in wood, pick here, there, many poisons. What for? I don't need. In pot here under table I have a little bit musquash—beaver poison—I keep covered so dog won't eat. This grow in wood, and anything come along and eat, little by little legs get stiff, body get stiff, no move, no breathe, then die. Once I remember deer eat, but not much. Get all stiff, lie down, look like dead. Along come Indian boy, cut off hide of deer. Get deer three-quarters skinned, suddenly deer him wake up, deer run off—without skin, no—not this much!" Sarah spread out her hand.

"No!" I burst out. "That's horrible!"

"It happen. Musquash bad medicine."

"Good! I come for bad medicine." A woman stood in the doorway at the other end of the shed. She leaned forward in a half-crouch, taut and intent.

"What you want?" Sarah said harshly.

"I just come to talk," the woman said, and edged into the shed.

"I already tell you no, many times. What you want talk for?"

"I . . Mrs. Mike," the woman caught sight of me and raised her head. "How are you, Mrs. Mike? I am Mrs. Marlin. I just come by to talk," she added defensively.

"Mrs. Marlin!" I cried. "I've wanted to see you, to thank you."

"Thank me?"

"For my flowers. They were lovely."

She lifted a thin hand to her face and looked at me wonderingly. Mrs. Marlin had that fragile exotic beauty that comes of the mixing of many races. Her eyes were deep blue, yet the sockets they were set in were slightly slant. Perhaps a Russo-Chinese prospector had met the French-Indian *klooch* that was her great-grandmother, and touches of Scottish and Irish had been added since. There were faint echoes of all races in her beauty, and this made the whole in some way inharmonious. It was an alien loveliness that delighted the eye but disturbed the soul.

"Flowers?" he paused. "I remember. I planted garden for you, Mrs. Mike. It is pretty, no?"

I stood looking at her, trying to think of something to say.

"They die?" she said. Then, nodding her head. "They die. I knew. What I touch . . . it dies."

Sarah stepped forward. "You go now!"

Mrs. Marlin sat down stubbornly on the cardboard box.

The rustling inside began again, but she didn't appear to hear it.

"I think she wants to speak to you alone," I said to Sarah.

"She not belong here. You go!" Sarah shook the young woman roughly.

A heavy cloud passed over the sun, and it became suddenly dark in the shed.

Mrs. Marlin spoke in a sly simple way. "You make death medicine, give me."

"I have no death medicine," Sarah said. "Who you want kill?"

"No man . . . no woman," Mrs. Marlin crooned.

I leaned forward. Under the table my foot kicked an iron pot. Beaver poison? I remembered. Little by little the legs get stiff, the body gets stiff, you look like dead, then . . .

"Law get you if you kill. Redcoat get you." Sarah was saying.

"I no kill person . . . just . . ."

"Animal?"

Then, after a long pause, "I think I know who is this no-man-no-woman," Sarah said ironically. "No. You right. Law not get you. Redcoat not get you. Very easy . . . if I help." Slowly Sarah's large hand closed on the woman's shoulder. With a jerk she pulled her to her feet. "But . . . I not help!"

Mrs. Marlin shook herself free. "I ask you ten, twenty time," she said bitterly. "You not help, I do myself, with knife maybe, with this hand maybe . . ." And she held out her trembling right hand, the fingers clawing in a terrifying gesture.

They stood there facing each other, motionless, silent, eyes expressionless, a violent wordless battle going on between them. I saw Sarah's face fall slack, saw the heavy wrinkles in her cheeks deepen.

"Yes," she said at last, in a voice so low and husky that I could barely make out the words, "I give."

Mrs. Marlin said nothing. Her lips parted slightly and bared her clenched teeth, her eyes widened, and she turned the clawing hand palm up. That was all.

Sarah took a jug out of the cupboard, fished around for a

184

small bottle, and carefully poured a sticky black syrup from one to the other.

Mrs. Marlin seized the bottle and silently fled.

Sarah immediately lit a fire in the stove. After a few minutes she choked it down and covered the hot coals with a bunch of dried sweet grass. Thick white scented smoke poured out of the stove, and Sarah passed her hands through it again and again with a washing motion.

"What are you doing?" I asked.

"I make myself clean."

After a while she said, "You should know what this about, Mrs. Mike."

"I don't want to," I said. "I think I'd better go home. I don't feel very strong."

"Mrs. Mike," Sarah said gently.

"Well, I'm afraid for my baby," I said defiantly. "This has been a strain."

"Don't worry about your baby, Mrs. Mike. You love, you want to have, you will get. She too, that woman, will have child. But she hate, she don't want. She tell you herself, she want kill it. Kill it before it begin to live. Not one look does it get at world, at bright sun. No, not one yell does it make for show its own strength. No, into ground she put it, before it have one chance to walk on ground." Sarah stopped and added heavily, "Me, I help."

"No, you can't," I whispered. "Take back the medicine."

"Many times before, woman come ask me for to help kill baby. I say no. I bring maybe five hundred baby into light, only lose one. I not help kill them. All right. Two, two-three year ago, Indian woman come. Have some reason, not want baby. I say, no help. She go away. She do nothing. Just sit and hate child. Hate all day. Not sleep. Hate all night. Day come when child is born. She reach down to kill him, to choke him. Pull him out by head. Twist head. Break arm. Crush little fingers. Bend soft back. Old, old woman take away broken baby."

The cardboard box was moving. Sarah put her hand on it, to steady it. But the rustling inside continued.

"Old, old woman give me child. I keep. I try fix. But can't fix good."

For the first time I noticed the air holes punched in the

185

box. Then I understood. That's where she kept it, that broken, misshapen child. I watched, horrified, as the box rocked and swayed. I leaped up as it overturned.

The thing sat there. It was a giant frog, blinking at us. Sarah took advantage of its surprise and clapped the box over it again.

"What did you do with that baby?" I asked. I was shaking all over.

"The baby? Oh, him not live long." The good witch sighed. "Just as well, I not fix too good."

## CHAPTER EIGHTEEN

The big event of the winter was the Edmonton mail. I had a letter from Uncle John, and a letter from my mother, and a package that was marked DO NOT OPEN UNTIL XMAS. It was the first package I'd had from the outside since my marriage and, as Christmas was long past, I opened it. First I untied the string and put it in my string bag. Next I unwrapped the paper and put it in the cupboard. Then, when I couldn't draw out the excitement any longer, I permitted myself to look into the box. Out came handfuls of corrugated cardboard padding, and something at the bottom flashed. It was a mirror—the size of a baking pan, with a Boston label pasted on the back, and my face smiling up at me in front. I could hardly recognize myself. The face in the glass was my mother's, younger and stronger perhaps, but not at all like that of the skinny child who had come to Calgary for her pleurisy. In the box was a little note: "My darling, Merry Christmas and a Happy New Year to you both, Mother."

I opened my mother's letter.

She wrote of many things: her new curtains, the hot summer, the coat she had had remodeled, the scarcity of eggs, the mysterious disappearance of two good silver spoons, the bronchitis my sister had in August, the trouble her stove was giving her, and the way Boston was getting dustier all the time. She didn't say she missed me, she didn't say how badly she wanted to see me; but I felt it, and in all the chatter about eggs and spoons I saw my beautiful mother standing in the doorway waiting for a girl who would not come, who was raising her own family in a cabin four thousand miles away. As I read, my life in the North wavered and flickered. It seemed to me that it was a wild dream, with all the inconsequence and crowded incident of a dream. My mother and our home were suddenly so real and present to me that I almost heard the clatter and roar of traffic in the streets of Boston.

Mary Aroon wailed, and Boston vanished.

To almost every cabin of Grouard the winter mail brought a warm breath of the civilization south of us. Mike had a circular from Winnipeg warning against an epidemic of smallpox moving east from British Columbia. Along with it came a case of vaccine which he was to put in cold storage until further notice. Louis Carpentier got a package of dried dates from his cousin in California. Mrs. Marlin received a check from her late husband's family. Old Irish Bill received six months' issues of the *London Mathematical Gazette*. There was a postcard for Baldy Red threatening him with half a dozen kinds of destruction if he should ever show his face in Edmonton again. It was signed "Emily." And there was a heavily sealed letter for Mr. James McTavish informing him that he was an earl and peer of Scotland.

The McTavish brothers lived in a tiny cabin down by the lake. They were extremely poor and unlucky. If James McTavish went fishing in the lake, the other boats put in to shore; no fish would bite that morning. If Allan McTavish trapped a rabbit, it would be sick; if he shot a moose, it would rise and charge when he came up to it. Their credit at the store was good, but their accounts were always on the debit side of the ledger. An amazing piece of good fortune like an earldom could not fall to *our* McTavishes. We were all sure it was a mistake.

But Mike examined the papers with the stunned brothers, and when he came home that night he told me it was true.

"James McTavish is an earl, all right, Kathy. And he's the owner of a castle and a whole village in Scotland."

"Lord McTavish," I said. "Somehow I can't picture it."

"It took a remarkable number of deaths," Mike said,

187

grinning, "but one way or the other all the other heirs are gone, and only James McTavish and his brother are left."

"And what is Allan, now that James is an earl?"

"Why, just the younger brother of an earl. That's all."

We both laughed. Allan would never get used to that. He was the younger brother in fact, but not in spirit. In the early days the brothers had taken turns at trapping and housekeeping. One did the hunting, the other cured the skins; one caught fish, the other cooked them; one drove the sled, the other mended the harness. Gradually James McTavish began to shift the active labor to his brother's shoulders while he sat home with his books and his pipes and his domestic duties. True Scot, he kept his house as neat as a pin, and there were even some who called the little man Mrs. McTavish behind his back. Now he was an earl, and his domineering athletic brother was only an earl's younger brother. It wouldn't last that way. We all knew it.

In the morning the brothers called on me to say good-by. They were leaving for Edmonton immediately, thence to Winnipeg, Montreal, Liverpool, Edinburgh, and their earldom.

James showed me a threadbare plaid skirt, carefully patched. "The tartan of the clan," he said. "I expect to wear it at the ceremony."

"What ceremony?" I said.

"They will ask me to take an oath of loyalty to the king, I have no doubt."

"Not in that rag, Jamie," said his brother. "It's not fitting for an earl to have patches in his pants."

"I'm not ashamed of honest poverty," James replied stubbornly.

"You're not poor," Allan went on. "You're the owner of a castle and a mountain and a glen and a village." He turned to me with a worried expression. "We've been racking our brains, Mrs. Flannigan, trying to figure what that comes to. Ten thousand pounds, would you say?"

"I don't see how I can possibly guess unless I know how big the mountain is, and how many houses are in the village, and I'm not even sure what a glen is," I answered helplessly.

"Mrs. Flannigan," Allan said, "the letter said there was a

188

castle. Not a cabin, mind you, which is one room, or a house, which is three to ten rooms, but a castle, that's at least fifty rooms. Now, a fifty-room castle is a valuable piece of property."

"There are castles in Scotland," James said sourly, "which are just rocks falling into the road. The rats wouldn't give you three cents for the lot." He grimaced. "I have a feeling it's just such a castle we've got."

"Fine talk for a new-crowned earl!" his brother stormed. "And the mountain and the glen? What of the mountain and the glen?"

James smoothed the worn tartan with his dry, spare, hand. "A mountain and a glen! And who is to buy a mountain and a glen? What market is there for mountains? A mountain is worth that—" He snapped his fingers. "This is no mountain such as are in the Yukon, full of silver and gold. It's a Scottish mountain, full of furze and wild goats. That's the kind of mountain we've got!"

"But a village, Mr. McTavish," I interrupted. "A whole village full of people is worth something!"

"That's what I tell him, morning, noon, and night," Allan said.

"Precisely what *is* it worth?" James said. "Am I to sell the people? Mrs. Flannigan, a Scottish village is a liability. School, church, poorhouse, infirmary—money out of my pocket, that's all; money out of my pocket."

"Ridiculous!" Allan said.

"You'll see, Allan. That's all this village will be, money out of my pocket." Lord James McTavish shook his head dolefully.

I was half-convinced. "Maybe it isn't such a good thing to become an earl," I said.

"There have been earls of Scotland, leaders of a thousand men, so poor a bowl of porridge was food for the day," James said emphatically.

"Mr. McTavish," I said, "maybe it would be better if you didn't go."

"My duty, Mrs. Flannigan, my duty to the clan."

Allan broke in with a roar. "It's all a lot of nonsense! He has every intention of going. Do you know what it's all about, Mrs. Flannigan? It's all about that miserable tartan. Fifteen dollars I want him to spend for a new one in Montreal, that's all, and he says he can't afford it."

"I have no the money!" James said.

"What about the old coffeepot?"

"There's nothing in the old coffeepot but twenty dollars to bury us when we die."

"We'll be earls before that! You'll have enough money to bury yourself twenty times over." Allan furiously snatched the plaid from James's hand and thrust it at me. "Look, Mrs. Flannigan, the earl's dress, with a mark on the seat of the pants they'll see as far as London!"

In truth, it was badly patched. The material was the same, but the stitches were large and loose, and the stripes weren't lined up right. I looked at James McTavish, but he only looked down at his feet and muttered, "I have no the money."

So it came about that I patched the tartan of an earl and lord of Scotland and sent him off to his coronation.

I was giving Mary Aroon a bath, and it was quite a job. Oh-Be-Joyful poured in the third kettleful of water. I tested it with my elbow. Mary Aroon sat and watched the whole process. She knew all this preparation was for her bath. And it pleased her to see her big giants running around like this. When I finally decided the water was the right temperature, I lifted her in. She laughed and chortled and waved her little fists. She loved her bath, as she always had an audience. Today it was Oh-Be-Joyful who leaned over the tub and swirled the water around in exciting ripples and splashes that made Mary Aroon gasp and gabble in that unknown tongue of hers. She was a plump, healthy baby who kicked her legs at you with energy. Her little back was strong now, and she sat in the tub by herself, my hands an inch away but not touching her.

She was in the midst of her bath when an Indian threw open the door, letting in cold drafts of air.

"Shut the door!" I yelled. But he didn't, so I jumped up myself and slammed it to.

"Sergeant Mike, Sergeant Mike!" the Indian said in a voice of terror.

"At the office."

"Him not there." The man opened the door.

"What is it?" I cried.

"Larry Carpentier, him in bear trap!" He was gone, the snow closing around him and covering even his tracks. I sat down slowly.

Larry, Sarah's boy! They'd be taking him to her cabin. Oh-Be-Joyful lifted Mary Aroon from the tub and wrapped her in a blanket. She came to me holding the baby.

"You go?" she asked.

"Yes." I got into my furs, my fingers working automatically at the buttonholes.

"You think him hurt bad?" Oh-Be-Joyful asked.

"I don't know. Get the baby dressed, Oh-Be-Joyful. Feed her at four."

I walked on snowshoes out into the white crisp world. The sky was a pale winter one. The trees were hung with frost lace. Icicles like sharp daggers pointed down at me. I tried to hurry, but the snow was so soft I was afraid of floundering.

Poor Sarah, Seventeen children, six raised, and now this! A bear trap. They had them at the Company store. Terrible things. Two sets of steel jaws with teeth six inches long that interlocked, that bit in, that mangled. I tried not to think of Larry, of anybody, even a bear, walking into the pan, the flat part of the trap where the powerful springs are concealed. Forty pounds they weighed, the ones in the store. I shivered inside my buffalo jacket seeing the jagged jaws closing on the flesh and bone of Larry Carpentier. Funny, too. It wasn't the season for bears. It must have been an old trap someone set and forgot, or couldn't find.

And it had to be Sarah's son. Big strong Sarah, her back was used to bending under troubles. And Larry. It seemed to me that Sarah spoke more of Larry than of the others. He was a mild-mannered young man of twenty-five. He caught wild horses up in the Yellow Pass and bred the strongest sled dogs in the North. He had a well-stocked barn, and cattle. In the summer the trappers bought the fruit he raised, especially plums and strawberries.

The smoke of the Carpentier cabin darkened the sky in front of me. A scream, a terrible scream came from inside,

191

then another. I tried to undo my snowshoes. My hands trembled. The mittens were stiff with ice. Again the screaming. A man's screams are terrible. With my heart beating so it choked me, I pushed open the door and stood, staring.

Larry lay on the table, and all his blood seemed to be beside him. From his foot to his knee, he was held by a rusted steel trap, the teeth of which clamped together, cutting entirely through the leg in thirty different places.

"Water," Sarah said, without turning around. "Boil it."

I couldn't move because then I saw what she held in her hands. It was a saw. She raised it. Larry's eyes followed the motion. She set the saw in the groove she had already made in the flesh above the knee. Back and forth. I saw the sweat break on the boy's face. I heard the crunching of the leg bone. Again the screams. The terrible agony of his screams.

"Water," Sarah said.

I moved forward. I pumped, I filled a kettle. I lifted it to the stove. The cries drew me back. His nails dug long furrows in the wood of the table. His dark eyes rolled back under his lids, leaving white, unseeing holes. The smooth muscles moved in Sarah's arms. Back and forth, back and forth. The trap bumped and clanged against the table. Sarah's strong man's hand pressed the saw's teeth deeper into the wound. It quivered, it quivered like jelly. A strange laughter stirred me. Mother and child, I thought. Mother and child. Then Sarah began hacking. The bone chipped and splintered. I looked at her face, at the clamped lips! I looked at her hands. I thought, how can she do it! I looked again at her face, relentless and calm. Then I understood. Sarah had gone mad. The good witch was evil. Her boy lay under her hands, twisting, screaming, while she hacked at him calmly with a saw. I stared at a flap of hanging flesh. It grew, it grew until it covered the whole room and had wrapped me in its soft bloody folds. The color deepened. It turned black, but I knew it was still blood. The screams faded, receded, became a buzzing that finally turned into a voice. It was a voice I knew, that I had hear before. I felt comforted. I wanted to understand the words, that came over and over again. It was my name, "Mrs. Flannigan."

I opened my eyes and looked into the face of Bishop

Grouard. I struggled to get up, but his firm hand on my shoulder kept me down.

"You're all right, my dear. Easy now. That's it."

I raised myself slowly into a sitting position, and he propped a pillow behind me. There were no more screams. Only a low moaning came from the boy on the table. For he still lay there, and beside him lay his leg.

Mike stood over him with the saw in his hand. As I watched, he lowered it, wiped his face with the arm of his jacket, and turned to Sarah.

"It's off."

Sarah nodded, dabbed at the stump with water, cleaning and washing. Then she wrapped it in a steaming flannel poultice which she clamped into place.

Mike walked up to the head of the table and put his hand on the boy's shoulder. "You'll be all right now, Larry." Larry tried to speak, his face convulsed with the effort, but no words came.

Mike made a shrewd guess. "Don't worry about a thing. I'll look after your stock until you're up and around." The boy sighed. His face relaxed. Mike moved softly away. "Don't worry," he said to Sarah in an undertone.

Sarah was heating another poultice and measuring clear drops of fluid into a dish filled with something that looked like mustard. She nodded when Mike spoke to her, but did not look up from her work. Poor Sarah. My heart overflowed for her. I hadn't been any help to her. Not any. What strength was in her, in her hands and in her soul! I was ashamed. Not for having fainted, but for having been mad myself, and I must have been, to have had such thoughts about her.

Mike walked over to me and helped me to my feet. The Bishop rose too, and the three of us went out together. We buckled on our snowshoes silently, without looking at each other. We had gone maybe a quarter of a mile, when Bishop Grouard said, "A wonderful woman. A heroic woman."

"Amazing strength," Mike said. "That leg bone was really hanging by shreds when I took over."

"Where were you?" I asked.

"Out on line inspection. The telegraph was on the blink

most of last winter. I want it open the year round, and I thought if I kept check on the wires . . ." His voice trailed off, and we walked in silence.

"You mustn't worry, Mrs. Flannigan," the Bishop said. "We'll take care of them. We'll see that Mrs. Carpentier has a hot supper tonight, and Larry too, if he's ready for it. And for as many nights as there's need."

"Oh, no. I want to do that for Sarah. I *want* to. She saved my life."

"Sorry, but I'm going to be stubborn about it, Mrs. Flannigan. You see, we cook *en masse* up at the Mission, and another dish or two to fill is nothing."

I didn't say anything. I didn't even thank him. He must have seen that I was crying, because he said, "We'll have him up and about. I feel confident of that. So confident that I'm starting to work on a wooden leg."

Mike shook his head. "I don't know. He's weak, to say nothing of shock. Must have been a couple of days in that trap before they found him. He'd started up to the Yellow Pass about a week ago. So no one missed him at this end. In fact, I didn't expect to see him for a couple of months.

"The way the Indians found him, they heard a gun go off and went to investigate. Larry was lying there, shooting into the bush. He said he was being attacked by a lion. But there were no tracks. He must have been delirious by that time. His leg was already turning black and gangrenous. The Indians tried to pry open the trap, but it was old and rusted. They thought from the condition of the thing that it had been set a couple of years ago and lost. That sometimes happens. They're so cleverly hidden. Anyway, they wrenched and pulled and jiggled at it until Larry passed out. That scared them, and they decided just to bring him in as fast as they could, trap and all. Which was probably the smartest thing they could have done, because they had no disinfectant, no way of stopping the bleeding even. So they brought him in, and it wasn't too tough on him because the leg was partially frozen. They brought him to my office first, and when they couldn't find me, they took him home. His mother saw at a glance that the leg was past saving. So she did the smart thing, the thing one in a million could do.

194

She cut it off. She made a clean job of it too, and if anyone can pull him through, it's Sarah."

I knew Mike was right, of course, and no one had more faith in Sarah than I had. But I couldn't see how that boy could live with that poor mangled leg—and the blood that had poured out of him.

"Has a man ever been caught in one of those traps before?"

Bishop Grouard sighed. "Plenty of times, my dear, plenty of times. Fifty or a hundred years ago the English designed a man-trap twice the size of this one, with teeth nineteen inches long and weighing about ninety pounds. It was used on large estates to catch poachers."

I held onto Mike's arm. "Did they—did they always die?"

"Usually. At least they were always maimed and crippled to such an extent that future poaching became impossible, and that's what the owners of the estates were interested in."

Things moved. A gray rabbit hid behind a bush, the clouds blew into each other in their hurry, and the collision was without sound. We ourselves moved noiselessly along. Everything was smothered and blanketed by the snow. The only sound I could remember was the low moaning in the cabin we had just left.

Thinking of Sarah's child brought to my mind the picture of Mary Aroon as I had left her, kicking her plump little legs in the bath water. I remembered how those legs waved in the air and danced. Then I thought of taking a saw . . . No, I couldn't. Not even to save her life, I couldn't. And I knew I was not the woman Sarah was. And not the mother, either.

"Kathy, what is it?"

"Nothing, Mike." I smiled at him, but I guess the smile wasn't much of a success because he wrapped a big fur arm tightly around me.

When we came to our house, I asked the Bishop in, but he shook his head and held out a fur mitten to us. "It was good of you, Sergeant, to put the boy's mind at rest, but just the same you've cut out a job for yourself, looking after the stock."

"All in the line of duty. Article 37, Section C, in the

195

Mounties' *Handbook of Regulations*. Anyway, you're the one that's taken on the big job . . . making him a wooden leg. Are you really going to do it yourself, Bishop?"

"Oh, yes. All in the line of duty. See the Gospel according to St. Matthew, Chapter 25, Verse 40." Bishop Grouard smiled at us and walked on.

"He's a fine man," Mike said, looking after the snow-encrusted figure of the old man.

That night, when the supper things were cleared away and Mike was out tending to Larry's stock, I got down the book of *Regulations* Mike had referred to. I thumbed through it carefully and then shut it with a smile. There was no Article 37, Section C.

I peeped in at Mary Aroon. She was sound asleep, and that was good because there was still another book I wanted to look in. I got out the Bible and opened it. There *was* a Chapter 25 in the Gospel of St. Matthew, and at Verse 40, I read:

"Inasmuch as ye have done it unto one of the least of these my brethren, ye have done it unto me."

## CHAPTER NINETEEN

We owned half a cow. Larry tried to give us the whole cow, but Mike wouldn't hear of it. After an hour's arguing in which Larry threatened to take off his new leg and hit Mike over the head with it, they finally settled on half a cow. The cow gave ten quarts of milk a day, and five belonged to us. Mike insisted that I drink a glass at each meal, and one before I went to bed, while I was carrying the baby. I think he bullied me a lot because whatever he wanted me to do was somehow tied up with the good of the baby, and of course he'd get his way.

By the middle of May, Larry was quite comfortable on his wooden leg, and whenever I went over to his barn to milk Bessie, he was there, hopping around, grinning, stroking Bessie's head, and telling me wild stories about her: how in the icy winter of 1907 her milk froze in the pail, and he carried it home in a piece of paper or a pan.

196

One day I invented a game for the walk home. The object was to see how far I could swing the milk pail without spilling a single drop. But as I came within sight of the house, I saw a strange Indian sitting on my porch. I changed the pail to my other hand and walked on slowly to meet the trouble I was sure he brought. He stood up when he saw me.

"Sergeant Mike?"

"He's not here."

"Big trouble. Must find."

I set the pail down. "What *is* the trouble?" I asked.

"Must find Sergeant Mike quick."

I saw there was nothing more to be got out of this fellow, so I gave in. "He's at the reserve. I'll take you."

"Me find." He walked down the steps.

"I'm going with you," I said firmly.

I looked at him out of the corner of my eye as we walked. He had the light springing step of the woodsman and the keen eyes that noted automatically how soft the ground was and how old the rabbit tracks.

"Where are you from?" I asked.

He pointed in a northerly direction.

"What tribe?"

"Blackfeet."

"That's a long way away. Sergeant Mike has no authority over the people of the Blackfeet. You must have a sergeant of your own."

The man grunted. I thought a while. We had heard that there was smallpox among some of the tribes. In fact, that's what Mike was doing today, vaccinating the whole Indian Reserve.

"Have you sickness?" I asked.

"No sickness," the Indian replied.

He's probably lying, I thought. They've sent him for help, and he's afraid to tell me. Well, if it was sickness, Mike wasn't going. I wouldn't let him.

"Sergeant Mike's not a doctor," I said. The Indian said nothing.

We walked in an unfriendly silence to the reserve. I noticed as we approached that the village was awfully quiet. There were no children playing in front of the tepees. There

197

were no old men squatting in the doorways smoking. No women's voices calling, laughing. No sound of loom or kettle, nothing. It was a dead village.

I looked into the tepees, throwing back the heavy entrance skins. Nothing, no one. But things looked natural, as though they had been left but a moment before. The fires were not out, needlework was left upon the floor, dogs bristled and growled at us. I opened the doors of the cabins, but again everything was deserted.

The Indian peered over my shoulder. He was evidently frightened, for he fingered the charm pouch around his neck, and his eyes rolled nervously. He must have thought the entire tribe had been spirited away by Gitche Manito. And even so, his deductions were more positive than mine because I simply didn't know what to think.

I was wondering where Mike was. I peered into the shadowy forest that crept up to the edge of the village, and I distinctly saw a face watching us from behind a bush. Was it a child playing a game? It couldn't be. This face was lined, was old. As I looked, the bush trembled and the face disappeared. I stared into the woods.

Dark shapes glided like spirits among the trees. And though there was no wind, bushes and leaves rustled in the strangest manner. The Blackfoot at my side was walking very close to me and casting terrified glances at the shadow shapes.

I felt eyes on us, many eyes, the eyes of the village. I was walking fast now, as fast as I could without running. Suddenly I heard a welcome sound. A baby was crying. The noise that came from somewhere in front of us was not a spirit wail, but the wail of a very real human baby, bawling at the top of its lungs. I turned toward the sound, into the woods; and there, behind the last tepee, was Mike. Beside him sat the crying baby, and three feet in front of them was the mother.

Between Mike and the young mother was a large jagged boulder. Mike was talking to the woman, and as he talked he slowly circled the boulder toward her, and she just as slowly circled away from him. It took them five minutes to complete the circuit, and all the while Mike kept up a steady one-sided conversation. The woman stared at him with large black eyes, not at his face, but at his hands. I looked too and saw that in one hand he held a small glass tube and a piece of cotton. In the other he clutched a shining scalpel which he pointed straight at the young woman. I didn't blame her for backing away, and I didn't blame her for not listening to Mike's soft words.

"It won't hurt," he was saying. "It won't hurt you at all. It's good medicine."

And all the time the sharp, wicked-looking blade chasing her slowly around the rock. Suddenly Mike stopped circling. The girl stopped too. Mike smiled reassuringly at her from his side of the rock. The young woman watched him warily, trying to determine what that smile meant. She reached her conclusion a moment too late, for Mike took a running jump onto the rock and dived off the other side on top of her. As they went down, I heard him pant, "This won't hurt . . ."

He had her pinned flat with his knees and arms. All she could do was roll from side to side and bite when his hand got close enough. His knife scraped on her upper arm. She yelled and screamed and tried to draw away from the uncorked vial, but in spite of her wriggling, Mike managed to get most of the fluid into the scraped place. When she saw he had succeeded, the woman's screams redoubled.

Mike got up from on top of her and removed his cap. "I'm sorry," he said, "but everybody's got to be vaccinated. It's orders."

The young woman rocked back and forth, holding her arm. Her baby had stopped its crying to listen to hers. And the baby was not the only spectator. Curiosity had brought the distant shadow shapes in closer.

Mike carefully wiped the scalpel and walked to a tree stump on which his supplies were laid out. He selected another tube and tore off a fresh hunk of cotton.

"Who's next?" he asked, looking into a bush that shook nervously.

"Come on out, Johnny, you're a brave boy. There's nothing to this. It won't hurt." Mike advanced slowly on the bush. Two bright eyes watched not him but the gleaming knife and the mysterious glass bottle. Mike pounced, but Johnny was quicker. He bolted from under the bush and dashed into the forest, paused at a safe distance, and looked to see if he were being followed. He was. Mike decided to use psychology. He put the scalpel and the glass tube behind his back.

"Johnny, Johnny," he coaxed.

I could see he wasn't going to get anywhere with Johnny, so I called to him.

"Kathy," he said, coming toward me, "what are you doing here?" And then excitedly, "Darling, I'm so glad you've come."

"Why?" I asked suspiciously, for I didn't like the way he was brandishing that scalpel.

"Why, now I can vaccinate you, and they'll see there's nothing to it. They just cry from fear."

"They do? Well, I'd like to oblige you, Mike, but you see I've already been vaccinated."

"Oh." And then his face brightened. "How long ago?"

"Well, I don't know exactly. Why?"

"If it's more than seven years, you need a new vaccination," and he started uncorking that little glass vial.

"Oh, no," I said hurriedly. "It wasn't that long ago. It was just recently. Just before I came out to Uncle John's."

"I thought you didn't remember when it was."

"Well," I said, "I remember now."

Mike put the cork back grudgingly, then his eye lighted on the Blackfoot. He smiled at him ingratiatingly.

"Now, there's nothing to this, nothing at all."

"Mike," I said, "you can't. He's not your Indian. I mean, he's a Blackfoot."

The word caught Mike's attention, and the Indian was saved.

"Blackfoot," Mike repeated, and looked at the man with interest.

The conversation that took place between them I couldn't follow. It was in a dialect I didn't understand, but every now and then I caught a Cree word. And then I caught a word that meant something more to me. The word was "Cardinal," and what it meant was trouble.

Mike put an arm around me. "Well, Kathy, I'll be leaving as soon as we can get me packed up."

"Oh, no, Mike."

"I'm afraid so, darling."

"But why?" I said, hanging onto him. "Is it on account of that Cardinal?"

"Yes." Mike started packing up the vials.

"You should have put him in jail when I told you. What's he done now?"

"Same thing."

We started back through the still-deserted village, the Indian following us.

"Trap robbing?" I asked.

"Yes. A refinement of it. He substitutes poor fur for good."

"Are you going to arrest him?"

"Yes. This time I've got all the evidence I need against him."

"But why can't Constable Cameron arrest him?"

"He's got to stay here and vaccinate these people." There was grim satisfaction in Mike's voice. "If he can."

"I don't see why you don't finish vaccinating and let Cameron bring him in."

"Because," said Mike, "if I were betting on who'd outsmart who, I'd bet on Cardinal."

I sort of agreed with Mike, although I didn't say so.

When we got to the house I had Oh-Be-Joyful feed the Blackfoot while I got Mike's supplies together. Tins of beef and tea and another pair of mittens, an extra buffalo robe, for he was going into the Far North.

I walked out front and watched Mike strap the things to his horse. He would ride to Peace River Crossing, pick up another Mounty there, and make the rest of the trip north by canoe.

"When will you be back, Mike?"

Mike cursed under his breath at a slip knot that for some reason didn't slip. "Two months, Kathy, for sure."

I reached out a hand and steadied myself against the porch rail.

"I'll put in a few more tins," I said and went into the house.

Oh-Be-Joyful was washing dishes in the kitchen, so I closed the door of the storage room behind me. I looked up at the rows of cans, trying to select those that would be most nutritious. But the bright labels blurred and swam in muddy colors before my eyes. I leaned my head against the edge of the shelf and cried silently.

Months didn't mean anything to him. He'd said it just like that . . . "I'll be away two months." He was going because he wanted to, because it was adventure. He didn't think about me, about us, that it wasn't so easy to have a baby, that maybe I'd be dead even.

"Mike," I said his name out loud, "Mike, don't you love me any more? Don't you care that I'll be alone, that I'm scared?"

I dried my eyes with the hem of my skirt. I had to be getting back. He'd be wondering why I was so long. I took down three more tins of beef, some soup, and more tea. "He's a man," I told the girl in the sunbonnet on the box of tea. "He hasn't even thought about it yet. It hasn't occurred to him. He'll feel awful when he remembers. He loves me." The girl on the label kept smiling. "He loves me," I said again and began to cry.

"Kathy!" It was Mike calling. I rubbed my tears away and took a deep breath before I answered him.

"Here I am," I called, "in the pantry."

I listened to his steps as he crossed the kitchen, and I couldn't help smiling a little because he's such a big man.

He opened the door. "What are you doing in here, kitten?"

"Getting more food. It would be awful if you ran short."

"Darling . . ."

"Yes, Mike?"

He reached out his arms to me. When he was through kissing me, I still stayed there with my head against the red of his jacket.

"Kathy, if you don't want me to go, I won't."

"Really, Mike."

"Of course, really."

I reached up my arms and slid them around his neck. "No, I don't trust Cameron to bring him in. You have to do it yourself, Mike."

202

Mike held me very tight. "Kathy."

"Of course," I said, "you're his superior. If he fails, the blame is on you."

"Remember the other time, Kathy?" He was speaking very softly, his lips against my hair. "Remember I promised you you wouldn't have the baby on the trail?"

I nodded.

"Well, I'm going to promise you something this time. I'll be with you. I'll be back. If I wasn't sure that I would be, nothing could drag me away from you now, understand?"

"Oh, Mike."

"In the meantime, Oh-Be-Joyful will be with you. And in case you or Mary Aroon is sick, there's always Sarah, thank God. We've very good friends here, Kathy. Don't be afraid to go to them."

"Mike, it's just you I'm worrying about. Be careful."

"Listen, girl. Don't come out. It's no good standing and watching a man ride off. It gives you a lonesome feeling."

I was glad Mike said that because I hated the idea of seeing him swallowed up by the outdoors. Here in my own house I could pretend that he hadn't really gone. I closed my eyes and lifted my face.

"You're beautiful," Mike said.

"You never used to say that before we were married."

"Well, you weren't beautiful then. You were too skinny, and had too many sharp places, elbows and things."

"What things?" I asked.

He laughed and seized me. "But you're beautiful now. Ever since the baby, you're softer and lovelier all over."

His mouth was warm and rough and wonderful. Then he pushed me away from him, looked at me, and drew me back again by the shoulders. This time he gave me a big brother hug that meant, "Be good, Minx, take care of yourself."

I knew he was going now, but I wouldn't let him, not just yet, just a minute more.

"Mike," I said, "will you still love me if I say something?"

"What?" he asked.

"Damn Cardinal!" And bless Mike, I said. Only not out loud, because men don't like that kind of thing.

He smiled at me with those blue eyes and ruffled my hair with those big hands. Then the pantry door banged to, and I was alone.

Mike kept his promise. He was back in six weeks, with Cardinal riding beside him, the same dirty yellow handkerchief knotted around his neck.

That first evening was a happy one. I'd fed Mike a big dinner. After such a trip I felt that even our criminal deserved a real meal, so I sent Constable Cameron over to the jail with a supper for Cardinal.

Mike sat in the big arm chair with Mary Aroon on his lap. I curled up on a buffalo robe with my head on his knee. Mary Aroon began to laugh, for Mike was making shadow pictures on the wall for her. He made a rabbit that wiggled its ears, and he made a billy goat that wiggled its long beard.

"Tell me how it was, Mike."

"How what was?" And he made a little old woman with a pack on her back.

"About how you captured him," I said.

"Oh, that. I just went up to his shack."

"Did you have to do any fighting or shooting?"

"No; he saw me coming and beat it. But he didn't go far. I heard him walking around the cabin that night. And in the morning I saw the tracks he'd made. There was still a thin layer of snow up there. Well, there was a night and two whole days that he stayed out with no food and no blanket. But the second night he called to me through the window."

"What did he say?"

"He said if I didn't go away he was going to shoot me and then burn down the house. I asked him, 'What about the buttons?' And he yelled in, 'What about them?'

" 'Well,' I said 'they won't burn, and if there's a button left, or a tooth or any part of a bone, you'll hang. Because everybody in Grouard knows I came to bring you in.'

"He didn't say anything, so I figured he was thinking that over. I fanned up the fire nice and bright and put on a kettle of tea. As I did it, I was thinking what a good target I made. When the water started boiling, I walked out on the porch and looked into the darkness where he'd been talking. I couldn't see a thing, but I talked as though he was right close by that first pine. 'Come on in, Cardinal, and have some tea. We'll talk it over.' And he did. He stepped out from behind that pine.

"'You're right, Sergeant, about those damn buttons,' he said.

"'Yes,' I said, 'I guess I am.'

"So we had tea and after a while dinner, and then sat around the rest of the evening. That's all. In the morning we started home."

Mike crossed his legs and slid Mary Aroon along them until she was sitting on his foot. He held her tiny hands in his big one.

"Now we're going for a ride." He swung his foot out and back very gently, out and back, and began to chant, "This is the way the ladies go, nimety-pin, nimety-pin." And then, swinging his leg with more force, "This is the way the gentlemen go, gallopy-trot, gallopy-trot." By the time he got to how the farmers go hobbly-hoy, he was wiggling his foot all over, and Mary Aroon was bouncing around as though she were riding a bucking bronco. She shrieked and yelled her delight and got red in the face from excitement.

Mike stood up and lifted her into the air. "Now you're flying," he said.

Just then the door burst open, and Cameron stumbled in. "He's dead!"

The shout brought Oh-Be-Joyful from the kitchen. We all stared at the man.

"Murdered! There's a hunting knife stuck clear through his throat."

"Just a minute," Mike said. "Who's dead?"

"Cardinal. That's what I'm telling you. I walked down there with his dinner, and he's sitting on the bench with his head thrown back against the bars. I thought he was sleeping. But when I got close, I see he's been stuck right through the throat. What a mess! And the knife still in him."

Mike got into his jacket.

"You should have seen it," Cameron said to me. "He was laughing. His mouth's wide open in a kind of twisted laugh."

"Laughing?" Mike said, and then, "You said it was a hunting knife. Have you ever seen it before? Do you know whose it is?"

205

"It's got Jonathan Forquet all over it, plain as though it was written."

"What do you mean?"

"The handle's all carved up. A whole hunting scene winding along. It's Jonathan's work, all right. You know he can't keep from whittling. He cuts designs in everything he owns."

"All right," Mike snapped and gave a quick look at Oh-Be-Joyful. "Let's not jump at conclusions." He started for the door and then turned back to us.

"Oh-Be-Joyful, I want you to think hard and answer me truthfully. Have you ever seen a hunting knife such as the Constable describes in Jonathan's possession?"

Oh-Be-Joyful stared straight in front of her. "No," she said.

"There's plenty of people around here can identify Jonathan's work," Cameron said.

Mike opened the door. "Come on, we'll take a look at things."

Oh-Be-Joyful continued to stare at nothing long after they had gone.

"Jonathan didn't do it," I said. "He wouldn't kill a defenseless man." But I knew that by tribal law Jonathan had the right. "Besides, he's too clever to leave his knife there." But at the same time I thought: Isn't that just like Jonathan to boast silently with a knife, to leave it as a taunt? I tried to reason myself away from the thought. I reasoned out loud to Oh-Be-Joyful.

"Even if it is his knife, that doesn't mean anything. Everyone knew of his quarrel with Cardinal. They'd know he'd come under suspicion. So they'd steal his knife and leave it at the scene of the crime."

I thought myself that that conclusion was a little weak. It would be no easy matter to steal from Jonathan.

Oh-Be-Joyful said suddenly, "When they bring the knife, it will be Jonathan's."

I looked at the girl. She stared through the walls of my house. Across a mile of grassy path she stared into the cage. The cage was before my own eyes too. The last time I had been in it was when Baldy occupied it. I shuddered to think that through those bars, the bars I had so often slipped between, a killer had struck. I remembered Cameron's voice. "Through the throat," he'd said. "Clear through the throat."

"Jonathan didn't do it," I said again, and this time with conviction. Because the picture wouldn't come. I could put the knife in Jonathan's hand, I could even raise it, but I couldn't make him stick it in. Not Jonathan. A shadowy deformed shape took over at that point.

"If he did," Oh-Be-Joyful said, "if he did do it—" She had to stop. "If he did," she said again, "they would put him in jail forever?"

"But he didn't do it," I said.

"He didn't do it," she repeated after me. Saying the words out loud like that helped her believe them.

I was not surprised that, when Mike and Cameron returned, Jonathan walked between them. The three men entered without a word. Mike took off his jacket and flung it over a chair. All eyes watched his movements.

"Well," he said, "it's got to be talked out."

"You've got it," Cameron said.

Mike reached into his pocket and brought out a carefully wrapped object. He held the paper by a loose edge, and the weight of the knife brought it tumbling out of the wrapping onto the table. I stared at it. The blade was clean now, but a dark spot stained the head of the stag that ran around the handle. In fact, I noticed with a shiver that it stained the stag's throat.

"Oh-Be-Joyful," Cameron said, "look at the knife."

So that was why they'd brought Jonathan here instead of to the office. They meant to work on him through Oh-Be-Joyful.

"Look at the knife," Cameron said again.

Oh-Be-Joyful looked first at Jonathan. But he made no move, gave no hint. Her eyes traveled slowly, unwillingly to the knife, then back to Jonathan.

"Well, it's his, isn't it?" Cameron asked.

She looked beseechingly at Jonathan, but he only smiled at her. She turned to me. "Mrs. Mike!"

I stepped up and put my arm around her. "It's all right, Oh-Be-Joyful." I looked defiantly at Mike. "You don't have to answer if you don't want to."

Cameron got red in the face.

Mike said, "I think Jonathan will answer any questions about the knife himself." And turning to the boy, he asked, "Is it yours?"

Jonathan did not hesitate. "Yes," he said.

Oh-Be-Joyful slipped out of my arms and went and stood by Jonathan. Together the two of them faced us.

Mike said, after a pause, "Sometimes you make knives to sell, don't you?"

"Yes."

"Is this one of those?"

Jonathan regarded us with that crooked smile. "No," he said. "It is mine."

"Have you loaned it to anyone recently?"

"No."

"Has it been constantly in your possession?"

"You think I kill Cardinal?"

"I don't know. Somehow I don't think you'd do it that way."

"Why wouldn't he?" Cameron asked.

"My hunch is all the other way." Mike was watching Jonathan closely.

"In fact, if you tell me you didn't do it, I'll release you and look elsewhere." Mike paused, but Jonathan said nothing. "Otherwise I'll have to hold you on a murder charge. That will mean spending the summer in the cage. I couldn't take you out before the snows next winter."

We all looked at Jonathan. Mike had given him every chance. Surely, if he was innocent, he would speak now. He didn't.

I walked over to him, closer than I would if I thought for a moment he was a killer. "Jonathan Forquet, would you have us believe that you cut that man's throat while he slept?"

"I did not say that."

"No," I said, "but you didn't say you didn't, either."

He didn't answer me, and that made me mad. "You heard Sergeant Mike. All you've got to do is tell him you are innocent."

"Yes," said Mike, "that and an account of your actions this evening will satisfy me."

208

Cameron grabbed Mike's shoulder. "Sergeant, you're crazy! What's to prevent him—"

Mike threw his arm off, and the movement silenced him.

"Well, Jonathan," Mike asked, "what do you say?"

Jonathan was not smiling now. He looked coolly at us, one after the other. Then he spoke.

"When north wind forget he north wind and blow from south—when the mad sickness of the wolf come on me, so that I run in circles and bite my own flesh—then will I make account to Sergeant Mike."

"That was a pretty speech," Mike said, "and you'll have all summer to sit and remember it. You're under arrest."

"No!" Oh-Be-Joyful sprang between them. "He did not do it," she said to Mike.

Jonathan looked at her almost tenderly. "You good *klooch*. You do not want me spend summer in cage with mosquitoes, with bull fly."

"Tell them you did not kill him."

Jonathan looked at her thoughtfully. "Did I not?"

"No," she said, but her eyes were not on his.

"Think," he said. "My knife and my hate. Did I not?"

Oh-Be-Joyful stood with her head down, and her tears dropped on the floor.

## CHAPTER TWENTY

There were a lot of things on my mind. Sarah kept telling me to relax. I tried to. I watched the northern lights dance outside my window. They flashed and quivered, forming arcs and ribbons of colors.

"The spirits are dancing there," Sarah said as she set the kettle to heat.

Oh-Be-Joyful came to the door with the sweet oil Sarah had sent her for. Her eyes were wide and frightened. Sarah took the bottle from her and chased her out.

I was very sorry about Oh-Be-Joyful. I had tried to tell her how I felt, but she wouldn't let me. It had lain between us these weeks. She did what I asked her and more than I asked her, but silently, with no words and no laughter. When she was not in the house, I knew she was standing before the cage. She would stand for hours pressed against the bars, but they never seemed to talk together.

"Take deep breaths, Mrs. Mike. Relax."

"Mike," I said. "Mike!"

I felt him take my hand in his. Love is pain, I thought, all love, and I cried out against it.

I heard the sobs, I felt the tears. I thought they were my own. But in a little bit, when I was easier, I saw that Oh-Be-Joyful had her cheek against my hand, and that the tears were hers.

"Mike didn't want to arrest him," I said.

"Me, I am crazy. I thought everyone against him."

"You're crazy now to say such talk." And Sarah lifted her to her feet. "Mrs. Mike must rest."

But Oh-Be-Joyful still clung to my hand. "Oh, my sister," she said to me in Cree, "oh my more-than-sister, forgive me."

I smiled at her. She seemed very far away. The northern lights made a robe for her. A curtain of colors shone between us—shone between me and the world.

The bright pain, the dazzling, screaming pain of many colors entered me, was tearing me. A new life. I was exultant, I was despairing.

A wailing filled the air and a moaning. I heard Oh-Be-Joyful's voice from the other side of the door, angry, pleading. But the sounds of wild grief, of lamentation, continued.

Suddenly a woman flung herself on the bed beside me. Mike's hand slipped from mine. He's taken her out, I thought, and then I wondered who she was.

A mosquito whined in the air and kept settling on me. I turned and twisted and writhed. Mike came back and killed it. I wanted to ask him who the woman had been, but I began to breathe the pungent odor of the woods, and I heard my good witch say, "Make nice baby come fast."

It did. For the next time the sky-curtains closed over me, throbbing with gold and purple pain, with agonizing violet and red—the boy was born. I lay with my eyes closed and let Sarah's hands work over me. They kneaded me into shape, they soothed and cleansed.

When I opened my eyes next, my son lay in the shelter of my arm. Mike was standing over us. He put a big finger

210

down to the tiny bundle, and the baby grabbed hold. With the movement he grabbed hold of my heart too.

Sarah smiled broadly. "The northern lights danced for him at his birth," she said.

Mike laughed. "It is a good sign. He'll wear a red coat too, this little one."

Suddenly there came a high, piteous wail, followed by the moaning I had heard before. I wasn't out of my mind now, surely I wasn't. I clutched Mike.

"No, Kathy," he said, "it is nothing. Poor Mrs. Marlin is out there wanting to see your baby. We sent her away once, but she must have come back again. Oh-Be-Joyful is stationed just outside the door. She won't let her in."

"Did she come in the room before? Did she lie down on my bed?"

"Yes," Mike said, "before anyone could stop her, but she didn't mean any harm. She just wanted to see the baby."

"She shall see him," I said. "Sarah, let her come in."

Sarah shook her head. "Too much excitement no good. You rest."

"Please, Sarah. I want to show him off."

Sarah grunted an Indian grunt of disapproval and opened the door. Mrs. Marlin stood on the threshold, her voice uplifted on a keening note, her body rocking in sorrow. The opening of the door confused her. She broke off her wailing and peered uncertainly at us.

"Mrs. Mike say you come see baby."

"Oh, can I see too?" Oh-Be-Joyful asked.

"No, too much."

I smiled at Sarah, who stood like a watchdog over me. "Let her, Sarah."

At my word, Oh-Be-Joyful bounded into the room. She looked with wonder at the blanketful of baby tucked in my arms.

"Oh," she said. "The little brave, the little warrior."

"You can hold him," I said because I saw she did not dare to ask.

She darted a quick look at me to see if I meant it and then, with her breath held, she lifted him.

I sighed a little. I felt sleepy and contented. I watched with half-closed eyes as Mrs. Marlin timidly approached

Oh-Be-Joyful. Something about her caught my attention. She moved slowly as one in a trance. Only her eyes were awake and alive. They were bright and large and swollen from crying. But it was the look in them, the avid, hungry way they fastened on my baby, that frightened me. I tried to tell Mike, but I wasn't quick enough. The suddenness of the woman's movement paralyzed me. With a darting gesture of the hand she took the baby from Oh-Be-Joyful.

Mrs. Marlin backed toward the door, the baby in her arms. But Sarah reached it first and blocked it with her body. Mrs. Marlin edged off to the far wall, keeping us all in front of her.

"What the hell!" Mike jumped up and strode toward the woman. In her fear she clutched the baby tighter. I half raised myself against the pillows. "Mike, don't!"

My words stopped him. "Yes," he said, "you're right."

Oh-Be-Joyful looked questioningly at me. I nodded to her, for I saw that Sarah could not leave the door and that the woman was afraid of Mike. I watched the girl approach. Mrs. Marlin watched her too. She crouched against the wall, ready to spring, to rush them all.

Oh-Be-Joyful stopped within five feet of her. She smiled and held out her arms. "Give me the baby."

Mrs. Marlin didn't answer.

O God, I thought. She doesn't even understand.

Oh-Be-Joyful still smiled. "The baby is not yours," she said gently.

This seemed to rouse the woman. She strained the child to her.

"Mine," she said.

"No, the baby is not yours." Oh-Be-Joyful said it slowly and patiently as though she were teaching the words to her.

Mrs. Marlin began to cry and rock her body. "Mine," she moaned. "Mine."

But in another moment she was smiling and telling Oh-Be-Joyful that she was going to have a baby.

"In July," she said. "Isn't this July?"

No one answered her.

"Yes," she said slowly, "it is time." She turned dark eyes on Sarah. "Where is my baby?"

I remembered the black liquid she had carried away from Sarah's shed last January.

"Where is my baby?" She was no longer asking it. It was a song to her now.

She cradled my son close in her arms. She crooned to him. "My baby dead. You are my baby. My baby went out from me when black medicine went in. My baby's spirit go into you not yet born. You are my baby."

Mike edged a little closer to her. Oh-Be-Joyful held out her arms again. The woman laughed at them and jiggled the baby up and down. The movement slowed to a rocking motion, and she began to moan again. Her tears spilled onto the baby's white blanket. Her voice was a broken murmur.

"Dead, all dead, everything dead. Baby dead, father dead. Everything I touch dead. Dead, dead, dead." She sang it to the tune of an old French nursery rhyme.

"I'm not *klooch*," she said, turning on us, "not Indian. I got married in a church to American husband. American man. But he died of coughing sickness. Everyone die. I'm not *klooch*, not Indian for every dirty 'breed put hands on. I tell him go away, leave alone. I'm widow of American. But when him drunk, come roaring into my house, throw me on bed, sometime on floor. Then he don't come no more. Maybe go trap line. I got baby in me, his baby. I'm not *klooch*. What should I do? I go to Sarah, get black medicine for kill baby. But when I'm home I think little baby, pretty baby, want live. I think I want baby, soft little baby to hold. I put bottle away. I think, when he come back I tell him I no *klooch*, him marry me in church maybe. Then pretty soon he come back. Sergeant Mike bring him, put him in cage. I go see him. I say, 'I'm not *klooch*, not Indian. I tell him how his baby make me big. He sit down close to bars, he say, 'You all right. Government she pay five bucks a year for kids born on reserve. You stick by me, I make you rich woman!' He throw back his head and laugh. Laugh at me, but I no *klooch*. My knife she lie in my belt. I take, I stick, like I stick my pig last summer in the throat. Red bubbles come out his mouth. The mouth she still laugh. I go home and drink black medicine. I get much sick. My

213

little baby gets dead. Dead, dead, dead." She sang the words as a lullaby to my baby.

"Cardinal," Mike said.

"Cardinal," she repeated and spat.

Oh-Be-Joyful looked at Mike with shining eyes.

"Wait," he said. "She may have imagined it. Where did you get the knife?" he asked her.

"Knife?" She no longer remembered what she had told.

Mike said, "You're not a *klooch*. He laughed at you. You stabbed him with the knife. Where did you get the knife? Think. Where did you get it?"

"My knife," she said, "mine."

"Jonathan Forquet stacked wood for you this winter."

"It's not his." She began to cry. "He gave it to me. He said I could have it."

"Yes," said Mike, "you can have it. If you give me the baby, you can have it."

"To keep?" she asked.

"To keep."

She handed him the baby.


### CHAPTER TWENTY-ONE

It was the time of the first fruits of the corn. The Indians were preparing a great feast, and I had undertaken to be on the food committee. During the last week every Indian for three villages around had come to me and asked me to write down his name on the list. After his name would come the food that he pledged: half a deer, a whole deer, two beavers, or maybe seven rabbits. But, as all these animals had yet to be trapped and killed, it was really difficult to determine what our exact menu would be.

The children had been gathering firewood for days, and this was now neatly stacked under the great iron pots that hung from poles in the clearing.

The food began arriving. Black Feather was entered for one brown bear. He brought me two ducks and a string of fish. Strong Bow, who was down for half a moose, came in with a long story and a baby porcupine. But I didn't care as long as the food piled up. The women arrived before noon, and the carcasses were divided and apportioned among them for skinning.

That evening I laid out the lynx-paw robe lined with red velvet that Mike had given me when Ralph was born. I didn't have any relatives called Ralph, and neither did Mike. We just called him that because it was the prettiest name we could think of. I also got out the suit of white caracul Chief Mustagan had given me when we left Hudson's Hope, and called in Oh-Be-Joyful.

"Would you like to wear it tomorrow?"

She smiled and shook her head.

"But look," I said. "It will just fit you."

She ran a caressing finger over the white fur.

"Try it on," I suggested.

She shook her head. "I don't think I go."

"Of course you're going," I said. "Everyone is going."

"I thought I stay with the babies," she said.

"Well, you can't stay with them because they're going too. Besides, you don't want to miss the games and the feasting and the dances. It's going to be fun."

She didn't say anything. I pretended not to notice.

"Try it on," I urged again.

She did, listlessly and indifferently. But when she saw herself in the mirror my mother sent me, a little color came into her cheeks. She did look beautiful with the white fur framing her face and throat. With a sigh, Oh-Be-Joyful turned away from her reflection.

I wondered, as I'd wondered the month Jonathan had been out, what was wrong between them. When he had been in jail she had been with him every hour she could spare, but since he had been released, she had not seen him. Once he had come to the house, bringing a wild pheasant, and she had stayed in her room. Once he had stopped by and talked to me of a small herd of bison he had seen in the vicinity. He had spoken with his eyes on her door, but it had not opened.

Oh-Be-Joyful slipped out of the caracul suit and folded it carefully on the bed.

"Take it into your room," I said.

"Thank you," she said. "It is so pretty."

I turned back the bed and laid out Mike's slippers. "I suppose Jonathan is in the games," I said, fluffing up a pillow.

"I don't know," she said, and fluffed up the other one.

"What's happened?" I asked.

She sat wearily on the bed. "In summer the deer stand in river many hours. The bear roll in mud until it coat its body. Why?"

"Why?" I asked, a little impatient at this Indian indirectness.

"So deer fly, bull fly, and mosquito do not make them mad. Why then you think Jonathan sit in cage through the hot days, his body bitten, his feet taking two steps, then back, then two step? He whose feet go in all the paths of the forest?"

This was not a new question. I had asked it of myself many times.

"Well, it's hard to know Jonathan," I said. "Hard to understand his reasons. He lives by some inner law of his own. Of course he didn't tell Mike he had given Mrs. Marlin the knife because he didn't want her punished. He didn't understand that she wouldn't be killed or imprisoned. And you couldn't make him understand because he's never seen a hospital. He didn't know that she'd just be taken care of."

Oh-Be-Joyful shook her head impatiently. "Yes, about the knife. You understand about the knife. But Sergeant Mike he say to Jonathan, 'Tell me you do not do it, and you go free.' "

"He's stubborn, that's all. Mike wanted an accounting of his actions, and rather than give it to him, he went to jail. It doesn't sound reasonable," I admitted, "but it sounds like Jonathan."

Oh-Be-Joyful seemed to speak to herself: "I thought he kill Cardinal. Jonathan, he know what I think. And that is why he say nothing, why he went to sit in jail."

"I don't understand it yet."

"He would not say, 'I don't sneak up on man in cage, I don't bring him to the bars with my talk, I don't kill man with knife, who has no knife'—these things he would not say. He wanted that I should *know* him. But I did not know. I know only Cardinal is his enemy. I know the knife in

216

Cardinal's throat is his, and most I know the never-forgotten anger in Jonathan."

I began to see into Jonathan's mind, to follow the circuitous courses of his thought. His conception of love seemed strange and mystic. He wanted his woman to understand him, not with her intellect, not with her emotions, but directly, soul to soul. The things he had done, the things he would do, she must know as well as she knew his face. She must know he would kill Cardinal, but not murder him. Jonathan would not help her to this knowledge. Instead he let Mike put him in the cage, where he sat, proud and haughty, under the stinging swarms of insects. He remained motionless for hours at a time, staring into the cool distant green of the forest, but when Oh-Be-Joyful came, bringing fruit and milk, he said nothing to her. He waited for the day when she could speak, when she would say to him of her own accord, "You did not kill Cardinal."

Much of this Oh-Be-Joyful understood now. And she was ashamed before this man of stern pride whom she loved. Indirectly his days of stubborn suffering had accomplished what she had desired: Oh-Be-Joyful "knew him," as she put it. But between them were still the days of torment and suspicion, and the insult of her long-unresolved hesitation.

I tried to comfort Oh-Be-Joyful. "He wanted you to know him all at once," I said. "But it takes years of living together to really know a person."

"If I loved him enough, I would have known *then*. How can I look at him? If he sees me, he must think of those weeks, and I must think too."

"You mean a great deal to him, Oh-Be-Joyful. It was for you he did it. It will be all right again."

She raised dark eyes to mine. "How can I know him when his spirit dance on the mountaintops?"

I laughed at her. "He's no spirit," I said. "He's a willful, stubborn boy who follows his own paths."

"But you like him?" Oh-Be-Joyful asked anxiously.

"Yes, I do."

She smiled and gathered up the white furs.

I woke in the morning to the throbbing beats of a drum.

"Happy first fruits of the corn," I said and reached over to kiss Mike awake. But he answered me from across the room. I opened my eyes at that and saw that he was already half-shaved.

"How come?" I asked, sitting up and yawning.

"I've got to be on the spot when the Indians and the 'breeds start sifting in from the other territories."

"If I hurry like everything, won't you wait for me?"

He kissed me on the head.

"The games won't start till about nine-thirty. You could wait for me if you wanted to."

"Kitten," he said, "did you ever hear of the massacre of 1897? Well, it was the feast of the dog. A feast very similar to the feast of the first fruits of the corn. Only instead of opening with foot races, it opened with the medicine man tearing a live dog to pieces. Then followed feasting and ceremonial dances. You see, it's much the same program laid out for today. Only there was liquor snuck in, and by evening there were sixty-eight scalps taken."

"I don't believe it," I said, "but I'm not the one to stand between a man and his work. You'd better get down there and keep an eye on things."

Oh-Be-Joyful and I hurried the children through breakfast, but even so the foot races had begun by the time we reached the village. There were a dozen young men competing. Oh-Be-Joyful looked quickly from one to the other, then her interest in the game was over.

But the excitement of the shouting crowd got into me, and I found myself yelling, *"Kenipe, Kenipe!"* to a young man who didn't *kenipe* fast enough, and came in fourth.

After the races there was some shooting. It was done with rifles, the marksman shooting down a pine cone or breaking a stick tossed into the air. One boy missed repeatedly with his gun. Grabbing up his bow and arrow, he waited for another chip of wood to be thrown and pierced it before it reached the ground.

Somewhere a solemn chant started. It was taken up by the men, who formed themselves into a long line.

"What are they singing?" I asked Oh-Be-Joyful.

"It is the gambling song. They are going to play the wheel-and-arrow game."

218

The men began divesting themselves of bows, bracelets, headdresses, belts, and placing them in piles in front of them.

"They are betting those things."

I watched as a large wheel was rolled along the line of men who attempted to toss an arrow through a spoke as it passed them. If they failed, the little pile of trinkets at their feet was taken away. If they succeeded, they received fur for fur and bead for bead what they had bet.

A drum broke up the gambling and summoned the people to a gigantic lodge erected for the occasion. It had been built of willow boughs.

Mike was outside holding on to a bottle and arguing with Baldy Red. "Now, you know better than this, Baldy."

"Sergeant, you haven't a legal leg to stand on."

"How's that?" Mike asked tolerantly.

"This here's three-fourths tobacco juice. Now, there's no law that says you can't drink tobacco juice above the 50th parallel."

"How about the other one-quarter?" Mike asked.

"Hell," said Baldy, "that's flavoring." But in spite of his protests, Mike kept the bottle. He guided us into the lodge and sat us down in a corner. While the people filed in he told me about the ceremony.

"It began in the old days when Earth Man, who was the first man on the earth, heard the first thunder. After the thunder came the rain, and the rain ripened the first fruits. Since that time, whoever hears the first thunder calls for a feast."

Everyone had crowded into the lodge, and all eyes were turned expectantly toward the entrance. An old man came in, he who had heard the first thunder. He walked to the center of the lodge and squatted beside a rectangular pit. Handfuls of sweet grass were passed in and placed in the pit. A fire was lighted there, and the old man purified his hands by holding them to the smoke. When this was done he began to unwrap the pipe. It was covered with many layers of furs, and there was a song for each layer, so it took quite a while to get it unwrapped. The stem was brilliantly plumed with many feathers. The old man pointed it toward the sun, toward the earth, and in the four directions of the world, asking health and happiness and long life. Now five hot stones were passed in and laid upon the smoldering sweet grass, one in each corner and one in the center.

"They represent the thunders," Mike whispered.

An ear of corn was set on each stone. Then the old man dipped a blade of grass into the water and sprinkled the corn and the stones. He sang four songs, and the people sang after him.

The giver of the feast invoked Gitche Manito and gave thanks that men again ate corn. The sun was asked to work faithfully to ripen the yet-unripened stalks; they reminded him that he was put there for that purpose. The thunders were asked for rain, and the earth was asked to bring forth more corn, that the children of men might grow old.

The lodge door was opened. We walked out and received an ear of corn from the great kettles that were used only on this feast day. The people drifted into groups, eating and talking. A little boy ran around holding his stomach and crying, *"Meesook, meesook."* Everybody laughed. The word meant dinnertime. The women were busy turning spits of buffalo tongue and deer meat. I felt responsible for the food and was relieved to see that, no matter how many times they went back for more, there was more there. At last even the hungriest were filled up.

Stories were told, and little knots of listeners formed. The women exchanged the gossip of the villages, and some who had come farthest spread out their blankets and slept. The children both napped, so I decided we could stay for the dancing.

Dusk was setting in when the weird gambling chant arose again. Mike played for a while and lost a knife. This time it was a game played with two bones, one painted red and one black. You try to guess in which of your opponent's hands the red one lies.

"Funny," Mike said. "The colors are the same as roulette," and after he'd lost the knife, "and I always had rotten luck in that too."

The pulsating beat of the drums led us away from the games and up to the circle of dancers. All day Oh-Be-Joyful had followed me around. She bent her head over Ralph and moved silently through the festivities. Nothing touched her. She did not see the glances of the young men. Her feet did not quicken to the throb of the drums.

The first dance called for the maidens and the young men of the tribes. The girls gathered at one end, and the young men faced them across a circle of space. A girl ran up to us and caught Oh-Be-Joyful's hand.

"Mamanowatum," she said.

Oh-Be-Joyful shook her head, but now a dozen young women were around her.

"Come, come," they said, "the eagle moon is filling out," and they pulled her unwillingly into the dance.

She looked back at me. "Mrs. Mike!"

But I would not help her.

The line of girls danced forward to the line of boys. On toe and heel they moved, and Oh-Be-Joyful moved with them. Then the line of girls swept back, and the young men surged forward, step, hop, step, in exaggerated rhythm.

A harmonica, playing "The Red River Jig," cut in upon the austere pattern of drumbeats. The 'breeds and whites had started a dance of their own. A little way back they cut pigeon wings and did the double shuffle, leaping and springing in the air. They drew a crowd of their own, that clapped hands and thighs in time to the harmonica. A fiddler joined them.

I turned back to the Indians. The commotion had no effect on them. They pounded their feet into the ground in unbroken measures. Oh-Be-Joyful, dancing in her white furs, was transformed with joy and beauty. She did not laugh or smile, but she could not keep the excitement from her eyes. The young men and the young women rushed together and fell back. Jonathan was dancing with the men. Fiercely, exultingly, he leaped and crouched in the prescribed positions of the dance. A murmur ran through the watchers. I heard an old man tell another, "Like a thistle he leaped among them."

Suddenly the line broke. The women wove among the men. As Oh-Be-Joyful passed them, boy after boy called to her. But she moved as swiftly as the restricting patterns of the dance allowed her. She stopped in front of Jonathan and, lifting the scarf from her head, threw it around his

221

shoulders. The other girls did the same, each catching a young man with her shawl. Everyone laughed and whooped and shouted.

Most of the couples broke up, a few walked away together. But Jonathan and Oh-Be-Joyful stood where they were when the drums had stopped. I didn't see him ask the question. I didn't see her answer it—but when Jonathan walked across the village, she went with him. At the edge of the wood he stopped and caught some branches from her path. They swung back into place, and she was gone. She had followed her maker of canoes. He would build her a tepee of willow; they would lie on balsam and on furs. She would follow his steps through the paths of the forest.

Oh be joyful, Mamanowatum.

## CHAPTER TWENTY-TWO

I sat down to darn socks and wondered where the time went. Here it was January 1911, and I hadn't heard from Oh-Be-Joyful for nearly a year and a half. I'd had less trouble over her disappearance than I expected. The Mother Superior had sent plump Sister Teresa to see me. Over tea and bannocks she mourned that even if we found Oh-Be-Joyful, it would probably be too late, didn't I think so?"

"Too late?" I asked.

"Well, you know what emotional creatures they are."

I nodded gravely and admitted that it probably was already too late.

That was two summers ago. I couldn't expect Oh-Be-Joyful to visit me, or even write. Who was there to carry her letters? But I kept hoping there was some way she could let me know she was all right, and that Jonathan—that Jonathan had made a life for her as Mike had for me.

At the desk Mike was making out his semiannual report. It was only nine in the morning, but he was working by candlelight. In winter our mornings were dark until eleven. I didn't like getting up in the dark. I'd just as soon have been as lazy as the sun. But the babies woke up at seven-thirty, and that was that. I finished the dishes and settled down to mend a pair of Mary Aroon's overalls.

"Damn!" Mike said. I was startled. Then I heard it too, the low, drawn-out howl of a wolf. I bent my head over my sewing because I didn't want Mike to see me laughing. But it was really funny—Mike and that wolf. The wolf had been hanging around for a couple of months. I'd seen him several times, a big fellow with a silver-gray coat and a limp. What he wanted at our place I don't know. We had no cattle at all, our half of Bessie being kept with Larry's half in Larry's stable. In fact, Larry did a good deal of complaining. After visiting us, the wolf would drop by his place for dinner. Apparently he had learned the sound Larry made when he called his turkeys. The wolf would hide behind the trough or a barrel halfway between the feeding ground and the turkeys. Then as they streamed by he'd pick off any loiterers.

Mike had said, and this was two months ago, that he would come over and help Larry shoot the marauder. So he went, and sure enough, as soon as Larry gave his turkey call, old wolf hove in sight. However, this time he didn't come up to the trough, or even as far as the apple barrel. In fact, he didn't come into the clearing at all, but slipped back and forth, a gray shadow among the trees. Mike said he was gunwise and wouldn't come in while they were holding rifles.

To test this theory, the men put their guns in the kitchen, and while they were gone the gray wolf got another turkey.

Since then Mike had made up his mind to get him. He knew this was a wise old wolf, and he prepared his bait accordingly. He set aside a plump juicy rabbit and carefully stirred three-eighths of an ounce of strychnine through its flesh, blood, and entrails. Mike wore gloves while doing this to kill his scent, and as a last artistic effect he bought a vial of oil of anise from Sarah and sprinkled a trail of it leading up to the poisoned carcass. Turning in, that night, he said with satisfaction that he estimated the wolf would be seized with convulsions about two hundred yards from the bait.

The next morning he took care to be out early so the dogs wouldn't get sick eating the dead wolf. But the rabbit lay undisturbed where Mike had put it. There were wolf tracks, though, and Mike was partly consoled because they did come in along the oil of anise trail he had laid. Apparently the wolf had drawn in close to the bait, had circled it once, and then hoisted a leg over it. Mike pointed out the yellow stain in the ice.

"Look at that!" he said indignantly.

"Maybe he had to," I said.

"He didn't have to. He did it to show what he thought of that trap. It's a typical wolf way of expressing contempt."

"Mike," I argued, "wolves are just like dogs. I'm sure there's nothing personal in it."

"There is," Mike said, "and I'll be damned if I'll let a wolf sneer at me."

"Mike," I said, "it's ridiculous to get worked up over what a wolf thinks of you. Besides, animals don't know how to sneer."

"Oh, no? I once saw a couple of male wolves fight. As soon as one went down, the victor stood over him and deliberately lifted a leg."

"But how do you know he did it maliciously?"

"I could tell by the look on his face," Mike said stubbornly. And from then on he was doubly determined to get the big silver wolf.

He consulted with the Indians and dug pits. They were carefully constructed pits and represented a good deal of labor, as they were five feet across and twenty feet deep. But, although gray wolf investigated them and expressed his opinion of them in the usual manner, he never fell in. Mike returned the taunts of the wolf with craftier traps and more tempting poisons. But in the morning the gray wolf's contempt was clearly discernible in the snow.

In spite of Mike's efforts, the lame wolf had adopted us. One morning I saw him cavorting around our back yard with a thistle in his mouth, shaking it furiously, dropping it and capering after it again. He was such a handsome creature that I was secretly glad Mike hadn't succeeded in killing him.

We'd always know when he was around because the dogs went crazy. Especially Juno, who returned howl for howl in a way that made me wonder how far back you had to go in her ancestry to find a large silver wolf.

Mike went on with his report. It was going slowly because he was using his best penmanship and literary style. The wolf continued his sad wailing call, and Mike frowned deeper in an attempt to concentrate.

Ralph began to cry. Mary Aroon had taken his rag doll away from him.

"Mary Aroon," I said, "shame on you for taking the baby's doll. You give it back to Brother like a good girl."

She regarded me silently, and I saw her little fist tighten over the doll. She ran to Mike and threw herself against his knee. The impact was so sudden that the tail of the "Y" he was writing went shooting up into the clear space between the lines.

"Kathy," Mike said angrily, "can't you keep her away when I'm busy?"

I felt hurt. I couldn't be expected to run after her every minute, especially when I had a lap full of sewing.

"She's your child too," I said and hauled her back. "Now you keep away from there, Mary Aroon. Your father's busy." I went back to my sewing.

The baying of the wolf sounded closer. Juno lifted her head off the hearth and sang out a dismal answer. Mike said he could detect the difference between a wolf and a husky howl. But I couldn't, and it startled me to hear the answering cry come from behind my back. Poor Juno! I turned to watch her. She was going to have a litter any day now, and I suppose that's why a wolf in close to the house worried her. I bent down and petted her, but she still whined nervously.

A wail of despair came from Mary Aroon. I whirled around.

"Now you've done it!" Mike yelled.

And it was true, she had done it—the bottle of ink was rolling uncorked across his carefully made out report.

Mary Aroon raced past me screaming bloody murder and making for the bedroom. Mike made a half-hearted attempt to blot the paper, then jumped up and ran after her.

He never had spanked the children before, but I knew by his face he was going to now. I was so scared that I ran after Mary Aroon, Mike right behind me.

Mary had thrown herself face down on the bed, a strategic error. With some vague notion of protecting her, I threw myself, face down, on top of her. Mike didn't hesitate an instant. I don't know if he even knew who was on top, but I got the worst spanking of my life.

I cried, Mary Aroon cried, and Mike—well, there were tears on his face and he was making some half-smothered sound and shaking all over. I thought, and I've always thought he was laughing. But when I accused him of it he became very grave and begged my pardon. I remained sulky. He went further—he promised to devote the afternoon to me. What did I want to do?

I thought about it and decided I wanted to take the children out in the new sled he had made for them.

Mike dressed Mary Aroon because, being older, she stood still better and was easier to handle, and I dressed Ralph. We stripped them to the long wool underwear that went down to wrist and ankles. Over this came the outdoor underwear, which was red flannel and covered the other completely. Next came the little lumberman's shirt which I made by the dozen from Mike's. Then miniature mackinaw pants. Sometimes I longed for ruffles and bows, the dotted swiss and fine linens that my babies would never wear. We tugged on hip-length beaver coats, beaver caps, and beaver mitts that came to their elbows and had a string through them so they couldn't be lost. Then came the footwear. Three pairs of wool socks and over them the larrigans.

By this time the children were panting, and we set them down outside to wait till we got dressed. They looked as roly-poly as a couple of little fat bears.

While Mike was pulling on his red flannel union suit over his white wool one, I began to laugh. He looked like a red gander. I kept on laughing. I fell down on top of my furs and laughed till my stomach hurt. When I feel like laughing, all the funny things crowd into my brain together, and the funniest thing of all was my spanking.

"Did you know who was on top?" I asked him.

"No," said Mike, "and I didn't care." He pulled my cap over my ears. "Come on."

The snow was hard-packed and icy. It made wonderful

sledding. Our sled was an old wagon Mike had found in the back room of the store. He'd taken off its wheels and put on runners. The only difficulty had been that, because of its tall wagon sides, only three of us could get in at a time, and even then the grownup had to sit crossed legs. But Mike had remodeled it by cutting a foot-high hole in the back side. Then the way we worked it was this: First Mike would get in, lying full length on his stomach, his legs sticking out the hole. Then, with the baby in my arms, I would flop on top of him, my legs also going out the hole, just on top of his. And Mary Aroon would climb in and squeeze down wherever she could, usually in my ribs. We were ready then for the flight downhill. It was really a long gentle grade, but with Mike whooping and the wind stinging our faces and whipping our clothes, it seemed wild enough. The children arrived at the bottom breathless and glowing.

"Give me this apple," Mike said, pinching Mary Aroon's red cheek.

"No!" she shouted.

"Well, what about this little cherry?" and he pulled her nose. That was her cue for the attack, and she pushed him into a snowbank. They wallowed and rolled until I decided they had enough snow in their mouths and down their necks for one day. I bundled the children into the sled, and Mike and I started for home at a brisk pace. Mary Aroon began fussing. I told Mike not to notice it. But he was afraid she was cold and went back to see if the robe was tucked around them.

"Holy St. Patrick!" he said and pointed. Ralph was sitting playing in the snow about ten feet behind us. He had evidently fallen out the hole. I rode the rest of the way in the wagon. I held the baby tight in my arms and tried hard to explain to Mary Aroon why this time she got praised for crying.

We hadn't started for home any too soon either. The Windmaker was driving gusts of snow into our faces.

"Look at that," Mike said as we came into our yard. He kicked with the toe of his boot what I thought was dog dung and muttered, "Wolf!"

"It's probably one of the dogs," I said to soothe him.

Mike stood down and examined it. "There's hair in it," he said. "That's the way you tell the difference between wolf and dog. A wolf's has the hair of game animals in it." He straightened up.

"I don't like it. Why, he came in practically to our porch. I'm going to quit fooling around and really get that guy."

As if in answer, there came a lonesome bay. We strained our eyes in the direction of the sound. On a rock overlooking the frozen level of the lake stood a gray wolf. He was excited by the storm and calling a challenge to it.

"Is it our wolf?" I asked.

Mike snorted at my phrase. "It's the wolf I'm going to get, if that's what you mean."

"Maybe it's a dog," I said, peering through the confusion of snowflakes, "a renegade dog, one that's gone wild and now he's sorry and wants to have a home."

"Katherine," Mike said after a tense pause, "there are ways of telling a husky from a wolf."

"What ways?"

"Take the kids inside," he said, "and hand me out my rifle."

I did, and while I was rubbing Ralph rosy, I heard the report of Mike's gun.

"Dear God," I said, "make him miss." I wondered if I'd said it fast enough, or if the bullet had already struck down that beautiful and wise creature.

Mike came in, banged the door, and stuck the gun in the corner.

"Damn poor visibility," he said.

Later, when the children had been kissed and tucked in for their naps, Mike decided that maybe it would be a good idea after all to instruct me in the difference between wolves and dogs, just so I wouldn't be giving bones to the wrong animal.

"It's in the tails," he said. "A husky's curls. The ears are different too. A husky's droop, and a wolf's stand erect." He took several preoccupied pulls at his pipe.

"Do you realize, Kathy, that a ranch loses ten per cent of its net income a year because of wolves?"

"Really?"

228

"Ten per cent on an average-size ranch; that would mean a thousand a year."

"But, darling, there are no ranches around here."

"Larry Carpentier has turkeys. And what about Bessie?"

"That wolf hasn't bothered Bessie," I said.

"Kathy," said Mike, patiently, "have you ever seen the pitiless way in which a wolf kills a cow?"

"No," I admitted.

"Well, the cattle are in a tightly packed circle. The wolf makes a lunge at one of them, say Bessie, and frightens her away from the others. Then, when he has her separated from the herd, with one bite he disables her legs and pulls her down. Now, you wouldn't want that to happen to Bessie, would you?"

"No, and I don't see how it could. Bessie is just one cow, not a herd of cows. I don't see how you could separate her from—"

"My God," Mike said, "you've no imagination."

"Yes I have."

"But you don't picture it. The fangs of that wolf closing over Bessie, Bessie's eyes rolling. It's wanton killing. It's not as though the wolf were hungry. One meal a week or twelve meals evenly spaced all winter is enough to keep a wolf going. Why, I've known wolves to kill a cow for the sake of the calf she's carrying."

"All right," I said, "kill it. If you think you can kill it, kill it!"

Mike relit his pipe and asked me if we had any unskinned rabbits. He knew perfectly well we had because Bishop Grouard had brought us three.

"I've just remembered an old Indian method that I've never known to fail. It doesn't involve poison, Newhouse traps, or pits." He looked at me expectantly.

"What is it?" I asked.

"Just this," and he took out his hunting knife, "imbedded in the bait. When he satisfies himself that it's free of poison, he'll tear into it, and the knife will cut his mouth and tongue."

"That won't kill him," I said.

"No, but it will draw blood, and the smell of blood will draw in other wolves, maybe even a mountain lion. A wounded animal doesn't last long in this country."

Mike began pulling on his clothes. "You can't tell what will happen when they get infuriated by blood."

"When who gets infuriated by blood?"

"The animals."

"The ones that aren't there yet?" I asked.

"Never you mind," Mike said, "there's liable to be three or four dead wolves out there by morning."

He went out with a rabbit, a knife, and the last of Sarah's oil of anise.

While he was gone, Juno had her puppies. She gave little short high yelps when I took my hand away, so I stroked her and talked to her. And four blind wet puppies were soon nuzzling her. She had a fine time cleaning and licking them, turning them over and knocking them down.

They were plump active bits of fur, and I could hardly wait for Mary Aroon to wake up and see them. I'd been promising her these puppies for weeks.

I heard Mike outside stamping the snow off his boots.

"Mike!" I yelled. "Mike!"

He opened the door and looked in. "What's the matter?"

"We've got puppies!"

He grinned and came over, shedding clothes as he came. He looked at those puppies a long time, and the grin slowly faded from his face.

"Hmmmmm," he said at last and buttoned up his jacket. He reached for his cap and his gloves.

"Where are you going?"

"Out to bring in that bait."

"But—"

"Kathy," he said, "it just wouldn't be right for me to be killing the father of Juno's puppies."

Now it was my turn to stare at the puppies. They were gray, all four of them, silver gray. And their tails, what had Mike said? A husky's tail curls. Well, theirs stood out straight and pointed. And their ears were erect, not flopping over like Juno's.

"Holy Mother of God," I said and sat slowly. "We've got wolves in the house."

"They're only half wolf," Mike said.

I looked dubiously at Juno. "Three-quarters."

"It doesn't matter. A lot of the Indians purposely mate their dogs with wolves to keep the breed fresh. You remember Louis Carpentier had a full-blooded wolf in his team for a while. It didn't have the stamina, though."

"But these were to be the children's."

"We'll call them theirs. They have to be kept outside anyway, the kids won't see much of them this winter, and in the spring there's bound to be more puppies."

I nodded, watching the little gray wolves nurse. A low sad howl drifted in to us, and Juno pricked up her ears. It came again and she answered.

"You better get out of there, Mike, before he finds the bait."

I helped him into his coat. The air was almost solid, and in a moment it had dropped a curtain of snow between us. I walked back to Juno and her little wolves, smiling. For two months he had tried to catch that wolf. He'd laid some ingenious traps too. But now I knew he would always think of himself as saving that wolf's life; although why this particular trap should work when for two months none of the others had, I didn't know.

## CHAPTER TWENTY-THREE

The McTavish brothers returned to Grouard dressed exactly as they had left, with nothing to show the change in their fortunes except a case of books. It was rumored that they had a fat account in a Winnipeg bank—the proceeds of the sale of the earldom. This James McTavish angrily denied.

"Not a penny did I get out of the whole transaction," he would repeat. "And I'm out a hundred and twenty pounds passage money."

However, it was noticed that the brothers began to live a little better, and that instead of his semiannual sprees, Allan permitted himself to get drunk once a month now.

James asked me to come down to their house and pick out any books I might want to read through the winter. There were about fifty volumes spread out on the floor in black, brown, and russet leather bindings, some with titles

231

stamped in gold. I had never seen books like that. I opened a copy of Burn's poems, and stared fascinated at the elaborate end-papers covered with swirls of color and flashes of silver. The paper was as thick as cloth, and the initial letters long and curled.

"There's Sir Thomas More, and Shakespeare, and Tyndall on *Sound,* and Bobby Burns, and four or five Bibles, and Knox's *Sermons,* and Carlyle, and Johnson's *Rasselas,*" James said.

"It's wonderful just to touch them," I said.

"You can have any you want, Mrs. Flannigan."

"Are all these from your castle in Scotland?" I could not repress my curiosity.

"Aye, and the only thing worth more than a lead two-bits," James said, and started to spit. He looked at me and checked himself. "That damn pile of stones," he added bitterly.

Allan McTavish put down the fishing line he was unsnarling and squatted down beside the pile of books.

"And what good these are going to do you is more than I'll ever know," he mocked his brother. "Sir Thomas More and Shakespeare! You that's been reading paper-backed novels all your life."

"They're good books," James said, "and tooled leather covers, and after crossing three thousand miles of ocean, I'd be a brainless fool if I didn't get something out of it."

"Well, you got to be an earl, didn't you?" I said.

"No, I did not."

"But you said . . . and I mended your tartan, and everything . . ."

"I turned it down, Mrs. Flannigan. I changed my mind the day before I was to sign the papers. It wasn't for me, Mrs. Flannigan. To sit in a pile of stones on a poverty-stricken hill, and the only company a score of dead McTavishes in the Mausoleum, and the people speaking a murderous Scottish it would take me ten years to figure out. No. My shack in Canada looks better to me than that pile of stones ever did!"

"For once he's right," his brother said. "There's something in this country that nails you down and keeps you here. But lugging the case of books was a fool stupid thing."

232

"Pay no attention to him, Mrs. Flannigan, but take what you please. It'll be good reading these winter nights. Take one with pictures."

I searched carefully and was tempted by a beautiful brown and gilt edition of *Famous Scottish Judges,* and by a sturdy *Complete Works of John Milton,* but I fell when a book opened to a five-color map of Manchuria and Inner Mongolia. I never could resist maps of strange places, and I walked home from the McTavishes carrying *The History of China,* Vols. I, II, and III.

Mike was astonished. "Couldn't you find anything lighter?"

I told him that China interested me very much, and that I was going to read the whole thing from Mythical Times to Modern Times.

"Well," he said helplessly, riffling the pages, "I suppose you know what you're doing. But why China? I should think you'd be more interested in a history of Ireland or Canada."

"China," I said, "is the seat of the world's oldest civilization."

Mike burst out laughing. "So you already read the introduction on the way over."

I had, and I could hardly wait to get into the first chapter. That night I lit a bear-grease candle and opened to the "Age of the Five Rulers."

For weeks I lived in two worlds. I felt that if I stepped out of my door I would see, not the Alberta prairies, but the plains of Fukien. Jade and lotus and porcelain were words I murmured to myself while I worked. I cannot explain the overpowering fascination that dry, long-winded history had for me. Perhaps it was that so much time had passed since I had read any book. Perhaps it was the pictures of cloudy mountains and twisting rivers that rewakened the desire to wander in far places that always slept in me. Or perhaps the amazing people I could be while smoking meat and making soap.

One day I was the tyrant Shih Huang Ti, who built the Great Wall and burned the great books and in the end was laid to rest on a bronze map of the empire flowing with rivers of quicksilver. I ruled my brood with a strong hand that day and demanded of Mike an accounting of his actions as sternly as any monarch interviewing his chief general.

And the next day I might be a Taoist priest or a young beauty from Szechwan waiting to be married to the Crown Prince. But most of all I enjoyed playing the life of Yang Kuei-fei, a "subverter of Empires," a charmer of princes, whose feet were washed by the Emperor, whose candy was fetched by an army from the other end of China, whose parrot was buried in a silver casket to the accompaniment of Buddhist hymns.

I was working fourteen hours a day, and it made it easier to fancy myself a silken favorite lounging in the royal summer pavilion and scattering jewelry on the floor that my courtiers might help adorn me.

I hummed Mary Aroon to sleep with a patchwork tune which I pretended was Yang Kuei-fei's own song. "The Rainbow Skirt and Feather Jacket," but which in truth sounded much like the "Londonderry Air" with bits of "Killarney."

It was my delight to imagine that outside my bedroom window spread the gardens of the Emperor's summer palace. The rustling of the wind was to me the noise of the artificial brooks winding through a conventionalized landscape of miniature hills, set with marble benches and carved stone birds. The tall pines were stately pagodas, and Lesser Slave Lake was covered by lotus flowers. I was Yang Kuei-fei, imperial concubine, jeweled and scented, dressed in rich silks, surrounded by musicians and lantern-bearers, supping on jade-tinted fish, and casually listening to my praises sung by the revered poet Li Po. This Li Po gaily defrauded out of his due measure of rare wine granted him by the Emperor. As reward for his verses, Li Po was to have two-score cups of the treasured imperial cordial, unbelievably ancient, and the color of peacock's eyes. I, Kuei-fei, gave the cellarer a jewel-encrusted false-bottomed cup to measure out the wine with. Li Po received only two-thirds of his due, and I appropriated the rest for the delectation of myself and my Mongol lover, An Lushan.

One night Mike asked me why I was so abstracted. Or to be more exact, he said, "Come out of that daze, Kathy." I

234

didn't dare confess my double life, but I told him the story of Yang Kuei-fei, hoping that it would charm him as it had charmed me. Mike only laughed.

"Kathy, it's a great career you'd have had on the stage if you'd stayed in Boston. When you talk about China, you almost make me believe those people are your relatives and close friends." He put his arms around me. "Surely it's not so serious that they buried the white parrot, that tears have to come into your eyes."

"But I—I mean Yang Kuei-fei loved it so much. It's sad, isn't it?"

Mike shook his head. "Try as I can," he chuckled, "I just can't work up a tear over a fifteen-hundred-years-dead parrot, white, black, blue, or yellow. What really interested me was that trick with the wine cup. Now that explains a lot." He winked at me and lit his pipe.

"That explains what?" I said after a while, knowing that I would have to ask him.

"Well," Mike said, "Irish Bill down at the Hudson's Bay store gives four cups of sugar for a beaver skin. Now, all of a sudden, James McTavish is offering the Indians seven cups. I thought it was kind of generous of him, but now . . . I would like to take a look at the bottom of that McTavish cup."

"There!" I said. "That shows. It's not so different, after all, China and Grouard. People are really the same everywhere. McTavish's cup isn't covered with jewels, but I'll bet it has the same kind of false bottom as Kuei-fei's cup."

"Which goes to show . . .?"

"Which goes to show that people are the same all over the world, and that as far as actions and feelings are concerned, there isn't much difference between here and there, and that I wasn't so silly imagining myself in China."

"It doesn't show that at all, kitten," Mike said. "It only shows that James McTavish read the book before you did, and"—Mike grinned—"he got more out of it."

The children were in bed. Mike was laying out his favorite game of solitaire. He never won it. It was the kind where you lay out the deck three cards at a time, suits are built down in the array and up on the aces, and only the bottom card of each triplet is movable. I glanced from the picture on the cards, a lady with a lunch basket standing in front of a bicycle, back to a reproduction in the Chinese history. I'd finished the book a couple of nights before, but I was still acting the people and their lives, repeating the strange beautiful names. This morning, while I brushed my hair in front of the mirror, I pushed my eyelids slightly up and back. I didn't look Chinese, of course, with my red hair and blue eyes, but I did look exotic, maybe Mongol. Genghis Khan had red hair and Kubilai, his grandson, who ruled Cathay, had blue eyes.

I looked down again at the book. It was a painting, white against black. At the bottom, in print it said: "A Reproduction—The Sung Period—Attributed to Li Lung-mien." This picture wasn't new to me. I knew what it was about, a mountain waterfall. Just rock and water and a tenacious tree that grew from the rocks. Up the grade a man climbed. You didn't see him at first. He wasn't important. He blended with the scene, his back humping into the shape of the rocks around him. He was like the tree too. His fingers clung to a staff, and the tree's roots clawed into the earth, but the brush strokes were the same, a clinging to life. Yet the man didn't stand out, he was part of things.

I couldn't have the picture because it was in the McTavish's book. But I looked around the walls, imagining where I'd put it if I *did* have it. I saw that over the table was a magazine illustration of a fat baby. Sometime or other I must have tacked it up there. I didn't like it any more. I didn't like the pink and blue cover it lay on. I didn't like the yellow curls and the doll-like face. I got up, took down the picture, and threw it in the stove. Mike looked up from his card game.

"I got tired of it," I said. I stood at his shoulder a minute, watching.

"If I could only get that jack out. Look at that, the ten of diamonds in the middle, and I can't free the jack."

"I don't know why you play that game, Mike. You always get mad."

"If I could only get rid of that five of clubs."

I saw he couldn't, so I walked back and picked up the book again. Only I didn't look at the picture. Not yet. I was

236

a sage, a philosopher. I looked with satisfaction at the bare wall. I was austere in my tastes. I owned this print in the McTavish's book. No, I owned the original. My good friend Li Lung-mien, the poet-painter, had given it to me. I kept it wrapped in a parchment scroll. I took it out only to contemplate it. I turned the book over, only allowing myself to look at the abstract beauty of individual brush strokes.

There was a curious sound at the door. Someone was pushing at it, hitting it with bare hands. Mike opened it. Wiya-sha stood there.

"Sergeant Mike," she said, "my baby sick. My baby choke."

The history of China fell shut in my lap. The woman stood outside, waiting; little sobbing breaths came from her. I brought Mike's jacket and coat.

"The gloves are in the pocket."

He nodded. "I'll be back as soon as I can. Don't wait up."

He brushed his lips quickly across mine and followed Wiya-sha into the night.

I hated these nights when pain and death took Mike away: sickness, a woman stolen, or a man shot. The shadows from the fire seemed longer, darker, they moved more violently, I didn't want to sleep until Mike was beside me. I moved around making things tidy and straight. I scrubbed a kettle. I set out the breakfast things. When there was nothing left to do, I undressed, folding my clothes over the chair. I went quietly into the children's room. They slept soundly, Ralph with his mouth slightly open. I was worried about that. I hoped he didn't have adenoids. He was a handsome little fellow. He had Mike's dark hair. But Mary Aroon was the real beauty. I just hoped the freckles on her nose would go away by the time she was grown up. I thought of Wiya-sha, of her sick baby. Thank God my two were healthy; they had never been sick.

I walked back into the front room. Mike had been gone two hours. I stirred up the fire and put on tea. He'd be coming home cold and in need of something hot. The floor was icy. I got into bed and curled myself into a ball. I felt lonesome. I wished Mike was here. I mustn't go to sleep—the fire's lit. I closed my eyes. I was warm now and drowsy.

Suddenly I was awake, very awake and listening. Someone was knocking. Mike wouldn't knock. I got out of bed and into a bathrobe. The fire was ashes and embers. There was someone at the window—Mike.

He called to me, "Don't open it, Kathy."

I walked to the window and stared out at him.

"I don't want to come in," he said. "Wiya-sha's baby just died of diphtheria. I'll sleep in the office."

"But, Mike . . ." I couldn't grasp it.

"If this is an isolated case, it will only be for five or six days. You'll walk down and leave my meals for me, okay?"

"Yes," I said "but—"

"If you need me, just hang a sheet out the window."

"You're sure it was diphtheria?"

"Pretty sure. Listen, darling. Don't worry. About the only precaution you can take is to swab your throat and the kids' with iodine."

"How?"

"With a feather. Dip it in the iodine bottle."

The glass was between us. A red coal smoldering in his hair made me think I was dreaming. But then I saw it was a reflection.

"If you need me, hang out a sheet."

"Yes."

"But when you bring the food down, don't come in. Just leave it on the porch."

"Will it be bad?"

"Maybe not. We'll know by morning."

By morning broken cries and lamentations drifting in from the village woke me. Mary Aroon was frightened and began to cry. I shut all the windows and locked the door.

"It's the wind," I told Mary Aroon.

"Why is it crying?"

"Eat your cereal."

I drew pictures for her, and she colored them with her crayons.

"Mama," and she held up my attempt at a hen which she had colored with barbaric reds and purples.

"That's very nice," I said, "but try to stay inside the lines."

238

She went at it again. I washed the breakfast dishes and threw out the cold tea that no one had drunk the night before. I splashed the water and rattled the dishes and tried to hum an Irish lullaby, but now and then a wild, despairing cry reached us, and always the moaning underneath. I found myself straining to hear it. Maybe it *was* the wind, or maybe it was the low, sad notes of old Bill's organ.

I put on Mike's breakfast. While I waited for the toast I looked out at the office. There was no sign of him. But there was a flash of movement over by the group of birch. It was a man running. He was naked. Naked in below zero weather. As I stared, he flung himself into the snow, buried his hands in it, pressed it to him like a covering. A woman ran to him, half-raised him. He reached his arms back longingly and plunged them into the snow. She pulled him to his feet, and, supporting him, they walked a few uneven steps. But his strength had been spent in that first wild flight. He sagged suddenly in her arms; his head fell across her shoulder. She lowered him to the ground, and with her hands under his armpits dragged him past scrub brush and trees until they were hidden. My toast was burning.

"Mama," Mary Aroon held up a pink tree.

"Yes," I said. "It's very pretty!"

By the time Mike's new piece of toast was done he was at the window knocking. Mary Aroon ran and held up the tree and the hen for him to see.

"Kathy," he said, "you've got to help me."

"Mike, are you all right?"

"Fine, but it's everywhere. They're lying four in a bed. Half of 'em don't have food in the house. Those who do can't stand up to get it. Get your biggest pots. Fill 'em with water and boil a couple of pounds of beef and a couple of pounds of rice in 'em."

"Yes," I said.

"When it's done, signal with the sheet and I'll come get it. Put it out on the porch. If you can spare any bread, put that out too."

"Mike!" I yelled it and beat the window because he was turning away. "You've got to have breakfast."

"Later."

239

"No, now. You're exposing yourself to all those sick people. You'll get sick too if you don't keep up your strength. It's all ready."

"All right." He walked away. I opened the door a crack and set out the food. When the door was safely shut, he came back and began to eat. I told him about the man in the snow.

"Poor devil, fever. Sometimes they do that."

I asked him what he was doing for them.

"Nothing. I passed out all the quinine I had. Now I'm giving them alcohol. It's a stimulant, and that's what's needed. But food is the best. If we can keep their strength up."

He left, but was back in an hour for the soup. I passed out the three pots. It took all my strength to lift them off the stove. I dragged them across the floor and set them on the porch. Mike carried the first two off. On his way back for the third, he told me the Mission was giving food too. It was closed and no one allowed inside. But Father Grouard set out food as I did.

"Sarah and Constance?" I asked.

They were all right, and tending the sick.

"Did you swab out the kids' throats?" Mike asked.

"Yes."

"Well, do it again." And he walked off toward the reserve.

The day dragged on. No one came near the house. Mary Aroon and Ralph took their naps early. They'd played hard and were ready for them. I tried to keep busy. There was a lot of mending to do. I dumped some miscellaneous socks from my work basket into my lap.

I don't know how long I worked. I don't know how long I sat there not working. I realized my fingers had stopped, and that I was listening. I had determined not to listen, but the low drone was hypnotic. It was grief. They were crying for their dead. I tried to picture grief, but I couldn't. Death was the long, black-robed figure with the head of a skull that stalked through posters. But you couldn't make a picture of grief. Grief was negative, not having.

The room darkened and I looked up. There at the window, with her back to the sun, a woman stood looking at me. Her hair was all undone, and the wind whipped it against her face and body. She held out a bundle to me, and her eyes pleaded.

I walked to the window. I could see how pale she was. Her eyes burned hollow with fever. I couldn't remember her name. I had seen her last week at the store and before that in the village. She lifted her bundle against the glass of the window. It was a baby. Dead and already stiff.

I ran to the door and started to undo the series of bolts I had fastened. Mary Aroon padded in from the bedroom, tripping over her long flannel nightgown. I snatched her up in my arms and threw myself against the door. It was still held by the latch. I set the baby down and frantically shot the bolts. Mary Aroon tagged after me as I ran to the window. I pushed her away. I didn't know—maybe she could catch it through the glass.

"Please," I shouted to the woman, "go back home. I can't let you in."

She remained motionless, holding out her baby as though that answered me.

"What do you want?"

The woman swallowed. She tried to speak. The effort made her choke. She spat in the snow, saliva with queer gray flecks in it.

"Go home. Lie down."

She pushed the dead baby toward me. Her mouth formed a word, formed it again and again. At last I understood.

"Medicine." She wanted medicine for the child.

"Go home," I said. "You're sick, go home."

She mouthed the word at me again, "Medicine."

She continued to look at me. She waited expectantly. She didn't understand.

"Go to Sergeant Mike. Sergeant Mike will give you medicine."

Her eyes dulled, and she shook her head slowly. She's been to Mike; poor Mike, the liquor must have given out too. Or maybe the baby was already dead then. The woman still watched me. I was the white woman. I was expected to do something. I couldn't stand it.

"I can't help you. Go away, go away!"

She turned obediently and walked off my porch. She

walked unsteadily and when the choking seized her, she fell. It was terrible to see her protect the dead baby from the jar with her own body. She made no effort to rise. Her face contorted as she struggled for breath; her body twisted and jerked. Strands of her hair beat at her like lashes. The spasm was still on her, but she looked straight at me and pointed up.

An owl flew over my house. I looked back at her. Was that what she meant, the owl? Her lips drew back, she was laughing at me. No, poor thing, it was only a gasping for breath that didn't come. She fell forward in the snow, across her child. The wind lifted her hair, it crawled uneasily about her.

I turned away from the two dead people in my front yard. I picked up Mary Aroon. She mustn't see. She . . . and all the time the face of the woman was before me. Why had she laughed? I felt it was a curse on me, an unclean thing. If only she hadn't laughed.

But it wasn't her laughing that frightened me so much, it was that bird. What was there—something about an owl —then I remembered. An owl flying over the house brings death. An old Indian superstition.

## CHAPTER TWENTY-FOUR

Ralph woke crying. The glands under his jaws were swollen. His throat looked red. I put Mary Aroon in our room and hung out the sheet. By the time Mike came, there were large grayish patches in his throat.

"Mike," I said, "do something."

Mike kept hot towels on the baby's throat, and he had me boil water on the stove so the room would be moist.

"Feed him all he'll eat, Kathy."

"No, I want some medicine," I said, and shuddered at the word. That other woman, she'd wanted medicine too.

"There's an antitoxin," Mike said.

"Do you have it here?"

He shook his head. "Take two or three months to bring it in, and the stuff's got to be fresh."

"It's not fair! Just because we don't live in a town."

Mike leaned over and felt the baby's pulse. He didn't say anything when he took his hand away.

I made soup, and when I brought it in Ralph was turning from side to side. Mike held the bowl, and I tried to feed him. But the pain in his throat wouldn't let him swallow.

"Ralph, baby, this is the train we're going to see Grandmother on. It goes to Boston, and this is the way to Boston, right down the little red lane." Only it wasn't a little red lane. The white patches covered it, and it was turning a thick yellow. I drew back frightened.

"It looks like leather."

"It will be all right, Kathy. The disease is just running its course."

"Don't lie to me, Mike," I said.

"I won't, girl,"

Ralph choked. He was fighting for every breath.

That night Mary Aroon held onto her throat and cried. "Mama," she said, "Mama!"

I tacked up her pink tree and the purple and red hen where she could see them. I put the gingham bear on her pillow and fed her.

Ralph began to cough saliva; it had gray dots in it. The little body twisted. Every organ in him strained for air. Why couldn't I put my own breath into him? Why?

The hoarse rasping sound gave way to a gurgle. Ralph struggled and lay still. Mike bent over him. When he raised his head, I knew. I guess I'd known before. He put his arms around me, but I broke away.

"No!" I said. "No, no!"

Seven hours later, we lost Mary Aroon. I told her we'd go on the sled again, that she could keep the puppy in the house, that he could sleep on her bed. I promised her anything, anything. But the yellow membrane grew in her throat, choking her. I kept the compresses hot. But, suddenly, the writhing stopped.

"Kathy," Mike said.

"But she's never been sick! She's never been sick a day in her life!"

He tried to lift me up, but I clung to her, still promising her the puppy, a rag doll, stories.

"Kathy," he said, "Constance's girl, Barbette, she's been sick since yesterday."

I didn't answer him. I cradled Mary Aroon, I whispered pleading words to her.

"Kathy, don't!'

"All right." I stood up.

"Darling, you can't do any good here. Go to Constance."

Mike, this was Mike, wanting me to do something. I loved Mike, so I packed a basket, I put in the right things; but all the time anger throbbed in me, a terrible anger against this country, this Grouard.

"Mike," I said, and I was careful not to look at him, "if we'd been in a town—"

"Don't, Kathy. You mustn't think like that."

He walked with me, carrying the basket. I couldn't believe they were gone. My babies. Where had they gone to? Was Mary Aroon wandering through a hazy unreal world looking for her mother? And the baby, he was too little even to do that. Or was that the end? Were they only allowed to live a few months and then, nothing? Why? What was it about? I thought of the Chinese painting, the little man, the unimportant man.

"No, it couldn't be like that."

"Kathy, shhh! I love you."

I didn't know I'd spoken out loud.

We walked to Constance's house.

Madeleine sat with Timmy on the steps; she was blue with cold. They watched us go in but didn't say anything.

The fire had gone out. I shivered. Barbette lay on a bed at the far end of the room. Constance was on her knees beside her. She got up slowly and smiled a weary smile.

"Yes," she said. "The food. You brought food. We will take it into the village. There is no need here."

I leaned against the door. It seemed natural to me that Barbette was dead.

After a while Constance spoke again.

She started to ask me about my children, I could see that she did, but she stopped. Mike stood slightly behind me. He must have made some sign.

She put on a sweater, a jacket, and a coat. Mike went out

and I heard him say to Tim, "Stick around, I'm going to need you."

He was back in a moment with a couple of sticks. "If you're going into the village, Kathy, I want you to take these. The dogs are dangerous. They haven't been fed for a week."

I nodded and took the sticks from him. There was an ache in me for Mike. I thought of myself holding him, kissing him, drawing the pain out of him. I thought of it, but I knew I wouldn't do it, that I couldn't do it. I went out with Constance. Timmy came around the side of the house with a shovel in his hand. I tried not to see.

We walked on a long way.

Once Constance said, "My dear—" and then, "O God!"

Once I changed the basket to my other hand.

The crying and the moaning closed around me. The first house I walked into, they were all dead but an old woman who sat on the floor, her head covered by a blanket, mourning. I put a half-loaf of bread beside her and went out.

The scene outside the next cabin held me. It was like a drawing I had seen in one of the McTavish books—a vision of William Blake's—and everyone knew he was mad. Out the window hung a pair of legs. And in the snow a young man kept clubbing a snarling phantom of a dog. I grasped my stick in both hands and walked toward them. The dog turned on me. I struck it on the nose and it backed off, whining. Another dog, lean and gaunt and ragged, crawled as close as he dared, on his belly. The two watched, their saliva dripping, while the man lowered the body of a girl into the snow. Lifting her, he climbed on the roof and laid her down.

I looked at the roofs of the other cabins, and for the first time saw the rows of feet. I saw then that there were bodies lashed to the trees too. That's the way Mike kept our meat in the winter. Best refrigeration in the world, he'd say. Only you had to be careful to pick a thin-trunked tree or a sapling so a cat or a bear couldn't climb it.

Here and there what I thought was a shadow detached itself from shadow and jumped, yelping at the trees. The creatures would fall back whining their disappointment and their hunger. Luckily most of the dogs were away with the trappers. Only the females with pups had been left, but now these pups were half-grown, and starving. The Indians fed them twice a week, which was only enough to keep life in them. But who could do even that now? Who could fish for them when sickness was a whirlwind among the people?

The mangy animals at my feet had inched forward. I flailed out with my stick and they cowered. The young Indian slid down from the roof and turned into the empty house. I put the other half-loaf of bread inside the door. He shook his head. "Where her shadow go, I follow."

The soft Cree words hurt his throat. He choked. Why had I not seen how gray his face was? He stumbled and half-fell onto a bed of skins. I rekindled the fire, went to him, but he motioned me away.

"Let me at least bring you warm soup." He shook his head. I sighed and turned away. As I reached the door, he called me back. "Mrs. Mike!"

"Yes," I said. "Let me make you easier."

"The dogs."

I didn't understand.

"The dogs," he said. "They break in maybe."

"I'll wedge the door."

"Yes," he said, "for I must lie here many days. Sergeant Mike, him have one, two, maybe three men help him. We die too fast . . . is not enough."

I wedged the door. I remembered that for the ever-after world of the Crees, they must keep their bodies intact. It would not do to appear before Gitche Manito mauled and torn by huskies.

I hurried past the rows of bodies waiting for Mike's shovel, and into a tepee where three children lay tossing. I hauled water, I set it to boil. It was a poor home; they had only manure to burn. I wrung out compresses. I forced soup down swollen throats. Sometimes the little dark faces blurred, and it was my own two I was fighting for.

A child twisted into a terrible knot and died. The mother covered her head and moaned.

"On the gray wings of dawn she went."

246

Yes, the sun was up, but the light from it was cold. The dead in the trees looked at us. The living writhed and choked and spat. And I moved among them, empty. Pain, tiredness, nothing touched me. Once a pair of little arms reached out to me, and I thought: Why these? Something hurt in me when I looked at the two children who were going to live, that were getting better.

I went for more water. Famished shapes slunk after me, but they kept at a distance. I didn't have to use my stick.

I should have felt sorry for these starving animals, but I didn't. I didn't feel anything. "Poor dogs!" I said, and I remembered that I had always had dogs and always loved them. But it meant nothing to me. And then I couldn't remember what meant nothing. I just knew the pail was very heavy. I followed my own footsteps back. I filled, poured, dipped, wrung, cooked, fed.

An old man carried in the body of an old woman. "I been to hill of white crosses," he said. "Snow much deep, ground much hard for old man."

His daughter, the mother of the three children, said without turning, "Put her in tree."

Tears ran down the old man's face. He picked up his burden again and went shuffling out. A moment later there was a cry. I looked out. A dog was tugging at the small shrunken corpse. The old man pulled and fought, but it was torn out of his hands. The dog ran off, dragging his prize, growling in his throat. The old man stumbled after him. The dog dropped the body, and with his eyes on the old man, began rending and tearing it. The old man, sobbing, flung himself on the dog, beating it with feeble hands.

I came at the dog with my stick, but by the time I reached him, the old man was mangled.

A gray dog moved in and fought the tawny one, and while they fought I pulled the old man away. I dragged him to the tepee, but he was dead, and the gray dog was dead. I turned away from the sight of the tawny one as he stood bristling over the shriveled corpse.

Some time after that, Sarah found me. She took me back to Mike. Part of the way she carried me.

# CHAPTER TWENTY-FIVE

The cribs were gone. I never asked Mike what he had done with them. Mary Aroon's crayon drawings were gone, too. I waited until Mike was out and then hunted the house over for them. I guess I was glad that I didn't find them.

Mike was gone every day. He and Tim and Tim's father, old Georges Beauclaire, buried half a village that week. It was mostly the children that went, and the old people.

The second night Mike had taken me up the hill. We had walked between the rows of white crosses. Was the sorrow of other days like the sorrow of now? Did each neat white-washed cross mean empty pain?

A little past the summit of the hill, a new row had been added. These crosses had not yet been stained or salted. But cut into the wood I read the name Mary Aroon Flannigan, and next to this, Ralph Flannigan. My two babies lying on this bare, windswept hill! I knelt down and laid my hands on the snow. I remembered the day, almost three years before, when Mike and I and our baby daughter had ridden into Grouard. I remembered seeing this hill and the bright crosses. Hadn't I known then for a moment? Hadn't I seen myself wandering through the rows that stretched horizontally, then end to end, and then crisscross in shifting geometric patterns?

I had been afraid when Constance had told me of her children, the one she hadn't named and the others. What warning could be plainer than her words, "The women here speak of their first family, their second and third families." Why hadn't I taken my children then, away from this country that had killed them? Why hadn't I taken them to antitoxin and doctors, out of these frozen winters?

I got up and followed him home. What had happened to us, to Mike and me? I wanted to reach out to him, but I couldn't. At first I didn't know why, and then I realized that I was blaming him. Did he feel it? Did he feel the thoughts that lay there, heavy and unspoken between us? He had very little to say to me. He was sweet and kind and patient, only he'd look away from me. And when he thought I was busy with something else, he'd stare at me. I couldn't sleep because of the way he'd look at me. But there was a bitterness I couldn't force back. He'd known. He'd lived in this country. He'd seen what it did to families. Every winter he'd seen children die in epidemics. He knew how virulent even a simple disease like measles was among the Indians. And he knew that in all the Northwest there was no help. He hadn't had the right to bring a wife into this country. He hadn't had the right to have children.

Eight days later the last of the graves had been filled in. I went with the women to whitewash and salt them. I moved, I worked in a kind of horror. I was beginning to realize my children were under there.

It was almost dark when I got home. I stopped outside the house in surprise. There was music coming from it. Such longing was in it, such hunger and desolation, that I stood there crying.

When I went in, I hurried past Mike, not wanting him to see my face. It was an old accordion he was playing, the accordion which had hung in Irish Bill's store for over a year. When he saw me, he stopped. The thing dangled awkwardly from his knee. I don't know, maybe if he had spoken to me then— But he went back to his music. I noticed it was a different song, that he played more self-consciously and made mistakes.

That night I knew I had been living in a daze. Mist and fog had mercifully wrapped themselves around my thoughts. All the time I had been listening for laughter and voices that I would never hear again. Why had I delayed giving away the children's clothes? Why did they still hang in the closet?

That night and for two months after I sat in the room with him. I don't know what he found to do in the daytime, but he kept away from the house. I wanted him, I longed for him, I couldn't stand the loneliness. Sometimes I counted the minutes out loud. Then he'd come.

"Hello, Mike," I'd say.

"Hello, Kathy." And if dinner wasn't ready, he'd go and get his accordion.

While I scrubbed the potatoes and put them on to boil, I went over the things I was going to say to him. But when I was sitting facing him, my heart pounded and I would jump up for salt or to bring milk to the table, or maybe I'd forgotten the napkins. Anyway, what was there to say? Everything went back to four years shared and known together. Each day, even the happiest, was now an entrance into a labyrinth of pain and bitterness.

After dinner I'd sit and listen to him play. He brooded in his music. I brooded in myself. I was alone. Mike was lost to me as surely as the children were. Night after night I listened to his music, hating it. Night after night I stared into the snow, hating it. I watched it melt. I watched the trappers come home. They gashed their feet and ankles and covered their heads with their blankets. The sound of mourning mingled with the sound of that damned accordion.

Spring came. A birthday present, four months late, came from my mother. I was twenty years old. Most girls of twenty were engaged or brides. I laughed when I thought of it, because everything for me was dead. Mike looked up when I laughed, but didn't say anything.

The accordion was driving me mad. When I was alone with it in the daytime, I wanted to smash it, break it into pieces. It had taken the children's place in his heart, and my place.

It was another night. I watched him reach for it again. I knew I was going to stand up and scream. I didn't because they brought a man in just then. They were carrying him on a door. I washed the blood off his face before I saw his eye was almost out, just hanging. I cut the jacket and shirt off him. Mike worked over his face. And somehow Sarah was there and putting on poultices. He was Randy Nolan, new in the territory. He'd come in with the trappers. When I looked at him again, his eyes was in place, and Mike was bandaging it. One of his ribs was broken off and was sticking out through the flesh, and across the others were long, bloody slashes.

"Bear?" Mike asked.

Steve Brooks slumped into a chair. "Where in hell's your whisky?"

I got him some. He didn't bother with the glass I'd

brought. When he'd had a long drink at the bottle, he asked Mike, "Well, what do you think?"

Mike didn't answer. He was occupied with an arm that hung at an odd angle from the socket. Steve Brooks went at the bottle again.

"Save some," Mike said. "I want to bring him around when I've got this arm set."

"Listen," Steve said, "I was with him, out in the canoe, shooting ducks." He paused for another drink. "Joe there was with us." He pointed at the Indian who had helped bring Nolan in. "He'll tell you what I said. I said, 'Don't shoot that damn bear.' Yeah, there was a bear on shore, a grizzly, sort of a yellow one. Reared right up when he saw us. Make a good target, except we was in a lurchy old canoe."

He had another go at the bottle. "Where was I? Well, it don't matter. Anyway, Randy shot him and the bear rolls over dead. Don't move or nothing, see? So we paddle in, and Randy jumped out before we're even beached and goes racing up to where that bear is lying. Well, you can see what happened."

I insisted that he should not be moved, and Sarah agreed with me. I welcomed that work the sick man brought me. I had something to think about, something to do. The first week he was unconscious most of the time. The second week he lay moaning. I didn't think much about whether he'd live or not. I thought more about giving him sweetened warmed milk with bread softened in it—or about making the broth nourishing. After a while Sarah let me even change the poultices. It was amazing to see how they drew the angry red from the newly formed scar tissue.

Then he began to talk to me when I came into the room. He hardly spoke above a whisper. He talked of cities, Chicago. He'd been born in Chicago.

"Been all over," he said. "Once I been to Los Angeles."

"Have you ever been to Boston?" I asked.

"Sure. Got a sister living there." Before I knew what I was doing, I was telling him about my mother and Uncle Martin and my two sisters.

"She always has a canary, and his name's always Pete,

251

and the dogs are always Juno. And there's a room on the top floor full of flowers, and she keeps it just for—" I stopped, ashamed of myself, for I could see I'd tired him.

But we talked again. In the morning when I brought him poached eggs, it was parks and theaters and restaurants we discussed. I described the block I'd lived in, and the house, red brick, and even the stone steps leading up to it. He told me that his sister was married to a traveling man. That she was lonesome and always writing him to come, and that she had a kid he'd never seen.

"Randy, she calls it. Named it for me. Can you beat that?"

He'd always been a rolling stone, he said. But he cursed the day he'd ever rolled into this devil's country, begging my pardon.

Finally he was able to have a pillow under his head, and then two. But he didn't get his strength as he should have. The wounds were closed and no longer draining, but he lay listlessly week after week. Sometimes he'd curse the country and sometimes the bear, but usually he'd just lie there. It was plain he'd never recover the full use of his arm, but his face was not going to be disfigured as I'd thought at first. I was glad of that. It would have been a shame in such a young man.

He thought I was wonderful to take him in and care for him. He didn't know the gap it filled for me. He didn't know I would slave night and day just to hear him tell about the concert he'd heard at Symphony Hall, and what the latest things in clothes were, and that almost everyone had a motor car now. They went awfully fast, twenty-five miles an hour. And the day would come when they wouldn't have to be cranked, either.

I had a plan that excited me and frightened me. I led the talk back to his sister.

That night before dinner I sent a telegram to Agnes Lentfield, Boston, U.S.A.

The next afternoon Mike came in with a wire for Randy Nolan. I acted surprised and said that someone must have written his family.

Mike said, "Kathy, don't you trust me any more?"

"I don't know what you mean."

Mike looked steadily at me.

"Oh, for Heaven's sake, Mike, what if I did send the boy's family a wire? Someone should have sent it long ago. They've got a right to know. Why act so tragic about it?"

He didn't say anything, and I was glad because I didn't want to quarrel. I wanted to know what was in that wire. I walked into Randy's room with it.

"It's from your sister," I said.

He took it from me and tried to open it, fumbling with his good hand.

"I'll do it for you," and I tore it open. Purple block letters: RANDY DEAR STOP MUST COME WHEN FIT TO TRAVEL LOVE AGNES.

"She wants you to come." I showed it to him.

"Well, I don't know," he said.

"What do you mean—you don't know? Of course you know. That's what you've been wanting."

"Yeah," he said, "but what about her kid? Probably won't get no rest with a kid around. And, anyway, I don't know if I'm fit to go yet. It's an awful pull from here to Edmonton, to Boston."

I persuaded him that he was fit. I reminded him that little Randy was named for him. That he was his own nephew whom he'd never seen. At last he agreed to the trip.

"Say," he said, "how'd Agnes find out about me?"

"Oh," I said, as casually as I could, "she was your nearest of kin. We notified her, of course."

"But she isn't my nearest of kin. I've got a mother and—"

"I know, but she's your favorite."

He started to protest.

"Look," I said, "I'm not going to hear any more out of you. Too much excitement is a bad thing."

So I settled him for sleep and went in to have it out with Mike. He was polishing his accordion, and for once I didn't care. I poked up the fire a bit.

"The telegram was from his sister," I said.

He didn't say anything.

"She lives in Boston," I went on.

"Boston?"

"Yes, and she wants him to come right away."

"You mean to Boston?"

"It would be the best thing in the world for him."

"Would it?" He was looking at me strangely.

"I think so," I said.

"Why?"

"Well, it would be good for him to get out of this country."

"What's wrong with this country?"

"He ought to have medical treatment. He ought to see a doctor."

"He's doing all right."

"Considering he's tormented by mosquitoes and insects and a hundred kinds of flies."

"I hadn't noticed any in the house."

"Well, they get in every time the door's opened and— Oh, what's the use, Mike? It's the country that's killing him. How can he get well here? How can he possibly get well here with the memories this place holds? . . . I mean, he ought to get in the sun. You can't put a sick man in this sun. Besides, the mosquitoes would kill him. But summer's short, and then it will be winter. And you know what that means. Dark all morning and the terrible cold and the glare. Then if there's sickness, it's the weak ones that go."

Mike looked at me for a long time. "He can't go by himself."

"I know." I talked very fast. I didn't look at him. "I thought I'd like to take him out. I haven't been out for almost four years. It would be a grand chance. I'd take him clear through to Boston, and see Mother and—"

Mike got up. "If you have to do this, Kathy, go ahead. God knows, maybe it's best. Maybe it will be good for you."

"It's not on my own account," I said.

"I know. I know. When will you go?"

"As soon as I can."

Mike sighed and lit his pipe.

There wasn't much to do. I packed my clothes and the first-aid kit. Randy was able to sit up, but Mike made a stretcher for him so that the trip wouldn't tire him more than need be. This time almost the whole journey was to be made by train. No more waiting for the winter freeze;

spring or summer you could go now, because the Edmonton and British Columbia Line was pushing deep into the Northwest. Of course they were still quite a way from Grouard.

Mike was explaining to me that the best way would be across Lesser Slave Lake to Sawarage, a hundred miles away. "There'll be a fifteen-mile portage that won't be easy with Randy on a stretcher. It might be smart to get a horse and wagon in Sawarage and make it with them."

"Whatever you say."

I looked at the trunk that stood open in the middle of the floor. It was packed with heavy rough shirts and men's pants, small size. I thought of myself in Boston explaining to my mother that I wore pants all the time. I unpacked.

"Well," I said, "I'd better leave a clean house for you. Sarah's going to get your meals and keep an eye on things."

Mike didn't say anything, but spread an old map out on the table.

I was happy, awfully happy, at getting away. And I told myself that, as I dusted and swept and scrubbed. I also told myself that Mike didn't seem to mind my going very much. He could have said more than he did.

"How far are you going with us?" I asked.

"I'll see you on the train, Kathy."

"That's very sweet of you, Mike. But I don't want you to have that long trip. It isn't necessary."

"It *is* necessary, it's necessary to me." He folded up the map and stuffed it into his pocket. He walked to the window and stood looking out.

"God damn it!"

"What?"

"I don't want you to go."

"But—"

"Listen, we haven't even talked it out. You haven't told me how long you're going to stay yet, and I have a feeling—"

"What, Mike? What's your feeling?"

"What's the use? You're going, aren't you?"

"Yes." What else could I say when he asked it like that?

That was in the afternoon. He went out to make arrangements about the boat. At supper Randy joined us. There

255

could be no talk then. And after supper Constance dropped in. She was terribly excited about my going "out." She insisted upon giving me the kerchief she wore on Sundays. It was real linen. After she'd left, Mike said we'd better turn in, that it would be a hard trip for me and I should be resting. I agreed with him.

I brushed my hair out in front of the mirror. I took a long time over it because Mike loved to watch me. I looked at him in the mirror and saw that he was watching me now. I smiled at myself in the glass. We would say our real goodbys tonight because in the morning everyone would be there to see us off—Sarah, the Beauclaires, Old Bill, everyone. But tonight it would be like in the old days; he'd kiss me and hold me and all the silences would be broken through.

He didn't kiss me or hold me. He said, "Good night, Kathy," very gravely.

I lay beside him for hours wondering whether or not he was asleep.

In the morning there was a lot to do. I already had the makings of sandwiches laid out. I just slapped them together. All right, I thought, that's the way he wants it. He hadn't spoken to me of the future, of when I came back. That was all right with me. I'd be glad never to set eyes on this country again. But maybe he thought there was still time; maybe he didn't realize these were our last moments alone. I finished packing the hamper and snapped it closed.

"I guess there'll be a crowd down at the lake," I said. But he was lugging out my trunk. I wasn't even sure he heard me.

Everyone was at the dock, and everyone had instructions for me. I was to look up a girl in Los Angeles and somebody's mother in Detroit.

"But I'm going to Boston."

So, I was going to Boston, it wouldn't be much out of my way, and they loaded me down with names and addresses and presents. If I got to New York there was a little restaurant on Seventh Avenue . . . And the things I was to bring back—dresses, pipes, pictures . . .

The sick man was lowered into the launch. Tim kept begging Mike to let him go as far as the train.

"If it's all right with Constance," Mike said.

James McTavish gave me a list of books I was to pick up second hand if I could.

"But, Mother, I've never seen a train." That ended it. Constance gave in, and Timmy came with us.

Bishop Grouard shook my hand, gave me his blessing, and if I got a chance I was to look up Father Grady at St. Anne's. And somehow, all the while, through the confusion, I was conscious of Sarah. She watched me as I smiled and joked, and her eyes were mournful. At the last, when Mike was holding out his hand to me and Timmy was yelling, "Get in, Kathy!" Sarah came up to me.

"Mrs. Mike," she said, "come back. You must come back."

Mike lifted me into the boat. I turned and waved, but the faces blurred into a wall of faces. And the shouting, calling, and well-wishing reached me as noise from which I could not separate a word. All the time I was thinking: How could she know?

The water cut me off from Grouard. I looked at the hill. We were too far away to see the crosses. Don't stand here, I told myself. Walk to the front of the boat. It would be symbolic, a looking forward. But I didn't go forward, not until I felt Mike looking at me.

There were wild geese honking and flying overhead. They flew in a pattern, making a V across the sky. There had been patterns for me too. A red brick home, mother, sisters, a yellow Pete and a brown Juno. I had broken that pattern for Uncle John's. Then Mike had carried me into a wild white pattern that had turned gray and frozen.

Randy and Tim and I laughed over my many and varied commissions. Mike smoked and listened. It took us ten hours to reach Sawarage. We were all cramped and tired. We split up for the night, various families taking us in. And in the morning we followed Mike's plan of renting a horse and wagon. The rail lines were only fifteen miles away. But what a fifteen miles!

The men who had taken us in the boat kept on with us. We couldn't have done it without them, for the trail was muskegged. We wallowed in mud, the four men pushing the

257

wagon from one watery rut into another. They laid boards and tried to keep the wheels on them. But every few minutes the horse would get bogged, sinking to his knees in the marshy places. By the time he had been pulled, coaxed, hauled, and kicked out of it, the slime had oozed over the boards, and once again the wheels would go slithering off. To make it worse, Randy gave advice from the wagon. I saw the boatmen look murder at him more than once. We ate lunch mired to the wheel hubs, and floundered on again. I couldn't believe train tracks had been laid on ground like this.

"Maybe it's a rumor," I said. "After all, have any of you ever *seen* the train?"

And then, there it was. In the midst of nowhere stood an engine, a caboose, and a car with seats. We investigated and exclaimed over everything. But not as much as the men who came out of the station exclaimed over us. I guess we were a sight, solid mud up to our hips, and the rest of us smears and splashes.

The railroad men were very hospitable. They took us into the station, which was a derailed box car, and fed us black coffee.

Mike asked them if it was true that, in bringing the line in, they followed the old buffalo trails. They said they did that as nearly as possible. The buffaloes always chose the easiest grades and cleared paths in heavily timbered sections.

They discussed the country, and Mike said it would open up once the railroad was in. "In ten years there'll be tourists and hotels for them to stay at. The vacationing bankers and holiday lawyers will ruin the hunting and trapping, God help us!" The railroad men nodded and spat and agreed with him.

"Although," said the engineer, "you raise mosquitoes in this country like they raise cows in Jersey, and they'll keep the tourists out better than anything." And he swore to us that the summer before he had seen big mosquitoes who couldn't get through the netting themselves, push the little ones through.

Mike laughed politely and asked about the fare. It was they who laughed then. "We can't charge you for the kind of ride the young lady will get. She travels as our guest, but at her own risk."

And though Mike argued till I was afraid they would change their minds, they didn't.

About that time we missed Timmy. Mike found him in the engine, fondling levers, gloating over switches, touching buttons and knobs.

We made a bed for Randy in the caboose. And Mike brought my trunk in. The small overnight case he carried into the car with seats. From deep inside a pocket he pulled out ten ten-dollar bills.

"Not so much," I said.

"I'll feel better if you have it. You may need it, you never can tell," and he stuffed the money into my hand.

Tim and the boatmen came up and said good-by. Suddenly I realized Mike was saying good-by too.

"I think you were right, Kathy, that the change will do you a lot of good."

The conductor looked in on us. "We're pulling out, Sergeant."

"Kathy . . ."

"Yes?"

"I want you to have a good time."

"I will."

"Sergeant!"

"All right. Kathy, I love you. I—" His arm went around me, clumsy and uncertain. I watched him walk away, and then he was outside and we were smiling at each other through the window. The train jerked forward. Mike walked along under the window. My last picture of him was standing alone, against the whole Northwest.

I stared out at the wet dripping country, my heart aching with the things said and the things unsaid.

The first hour the engine jumped the track twelve times. At each derailment the crew tumbled out and lifted it back on. It took us two days and one night to go two hundred miles. But there were a lot of diversions. There were contractors' tents all along the way where we'd stop for food and talk and black coffee. Then on again. If I got tired of sitting, I'd get out and walk beside the train and talk to the engineer about all the things I was going to do in the city.

259

Every once in a while the ground became slushy, and water covered the tracks. Then I'd hop on and look after Randy. I began to enjoy the trip, to look forward to Boston.

## CHAPTER TWENTY-SIX

Causeway Street. The North Station. Boston. There it was, gleaming in the rain, familiar and yet unreal. I had the same uneasy feeling you have in a dream when you speak freely and yet a bit dubiously to someone you have loved and who is now long dead. All through the trip with the sick man I had been fretting impatiently, burning to see my home and Mother. Now I was afraid.

My sister, Anna Frances, and Randy's sister, Mrs. Lentfield, met us at the station. There were introductions, talk about baggage, and hasty good-bys. Randy had stood the trip extremely well, and he was happy, confident that Boston surgeons would have him walking again. I felt I'd been right to bring him.

My sister had been watching me thoughtfully and saying very little. Mother was home, nursing a cold. Mary Ellen hoped to get down from Rhode Island. There were none of the questions I had been expecting about Grouard and Mike. Instead, my sister took my hand as we rode home in one of the new trolleys and said, "Mother is very happy you've come home."

"I want to stay a long time," I said carefully.

"As long as you want," my sister said. "This is your home."

If my sister was strangely silent, my mother was even more strangely talkative. She kissed me and smiled at me and spoke of a thousand and one things—of the elevated railroad they were building, of my sister Ellen's baby, of the awful weather, of guess whom she had run into at the library, of the good and bad habits of the boarders, of the difficulty they had had finding out when my train was to arrive—in short of everything under the sun except my four years in the Northwest.

My mother was looking remarkably young and gay. She

insisted her cold was much better, just seeing me had been the tonic she needed, so we ended up going out to lunch and taking in the town. Mother knew her Boston, and I had to admire everything, even the new bank building. After a while I was carried away by her gaiety, but even so I felt there was something forced and nervous about it.

The second day there was a homecoming party for me. Boys and girls whose faces I vaguely remembered crowded into my mother's living room. Someone played "Alexander's Ragtime Band" on the piano. I missed Uncle Martin's bagpipe, but he ruefully explained that the boarders couldn't stand its "outlandish noise," and it was gathering dust in the attic.

A tall pale youth called Dick or some other equally colorless name invited me to dance. My sister served sherbet and small delicate cakes. I ate them greedily. The food was the only thing that tasted real to me.

Dick made me sit down next to him at the piano while he sang "Oh, You Great Big Beautiful Doll" in an exaggerated comic style, looking at me and grinning after every chorus. A din of chatter and gossip filled the room. I got up and walked out on the porch. I couldn't stand so many people so close to me. I was overpowered by the noise, the perfume, the decorations, and by the glare of the electric lights. After the soft glow of candles, everything seemed harsh and artificially bright.

On the porch the air was cold and wet. It felt good. I strode into the drizzle. I turned my face up, and the rain caressed my cheeks. The subdued secret patter it made on the pavement soothed me.

"Kathy, what are you doing out here?"

Dick was standing on the porch, testing the rain with his outstretched hand. He drew me back under the eaves.

"Aren't you enjoying the party?"

"Oh, yes, it's nice," I said.

"I know how you feel. I like to get away from the crowd too." He looked me over curiously. "You're liable to catch cold. It's raining, you know." He laughed and leaned on the porch rail beside me.

"Well, how does it feel to be back in civilization?"

261

He edged closer and put his hand on mine.

"You'll think I'm kidding, but it was quite a blow to my young life when you moved away."

I drew back, feeling suddenly uncomfortable in my sister's full-skirted party dress.

"You're teasing," I said, trying to match his gay air. "Aren't you, Dick . . . it *is* Dick?" Now I was really confused and hardly ready to resist when he took both my hands and began to speak earnestly and rapidly.

"Kathy, you have no idea how beautiful you look in that gown. I'm quite an expert on color harmony, and take it from me, chartreuse is the perfect thing for your eyes and hair. I will always remember you as you are now."

I wanted to say this is my sister's dress, and I generally wear trousers, sometimes two pair if it's cold enough, and this talk of color harmony is ridiculous, and you know you don't mean a word of all that chatter, and please let go of my hands. . . . But a numb bewilderment was on me, and in a moment he was drawing me closer. When I saw that silly face bending down toward me, however, the spell broke. I laughed and pushed Dick away. I could see that he was as surprised as I was at my strength and roughness.

"Go in and play with the girls," I said. I opened the screen door and walked upstairs. I was gleeful. In Alberta I had been delicate, even pampered. Sarah kept a continuous eye on me. Mike saw that I had nine hours' sleep. Everybody knew I had to be careful because of my pleurisy. But down here in Boston I was almost indecently healthy and strong. For the first time since I'd left, I allowed myself to think of Mike. There were no men like him in Boston. Tall, yes, but not solid. Brilliant, but not enduring. I sat on the bed in my sister's room and smiled proudly. After a while, I cried.

The door opened softly, and my mother stole into the room. She put her arms about me. "Katie," she said, "you're lonely."

"It's all over now," I said. I rubbed my eyes with my hands and stood up. "I'd rather not go back to the party, Mother. I'd rather just sit here and talk to you. We really haven't had a chance to be alone."

"I wanted you to myself too, Katie. But I thought, after all those years, you'd like some fun . . . some gaiety."

"Mother," I said abruptly, "I love him. I always will."

"I know."

"I wish he were here."

My mother smoothed my hair. "We can work that out," she said. "I don't want you to leave home for a long time." She looked thoughtfully down at the floor. "Perhaps . . . Sergeant Flannigan would like to come to Boston.

"For a visit? He couldn't do that."

"I mean permanently," my mother said.

"No, Mother. In Boston, Mike would be just a cop."

"Katherine Mary." My mother spoke in a new firm voice. "The last thing I would ever do is to interfere in my daughters' lives. You were married somewhere off in the wilderness to a man I never met, and you've lived four years in a place I never heard of. I always dreamed of the day when you would have a big church wedding with your sisters and myself by your side. Well, that can't be helped. It's a wild thing you are, just like your father that went off to Australia and came back with a parrot on his shoulder. But it's not my happiness I'm thinking of now. You've lived hardly like a woman, stuck in a little cabin with snow outside and mosquitoes inside, with not two dresses to your name, and not a white woman to pass the time of day with, nor a doctor to care for your babies when they lay dying, far from your friends and your family. It's not good for you, Katie, and it's not right. I'm an old-fashioned woman, Katie. I believe a woman should stick by her husband. But this time it's different. If your man wants you, let him come here and get you. It's no blame I have for him. A man lives the life he has to. But I'm your mother. And I'm not letting you go north again to loneliness and the graves of your children!"

"I don't want to," I murmured.

"And now," my mother said brightly, "you're to forget all this. You're to remember you're only a child of twenty years, and you're to cheer up and smile. Surely you've worked hard enough and suffered long enough. Now, let's go back to the party."

"All right," I said, "I will."

So I went down and danced and talked and sang and drank punch, and though I didn't believe it was possible, my spirits began to lift, and when I went to bed that night I was too exhausted to think back or brood; so I went to sleep content, if not happy.

In the morning I gave my sister back her party skirt, and Mother took me out and bought me one.

"Would you like to go to the theater tonight?" she asked.

"Yes," I said. "Tonight, and tomorrow night too."

There were weeks of plays, operettas, and musical comedies—color, movement, and song reaching out from the stage and holding me entranced. *The Red Mill, The Dollar Princess* . . . It was after *The Chocolate Soldier*. Mother and I were riding home on the "L." The tunes I had heard were running through my head, the full taffeta skirts were still whirling. Mother was speaking of the boarders, and I wished she wouldn't. I wished she would let me waltz and coquette with the twelve tall, gold-braided, uniformed men and sing with the pretty powdered women. It was about Miss Ivy that she didn't know what to do.

"She has a perfectly good position. Why, she earns more than Mr. Monts. Of course, when I took her in she wasn't earning, but now it's different. She can afford to pay for her room; after all, it's the nicest in the house, and I think she should."

The blue painted sky with its white clouds gave place to the real one, black, wet, and drizzly.

"Why don't you ask her to pay, Mother?"

"Well, I've hinted at it. But you're right, Katherine Mary, and I'll be asking her straight out."

I was ashamed of myself for being so thoughtless. Mother'd done so much for me since I'd been here. It wasn't right. She was middle-aged and working hard for the little she had. When we went to *The Pink Lady* and *Quaker Girl,* I took Mother. We saw *Peg o' My Heart* too, so sweet and Irish, with love going all the wrong way till the end.

We went to all the shows, and there were plenty, for Boston was always the big try-out town. But the most thrilling evening was the one spent at the Boston Theatre. Sarah

Bernhardt was playing, and the Washington Street entrance was jammed with pushing sables and prodding minks. Mother and I went around to the side and into the theater by a sort of tunnel. The galleries were steep, and we climbed to the very top, so high that I got vertigo and pictured myself crashing into the orchestra. Funny, at Hudson's Hope I scaled the highest, most dangerous bluffs and wasn't afraid.

Well, I couldn't tell you much about the play, but every movement of that woman is engraved upon my mind. She was tall and very slight, with a mass of red hair piled high on her head. She hypnotized the entire audience. We strained forward to catch each inflection of that clear, high voice. The other actors annoyed me. I waited for them to finish, that she might answer. What a night! After that I piled my red hair high on my head.

"I tell you, I left it in my room." I paused on the stairs, uncertain whether or not I should go down. I didn't like Miss Ivy. She spoke in a shrill excited way, and since she had been paying Mother five dollars a week it seemed that her voice had gone up another octave. Mother'd already seen me, so I walked on down.

"I'm sure you've mislaid it," Mother was saying.

"Good Heavens, is something missing?" I asked.

Miss Ivy ignored me. "I couldn't have mislaid all *three* of them."

"Three of what?" I asked.

"The *Atlantic Monthly*," my mother explained. "She saves them, and now she can't find the last two issues, and—"

" 'Can't find' is one way of putting it. Why I never even laid eyes on this month's copy. That is, just barely. I hate to accuse anyone in this house, Mrs. O'Fallon, but it seems plain that someone has entered my room, and do you know, I had left a gold ring on the wash stand. It was just fortunate they didn't see it."

My mother looked very pale and very angry. "I refuse to listen to such insinuations. There's been nobody in your room except myself, to clean. And I think it's just possible that in clearing up after you, I threw out the papers you're missing. If I did, it's your own fault for keeping the room in such a litter."

"Litter! Well, I like that! Not only is there no privacy here but—"

I mumbled something about going down to the corner and shut the door on Miss Ivy's list of injuries. It was good to get off by myself and not have to look at graveyards and Emerson's home or Julia Howe's or Booth's or anybody's, but just wander without bothering to *go* anywhere.

There were bicycles on the street, but not many. Mostly there were shining black motorcars that honked impatiently at nervous, traffic-leery horses in blinders.

I hesitated which way to go. I'd seen the downtown district with its steel and cut stone and marble. I'd walked along the Back Bay Fens and wondered why the houses all had their backs to the water. So now I turned toward Beacon Hill. I looked in through tall iron gates at expanses of green lawns, at stone mansions. I passed brick walls that towered over me and imagined the lawns and the houses. I caught glimpses of wonderful flower beds and shaded walks. Once some elegant young ladies were playing croquet and missing the wickets. Once a gardener nodded to me, and I nodded back.

From the other side of a fence a black spaniel kept pace with me, barking. I laughed when I thought of this little dog beside my Juno, or imagined his shrill yelp lifted against the baying of a deep-chested wolf.

It was getting awfully warm. I felt hot and thirsty, and there was nothing around me but estates. Well, I thought, I guess they can spare a glass of water. I had to walk another quarter of a mile to find one that had no wall. I turned in at the driveway past all the "Private" and "No Tresspassing" signs.

Rows of flowers lined the drive. They were beautiful, but you hadn't the pleasure of hunting for wild violets under their leaves. These violets were planted to be looked at. There were no surprises, either; in the pansy row there were pansies, and in the jonquil row, jonquils.

The drive took me up to a gigantic stone house, very massive and very ugly. I hesitated about which door to knock at. I wasn't going to go around to the back, yet I didn't like the looks of the front door. I just knew it would be opened by a butler or a maid in a frilly cap. I decided to try the side door. But I might as well have saved myself the walk, for it was opened by an elderly man in evening dress, white gloves, and a green striped shirt who lifted one eyebrow, a trick I had practiced but never perfected.

"You wished something?"

"A glass of water, please. I'm thirsty."

"I'm terribly sorry, Miss, but didn't you notice the signs? Madame would not—"

"All right." I walked down the steps.

"But if you're really thirsty—"

"Never mind." I walked back the long flowered path and back the five miles to Mother's. I couldn't understand. The water was free, it was supplied by the city. I thought of the hundreds of trappers' cabins throughout the Northwest, the doors left open, the food there for you, the wood cut and stacked.

When I got home I found they were waiting lunch for me. Mother was in the parlor adding and re-adding the items deductible from her taxes. In keeping house, I had never had to bother about rent, mortgages, taxes, assessments, any of those things.

Anna Frances told me to hurry down, everyone was hungry, and she was putting on the toast.

As I washed my hands and face I noticed that they needed it, which proved there was as much dirt on Beacon Hill as any other part of the city. The thought restored my spirits.

A wail from Anna Frances brought me to the head of the stairs. "Oh, Mother, weren't you watching the toast?"

"Why, no. You put it on, dear."

I ran down. Everyone was at the table. I slid into my place, but not quickly enough. My sister waved a black square of scorched toast at me.

"You could have hurried. I told you I was putting it on."

Mr. Monts turned to Miss Ivy. "She's always burning the toast."

"I've never made toast in this house before, so I don't know how I possibly could have burnt any."

267

"Why don't you scrape it off?" Mother asked. "It's not so bad when the black part's scraped off."

"Oh, it's no use!" Anna Frances carried the toast into the kitchen and dropped it into the sink.

Mrs. Ellison shook her head. "It's wicked to waste food like that."

"I took a walk to Beacon Hill," I said, smiling around on everyone. But it didn't work because Miss Ivy, who had sat drumming her fingers on the table in an effort to think, said suddenly, "You did too make toast, Anna Frances. It was three weeks ago Friday, when that young gentleman friend of yours was at the house." Then, turning to Mr. Monts, "I knew she had. And you're right, she burnt it then too."

"It's not the burning of it," Mrs. Ellison said, "it's the waste."

"If toast can't be a light, even brown," Mr. Monts grumbled, "it's better to eat bread."

Anna Frances began to cry.

"For Heaven's sake!" I said, jumping up so hard my chair fell on the floor. "All she did was burn a piece of toast. So you'll go without—or if you must have toast, you'll toast it yourselves."

"We don't have kitchen privileges," Mrs. Monts said haughtily.

Mother said, "Sit down, Katie." And I would have, but just then Miss Ivy began fanning herself and saying the smoke from the burnt toast in the kitchen was just reaching her, that it was making her ill. That she was sensitive to smoke.

What would she have done, I wondered, if she had stood all day in the river with her skin blistering? That smoke she couldn't have waved away with her hand.

I turned from the table and the faces of the boarders. With a third of a village dead there hadn't been this much commotion. When you've seen bodies lifted from the wells and root cellars that were charred as black as the toast they complained about, when you've seen little Tommy Henderson with his skin flaking off in cinders, and then hear the same words that describe those memories describe the smell of a kitchen or the condition of a gas range—then you real-

268

ize many things. I knew now how alien these people were to me, how different their whole pattern of thought. Even my mother and sister were irrevocably separated from me. They could never know any part of my life up there. They could never know my children or my husband.

My husband. That was why I was crying. I'd been seeing Mike as I'd seen him last, standing alone against the Northwest. I understood now. It was the country, the country I was homesick and longing for, that made him *Sergeant Mike Flannigan.* I'd been unjust, I'd been wrong. I knew it now, and I had to tell him. I had to have his arm around me and his voice telling me the wonderful things about the stars and wolf dung. But mostly I had to explain, to get him to understand the things that had piled up in me. I had to tell him that after the children died I thought I couldn't stand it, that I had to get away.

"But the only thing I can't stand is not being with you, not being yours again. Mike, you must let me come back into my own place. I'll never leave you again. I couldn't, you're my life, this is my life . . ." And I spread my arms taking in the miles of endless snow.

He met me at the train. He had put bells on the dogs. Wrapped in a buffalo robe was a little new Juno the Second, whose eyes were hardly open yet. And the big Juno, the team leader, had almost broken the traces to get at me.

And now I was beside Mike in the cutter. Mike! His voice was low and choked up. He'd start to say things, and then he'd stop and just look at me. Then I'd forget what I was saying and just look at him. After a while I told him about Boston and the boarders. He laughed when I came to the toast and said, "When little things are so important, it's because there aren't any big ones."

"But everything's big here. Why, look at those firs and all the miles between things, and, and—look at you," I added. His arm tightened around me.

I tried to tell him how wrong and confused I'd been about everything. But he wouldn't let me. He kept kissing me, over and between and through all the words. He was so good to me and wonderful that it made me cry. I cried, too,

269

because of his lonely nights with no children and no Kathy. My tears turned to sleet, and Mike had to stop and wipe my face.

"Mike, promise me, we'll live together all our lives and never be away from each other."

He held me. The reins dropped, and Juno had to pick her own way.

"We'll start over, won't we, Mike?"

"Sure." And he made me imitate Miss Ivy again.

I had to know all about Sarah and Constance and Timmy and old Georges, and could you get more things at the store with the train so close.

All of Boston now seemed as unreal to me as the plays I'd seen there. After landscapes that were trimmed and raked and pruned into existence, it was thrilling to skim across unbounded open country. The snow shone and sparkled. The sun struck here and there among the fine particles, touching them with cold fire. I didn't think how beautiful it was. I thought how many times I had watched it before. And now for the first time it was familiar; I recognized it just as I recognized the way the air smelled.

Mike had been watching me, and now he said, "How does it seem to be home, Kathy?"

That's it, it was home.

That night at Sawarage I woke myself up to make sure I wasn't dreaming, that Mike was really beside me. I kissed the pillow close up near his cheek because I didn't want to wake him. He opened one eye and grinned at me.

"Don't waste 'em, kitten."

It wasn't until late the next day that we got home. Icy branches arched like crystal domes above the cabin.

"There's nothing so fine in all of Boston." I jumped out of the sled and ran up on the porch, but Mike got to the door first.

"Listen, Kathy. It's in a bit of a mess. At first glance it won't look very good. I guess I'm not much of a housekeeper."

"Don't be silly," I said. "It can all be straightened out." Mike looked dubious, so I prepared myself for the worst and pushed the door open.

The house was scrubbed, polished and shining. I looked at Mike to see if he had been joking, but one glance at his face convinced me that he hadn't. Everything was in its place, and on the table was a steaming hot dinner.

Just then I heard the back door close. We ran to the kitchen in time to see Sarah striding off. We called to her, and she raised her arm above her head to show she heard. But she wouldn't call back or even turn to look at me.

Coming from the crowding, pushing, noisy world, I was impressed again by the delicacy of the Indian women. Sarah did not understand politeness; she understood that we must be alone—that this return was Mike's and mine.


### CHAPTER TWENTY-SEVEN

August 1914, and war. Mike got the news by telegraph the eighteenth of the month, but we had known it was coming since the fourth, when Britain had declared herself at war. It seemed strange that guns we couldn't hear and events we knew nothing of could reach into our remote settlement—but here and there men left their trap lines, sold their equipment, and rode the train into Edmonton.

It was by train that we got our month-old newspapers. We read them and were shocked, as the rest of the world had been weeks before. The news we received by telegraph in cold, blunt statements made it hard to picture blocked roads of streaming refugees and armies like juggernauts closing in. But these first war editions blazed with atrocities and published photographs of blurred dead bodies and emaciated living ones. I had never seen such tension and excitement as they caused. There were fifteen or twenty people waiting their turn at each copy.

More deserted trap lines, more secondhand equipment to be bought cheap at the store. Timmy came to say good-by and to ask Mike to look after his pony.

I couldn't help saying to him, "Tim, think of your mother."

"Father'll be with her. Besides, Paul, my brother in Edmonton, has enlisted, and he's got a wife. Besides, I have to go."

I looked at Tim, a young man now. I sighed and kissed him. The pony whinnied and nickered, and Timmy turned to wave. He wrote to Constance from Camp Valertier, from Quebec, from England, then from St. Nazaire, France. Mike and I got a postcard of the Loire River and one of a cathedral.

By the end of winter I had delivered five wires, "Missing in action," "Killed in action." I took them on snowshoes into the village and twice off to lonely cabins. I never said anything. I always tried to. But when I handed over the envelope, a man died. Even before it was unsealed, he died. There are no words against death. Death just is.

Sarah came into the office one day.

"Make me a cup of tea, Mrs. Mike."

That very ordinary request frightened me, for in all the time I'd known her Sarah had never asked anything of anyone. I put the water on and sat with her. Mike worked at the desk without looking up. I wondered if Sarah was ill. The water bubbled. I added the tea and let it simmer.

"Will you have some?" I asked Mike, but he shook his head and I poured only two cups. Sarah drank slowly and steadily.

"More?" I asked, getting up.

"No. It is enough." Then abruptly, "Constance's girl, Madeleine, she have babies, she die."

"Madeleine died?"

"I take two babies from her. She bleed. I make it stop outside, but inside she still bleed."

I watched Mike lay down his pen. "She had twins?" he asked.

"Yes. A boy and a girl."

No one said anything. We sat and drank tea. Mike returned to his ledger. It grew dark.

Three hours later the telegraph began to click, that click I had come to associate with death. It almost seemed as if we had been waiting for it. Sarah raised her head and watched Mike closely as he copied the message.

"MARCH 27—MR. AND MRS. GEORGES BEAUCLAIRE . . . REGRET TO INFORM YOU . . . KILLED IN ACTION . . ."

Mike stood up. "I'll take it over."

272

"No, I'll take it." He handed me the telegram. I wanted to crumple it, destroy it, tear the words to pieces. "I'll take it to Constance." I turned to Sarah. "Does she know about Madeleine?"

Sarah nodded. "She was with her. By now she home."

"Why? Why does it happen like this? Why both together and why to Constance?"

Before they could answer me, I went out. I knew there was no answer, and I didn't want any more of that silence.

Poor Constance, mother of sorrows. Already she was grieving, and then I'd come. But it might help her if it's me, I said to myself. Maybe she'll cry or say something then. It was strange: two taken and two given. Twins. No one had suspected it would be twins, not even Sarah.

Finally I was there. I knocked and went in. She came toward me.

"Constance . . ."

I was going to prepare her, to say wise and gentle things, but all I could do was to hold out the telegram. She stood looking at it, but she wouldn't take it. I put it on the corner of the table. I was glad to look away from those violet eyes, from the marble face.

She spoke through stiff lips, "Which one?"

"Paul," I said.

Next spring it was Timmy, and again I carried it to her. It felt unreal. I had done it all before. I couldn't be doing it now. She was preparing the babies' bottles; she turned to me smiling and saying, "Kathy."

I stood there where I had stood in the winter, by the corner of the table. Under my hand lay the first wire. It was unopened and thick with dust. She had never touched it. I put the second wire on top of the first and went out without looking at her. I guess it helped her not to have to see it written. Words made you know. They made it harder to dream and pretend. I know all about dreaming and pretending. Sometimes at night I still held Mary Aroon and Ralph in my arms.

It suddenly seemed strange to me, that silence about the dead. Mike and I never spoke of our children. All this time I had drawn back from any reminder of them. I had

273

forced my thoughts away, flinching if they got too close. Only recently had I allowed myself to think of them, and the pleasure had been more than the pain.

Now suddenly I wanted to laugh with Mike again about the time Mary Aroon got her head stuck in the porch railing. It had been awful getting her out, and later, when I was telling Oh-Be-Joyful about it, Mary Aroon put her head in all over again to show how it had happened. When we told Mike at dinner he had all he could do to keep her from going through still another demonstration.

I almost wanted to go back to Constance and tell her that after a while she would be able to think of Timmy, and each time the hurt would be less. Then I remembered her families, her lost families of children, and I felt ashamed. The day my own two had died, on the way to the village, she had tried to tell me something, had started to say something. It was this, of course. I smiled and told myself, "Katherine Mary, you are like a baby that is so pleased with himself for standing up that he doesn't notice anyone else has learned to stand too."

Mike was staring out the window. Timmy's little cayuse stood in the pasture with her nose laid along the fence. Mike walked to the stove and knocked the ashes from his pipe into it.

"Sarah was here. I don't know how the devil she knew, but she asked about Tim."

"Did you tell her?"

"She said, 'When they're little, sickness. When they're big, war.' "

I remembered the first time I'd seen Timmy. He came riding up with Constance Cameron. "He held the puppy up for me to see, and I held up Mary Aroon."

"Yes," Mike answered. "Remember that? She was bundled right up to her nose." He broke off suddenly and looked at me carefully for a long time. Then he smiled.

"Mike," I said, "it just came out. I was thinking of it and then I'd said it." He reached for my hand.

"On the way home I was thinking about the time she got her head caught in the porch railing. I wanted to talk about it, but I didn't know I was going to."

We sat together, the memories holding us silent. When words came we hardly noticed, they were so much a continuation of our thoughts.

"You used to say she was a born actress. Remember, Mike?"

"She was too. Remember the time Ralph fell off the bed, all the attention he got?"

"And a couple of hours later Mary Aroon fell off too!" We were both laughing now.

"Kathy," Mike said, "you're crying."

"No, I'm not." He held up his hand. It was wet with my tears.

"I didn't know it," I said.

We sat a long time watching the shadows of the trees stretch over the grass.

The world outside, the noisy quarreling world that sent us the wires of death, sent us a new death. Born in the dirt of European trenches, in the fall of 1918, the flu spread into the Canadian Northwest. And we died, again without doctors, serum, or help. Even the wild forest creatures died. The bear was the only red-blooded animal to escape it. But then, as Mike says, nothing affects bears.

I followed Sarah into the bedroom of the Beauclaire cabin. She closed the door and we stood in darkness, listening to the soft voice of Bishop Grouard. It came to us indistinctly from beyond the door, a low murmur, rising and falling in benediction, in prayer. His deep tones were punctuated by feeble responses, barely audible. The pauses were awful. They might mean she hadn't the strength to answer, or they might mean she was dead. I was getting used to the dark. I saw the big square shape that was a bureau; I saw the twins asleep in their bed.

Sarah's voice came out of the shadows. "Too bad. She live enough just to see her children dead." I couldn't answer her, and the darkness was thick between us.

After a while the Bishop called to us. He was pulling on his coat. In the corner by the door an Indian child stood crying.

The Bishop sighed. "I am needed in another home for

the same purpose." He turned for the last time toward the bed, but Constance lay with eyes closed, unmoving, unknowing. He went out, the child following him. Death was everywhere.

Georges sat huddled by the bed. But it was many hours before Constance moved or spoke. Once she opened her eyes and said, "I know I'm dying. But, Kathy, I'm so tired I don't care." Georges jumped up and began to plead with her. But Sarah only nodded. "She does not care. I know. At the end there are only the children, and when they go . . . nothing."

I smoothed her pillow. It was made from a flour sack. I smiled when I remembered the way I had first pictured Constance. What a shame to have put her in satin skirts heavy with brocade. I realized now that there was no place for the sapphire rings in golden settings that I had wanted for her. You would not encumber hands with jewels and have them mend and wash and handle babies. Constance's hands had always fascinated me. They lay, slim and brown, against the covers. You would not think there was the strength in them to make such a life, dig it out of nothing.

Why was I thinking everything in a new way? Where was the Kathy who had longed for finery and romance? Because she had once been me, was she closer to me now than any other?

More hours. I heard my mother saying, "There are those in this world born to sorrow." Why had I always pitied Constance? I couldn't understand it now. She had had sorrow: her family, all her children—gone. But death does not stand at the end of life, it is all through it. It is the fear of losing, the knowledge of losing that makes love tender. I remembered what she had said about the little things being the important things. I felt closer to her than I ever had. So much of what she had said came back to me. I remembered how she had talked to me that first day in Grouard. I hadn't liked it then, her emphasis on the fact that she and I were white, the only white women. There were already strong ties of love and friendship between me and my Indian neighbors. I had Sarah. But now I understood. It wasn't *that* she meant. She had tried to say, "You and I came to this country. We have known other things. The rest were born here, so they live here. But we chose it, you and I, and we are the only ones."

I bent over her. I wanted to say, "Yes, now I see. I understand you. And I can be a better friend than I ever was." But she lay so still.

We sat through the night. I felt stiff and cold. Sarah got up to prepare a fresh broth of herbs. But Constance remained motionless. Her lips were parted, and her breath came and went too gently.

I watched it grow light. Mike came to take my place, to beg me to sleep. She opened her eyes again, looked at all of us, knew us.

"Mike and Kathy, take the twins."

Georges threw himself across the bed, sobbing, clutching at her with his red hands. She patted him absently, as she would a child. She spoke. "It's cold," she said. And then, "Timmy, light the fire."

That was all. I cried against Mike's coat for one of the dearest friends I ever had.

All the while I was conscious of Sarah moving about, silently doing the things that must be done. She grieved, but who would lay out Constance's blue cotton dress, who would wash the body and prepare it, if not Sarah? So she went sorrowing from one task to another. At first I didn't try to help her. I didn't want to touch Constance. The body of a loved person is a terrible mockery. It says, "Look, I am still here," when you know she is not there. I had held those hands and kissed that mouth and combed that hair. I didn't want to do it again now.

Sarah passed me with a kettle in her hands. Her back was terribly bent, and her motions were slow. I had never before seen how old she was. But she didn't stop working. Her love for Constance wasn't wasted like mine in mourning and grief.

I shook off my numbness. I opened the door and went into the other bedroom. Two little figures stood on the bed. One had a shirt over his head which Mike was trying to pull past his ears.

"Here," I said, "you've got to unbutton another button."

277

"Then you'd have to take the whole thing off," he protested.

"There are times when it pays to start all over again, and this is one of them."

The child's feet started prancing, and a muffled sob came from behind the plaid shirt. I took it off and smoothed back the tousled brown curls.

"Were you scared in there?" I asked.

The boy shook his head.

"He was!" I turned from little Georges to little Connie. I was terribly startled to see the large lavender eyes of her grandmother looking out at me from that baby face. I had never realized how alike they were. Little Connie had the same delicate features, a haunting sweetness in her mouth. I wondered if I would find my Constance again in this four-year-old.

Although she was only standing in her underwear, I whispered to her that we could beat Mike and little Georges. We did, and then watched Mike struggle with her twin's coat. Every time Mike put it on, the sleeves of the baby's various shirts and sweaters were carried up into such a knot that the coat sleeve couldn't be pulled over it. Connie and I helped by putting all sleeve ends firmly in little Georges' hands. The coat went on.

We hurried them through the front room and out of the house. I went back to tell old Georges that he was to come to see the children all the time—that they needed their grandfather. I don't think he heard me. His eyes were sunken and almost closed. He seemed dazed. But maybe he was just thinking a long way back. Maybe somewhere in his mind a young man with a fifty-pound sack of flour on his back trudged barefoot beside a beautiful young girl with lavender eyes. I went out as quietly as I could.

Mike had kept the children busy building a snow man. We couldn't persuade them to leave it except by promising them a new one when they got home.

That night Mike played he was a bear. And when we went to bed the house was in a litter, a wonderful exciting litter of cut-outs and spilled jam and cookie crumbs. Mike caught me around the waist while I was cleaning up.

"Well, girl?"

"Oh, Mike—" I couldn't say anything else because I was crying and getting kissed all at once.

## CHAPTER TWENTY-EIGHT

It was wonderful having children in the house again. The long hours Mike was away were suddenly filled for me. The twins played well with each other. Of course it was up to me to get them started. But once I had set out chips and blocks from the kindling, they would spend intense hours piling them in stacks. I taught them little French songs that I had heard Constance sing. And at night when they roughhoused with Mike, I worked on a blue dress for Connie to wear Sundays. I thought I would make a blouse for Georges out of what was left. I worked late over it. Long after the children were in bed, Mike and I discussed them and planned for them. Mike thought it would be nice for Georges to be a Mounty, and I thought that maybe Connie would be a nurse. We decided that Old Irish Bill would give them music when they became six. The picture of a pretty white-starched nurse faded, and I saw Connie bowing instead to an audience at Symphony Hall and seating herself at the organ for another encore.

The blue dress was done. Connie hopped up and down impatiently while I buttoned it on. Then she stood back for me to see. I looked at her and burst into tears.

"Come here, Connie. I've got to take it off you."

Now it was her turn to cry. I promised her another dress, much prettier, any color she liked, only not blue. In blue she became her grandmother, her eyes became the same strange lavender. It broke my heart. I traded in the blue material for red, and that night started a new dress. While I worked, Mike read me the poems of Bobby Burns that we had borrowed again from the McTavishes. I loved to hear him declaim, "A man's a man."

It was one of these evenings when Jonathan Forquet walked into the room, holding in his arms a solemn-eyed baby.

"I come to my friends." He said it half-defiantly.

Jonathan was Jonathan. It had been eight years, but he had the same proud way about him.

"Is it your baby?" I asked, coming toward him. "Is Oh-Be-Joyful with you?"

He looked at me and answered slowly. "Can you not see that she is dead?"

Then I did see it. I saw it in the black eyes that looked hopelessly into my own. The lids were heavy . . . Jonathan had cried.

"The sickness?" I asked him. "The flu?"

"The sickness, it took her, Mamanowatum." He lifted the baby toward me, and before I knew it I had her in my arms. Jonathan watched me as I held her.

"From ten sleeps away I bring you. Mamanowatum, she call her Kathy. She want this winter come show you girl-child, come show you happiness. Now she no come ever. Only I come, say, 'Keep baby.' No want Mission for keep her. They not like me. They not like my father."

Mike came over to me. "We'll keep her, won't we, Kathy?"

"Yes," I said. "Of course."

Jonathan nodded "You are my friends. I knew. I come, bring furs once, twice, in the year. You sell. Feed, make clothes for girl-child." He hesitated. I knew there was something else.

He spoke in Cree: "Mamanowatum . . . many winters we are together, always the canoe sings in the river and the paths we walk are of happiness. You will say that to the girl child? You will tell her of the joyful heart of Mamanowatum!"

Mike patted him roughly on the shoulder. We stood in the doorway and watched him walk into the night. He was alone, as he had been before he knew the gentleness and the love of Oh-Be-Joyful. The baby reached out after him, but the little fist closed on emptiness.

I turned to Mike. Oh-Be-Joyful, the girl with black stockings sitting primly in punishment row . . . I saw her laughing, scrubbing a pot with the same intensity with which she had clung to that pile of pelts, Jonathan's present. I heard again the story of Fleet Foot, heard her chattering to Mary Aroon in Cree.

Mike crouched on his heels and looked earnestly at the round copper face of the baby. "She's a cute little mite." He ran a finger lightly under her chin, and she dimpled all over. Mike grinned back, "Hello, Kathy." He winked at me, "We can't have two Kathies. Let's call her Kate."

Kate. This brown Indian baby had my name, perhaps part of my destiny. "My more-than-sister," Oh-Be-Joyful had called me. And her child was closer to me than my own sister's. I murmured the name, "Kate." I pictured Oh-Be-Joyful saying it, bending over her child, thinking of me, whispering my name. She lived in the wild world of brilliant summer colors, she walked through the clean pine woods of the North, among the cries, the calls, the flapping of wings, the swaying of bush, surrounded by life, part of it, free in it; at the height of her happiness, her child in her arms, she had thought of me.

"Mike," I said, "it's very strange . . . and I want to cry. But what does it all mean?"

"Well, there's a pattern," Mike said. "The baby is Kate and you are Katherine, and it's right that you should have her."

"A pattern?"

"Yes. I don't mean the names exactly. But Oh-Be-Joyful was part of the pattern of your life, and things iike that don't just stop. Things from her life will come into yours, into ours, as long as we live."

I knew what he meant by this pattern. It wasn't something you could put into words, but you could sense it behind everything. If you tried to talk about it, all you could say was something trite, like water is always watery, and leaves are like leaves. But it did have a meaning. You could see that events were like the people they happened to. Oh-Be-Joyful's life had always had that intense emotion and pathetic grasping after happiness that my mother said was characteristic of those "who are not long for this world." Perhaps on another day I would laugh at this and consider it superstition, but this day, watching Oh-Be-Joyful's baby in Mike's arms, I saw the pattern too.

Stretched on the loom was the huge white cloth of the North. We were the threads. Short and long, our ways stretched across it, bright and dull: Oh-Be-Joyful, born

281

here, loving if because it was her home; Constance, coming because she hadn't a better place, because she must make a new life for herself; and I—I had come thinking I was different, that I could choose my own place in the world; but I was woven in as firmly as the others. There was a time when I had tried to run away. Everything up here had suddenly become too big for me. The great sweeps: winter, cold and white, the coldest and the whitest; summer, the northern lights hanging terrifyingly in the air. I had tried to escape, like Mrs. Neilson, who had gone back to New York, or Mrs. Marlin, who had gone insane.

But when I left Mike, I left myself, I left the Katherine Mary the North had made. I was part of Grouard. Sarah had nursed me; I had nursed Randy. Constance had mended my clothes; I had mended James McTavish's plaid. Oh-Be-Joyful had cared for and loved my children, and now it was I who was to care for and love hers. Mike was right: the pattern of a life isn't a straight line; it crosses and recrosses, drawing in and tying together other lives, as I do when I gather in the ends of my thread to make a knot.

"It's strange," I said, "but love for a place has to grow in you, the same as any other kind of love."

"Do you really love it, Kathy?" Mike said in a low voice, playing absently with the Indian baby. "You've had a hard time up here, and perhaps not a very happy one, and I can't promise that it'll be any different."

"I don't want it any different if it can be with you." I didn't move. I felt too much in love to touch him or even look at him.

"Mike, I feel almost like when I was a kid and ate all the Easter candy before my sisters got up. Look at me. I have everything. And then think of Jonathan with only emptiness in his life."

"He had what he wanted, and still has a part of it. And so did Oh-Be-Joyful."

"But for such a little while."

"They had it, and that's what's important!"

Mike reached up and pulled me down on the floor beside himself and little Kate. He rocked us each in a big arm.

"I'm thinking back a way, Kathy. Not very far, when you and I were alone too."

I began to see. The pattern of things half-formed itself against the jumble of incidents before I lost it again.

There was great excitement the next morning when the twins found out they had a baby sister. We told them they could celebrate any way they wanted. It wasn't hard for them to decide. They'd been after Mike for days to take them out in the snow.

Mike laughed. "Okay, Kathy, dress 'em up. I'll meet you on the porch." And he went striding off on some errand of his own.

When the last fur mitten was on the last twin, I sent them out to wait while I bundled up the baby and dressed myself.

It was a wonderful winter's day, clear and cold and dry, with the sun shining. I came up close to see what Mike was working over. It was our old sled. I thought he had burned it or hacked it to pieces, but evidently it had only been hidden, probably under the wood pile. He was oiling the runners and rubbing off seven years of rust. The twins were busy rubbing too. Mike looked at me over the heads of the children. "I just came across it the other day, and I thought they'd have a lot of fun with it." I smiled at him, and he smiled back, relieved.

"All aboard. Everybody in!" There was a wild scramble, and more arms and legs than I thought we possessed even collectively.

Mike swung into the wind. It was good to watch him striding through unbroken snow, but I was content—back here in the sled, keeping the children from falling out the hole.

It was a magic cutter. We sailed across a frozen sea. Georges was captain and yelled orders to Connie, who yelled them at the trees and drifts and clouds.

"Warm enough?" Mike asked when we were at the top of the hill.

"Yes."

The twins were pulling at him, demanding a snow fight, but he still looked at me, unsatisfied.

I tried to tell him. "It hurts a little."

"What hurts you?" Connie asked. "A pin?"

"No," I said. "Happiness."

283

## ABOUT THE AUTHOR

Three people are responsible for *Mrs. Mike*—Nancy and Benedict Freedman, whose names appear on the title page, and Katherine Mary Flannigan, the heroine herself, whose chance meeting with the Freedmans in Los Angeles inspired them to write a book about her.

Nancy Mars, an ex-ballet dancer and actress, married Benedict Freedman, a radio writer, in spite of doctor's warnings that she had only three months to live. That was in 1941. Since then, they've shared each other's lives completely—they write, cook and even paint the house together. So it was only natural for them to be interested in the story of another devoted couple—Mrs. Mike and her gallant Sergeant.

Mrs. Flannigan, a widow since the Sergeant's death in 1933, now lives in California. A spirited, cheery woman, she regards that pleasant State as a temporary setting and hopes to move to Vancouver, British Columbia—to be near her friends of the North country and to watch the Northern lights.